Andie Newton is a *USA Today*  fiction. Her work has been pu and has topped ebook bestselle holds a bachelor's degree in I University and a master's in teaching. When she's not writing gritty war stories about women, you can usually find her trail running in the desert and stopping to pet every dog that crosses her path. She lives in the beautiful Pacific Northwest with her family.

 instagram.com/andienewtonauthor
facebook.com/NewtonAuthor
x.com/AndieNewton
bookbub.com/authors/andie-newton

Also by Andie Newton

A Child for the Reich

The Secret Pianist

THE GHOST HOUSE

ANDIE NEWTON

One More Chapter
a division of HarperCollins*Publishers*
1 London Bridge Street
London SE1 9GF
www.harpercollins.co.uk
HarperCollins*Publishers*
Macken House, 39/40 Mayor Street Upper,
Dublin 1, D01 C9W8, Ireland

This paperback edition 2025
1
First published in Great Britain in ebook format by
HarperCollins*Publishers* 2025

A catalogue record of this book is available from the British Library

ISBN: 978-0-00-877647-3

To everyone who loves a ghost story.

Every night, we feel the dead walking beside us in the trenches.

The land is theirs now, and I fear I'm next.

— Luc Marchand, in a letter to
his mother, Verdun, 1916

Chapter One

Occupied France
Lorraine Region–May 1944

Vianne bolted upright in bed from a nightmare, dripping with sweat and certain she had heard her nephew scream. Without a moment of hesitation, she flung off the blanket and rushed toward him with her nightgown billowing behind her like a ghost. She barely noticed the sting of the cold floor beneath her feet as she descended the stairs to the hallway.

"Blaise—" She burst into his bedroom, expecting to find him cowering under his blankets, but instead found him standing unnaturally still and quiet between the parted velvet drapes, his misty breath blooming against the windowpane.

He didn't turn around.

"Darling?"

His room showed no signs of a disturbance, with the book of nursery rhymes closed on the nightstand where she had left it, the teddy bear slumped in its usual place, and the rocking chair unmoved. Nothing out of place—yet something felt terribly wrong.

She reached for his slate and chalk. He hadn't spoken a word since she took him in two months ago—after her dear sister was arrested by the Germans, presumably never to be seen again—but he would write. Was he sleepwalking? No, his eerie awareness and shifting eyes told her otherwise: he was awake and fixed on the fog.

"Blaise?" A dark shadow breezed across the far wall—too quick to explain—and he let out a shrill cry that had her reaching for her chest with the slate crashing to the floor.

He'd already scampered back to his bed and thrown the blanket over his head before she could catch her breath, but it was her heart that was pounding and nearly in her throat. She closed her eyes. That scream, still piercing her ears long after the room turned quiet again, was enough to send a terrifying shiver up her spine where it settled into every bone.

She checked on Sandrine, her elderly mother-in-law sleeping across the hall, and saw she remained undisturbed, thank God, only a slender rise beneath her favorite quilt.

Vianne comforted Blaise. "There, there…" she said, until he fell back asleep, but her heart was still beating wildly from the fright, too wild to go to bed herself. She crept over to his windowsill where the slightest breeze whistled through a crack in the glass.

Beyond the rusted old fence line, the forbidden forest of the Zone Rouge loomed—the site of the Battle of Verdun, a scarred wasteland wracked with skeletal remains that lay buried in sorrow.

A wave of loneliness crashed over her after placing her hand gently on her chest—not just her own, but a shared, aching grief as thick as the fog that rolled over the scorched trees and onto her property, blanketing the courtyard with ribbons of white. After a while, she was barely able to make out the iron gate that separated them from the old battleground.

Blaise's whimpers pulled her away.

"It's all right," she said, rushing back to peel the blanket away. His hair was damp and sticky against his temples, his eyes wide and glassy. "I'm here," she murmured, brushing his cheek with her lips. "I'm right here."

Vianne lay down next to him with his teddy bear and continued petting him. She chided herself inwardly. *Jumping at shadows and dropping the slate. You're his caregiver, Vianne. You have to be the calm one.* But even as she told herself it was nothing, she couldn't stop the prickle that crept up her spine, especially when her eyes wandered over to the windowpane, framed in soft moonlight.

In the morning, she did her best to start anew, and after changing for the day, she watched him quietly from the doorway. "Good morning," she said, but he barely stirred under his blankets.

Vianne broke away when she heard Sandrine trying to move on her own in her room. "Let me help you!" Sandrine wasn't only standing on her own, but dressed and ready for breakfast.

"I can walk a few steps without assistance," she said.

"I know you can." Every morning seemed to start off with Sandrine testing her strength, which always worried her. Vianne pulled Sandrine's coarse gray hair into a bun at the nape of her neck after helping her into her wheelchair.

Pierre, the dear sweet soul that he was, walked in and relieved her. He did not have to help Sandrine. He wanted to, and had been helping her for years. Vianne knew Pierre was worth more than she was paying him to help manage Chateau Ten; she just wished she had more to give.

"How are you this morning?" she asked, but really, she was asking how his guesthouse was holding up. She was aware he needed a new bed, and she had a suspicion his roof was leaking because he was always dressed in layers.

He rubbed his good eye, lifting his glasses where she noticed a scratch. "I'm good, you?" he said with a smile. His peppery, silver hair had turned dull since the occupation, and every day he was looking more and more his age, which was too old to be working such long hours.

"I see you chose the threadbare jacket this morning," Vianne said. "Is that what you wore to bed because of the chill?"

Sandrine watched them both from her wheelchair.

"It's my favorite," he said, nodding once. "Honest."

She wanted to demand that he sleep in the main house, but he'd always refused when she asked before, and she wasn't about to make a scene in front of Sandrine. "I don't deserve you, Pierre." She patted his shoulder. "None of us do."

The cook called for Vianne with a mad thrash of the dinner bell, even though it was morning. Pierre assured her they were all right and to go ahead, since Sandrine liked to take her time to breakfast, and spend a minute or two looking outside by the grand staircase.

Vianne poked her head into Blaise's room. Now, he was up and dressed, reading a pop-up book about planes, like any other morning, pulling down on the tab to make the propeller rotate. She kissed the top of his head before he shot up to show Pierre his book.

The smell of cooked eggs had grown strong in the hallway, but as Vianne approached the kitchen, she thought the cook had burned them. Élise was probably making a point about the oil, Vianne thought, which they'd been out of for two days.

Vianne paused in the kitchen doorway before entering. "Good morning!" She smiled.

Élise snarled over her shoulder. "What's good about it?" She scraped eggs from the bottom of the frying pan with a metal spatula, scratching the pan and wrecking the eggs.

"Please, use the wooden spatula. You'll ruin the pan, you know this."

"We have more problems than this spatula," Élise said. "We're out of nerve medicine, and how am I supposed to cook this family a proper meal without money for the black market? The rations are simply not good enough. I need more oil, oats, and sugar."

Vianne peered into the frying pan. "Looks like our hen managed just fine this morning. And there's bread from yesterday. We can make toast." She made a point to mention the butter on the table, which was enough to last the rest of the day.

"And what about tomorrow?" Élise continued scraping the pan with the metal spatula.

"Please, Élise. The wooden spatula."

Élise changed out the spatulas while Vianne set the table for six, including a space for Henri. "There are five of us," Élise said, her back to Vianne as she cooked. "Only five. Has been only five for quite some time."

"You know Sandrine will expect it." Vianne placed a fork next to Henri's plate and folded the linen napkin, making sure the crease was just so, when Blaise burst into the kitchen, writing on his slate, asking if breakfast was ready. "You have a few more minutes. Go pick out another book from your library," she said.

He used his hand as an eraser and quickly drew a heart, then ran off to his bedroom.

Élise's eyes shifted. "Why is he still using that thing? It is odd, don't you think? He's been here two months."

"He's a child, Élise." Vianne's voice was stern. "Show some compassion, will you? The doctor said he could start talking again at any moment. We can only imagine what he witnessed —what he heard."

"Yes, of course. It is all very sad—sad, indeed." She seemed to back down, switching the subject. "I heard there's a storm on the horizon, which means it will get noisy at night, and messy. It might scare him." Élise looked out the window where the skies were clear.

Vianne continued folding the napkins. She wondered if that was Élise's way of bringing up Blaise's cry in the middle of the night. She'd have to choose her words carefully to avoid saying too much, but she wanted to know if Élise heard, if only so she could make sure she didn't dwell on it.

"Élise…"

Élise had just cracked the last few eggs in the pan. "Yes?" The eggs sizzled with a few pops from the lack of grease.

"Did you hear anything last night?" Vianne asked.

"Like what?"

"I checked on Blaise in the middle of the night when I heard him stirring, only I scared him, and he screamed," she said, even though that wasn't quite how it happened. "I thought you might have heard. Sorry if you did."

Élise stopped scraping the pan, letting the eggs pop and crackle over the hot surface. "What was he doing up?"

Vianne refolded Henri's napkin, wishing she hadn't mentioned anything about it now. "I don't know. So, you didn't hear him?"

She pressed her lips together, which Vianne took as a no.

"You know, children don't just pop up in the middle of the night for no reason." Blaise was back with his book, and this time with his limp teddy bear under one arm. Élise waved him over, whispering, but talked loud enough for Vianne to hear. "Your auntie told you about the legend of the Sorrows, didn't she?"

Blaise shook his head.

"That's enough, Élise," Vianne said.

"The Sorrows are the lost souls from the Battle of Verdun, soldiers who died more than twenty-five years ago." She hiked her thumb toward the window. "Right out there." Her voice deepened. "Like sirens from the sea, the Sorrows cry. An eerie

7

melody tangled high, drifting through the night in play, whispering your name to steal you away—"

"I said, that's enough." Vianne guided Blaise to sit in his chair. Now, she'd have to explain when she didn't want to. "The legend of the Sorrows is a story adults tell children so they won't go into the Zone Rouge—not because it is true. It is forbidden to cross the fence for many reasons, but mostly because it's an old battlefield and it's dangerous. I told you not to open the gate, didn't I?"

Blaise went back to his book after nodding.

Vianne sighed. They were told the land wouldn't be habitable for three hundred years because of the gas mines, chemicals, and unspent explosives left behind from the battle. Pierre, who was pulled from his detachment in the trenches to develop chemical weapons, argued that it would take many more years than that. Aside from the hundreds of thousands of soldiers who lost their lives, nine whole villages were abandoned and deemed unhabitable because of the risks. You couldn't go anywhere in Belleville without still being reminded. It was an honor to say you were from one of the villages that died for France.

"Thank you, Élise. I could have done without that."

"The boy should know." She glanced at Blaise over her shoulder. "He should know the rest of the legend, too."

"He knows not to cross the fence. That is enough."

Élise scooped eggs onto all five of the plates, then paused with barely a spoonful left for a sixth. "You must tell Sandrine about Henri. It's sad listening to her mention his name and try to recall things. If you don't do it, I think I will."

8

"You will not," Vianne said. "Not while you are an employee at Chateau Ten."

Employee. Another thing Vianne had to tread carefully about. She didn't have Élise's wages for the week, and she knew it was only a matter of time before she asked.

Élise held up her eggy spatula. "Speaking of—"

"Good morning!" Pierre wheeled Sandrine into the kitchen, and right on time as far as Vianne was concerned.

"Oh, my, Élise, you burned the eggs?" Sandrine asked. "I'm sure our hen has plenty this morning. Get a few more, will you?"

Élise added the last eggy bits from the pan to Sandrine's plate. "That's all she gave us this morning, madame." She turned to Vianne. "The chickens are out of feed."

Pierre helped Sandrine out of her chair and the few steps it took to walk to the table. "I've got it. Let me do it." She ended up walking the last four steps by herself and they all sat down together, including Blaise, who was quiet as a lamb, praying silently over his plate of eggs with his hands folded.

"Amen," Sandrine ended, unfolding her napkin and placing it on her lap. "Where's Henri?"

Nobody said a word. Usually, if they kept quiet, Sandrine would forget she'd asked, but on this morning, Sandrine pressed the issue.

"Vianne, where's my son? Did he leave?"

Vianne set down her fork. "Yes." It was the most honest response she could give, without telling her the whole truth.

"Ah. I guess I'll see him at dinner. He never misses one of Élise's chicken dinners." Sandrine picked at her eggs with her fork, examining the consistency. They were burned, that was the cook's fault, but they had also been stretched with water, and that was Vianne's. "These look anemic."

"It's the rations," Élise blurted.

"The Germans have a tight leash on us all," Vianne added. "We aren't the only family that has suffered."

Sandrine sat up, blinking. "Germans?"

Vianne swallowed dryly, not knowing what kind of questions would spark other questions, then confusion. "Yes, the Germans."

"Germans in Belleville-sur-Meuse, Vianne?" Sandrine asked. "When on earth did this happen? Does Henri know?"

"He knows," Pierre said. "But don't you worry about the Germans. We are protected out here. They'll leave soon enough. Just have to be patient and wait for the invasion from the sea."

"Whenever that'll be," Élise piped. "Been waiting for ages."

Vianne shot her a look.

"Where's the keepsake?" Sandrine asked, which Vianne understood to mean her mind and memory were now somewhere before The Great War had ended. Sandrine searched her dress pocket, then looked under her plate and shook out her napkin. "It is good luck. It will keep the Germans away."

"You gave it to Henri, remember?" Élise said.

"Oh, yes," Sandrine said, scratching her forehead. "I did give it to him. How about some music? Good French composers like Chopin—Germans hate French composers."

"I wish it were that simple," Vianne said. "Besides, the gramophone is broken." Another thing Vianne didn't have the money to fix. She held her head in her hands.

"That's a pity. Must get that fixed if there are Germans in the village," Sandrine said. "Do you have a headache?"

Vianne sat up. "A slight one."

Sandrine felt Vianne's forehead to see if she was sick.

Of course, Vianne could not tell her the source of her headache. The chateau's guestbook never recovered after The Great War, though they were able to supplement their income with Sandrine's trust. But by the second war, they'd been at emergency levels.

Then tragedy struck in the form of Genevieve Lacroix.

Genevieve was Sandrine's dear friend, who regularly visited until two months ago, after which she went mad and told anyone in Belleville who would listen that the Sorrows existed and to stay away from the estate, calling it a ghost house, which only gave the legend teeth.

Vianne remembered the day vividly because it was the weekend after Blaise arrived, and she had the unfortunate duty of telling Genevieve to leave and not come back. Sandrine asked about her the following month, lamenting why her dear friend hadn't written, to which Vianne replied with silence and waited for her to forget. The truth was, Genevieve had written a letter, but Vianne folded it back up as soon as she realized Genevieve was still mad with delusions.

"I know what will perk you up," Sandrine said. "A visit to the bookshop."

"The bookshop?" Vianne asked.

"Yes, to see your friend. Colette, is it?" Sandrine asked, which meant she was now back to the present day. "Bookshops hold the answers to everything that troubles us. There's a lot of knowledge in the pages. You can smell it." She patted Vianne's hand on the table. "It will be good for you to go. Take Blaise."

Vianne turned to Blaise. "Would you like to go?"

He sat up in his chair, nodding.

"Then, we'll go." She smiled.

After breakfast, Sandrine let Blaise show her his pop-up book about planes while the rest cleaned up the table. Élise cornered Vianne near the sink while the tap was running. "My wages, madame. Today?"

Vianne took the dirty plate she was holding and rinsed it off, trying to think of an easy way to tell Élise she wasn't sure if she had the money or not. She had plans to balance the estate's ledger after breakfast. *Colette*. Why didn't she think of her before? It was the first of the month, and Colette owed her rent on the building Sandrine owned in the square, but Vianne rarely asked her for it on the day it was due because she knew Colette was struggling. However, she was also Vianne's close friend, so maybe Colette could pay on time? Maybe.

"I have plans to visit the bank today after I see Colette." She passed the rinsed plate to Élise for drying.

"Do that."

Vianne would just as well not have had a cook, but Sandrine liked Élise for reasons unknown. But also, Sandrine didn't do well with change, and Élise's absence would cause her stress, which Vianne absolutely didn't want.

Élise had been watching Sandrine talking to Blaise. "Have you ever considered that Sandrine is the way she is because of the toxins?"

Vianne turned up the tap.

"I'm just asking what is obvious. Some days, she's fine—

depends on which way the wind blows—and those winds are blowing through the twists and gutted valleys of the Zone Rouge. Not to mention the trees, where there isn't much resistance."

Pierre heard Élise. His eyes may not have been the best, but his hearing was impeccable, and he got up from the table to talk near the sink. "It's not the Zone Rouge," he said. "She has an affliction."

"How do you know?" Élise snapped back. "You're a retired chemist turned handyman. Not a doctor."

"Because I've lived here for a long time, same as you, coming from one of the nine villages—"

"Born in Ornes, thank you very much," she said. "The fifth village to die for France."

"And Vianne was born in Fleury. My point is, all three of us are all right, breathing the same air this whole time."

Élise completely dismissed Pierre's comment, turning her attention back to Vianne. "You know..." She gently lifted a lock of Vianne's hair away from her earring. "If you can't come up with my wages, I have always liked your pearls."

Vianne cupped her ears. "I said I'd have your wages this afternoon. And lower your voice!" she rasped.

"Make sure to see Henri for your wages today, Élise," Sandrine said from the table, and Vianne's jaw clenched.

Élise turned to Vianne, eyes wide. "I guess Henri will pay me," she said before walking away.

Pierre placed his hands on Vianne's shoulders, which allowed her to take a resetting breath. "Don't let her get to you."

Vianne turned off the tap.

13

"Easy to say."

"I'll get Blaise's bicycle ready. The tires need some air. They might be punctured. I'll check."

"Thank you." Vianne dried her hands, gazing out the window to the dilapidated fence the French government had put there twenty years ago, and the rotted hollow trees that looked more like hands without fingers reaching for salvation. She remembered the day when there were no iron bars, when the gardens were green with towering, centuries-old trees singing with birds. That was so long ago. Now, the only trees taller than the chateau's chimney were the poplar trees planted inside the Zone Rouge, and she couldn't even see them from her window.

She perked when a magpie landed on the fence post, squawking at the Zone Rouge and ruffling its feathers.

Pierre leaned in. "Blasted magpie. He must be the one tearing up the garden."

"It's been so long since I've seen a magpie." Vianne waved to Blaise. "Blaise, come have a look."

He took a few steps toward her, only to stop dead in his tracks, shaking his head and clutching his teddy bear to his chest.

"Don't you want to see?" She motioned for him to come forward, just one more step.

He retreated slowly, burying his nose back into his book and refusing to make eye contact. The magpie flew over the chateau's eaves while squawking madly into the wind.

"Vianne?" Sandrine said.

"Yes?" Vianne was still looking out the window.

"Will Henri be joining us for dinner?" she asked.

Vianne closed her eyes.

"He left."

Chapter Two

Vianne sat in her study, going over that month's expenses, and unable to ignore the stack of unpaid bills lying in the basket since last week. Her goal was simple: squeeze the budget far enough to pay her staff's wages and live another day. Blaise sat quietly on the rug reading a book with his teddy bear close by, and his slate even closer, tracking the text with his finger, then pulling the tab to make the airplane's wheels drop.

"Blaise, sorry for scaring you last night." She wasn't going to bring the subject up because she didn't want to upset him, but not addressing it also felt wrong, especially after his odd reaction to looking out the kitchen window. It crossed her mind that the German who arrested her sister might come for them by association. "Did you see something outside, darling?"

He briefly glanced at her, then went back to his book, flipping the page over as if she'd never asked the question.

She knelt next to him on the rug, sweeping a lock of hair

away from his hazel eyes—the eyes of her sister, which always tore at her heart.

"Someone in the fog, was there?" Vianne abruptly pulled her hand away when he nodded. "There was?" Her heart raced. "Who did you see?"

He began to draw the fence line and something else, but she couldn't tell exactly what. She stretched her neck, trying to get a clear view, but that's when his pace grew into a frantic white-out scribble to cover it up. "What are you drawing?" she asked, but that was one question too many, and Blaise snapped his chalk in half against the slate before darting away to the corner with his book.

"Blaise—" she said, reaching for his shoulder, but then thought better of it, and after a second or two, she walked mindlessly back to her desk.

Pierre poked his head in. "The tires on Blaise's bicycle are not punctured. I'll give it a pump of air and have it ready soon."

Vianne was still too stunned to talk.

"Madame?" Pierre said.

"Ahh…" Vianne looked at Pierre, then Blaise, who was still curled in the corner. She certainly wasn't going to talk to Pierre about what just happened in front of Blaise.

"Blaise, why don't you go to your bedroom. I'll come get you when it's time to ride into Belleville, all right?"

Vianne forced a smile as he dashed out. She had so many thoughts running through her head, including the most disturbing one.

"Something wrong?" Pierre sounded concerned, and rightfully so.

Vianne picked Blaise's limp teddy bear up from the rug and briefly adjusted the button eyes. "Close the door, please."

She told Pierre what happened with Blaise last night, his intense stare and piercing scream, then how he reacted with his slate moments ago. "You don't think…" She put her fingers to her lips. "The German who arrested my sister Marion has come looking for Blaise and me? Because why would someone be near the fence and gate?"

"But he's a child."

"And they are Germans," she said.

Vianne closed her eyes, remembering the urgent call she received from Marion's neighbor, telling her what had happened. Marion was ten years younger, and in many ways, Vianne had been more of a mother to her than their own, who had died shortly before The Great War. Vianne helped Marion when Blaise was a baby after her husband had left her, but Vianne wasn't there to protect her sister when she needed it, mainly because she had committed herself to helping Sandrine, and there was a part of her that felt guilty about that too.

According to Marion's neighbor, a German officer arrested her sister late at night, first with a thundering fist on her door before kicking it in and dragging her away. Blaise was found the next morning, hiding in a secret compartment in the back of the closet, clutching his teddy bear.

"Bastards. They probably thought the fog would conceal them. I can only imagine—"

"Fog?" Pierre shook his head. "It's been clear all week. A storm is on the horizon, but no fog last night or the night before."

18

"There must have been fog last night," she said. "I saw it settled among the trees."

She slowly took her seat behind her desk. If she was wrong about the fog, then maybe Blaise was mistaken as well. Yes. That was it. Children think they see things all the time, and she was too groggy-eyed to tell the difference between a patch of fog outside and the clouds in her eyes. He was also still recovering—it would be natural for him to imagine.

She propped Blaise's teddy bear on her desk to palm her eyes, but the bear's head flopped over. She adjusted his leg, and that, too, wouldn't stay. She finally set him face down with a groan.

"Could it be that he saw something else?" he asked. "A shadow, perhaps, in the fog? The Sorrows—"

"Pardon me?"

A smile flashed on his face, which Vianne took as his way to soften his question. "I'm sure it was nothing. Like you said."

"Yes. He could have been sleepwalking," Vianne added, though she was lying to herself because she knew he was awake.

Pierre gave a subtle nod, then left to go pump Blaise's tires with air.

Vianne tapped her pencil on her desk. She didn't mean to upset Blaise, even though that's precisely what she went ahead and did. She hoped the ride into the village would smooth things over, and of course, the visit to Colette's bookshop.

She took a deep breath and moved on to the bills.

At first, her figures were favorable, and she checked her math to make sure she hadn't made an error, playing with her pearl earring before moving on to twist a lock of hair. But with each new envelope she opened, her heart skipped a beat. Would there be enough? How much was she being taxed this month for the war?

The francs in the filing cabinet. Vianne shot up, opening the drawer where she kept her household fund for small purchases around the estate, and counted out the notes. She had enough to pay the cook, which meant she wouldn't have to rely on Colette's rent payment a day early. The relief she felt was immeasurable. She had been dreading asking her.

"Your bicycles are ready." Pierre had walked in just as she ripped open the last envelope with her letter opener.

"Thank you, Pierre," she said, now glancing over the bill. "You know, Sandrine was right. The bookshop will—" Her eyes grew wide looking at the amount she owed, and when she covered her mouth, Pierre stepped inside and closed the door.

"What is it?" he asked. "Bad news?"

She stood. "This can't be happening."

"Madame?"

She scrunched the bill in her hand. The taxes were due, and they were much higher than they'd ever been, which would not only drain her household fund of the francs she planned to give Élise, but everything left in the estate's account. "War contribution tax," she said out loud. "*Mon Dieu*, it's pure thievery."

Pierre leaned in to get a peek at the ledger, and she promptly closed her books. Keeping the estate's finances in order wasn't his responsibility.

"I know what is going on," he said, but she wouldn't look at him. "I want to help."

"No, Pierre. No."

"Don't pay me this week," he said.

She shook her head. "Out of the question. I owe you a new bed as it is, and your glasses have a scratch. Don't think I haven't noticed."

"I insist. If you pay me, I'll quit."

"You can't quit. If you do, we'll all fall apart. There'll be nothing left of Chateau Ten," she said, but what she meant was that not only would she and Blaise be devastatingly sad, it would break Sandrine emotionally as well.

"If Henri were here—"

"But he isn't, is he?" She sat heavily in her chair. The cat stretched out on the window ledge with the sun on his belly, basking in warmth, while she struggled to hold herself together, and what was left of her family.

"Vianne," he said, placing his calloused hand on top of hers to hold. "Don't pay me."

There was nothing else to say. Pierre was serious, and she had no choice but to accept. She still had a difference to make up, which would be satisfied with Colette's rent payment, but what if Colette couldn't make rent? Her stomach twisted.

She thought of some other way she could raise the funds, but it was nothing she hadn't already thought of in the last year when she realized they only had months left.

"I might have to take on a long-term renter, Pierre. It would be for half the cost, but these are desperate times."

"You risk alerting the Germans about the rooms we have available at Chateau Ten, only they'll billet every suite and the private areas without compensation. We've been so fortunate to have stayed hidden out here throughout this occupation."

"No German is setting foot inside Chateau Ten."

"You may not have a choice," he said. "Officers will find out, and they will force their way in. You know how it works. It's happened to my friends in Belleville-sur-Meuse, and to yours."

"Privately, I'll have to remind the French what we can offer and convince them it is safe. The nine villages died for France, but not Chateau Ten. We remain standing and alive. I sometimes wonder if the displaced villagers resent us for still living at the chateau, thinking we should have abandoned the estate out of respect, even if the government didn't demand it."

"Do you think so?" he asked.

"I do. I wish Sandrine had kept the chateau's original name, Le Grand Maison," she said. "Chateau Ten has an unsavory reputation by name alone, then add in the legend, and the leaking gas canisters in the forest… We can't win."

"She changed it because she thought it was patriotic," he said. "And you know, the gases aren't as close as people think."

Nobody knew more about the deadly toxins in the Zone Rouge than Pierre, since he developed most of them and had a hand in their storage.

"How close are they, and how many canisters?"

He stared out the window, arms folded. "The closest chemical stockpile to us… It's about four or five miles due north. Maybe a hundred canisters. Not all are leaking, but I'd guess most are." He turned to Vianne. "Don't worry, stigma or not, four miles is a good, safe distance. After the war, things will change. Remember, the chateau was once a place of luxury. Renowned for our suites and salt baths, and the expansive library in the west wing. Americans, Canadians. Everyone came. They will come again after this war." He patted her on the hand. "Go see Colette. Maybe all this worrying is for nothing. As for next month, perhaps the war will be over."

"Wishful thinking," she said. "Not that I'm opposed to it." He moved toward the door. "Thank you, Pierre."

He nodded once.

It had been weeks since Vianne rode her bicycle into the village of Belleville-sur-Meuse. As the wind blew her hair playfully over her shoulders, and Blaise made small, delightful noises from going downhill, she wondered why.

At the bottom of the hill, they stopped riding to walk their bicycles the short distance to Colette's bookshop. She stumbled once upon seeing Wehrmacht standing under Nazi Party banners hanging from a collaborator's shop, smoking and joking.

"That's why," she said to herself, then turned to Blaise. "Look straight ahead. All right?" She adjusted his collar and the slate he carried on a string around his neck.

She looked back once. The officers were still carrying on.

The last thing she wanted was to alert the Germans to his ailment. "I'll carry your slate. And your teddy bear…" She paused with the bear in her hands. Vianne normally would have thought he was getting a little too old to be carrying around a stuffed animal, but after what he went through, she decided he'd give it up when the time was right. "Keep it under your arm."

Vianne held her chin up, positioning Blaise and his bicycle near the gutter, separating the Germans from him. "Follow me."

As stressful as walking past German soldiers was, she would have never attempted to walk past SS officers on a smoke break because they were notorious for detaining Frenchwomen every chance they could get, insisting on car rides, a café visit, or a short chat.

Mme. Marchand waved to her from inside her patisserie as they passed. Her son's portrait hung on the wall behind her, barely visible through the glass. Luc died in the Battle of Verdun when he was nineteen years old, which Sandrine insisted on remembering by sending a bouquet of flowers on the anniversary, but Vianne had to resort to mailing a card last week because of money constraints.

Colette burst from her shop's door. "Blaise!" He dumped his bicycle to run into her arms for a big hug. "I have new books in the back for you."

Vianne propped both bicycles against the building while Blaise ran into the shop, past the bookcases, and into the back where he could discover and read quietly.

"Hallo, dear Colette." Vianne kissed her cheek. Colette's hair was dark as the night and curly as a young woman's, though she was in her mid-forties, like Vianne. "How do you manage this?" She touched Colette's hair, then her own, wishing she had the funds to keep hers presentable. "Not a strand of gray."

Colette smiled. "It's good to see you."

Renée Devereaux, who made a living off swindling customers with promises of fortune-telling, sat just outside Colette's door, listening and watching. She wore a ragged dress that used to be light blue but had lost all its color from years of wear. Nobody knew when she last washed her hair, despite numerous attempts to give her soap. Vianne nodded her hello as a courtesy, which drew an odd smirk from Renée.

Once inside, Colette explained that she would have shooed Renée away if she hadn't agreed to pay her a few coins a week for a seat on her bench, and the chair inside for when it was rainy.

"I thought she left Belleville a year ago," Vianne said.

"I don't know what brought her back. Business must be good for her here, or it was bad where she came from." Colette walked around her front desk. "I have something for you."

"You do?" Vianne assumed she meant the rent, which was relieving. She wouldn't have to suffer the embarrassment of asking her friend for it early, and she'd walk out of the little bookshop on Rue de Jardins with her head held high because she had managed to survive another day.

Colette placed a small yellow box with a pink ribbon on the counter. "For you." She slid it toward her.

Vianne's back was to the door, but she could smell Renée. She'd snuck back in and sat in the empty chair near the door, watching and listening, and somehow managing not to trigger the doorbells.

Vianne untied the bow. This felt a little over the top, but she smiled just the same. She lifted the lid, and in that split second, before she saw what was inside, she realized the box was too heavy for paper notes.

"It's chalk." Colette smiled. "Colored chalk." She pointed to them individually. "Green, blue, and black. I know that sounds like an odd choice, but black is very rare and worth a lot of money."

Vianne's smile faded.

"You don't like them?" Colette looked disappointed, and Vianne wasn't sure how to tell her she was expecting the rent instead.

"I got these on the black market from an old colleague—a librarian from Verdun. I thought Blaise would love them. I know you can only get white."

"Thank you," Vianne said. "I do appreciate it—"

"Are you blind, Colette?" Renée spouted. "She came to collect the rent. I'm sitting behind her, and I can see that."

"Oh…" Colette shook her head. "Of course. Yes, I'll see what I have…" She looked around her desk, opening the drawer, then patting her pockets, coming up with a few coins and even fewer notes. "I'll get you the rest at the end of the week. You've never been this punctual before." Colette counted the measly amount she had gathered on the counter.

"You don't have it," Vianne said.

"The truth is, the chalk was a gift because I was going to ask for an extension until the end of the week," Colette admitted. "But I will have it then. I promise. A friend of my husband's has asked to rent the room in the loft—this here is what's left of his deposit after paying my bills."

Vianne leaned against the front counter, palms to her eyes. "I need it today. Taxes on Chateau Ten are due tomorrow."

"A married woman, sharing space with another man,"

Renée said to Colette. "What does your husband say about that?"

Colette talked over Vianne's shoulder. "My husband was sent to the factory. Be quiet!"

"You can't send a letter? Women know how to write a letter to their husbands."

"Letters take weeks. What am I supposed to do, send a pigeon?" She turned back to Vianne, rubbing her arm tenderly. "Sorry, friend. I really am."

"Sell your earrings, if you need money so bad," Renée said to Vianne. "If you want some advice."

Vianne sighed. She wasn't going to respond to Renée. Talking to her always felt like she was gathering information, rather than listening. Colette and Vianne huddled closer for privacy.

"Those are the earrings Henri gave you, aren't they?" Colette asked.

Vianne nodded. "I can't give them up. It's the last thing he gave me before he left."

"Left," Colette repeated.

"What else would you call it?"

Colette hesitated. "I'm sure he'd want you to sell them if it meant saving Chateau Ten."

"I thought about advertising for a renter. But I'm cautious about the Germans taking an interest."

Vianne's attention turned to the roadster that pulled up to the tax office. The couple looked like cinema stars, him in a three-piece maroon suit, and her in a slinky, cream-colored dress and matching hat.

"What about them?" Colette asked. "They were in

yesterday for a rare book. They don't just look like money, they have it. He wore an especially interesting piece of jewelry around his neck—"

Vianne scoffed. "They are champagne in a glass, and Chateau Ten, in the state it is now *and* on the edge of the Zone Rouge, is ale in a barrel. Maybe I could do some sewing?"

"When have you ever sewn?" Colette asked.

"If I could just get some money, my life would change," Vianne said. "I'd manage to fend off the tax collector at least, and with the invasion we've all been hoping for, who knows what could happen? Good thing the taxes are paid on this building for the year. I fear that after the chateau, this one is next to lose." She looked from the rafters to the wood floors.

"Vianne," Colette said. "I've known you for a long time. I knew your sister."

"Know. You *know* my sister. She was arrested. She's not dead."

"What I mean is, I knew you before…"

"Yes, Colette?" Vianne had an idea of what she was going to say, but she wasn't in the mood, not when she needed money, which was the only thing on her mind.

"You are stuck. You've been stuck for so long, trying to save the chateau on your own. All by yourself."

"What would you have me do?"

"Ask for help. Sandrine has friends, and so do you. Then, maybe, after it's all said and done and you've saved the estate, you can move on. Be free to live your life without so much obligation."

Vianne had never asked for help, and she wasn't going to start now. "I need money, Colette. Not favors."

"The gentleman renting the attic loft—he was a professor in Paris once, and he's a widower. Maybe he has some ideas that can help? He's very knowledgeable."

A widower? Vianne knew what she was getting at. "Not now, Colette."

"If not now, then when? You know, there are plenty of people in Belleville-sur-Meuse who are worried about Sandrine, but I'm worried about you."

"I'm worried!" Renée piped.

They both looked at her.

"I'm warning you, mystic Renée," Colette said, finger sharply pointing. "One more word out of you and I'll ... I'll..."

"You'll what?" She laughed, then addressed Vianne. "Don't take on renters. It's your doom if you do. Nothing good will come of it." Her eyes narrowed to the couple across the street. "I can feel it."

"Outside, you," Colette said, stomping around the counter. "Now!" She opened the door for her to leave, but Renée only went as far as the bench, a foot from the door where she could still hear.

"Sorry about her," Colette said. "Business has been awful these last weeks with the influx of Germans, everyone is on their toes and bickering. New officers arrived just three days ago." She pointed across the street to where SS pulled up in a black Mercedes 770 with Nazi Party flags near the headlamps.

Vianne let out a soft gasp. They all looked the same with their uniforms on, though one stood out from the rest with his silver chevrons and shoulder boards. "Do you know where they came from?"

"You mean, did they come from Verdun?" Colette asked.

"I don't know." She paused, looking down the aisle to the back where Blaise was quietly reading with his teddy flopped on the floor. "How's Blaise? I see he still carries the teddy bear. Has he said anything about the night of the arrest?"

"Nothing, and he still only uses the slate to talk. Last night I woke to find him staring intently out the window, unable to break away. Then he screamed, and I'd never felt my heart beating so fast. It was terrifyingly shrill."

"He was staring into the Zone Rouge?"

Vianne turned away from the window, nodding.

"Has he done that before?" Colette asked.

"Not that I've seen. Marion's been gone for two months. I'm sure it will take some time before he's able to sleep comfortably again."

Colette set a stack of books on the counter for sorting. "I want to know what he saw out that window. You know the legend about the Sorrows. That friend of Sandrine's so much as confirmed them."

"Genevieve Lacroix?" Vianne's lips thinned. "Come on, not you, too, Colette." Vianne held her head again. "I believe in things I can see, as you should. I can assure you they do not exist."

"The forest is alive," Renée said on the other side of the window. "When it grows, you'll know it's too late." She pounded on the glass.

"All right, that's it!" Colette stomped outside and shook her finger at Renée. "You've lost privileges for the rest of the day, got it?" Colette kept shaking her finger until Renée got off the bench.

"That woman!" Colette had thrown open the door, letting

out an irritated little cry. "Not worth the meager coins she gives me."

"She must be worth it," Vianne said. "Or you would have told her to never come back."

Colette closed her eyes. "God, this war. The things we do."

"I better be off," Vianne said. "Sandrine might wonder where we are, and who knows what Élise will tell her." She called Blaise to the front. He wrote a few kind words on his slate to thank Colette for the use of her books since they couldn't afford to buy them.

Colette smoothed Blaise's hair behind his ear. "Anytime, love. Anytime."

Vianne kissed Colette's cheek before leaving, passing by Renée on her way to their bicycles leaning against the building. "Heed my advice," Renée said.

Vianne swiftly grabbed her bicycle by the handlebars. "Leave me alone." She helped Blaise with his, hanging his slate around his neck.

"Don't do it!" Renée shouted.

"Follow me, Blaise."

They rode away.

Chapter Three

That night, Vianne managed to avoid the topic of Élise's wages because shortly after dinner, Élise went to nurse a stomachache in her room.

Vianne wheeled Sandrine down the hallway once it was dark and helped her get ready for bed, slipping a nightgown over her head and brushing out her coarse gray hair. Candlelight flickered against the mirror. Vianne was waiting for Sandrine to say she didn't like the candles and to use the electric light, but when Vianne looked at the lamp, all she saw was another expense.

"You weren't supposed to be *my* caretaker." Sandrine shook her head. "I went and ruined things, didn't I, by getting older? It is too much, especially now with Blaise here."

Vianne looked up, the brush frozen midair in her hand. "You didn't ruin anything."

"It has been an adjustment for you, suddenly stepping into the role of a mother. It can't be easy."

Vianne couldn't deny that it hadn't been easy, and she

constantly worried about making wrong decisions when it came to Blaise's care. All she desired was to provide him a safe place to live, one of comfort and stability during a time of such upheaval and pain.

Sandrine patted Vianne's hand resting on her shoulder. "Withdraw some money from the account. Take as much as you need and hire someone. You deserve it."

Vianne forced a smile because there was no money to withdraw. "Thank you, madame."

"Would you buy me some flowers while you're at it?" Sandrine asked.

Vianne reached for the dark red rose on her nightstand that smelled stale and sour. "This one has plenty of life left. Even if you don't see it."

After helping Sandrine into bed, she carried the drippiest candle with her across the hall into Blaise's room, who had already fallen asleep with his teddy bear clutched tightly in his arms.

As quiet as the chateau was, it was even quieter in the kitchen where Vianne hung her head. There was nothing else to do but tell Sandrine the truth, she thought. They were on the verge of losing everything. Unless… Unless she followed through and posted an advertisement soliciting a renter, and by the grace of God, someone answered. But the question remained: how could she manage an advertisement without alerting the Germans about all the rooms she had, and the space?

Vianne wrote the advertisement anyway in the candlelight, pulling a pad of paper from the kitchen drawer and scrawling a few sentences out before she had a chance to change her mind.

The kitchen light flicked on. "Vianne?"

She whipped around, shoving the paper into her dress pocket. "Pierre?"

He looked as shocked as she was to find someone in the kitchen at that hour. "I'm terribly sorry. I didn't realize you were up."

Vianne was still clutching her chest, long after he walked to the sink for a glass of water. "Can you turn off the light?"

She turned toward the window, looking into the dark Zone Rouge where the rotted ashen tree trunks rose above the iron fence. Pierre joined her, and they were quiet, together.

She allowed herself to think about what their daily lives would be like if the Germans came, and each instance tore at her like a rabid, biting wind. She was at her last straw, but she didn't think she was on her knees just yet, which was why she was thankful for Pierre's interruption.

"We've weathered worse storms before, Vianne."

She tried her best to hold back her emotions. "I don't know what to do, Pierre. I'm … I'm lost. I've tried to be strong for so long, but truth be known, I'm not sure how many days we have left here at Chateau Ten. Maybe three. Maybe two. Colette, she didn't have rent, and won't have it for a few days."

Seconds passed in the quietness. Her head pounded, and now her eyes.

"You could pray."

Tears pooled in her eyes. "Pray?"

"We need to start talking about Henri in the past tense. Enough of this 'he left' business. He died more than twenty-five years ago in the Zone Rouge. Ask him for help. He loved you, and I believe our loved ones who've passed on are listening."

It hurt to hear Pierre talk that way, but he was speaking the truth. Henri died in the Zone Rouge. There wasn't a day that went by where she wasn't reminded, and when she let herself, she remembered the sweetness of the pink roses she carried on their wedding day, and the vows they took in front of their priest in the Fleury Chapel. Those few hours in front of their closest friends and family were full of so much promise.

It was the day after that her world fell apart.

Henri enlisted despite Vianne's objections since he had not been conscripted. He assured her that he'd be all right, and somewhere in her naivety, she let him talk her into agreeing. Then he left as if he'd be gone for a day or so, and not on his way to war, with a parting kiss on her cheek. The last image she had of him was in his uniform, rucksack over his shoulder, and his words, reminding her that he'd be back.

She dried her eyes with her palms, turning to Pierre. "There's only one problem."

"What's that?"

"I don't believe in prayer."

Knowing Vianne, Pierre should have expected as much. "Will you do it for me, then? You said it yourself, you've done everything. What will it hurt?" He gave a small smile.

"It won't hurt." Vianne did her best to smile back. "I guess."

Inside her bedroom, Vianne fully intended to get under her covers, say a couple of words into the air, and go to sleep. Instead, she found herself folding her hands at the window ledge and looking out past the scorched tree trunks as if she were standing at Henri's graveside.

Storm clouds brewed on the horizon, rolling slowly toward their property and shielding the moon but allowing just enough light for shadows to creep darkly up her wall. In the distance, she saw a yellowy spark of lightning. "Henri," she said, barely above a whisper, "I…"

She lit a candle, stalling for more time because she wasn't sure where to begin, or precisely what to say. But she had to say something. Vianne practically promised, and she wasn't about to lie to Pierre's face in the morning when he asked her.

She straightened, clearing her throat. "Henri," she said again, only this time much stronger, "I need—"

She stopped short of asking for help and instead told him how she'd let their expenses get away from her at Chateau Ten, and how she had sold an entire set of china and all the art over the years, except for the pieces in the foyer. The wine cellar had a few bottles left, but that was because nobody would buy the spoiled ones. She prayed for a miracle even though she didn't believe in them. She prayed for enough money to keep the estate.

"I have Blaise now. For so many years, I didn't have anyone to fight for, but now I do. I'll do anything to keep him safe and keep his home—"

Her door slowly creaked open, and what initially gave her a gasping fright turned into relief when she saw it was Blaise, half asleep and clutching his limp teddy bear by one arm.

"Blaise, darling." She'd fulfilled her promise as far as she was concerned, even though she'd left the prayer unfinished. She brought her flickering candle over. "Did I wake you?"

He nodded, and she ushered him back to bed.

She would place the advertisement after breakfast.

Vianne woke the next morning to Sandrine calling her name from downstairs. She pulled back the covers, and her feet met the cold floor, feeling groggy from being up so late. "Be right there," she called back.

She saw that Blaise was up and reading a book near his bed.

"How can it be morning?" Sandrine asked. "I feel like I just went to bed." She patted her robe pockets. "The keepsake. Where is it?"

Vianne sighed. She didn't have the strength to tell Sandrine, again, that she gave it to Henri more than twenty-five years ago, and it was buried somewhere in the trenches where he died, never to return.

"It's a key—a very special key."

"I know." Vianne briefly remembered the day Sandrine gave it to him, watching from a distance, a mother embracing her son before he left for war.

"Do you know what it looks like? Have you seen it?"

Vianne only knew that it was a key. She imagined it was gray and small enough not to get in the way. Élise said that before the war, Sandrine kept it in her jewelry box and polished it on Sundays. "I haven't seen it."

Vianne wheeled her mother-in-law over to the window

where she liked to sit and watch the clouds, but instead of showing interest, Sandrine suddenly seemed very far away and unreachable. "Madame?"

Vianne gently touched Sandrine's shoulder.

"Oh, sorry." Sandrine looked confused, then embarrassed. "I don't know where I was just now."

Vianne kissed Sandrine's cheek. Her condition was getting worse by the day, it seemed. The doctor warned that her deterioration would be slow at first, and then it would move at a rapid pace, but she was told that only a few weeks ago. Pierre came in seconds later, offering to take Sandrine to the foyer, while Vianne went to help with breakfast.

Vianne would have to tell Élise the truth about her wages, and she was debating whether to wait until after she cooked breakfast to do it. She took a few moments in the hallway to collect her thoughts before entering.

"Good morning," she said, finally walking in.

Élise was cooking eggs again, but this time, she was boiling them in a large stock pot. Vianne immediately started folding the linen napkins at the table. Élise handed Vianne Henri's plate to place in front of his empty chair.

"You know," Élise said. "Sandrine loathes boiled eggs. How are you going to explain it to her?"

"Explain that we're having six-minute eggs?" Vianne asked.

"Explain that you can't afford the oil for me to fry them in a pan."

Vianne continued with the linens, making sure the creases were just so. Pierre wheeled Sandrine up to the table, and

Blaise came running in a second later with the slate in one hand and his book in the other. Élise had just emptied the boiling pot of water into the sink, sending a cloud of steam up into the air.

Pierre leaned in to whisper, asking Vianne if she had prayed. Élise didn't seem to be paying attention, much less able to hear anything over the woosh of the water pouring into the sink, and Sandrine was busy talking to Blaise about his book.

Vianne was only able to nod once before Élise spun around and crossed her arms.

"I want my wages."

Vianne stood, finding her voice to break the news before stepping cautiously toward her. "I don't have it." Élise's face was stuck in one expression, and Vianne wasn't sure how to read her. "If you are willing to wait a few more days—"

"Élise," Sandrine called, searching the table. "Where is the salt?"

Élise shook her head in anger, not saying a word, but Vianne knew she had plenty to say.

Vianne pulled the advertisement she'd written last night from her dress pocket. "I'm soliciting for a renter. Just need to be patient," she said. "And if this advertisement doesn't work, well, we can talk about my earrings."

Pierre reached for Vianne's hand. "Not the earrings—"

"Where's Henri?" Sandrine said from the table. Blaise looked up from his book as if he, too, was wondering. Vianne would have to explain to Blaise later, though she thought he would have figured out by now that Henri did not exist, not anymore.

Élise turned to stare out the window as if considering Vianne's offer about waiting for the earrings.

"Élise, please. Sandrine needs you."

"Don't do that, Vianne. You know I have a place in my heart for that woman. It's you I have an issue with and how you run things around here."

"Does that mean you'll think about it?"

A knock on the front door interrupted them both. Pierre offered to go, but Vianne insisted she should answer it, mainly because she wanted to leave Élise with her thoughts and hoped she'd stay if she had a moment to think.

Vianne still had the advertisement in her hand when she looked out the front window to see who it was. It was that fancy couple she'd seen outside Colette's bookshop. Vianne hastily smoothed her hair into place, then looked again. They must be lost, she thought, but when they stepped away from the door to look at the fountain, then up at the estate, pointing in both directions and smiling, her heart sank. "Oh no…" she breathed. They must have heard the property was about to be requisitioned by the tax office.

The couple smiled big when she opened the door, their arms wrapped around each other. "Ah! Someone is home," the man said. "Excellent." They walked toward her, and with each step, Vianne's chest tightened.

He looked as expensive as he had yesterday, except this time he was wearing a tailored gray suit with pomade-slicked hair. She glittered in gold from her head to her toes.

"I am François Gaultier, and this is my wife, Monique. You are the proprietor of this estate?" He looked over Vianne's shoulder into the foyer, and beyond that into the kitchen where the noises of breakfast were rife. "Or, at least someone who can answer for the proprietor?"

"I am." Vianne's upper lip stiffened. The time had come—it was too late to save Chateau Ten. She only hoped the others couldn't hear them at the door—she'd like to break the news gently, especially to Sandrine.

"We were wondering if you had a vacancy for a stay of say…" he looked at Monique, discussing with nods and noises, "seven to ten days?"

Vianne couldn't believe her ears. "You want to rent a room?"

"Is that something you'd entertain? We thought—"

Vianne reached for her chest, suddenly realizing her dear friend Colette must have directed them to her. True, she said she was against approaching them yesterday, but now she was thankful. She wadded the advertisement in her hand. "You must have talked to Colette at the bookshop!"

They smiled.

"Yes, I'd be open. And, just to be certain, you are interested in Chateau Ten?" she asked because she still couldn't quite believe it.

François gave her a look, followed by Monique. "Madame, that is why we are here," he said.

Vianne exhaled. She was being obtuse. "Yes, of course. I'm sorry." She shoved the advertisement into her pocket. "I was on my way to the newspaper office today to place an advertisement. What timing! I will have to thank Colette."

"Good timing, indeed." He straightened his tie. "Would you mind showing us around? We need to make sure this fine estate suits our needs."

Vianne couldn't let them inside fast enough.

Monique's shining blonde hair looked soft and well taken care of, and she had a face full of makeup with a natural beauty mark near her eye. Good makeup, most likely from Paris. An opal necklace adorned her neck, and a gorgeous pair of blue earrings dangled from her ears. They did have money, more than their clothes suggested, or that roadster parked outside. However, it was François's necklace that caught her eye the most, with its shiny blackness and mirror-like reflection. Even Colette had mentioned it. She tried not to stare. It must be worth a fortune.

"This is the foyer..." Blaise's teddy bear lay on the bottom step. Vianne swiftly stuffed the toy behind the marble bust near the balustrade, putting on a smile in case they were looking, but their heads were turning every which way, commenting on the heavy wall tapestries, the crystal chandelier, and the landscape oil paintings. She was glad she hadn't sold what was in the foyer now.

Monique gently stroked the ornately carved newel post. "What a divine staircase." Her eyes went up and up and up.

"That leads to our private quarters," Vianne explained. "And the hallway downstairs as well. But over here..." Vianne walked toward the pocket doors.

"Do you have a library?" François asked.

Monique admired herself in the gilded mirror, turning her head to see her curls bounce.

"We do, and a well-appointed suite I think you'll enjoy." She opened the pocket doors that revealed the expansive west wing. "How much space will you need?" They followed her through the doors and down a switchback of corridors past the salt baths. Monique's heels tapped against the marble checkerboard floor while François's shoes sounded soft. "The entire west wing is available." She laughed, but they didn't laugh back in the slightest, and she wondered if they were considering. She would only be so lucky.

She took them to the King's Suite. "This is our best suite," she said, opening the door, but the doorknob nearly came off in her hand. She hoped the scented vanilla sachets on the sunny window ledge would distract them as she tightened the screws on the key plate behind her back.

Monique surveyed the entire room, running her finger over the bureau to check for dust, but Vianne always had a handle on that part. Chateau Ten may need fixing, but it was clean because she scrubbed it herself after she let housekeeping go, and she always made sure this particular suite was ready for guests, even after the guestbook had dried up, just in case.

They didn't say a word about the suite, the luxury bed linens, the goose-down duvet Vianne had been meticulously fluffing for years, or the private marble bathroom and clawfoot tub, and instead folded their arms.

"As you can see, it is spacious and has access to a private entrance down the hall to the outside," Vianne said.

"And that library I asked about?" François turned on his heel, tapping his chin.

Vianne wasn't sure how to read their reaction. Maybe they'd changed their mind about the chateau because the tapestries and rugs weren't as updated as they hoped?

She motioned for them to follow her. "This way." They followed her around the corner to the library. "The walls are deep green with hand-painted gold filigree, and the drapes are made from the finest velvet." She held the door open for them.

Monique gasped the moment she stepped inside, gazing at the ebony bookshelves that went all the way to the ceiling. "Oh, François..." She tapped across the parquet floor to the oriental rug, mouth hanging open, and set her handbag on the large mahogany writing table that took up most of the library. The gold and crimson antique oil lamp that Sandrine's mother had handed down was a nice added touch.

"This is magnificent!" François lifted his hands in the air as if it were the grand reveal.

This was the kind of excitement Vianne was waiting for. She held her breath, not just in anticipation of finally getting some financial relief, but because Monique had climbed the rolling ladder to the highest reaches of the shelves, and she wasn't sure if they'd hold. "Look at me, François!"

François playfully gave the ladder a push, and to Vianne's relief, the wheels didn't squeal, and the ladder didn't wobble.

Monique's gaze hung on the stained-glass lunette window before climbing down and turning to Vianne. "What a fascinating window. Doesn't let much light in, either."

"Thank you, and no, the decorative purples and blues keep it dark in here. That is why we have the oil lamp, but the chandelier uses electric light, if you prefer."

"Another crystal chandelier. How excellent. And you have coal for heat?"

"Yes," Vianne said, but she left out the part where she was past due on both.

"This is the place, François," Monique said. "What do you think?" They held each other while standing on the oriental rug as if Vianne wasn't even there. Things turned only slightly awkward when François gave Monique a full-mouth kiss that lasted several seconds, not that Vianne was counting, but it was quite extraordinary. She just hoped he wasn't going to throw his wife on the chaise after his kisses moved down her neck to her décolletage.

They both pulled away, gasping for air.

"We will take it," François said, which made Monique giggle with delight. "How much?" He pulled a wad of francs from his inside jacket pocket. Vianne tried to hide her bulging eyes from the sight of all that money, but it was nearly impossible. When he offered her fifteen thousand francs, she reached for the mahogany table to keep her legs from buckling.

"We want the entire west wing to ensure our privacy. Is that agreeable?"

"The entire west wing?" Vianne's heart sped up. "Yes, that's agreeable! I was only joking when I mentioned that earlier—"

"Sign here." Monique pulled a contract from her handbag while François was still counting, piling the paper notes neatly into stacks. "We are used to long stays, and we always travel with our own contracts. Protection for you, and us." Monique used her personal ink pen to write in the particulars about the west wing and Chateau Ten, where spaces were left blank.

Vianne looked over the contract's small print.

"As you'll read, upon signing, you agree to give us complete privacy and anonymity, especially during intimate gatherings with our guests."

"Guests?" Vianne looked up.

"Guests are all right, no? We will make sure your cook has

the proper funds she needs for a full pantry when we require her to cook a dinner party." Monique handed her the pen, which looked strange and foreign to Vianne. "It's a ballpoint pen. State of the art." She paused when Vianne looked unsure. "It works perfectly fine."

"It's not that." Vianne set the pen down on the table. "I'm sorry, but before I sign. I must request—" Vianne knew she had to be firm. "I have one rule myself. Something I'd like to add to the contract."

They both smiled, silly-like, as if whatever she had to say was inconsequential.

"You mentioned guests, but I can't allow Germans on the property. I realize—"

They burst into laughter. "We hate Germans. You won't need to worry about that. In fact, there's a clause in paragraph five to set your mind at ease." Monique flipped to the very last page of the contract. "Sign right there below my signature." She pointed to the dotted line.

Vianne took a deep, satisfying breath and gladly signed her name.

Chapter Four

Vianne bounded into the kitchen, eager to share the news, catching Sandrine and Pierre off guard. "We're going to be all right!" She gazed out the window, hand over her mouth in total disbelief.

"There's been an invasion?" Pierre asked.

"No, but something just as needed." Vianne whipped around, hands bracing the counter behind her. "We have some new guests. The Gaultiers—a charming couple. They have paid upfront for an extended stay and reserved all the rooms." Her eyes glowed. "The entire west wing!"

Blaise ran in from his bedroom with a book to show Sandrine.

"All the rooms?" Sandrine scratched her head while trying to juggle the book Blaise had thrust at her. "When it's just the two of them?"

Vianne nodded.

Pierre got up from the table to talk to Vianne near the sink. "Madame?" he questioned.

Vianne ever so slightly pulled the wad of francs from her dress pocket, giving Pierre a peek. "They paid me fifteen thousand francs," she whispered. "Can you believe it?"

Pierre leaned in, fingertips grazing the notes. "I didn't know that kind of money existed. Not anymore."

"All they asked for was privacy and a cook because they might want to entertain."

"Entertain who?" Pierre shoved his hands into his threadbare pockets. "What if they—"

"I already talked to them. The agreement was conditional upon no Germans being allowed on the property."

"You asked Henri for help—the prayer worked."

She touched his shoulder tenderly because she'd never asked for help. "Colette told them I was looking for a renter. We talked about them yesterday." She doled out a few notes for Pierre. "Here, I want you to get a new bed. And also, get yourself a new pair of glasses." Vianne wished she had enough to fix his roof, so he didn't have to wear that jacket any longer, but she thought it was best to pay her bills first and see what was left over.

"No—it's too much." He pushed the money back, but Vianne wouldn't have it any other way.

"Take it, Pierre. This is non-negotiable." She tried to sound tough, but she was rarely tough on anyone, much less to Pierre, who was the sweetest man she'd ever met. "Please. I need you to take it." She touched her chest. "For my heart."

He finally took the money. "Thank you, madame."

Now it was time to pay the cook. "Where's Élise?" She looked over his shoulder.

"She's gone."

"Gone?" Vianne asked. "*Mon Dieu*, did she quit?"

Before Vianne even thought about where to go looking for her, Élise appeared in the side doorway, a suitcase in her hand.

"Well, I'm off." Élise adjusted her jacket cuff, then looked at Vianne, head held high.

"Oh, thank God," Vianne said. "Élise, I have good news. You don't have to leave. I have your wages." Vianne started to pull a few notes from her pocket.

"Too late."

"Too late?" This wasn't the response she thought she'd get from Élise. She expected her to be elated. "You don't want your wages?"

"I want to leave," Élise said, but she didn't move one inch, which told Vianne she needed to sweeten the deal.

"I see." Vianne didn't want Sandrine to hear them talking, so she ushered Élise backward into the service hallway. "How much, Élise?" She flipped through the francs. Vianne didn't have time to count it, but she estimated she'd offered her at least another week's wage. "Will this convince you?"

Élise gasped. "Where did you get all that? Did you have it the whole time?"

"You heard the door, didn't you? They were guests, looking for a place to stay. Only they love Chateau Ten so much that they paid to use the entire west wing for over a week."

"The entire wing?"

"They want to host a dinner party, but the best part is they said they'd give my cook all the funds she needs to stock her pantry. You can get oil, butter, and anything else you want on the black market. Including that expensive nerve medicine you like to put in your tea."

Élise blinked once. "Are they German?"

"No. Absolutely not. Just wealthy. They only ask for privacy, so we'll need to make sure the pocket doors are always closed. Will you stay now?" Vianne pushed the money at her, but Élise remained still. "This is what you wanted, Élise. Don't be a fool." A moment passed, with Élise trying Vianne's patience. "Well, if that's how you feel…" She started to pull her hand back.

"I'll stay." Élise snatched the francs away to stuff them into her brassiere. "For now."

Vianne closed her eyes briefly, thankful Élise had come to her senses. She didn't want to think about what it would be like if she had to find another cook, worse, tell the Gaultiers that hers had quit while she was showing them around. "Thank you, Élise. Thank you. Things will be different around here now that—"

"I want the earrings, too."

"What?" Vianne cupped her ears. "But I paid you your wages, and you know Henri gave them to me. How can you be so cold?"

Élise shrugged one shoulder. "What am I supposed to do if you can't afford my wages again? I need collateral."

"A loan?" Vianne asked.

"I think that's fair. As long as I work here, I get to wear them exclusively. Agreed?"

Pierre encouraged her by nodding behind Élise's back. Vianne knew she had no choice. The Gaultiers needed a cook, and Vianne needed the Gaultiers.

"Fine." Vianne unfastened the earrings.

"Why are you whispering in the hallway?" Sandrine shouted from the table.

Élise clipped the pearl earrings to her earlobes, smiling at Vianne but talking to Sandrine. "Nothing, madame," she shouted back. "Nothing at all."

Élise had left Vianne a little shaken, but not deterred. She had saved Chateau Ten, and she deserved to celebrate just as soon as she paid off all her creditors. Vianne walked back into the kitchen with a smile on her face, turning to Blaise sitting at the table.

"Blaise, darling. Would you like to go to Belleville? I'll buy you a new book at Colette's. You won't have to just look this time, you can take one home!"

He nodded incessantly.

"I don't understand what is going on," Sandrine said. "And not understanding makes me worried. Why do we need to give them the entire west wing? Seems extreme, doesn't it?"

"They seek privacy, that is all, and we have been paid handsomely for an extended stay." Vianne knew she needed to change the subject before Sandrine thought too much more about their new guests. "I'll tell you what. When I'm in Belleville this afternoon, I'll stop by Madame Marchand's and pick up some desserts for you. Those strawberry cakes you like."

"Oh?" She perked. "How about some macarons?"

Vianne turned to Blaise. "Go get ready. We can take the car this time," she said, then addressed Pierre, "and I'll make sure it's full of petrol before coming back."

"I'll go bring the car around," Pierre said.

Vianne sat in the moment, feeling the bulge of the francs in her dress pocket and the financial freedom that came with it.

Sandrine reached for Vianne's hand. "Henri didn't come to breakfast, did he?"

"No, madame." Vianne kissed Sandrine's cheek. "He left."

Vianne walked into the tax office with Blaise shortly before noon. She was relieved to find no German officers inside, but just to be safe and not cause attention, she tucked Blaise's slate under her arm and gave him his teddy bear to hold. "If you need anything, tug on my hand," she whispered into his ear.

He nodded.

Sandrine's dear friend, Amélie, worked at the tax office and called Vianne over with a frantic wave of her hand. "I saw Chateau Ten on a requisition list for unpaid war contributions. Please tell me you are here to pay the bill."

"I am." Vianne and Blaise took seats at her desk.

Amélie leaned over her papers. "Thank goodness," she said. "I had a feeling when I saw you pull up in the car. If you have money for petrol, you should have money to pay your tax, or that was what I was hoping." She turned to talk to Blaise, whom she had never met. "And who is this fine gentleman?"

"My nephew." Vianne brushed a curly lock of hair away from his eyes. "Blaise."

"How lovely," Amélie said. "How long will he be visiting?"

Vianne straightened when Amélie's supervisor walked by.

She trusted Amélie but didn't want to discuss Blaise's story within earshot of someone she didn't know. "As long as he wants," she said.

"Such a dear." Amélie winked at Blaise, who tightened his arms around his teddy bear.

Vianne counted out the notes she pulled from her handbag. Amélie was staring, and Vianne thought she was wondering how she came into so much money. If Vianne didn't tell her the truth, or at least a story that sounded like the truth, she might infer her own.

"We have renters," Vianne said. "But please, don't spread that around. The last thing I want is for the Germans to hear about it, if you know what I mean."

"I do know what you mean. It would be Sandrine's death. My lips are sealed."

Vianne slid the money across the table to Amélie.

"I'm sorry, Vianne, and also tell Sandrine I'm sorry. I did all I could to shield you from the war contribution tax."

"I will tell her, thank you."

"You know, I remember Chateau Ten before it was Chateau Ten. The parties, the dignitaries. Oh, and the gardens… I don't think you could find a finer garden in France." Amélie counted out the money for herself, pausing on the last note. "That was so many years ago. Shame what has happened since."

"It is a shame." Pierre did his best to keep the gardens up, but it was such a vast estate, and she needed the help of at least three more hired hands to restore Chateau Ten to what it was before The Great War and live up to its original name of Le Grand Maison.

Amélie wrote out the receipt. "And the fancy dinners. Can't forget those. I remember when Sandrine's husband bought her that gramophone from America—San Francisco, I think it was. At that time, I'd never seen one before, much less listened to an entire orchestra coming from a horn. I hope she still listens. Such fond memories."

"It's broken. I hope to get it fixed soon, though."

"Here we are. Paid in full." She handed Vianne the receipt. "You just missed Madame Marchand."

"Oh?" Vianne tucked the receipt into her handbag with her money. "We're going to stop by her shop after my errands."

Amélie placed her hand on her chest. "That relieves me. Please, do check in on her."

"Check in on her?" Vianne snapped her handbag closed. "Why?"

"She wasn't herself, and I worry about her. I know Sandrine worries as well." Amélie lowered her voice so her supervisor couldn't hear. "She was saying some dark things." She shook her head as if she still couldn't believe what she heard. "Very dark."

"What kind of dark things?"

"Perhaps this isn't a conversation for the little one?" Amélie said, to which Vianne agreed.

She gave Blaise his slate so he would have something to keep him occupied and asked him to sit in the corner chair a few feet away. "We'll just be a moment." She waited until he took the seat. "As you were saying?"

Amélie leaned over her desk, her voice barely above a whisper. "She talked about reuniting with her son, which I think says a lot."

Vianne covered her mouth. "Reuniting with her son? Do you think she's entered the Zone Rouge?"

"I don't know. She thinks her son is one of the Sorrows because of the way he died."

"How did her son die?" Vianne always assumed it was during the battle with a bullet.

"You don't know?" Amélie asked. "He hung himself, traumatized by so many dead, his friends' bodies in the trenches holding the mud walls together. He wouldn't waste a bullet on himself."

"I didn't know. Tragic, indeed. Though you don't have to go too far to hear about tragedy in this village."

"That was the story she was told anyway. Of course, they had to leave his body on the battlefield after we abandoned our villages, so she never had a grave to mourn over, just like the rest of us."

"But to go into the Zone Rouge…"

"Is it out of the question to imagine? Hasn't there been a time when you've been tempted to mourn Henri on the very ground he fought and died? If I could get away with it, I'd go in." Her gaze drifted to the window. "I lived in Haumont—the first village that died for France, just like my brother died, but on the battlefield. He's out there, you know, somewhere in a trench, in the mourning ground. I sometimes wonder if he's one of the Sorrows…"

Vianne cleared her throat.

"The Sorrows are a myth, Amélie. It doesn't do any of us any good to think otherwise, and the mourning ground of the Zone Rouge is sacred."

Amélie nodded, looking down at her hands. "I respect your

opinion, I do. I'm only saying that sometimes the grief has been hard to overcome, as you know—especially around birthdays and holidays. Doesn't matter how many years have passed. Hurts the same."

Vianne felt bad for being curt. "I'm sorry for my tone. I didn't mean—"

"It's all right. You know I have a special place in my heart for Madame Marchand because she looked after my parents when she lived in Vaux, the eighth village to die. I'm just trying to look out for her." She patted Vianne's hand. "Anyway, you are under loads of stress, and I shouldn't be talking about such a heavy topic at work. How's Sandrine?" A couple took seats at the next desk along, waiting to pay their taxes. "I haven't heard from her in many months, when I was used to weekly visits."

Sandrine wasn't the same person Amélie had known even months ago, but she wasn't about to talk about her mother-in-law's private health information with strangers sitting so close. If word spread of Sandrine's actual condition, she'd have more to worry about than the tax office—what riches were left on the walls at Chateau Ten would be spoils for those who dared.

"She is doing well," Vianne lied. "You should come for a visit."

"I think I will. Give her my best until then, will you? Or, when she's in Belleville, have her stop by. You know I never miss a day of work. We can chat on my break."

Vianne nodded.

After getting petrol for the car, paying her bill at the Meuse Electric Company, and settling with the baker who'd been nice enough to carry a balance for her since last week, Vianne paid

Mme. Marchand a visit, pulling up right outside her patisserie. She couldn't deny the independent feeling of driving again and took a moment behind the wheel after turning off the engine.

Blaise wrote a question mark on his slate.

"Just enjoying the car. It's been so long since we had money for petrol. Are you enjoying it?" She winked. "Let's go buy some treats."

Blaise ogled the delicacies in Mme. Marchand's dessert case, and particularly the pink and blue macarons. Vianne's eyes went to the flaky pastries, remembering what they used to taste like before the rations. Beet sugar, margarine, and powdered milk had replaced the best ingredients. Poor Blaise, Vianne thought, probably couldn't recall the sweetness of a macaron made with real buttercream, as young as he was. She didn't have the heart to tell him they used to taste even better.

"Which colors do you want?"

He pointed to a pink one and a blue one.

Vianne smiled. "Pink and blue it is, and some yellow ones for Sandrine."

They waited, but nobody came to the counter, and they'd been in the shop for several minutes. Vianne checked her watch before ultimately deciding to ring the counter bell. Seconds later, Mme. Marchand's husband walked through the back curtain, which was a change—she rarely saw him tending to customers.

Vianne caught a glimpse of Mme. Marchand over his shoulder through the curtain slit, sitting in a chair behind the storage bins where they liked to take breaks. After their usual greetings, Vianne thought up a way to ask about his wife in a delicate manner.

"Is Madame available?" she asked, followed by a light smile. "I'd love to say hello."

He took his time boxing her order. He either didn't hear Vianne or didn't want to answer. Vianne began to take Amélie's dark comments seriously and grew concerned, especially after seeing Mme. Marchand pacing.

"She means no disrespect." A smile flashed on his face. "She had a tough day yesterday and is still not herself." He slid the pink pastry box across the counter.

"I'm sorry to hear that. Anything I can do?" She handed him more francs than the desserts were worth to make up for her lack of ration coupons. He slipped the extra into his pocket instead of into the register, without a mention either way.

"Did you see those people with the roadster yesterday?" he asked.

"The black roadster?"

"Yes. Belongs to a couple. They were in yesterday evening, just before closing, asking all sorts of questions about the Zone Rouge. They were nice, but it put my wife in a delicate state, as I'm sure you understand. The anniversary was just four days ago."

"I'm sorry, Monsieur Marchand. Truly. I'm sure they meant no harm."

Vianne thought the Gaultiers must have already talked to Colette, and after finding out about Chateau Ten's location, wanted to learn more. "They are new to the area. Actually…" She hesitated about confessing she'd taken on renters, then decided to just tell him the truth so that he'd know they meant no harm. "They are guests of the chateau. Very nice couple. They must have had concerns about the Zone Rouge and thought to ask questions."

He reached for his broom to clean up, never responding to what Vianne had said and disappearing behind the curtain. She wouldn't be able to ask Mme. Marchand anything today, unfortunately, but the more Vianne thought about it, the more sense it made that Blaise had seen *her* near the fence and gate.

She smiled down at Blaise, and they left, making the short walk to Colette's bookshop, passing by Renée the mystic sitting on the bench outside. Renée shifted, leaning forward with her arms on her thighs, getting a clear and long look at Blaise with his teddy bear flopped over the pastry box he held in his arms.

Colette threw open the door with a clang of bells.

"Vianne! I wasn't expecting you again this week. Come in." She looked pleased to see them, but that changed once they were inside. "This isn't bad news, is it? You know I can't—"

"Not bad news," Vianne said. "I'm here with good news. And a thank you."

"I like good news." Colette showed Blaise a selection of tattered, but well-loved children's books, which he could have a pick through when Vianne interrupted to say they were going to buy new ones. Colette's face beamed. "New? You don't say," she said, then turned to Blaise. "Well, in that case, have a pick of the bookshelves in the back. I think you'll find something you like there."

Blaise ran off to the back of her shop, where he was used to looking and not buying. "It's been a long day." She sat on the stool next to the counter. "A good day. But long."

"And you're celebrating with some pastries, I see." Colette pointed to the pink box. "I guess now is the time to tell you I need another day with my rent." She grimaced. "Do you mind? I told you the end of the week, but now it will be Monday."

"That's fine." She nodded. "Pay when you can. Our new renters have paid me enough to keep us in a favorable position for a while."

Colette sat down with a little gasp. "You did it. That's wonderful news!"

"They seem like the perfect guests, even had their own contract for me to sign, which I thought was astute. And they rented the entire west wing for privacy."

"I'm so glad it all worked out. How does Élise feel about it? Cooking for two more…"

"That's the other thing, they are giving her extra funds to stock the pantry for their dinner parties."

"Dinner parties? Maybe there is hope in this world after all," Colette said. "And thank you for the rent extension. Regardless of whether you don't need the money right now or not, you have a right to collect it, even if you are my friend."

"Well, it's the least I can do. And I'm the one who is thanking you!"

Colette sat up tall when Vianne got up to kiss her cheeks. "For what?"

"For sending the Gaultiers out to Chateau Ten." Vianne sat back down, hearing Blaise plop books to the floor in the back.

"Who?"

"The Gaultiers," Vianne said, but then wondered if Colette even knew their last name. "The flashy couple with the roadster. I would have never approached them myself, and for once I'm glad you didn't listen to me—"

"It wasn't me."

Vianne laughed, thinking she was being modest. "Well, of course, it was."

Colette shook her head.

Chapter Five

Renée had stepped a little too close to some potential customers on the pavement, begging for money. "Hold on." Colette dashed for the door to scold her, leaving Vianne breathless with more questions.

"Wait—" she said, but Colette was already outside shaking her finger at Renée. "Then who did?" Vianne said to nobody.

Vianne quickly thought back to her first interactions with the Gaultiers—from the moment she peeped out the window and saw them looking at the fountain until she'd signed the contract. They said Colette told them about her rooms for rent, didn't they?

She tapped her fingernails on the counter, waiting anxiously for Colette to come back inside, and when she did, she wasted no time bringing the subject back up.

"But it must have been you!"

"Your renters?" Colette retied her apron. "I wouldn't lie to you. You know that."

Vianne was at a loss. "Tell me again about when they came into your shop. What did they do, or say?"

"Well, it was the afternoon, and they were dressed like they'd just come from the theater. Swanky and glittery with all sorts of jewelry on. They asked about a rare book, so I showed them my private collection since they looked like they could afford it. They spent about twenty minutes here. Bought a book. No change—"

"What book?"

"I'd have to look, and my ledger is in the back. They said nothing about Chateau Ten or needing accommodation. I just assumed they needed a place when we saw them outside the window yesterday, being new to Belleville and all. Renée knew you were considering renters. You think she could have told them?"

Vianne shook her head. "They don't look like the type that would listen to a mystic. They're sophisticated. Besides, Renée warned me not to take on a renter. If we ask her, she'll pipe up about how she warned me."

"It must be a coincidence. Or luck. Or..." Colette's eyes slowly met Vianne's.

"Or, what?"

Colette shrugged. "Nothing." She reached for the pink pastry box, tracing its edges with her fingertip. "It is odd, though. Your estate is hidden from all the roads, and the citizenry of Belleville-sur-Meuse wouldn't have suggested it, not without first telling them that it's as close as you can get to the forbidden forest without standing on a grave—"

"Roadsters are meant to drive. They must have been

looking for an estate on the country roads, and they found one. I misunderstood them. Let's change the subject."

"If you say so."

Blaise was still in the back, trying to find a book.

"How was Madame Marchand?" Colette asked.

"I don't know."

"Didn't you see her?" Colette patted the pastry box. "You were just there."

"Her husband helped me. But Amélie did tell me something disturbing." Vianne cupped her mouth because even though Renée was away from the window, she didn't put it past her to read lips. "She said Madame wasn't doing well. Her exact words were that she was having some dark thoughts."

Colette's mouth fell open. "That's awful. About her son?"

"It occurred to me ... Blaise wasn't sleepwalking or having a nightmare the other night. He saw Madame Marchand entering the Zone Rouge from out his window, and that's what made him scream. As awful as the image is to think about, with her purposely wandering into the forbidden forest, it's also relieving to know the truth."

"Talking is not the same as doing. That's a sacred place, and she'd risk offending the entire village—she'd never have another customer again if someone found out." Colette was once again distracted by Renée talking to potential customers and convincing them to give her a few coins. "Not again."

Colette burst outside under a clang of bells, shouting Renée's name, which brought Blaise running in from the back of the shop in a panic from the noise, his slate in one hand, and a new book he'd picked out in the other.

Vianne assured him everything was all right, then had a look at the book he wanted to buy, but Blaise's eyes were on Renée and Colette fighting it out on the pavement. She handed the book back to him when she noticed his slate. There was writing on it. "What's this?" Answers to questions he was asked—his name and who he was with.

She stood, looking down the middle of the shop to the dark back. "Blaise," she said, her heart hammering at the thought of him talking to a stranger. "Who were you talking to?"

He looked up with one blink of his big hazel eyes under a lop of blonde hair.

"You were talking to someone." She turned the slate around to show him his own writing. "Who?"

He pulled his thumbnail from his mouth, pointing fleetingly down the long aisle to the back, where she could barely make out the divan and some chairs for reading.

Vianne was sure she'd know if Colette had customers in her store this whole time. Wouldn't she? She looked out the window to get Colette's attention, but she was still busy with Renée.

"Stay here." She placed Blaise's hand on the counter for him to hold onto so he wouldn't follow her and started down the aisle, carefully creeping between the tall, full bookcases. "Hallo?" she called, followed by a pause. "Who is there?"

Vianne reached the end of the aisle. The books Blaise had been picking through lay on the floor from a tumbled book tower. "It was no one," she said to herself, followed by an exhale.

She bent down to pick up the books, stacking them in her arms to put back on the shelf, when a man appeared before

65

her from the darkness, handing her one of Blaise's discarded books, nearly scaring her into the next bookcase.

She dropped all the books to clutch her chest. "Who are you?"

He was still holding the book out for her to take when Colette threw open the front door and walked back into the shop.

"Colette!" Vianne yelled. "Hurry!"

Both she and Blaise were by her side seconds later. Vianne wrapped her arms around Blaise to keep him safe.

"This man was talking to Blaise."

He held out his hand for a shake. "I'm Max." He was dark-haired and blue-eyed, an interesting combination.

"Vianne, this is Max Durand," Colette said.

"Yes, as I heard. Twice now."

"He's a guest," Colette said.

"That still doesn't explain why he was talking to Blaise."

Max dropped his hand and genuinely looked apologetic. "Oh, ahh… Sorry. The boy asked me a question about a book—" Max wrote in the air with his hand "—on his slate, and we got to talking. Was I not supposed to…" He looked at Colette, who put her hands out in an attempt to defuse the situation.

"Vianne, this is the professor I told you about," Colette said. "The one renting my spare room. The one who is paying me, so I can pay you." She smiled with a slight stress in her eyes.

"Oh. I see." Vianne slowly loosened her grip on Blaise, who returned to building a book tower on the floor. "I'm protective.

I hope you understand. He's just a boy, and I thought we were alone."

Max seemed to understand, looking at the slate and acknowledging that Blaise didn't talk, and that was enough to be protective about. He apologized again.

"He's a war hero," Colette said.

"Well, I don't know about the hero part." He held his hand out again for Vianne to shake. "Let's try it again. I'm Max. Glad to meet you."

"Vianne." She shook his hand this time, and in that second when their warm palms met, she realized it had been ages since she'd shaken a man's hand who wasn't trying to arrange a payment plan for her bills. She pulled back a little too quickly. "Sorry," she said, without saying what she was sorry about. "Nice to meet you."

Blaise set his teddy bear on top of his book tower, and that was enough to send it crashing to the floor. Max helped him pick the books up, giving Colette enough time to whisper to Vianne while he wasn't looking.

"He's a widower, remember?" she said, then mouthed, "You'd be perfect together."

Vianne gave her a look. That was the last thing she needed, among so many other things.

Max stood up after helping Blaise. "Did I miss something?"

They both smiled. "No."

There was an awkward pause between them because clearly, he had missed something. Colette jumped in. "Tell her why you're here, Max. She might find it fascinating."

Max pulled a worn, leather-bound book from a shelf. "I'm

researching a secret society heavily involved with the Nazi Party—some say they started it. All my notes are in here."

"Secret society?" Vianne asked.

"An occult."

"What's an occult?" Vianne asked.

"A devilish organization that believes in apparitions, deities, and powerful ancient relics."

Vianne fought hard not to erupt with laughter after hearing something so ridiculous. "Sounds ambitious." She didn't know what to make of him. He wasn't German, and that's all she cared about. "Well, good luck." Blaise was engrossed in building his book tower, but Vianne thought now was a good time to leave after finding out what Max was researching.

She gave Colette a few coins for the book, who promptly slipped them into her pocket after handing her a bag for the purchase. She looked at her watch.

"Do you have to leave already?" Colette asked.

"We've been gone a while and with our new guests…"

"Guests?" Max asked her.

"She runs a chateau at the edge of the Zone Rouge and had the most peculiar guests show up this morning," Colette said, then turned to Vianne. "And the more I think about it, the more I don't know about them, Vianne. They just showed up? All on their own?"

Vianne closed her eyes. She thought they were done with this.

"The Zone Rouge?" Max asked. "Chateau Ten?"

Vianne was surprised he knew about the chateau. "You've heard of it?"

"Yes, actually. I have a friend who lives near there."

"We're the only family. Not a soul for miles, except up the hill."

He scratched his head. "I could have sworn…" He dropped his hand. "You don't know Pierre Boyer, do you?"

"Pierre?" Vianne should have known. "I must eat my words. He works for us, but he's like family, and I didn't think about it. How do you know him?"

"Through my father. They were both chemists in the war. Tell him I said hello, will you?"

Vianne liked that Pierre knew Max, and suddenly felt even more embarrassed for reacting harshly when she first met him. "I will," she said. "It would be lovely if you visited him at the estate. He doesn't get many visitors."

"I plan to. Thank you." He sat on one of the cushioned chairs where he lit candles due to the lack of natural light. "I have to ask. What is it like living so close to the Zone Rouge?"

Colette stepped closer to Vianne, coaxing her to take a seat opposite him on the divan instead of leaving. The space was inviting, as much as she resisted taking a seat, with deep blue walls and soft, goose-down cushions on the divan and chairs. The candles were a lovely accent, even if they were necessary for light.

"Well," she said, sitting with the book bag in her lap, "fairly normal. I live with my mother-in-law."

He looked at Vianne's bare ring finger. "You're married?"

"I was. He left—" She caught herself with a brief close of her eyes. "He died. Many years ago. Battle of Verdun." She'd never spoken that way before, and saying it out loud had shocked even Colette.

"I'm sorry."

69

Vianne could tell he truly was sorry to have mentioned it, and she thought it was best to just continue with what her life was like, save them both from the discomfort of talking about their dead spouses.

"My mother-in-law, Sandrine, she gets along with my help and Pierre's. My nephew, Blaise, also lives with us and enjoys it there. Not many guests these days, but hopefully that will change after the war."

"And you haven't suffered any effects of the Zone Rouge? The gases, the toxicity of the battlefield, being so close?"

Vianne shook her head. "We are perfectly healthy."

"Sandrine isn't," Colette said, which got Vianne to turn her head. "I'm just being honest."

"That's not because of the Zone Rouge, you know that. Otherwise, I would be sick, and so would Pierre. And our cook has been there the longest, next to Sandrine, and she's as robust as they come. We have many suites, a garden, and a magnificent library."

"Well, if I know Pierre, from what my father has said, he wouldn't stay if he thought it was bad for him."

"No, he wouldn't," Vianne said, though she knew Pierre would absolutely stay and watch over her and Sandrine.

"Sounds like a wonderful place."

"Try telling that to the people of Belleville-sur-Meuse. That, and the legend of the Sorrows in the Zone Rouge hasn't helped our chateau in the least."

"The Sorrows?" he questioned, looking quite confused.

"Forget I mentioned it. People need stories. That's all it is. Tall tales and stories."

"Vianne." Colette cleared her throat. "If you don't tell him about the legend, I will."

Vianne shook her head. "Blaise will hear. And besides, I'd rather you not."

"I'll whisper." Colette turned to Max. "It's said that in the deepest part of the Zone Rouge, the ghosts of fallen soldiers, sorrowful and resentful, roam the land at night, mourning their comrades and the lives lost."

"Colette…"

"Blaise can't hear us, Vianne," she whispered.

"Has anyone seen a Sorrow?" Max asked.

Colette motioned him closer. "There's one, and she confirmed what everyone has feared for over twenty-five years, including the rhyme they sing."

"What rhyme?" he asked.

Vianne kept glancing at Blaise to make sure he couldn't hear because, at this point, she was powerless to stop Colette.

"I don't remember it word for word," Colette said. "Like sirens from the sea, the Sorrows cry. An eerie melody tangled high—"

"Like sirens from the sea?" Max repeated.

Colette shivered. "They chant it through the trees, and once they learn your name…" She ran a finger across her neck, gesturing.

Blaise's book tower crashed to the floor, startling them all with a jolt.

Vianne huffed. "It's an absurd story, made up by the displaced people of the nine villages, people who don't respect the dead, or the soldiers who died for us. Yet they proudly say their village died for France. Plainly, it's what adults tell children to keep them out of there because it's dangerous. That's all. They should have been more careful with their storytelling. And the rhyme changes depending on who you talk to."

"It may change," Colette said. "But the message remains the same."

Max looked intrigued. "And you said someone has verified their existence? They actually saw a ghost?"

Colette gave an exaggerated nod.

"Who? And are they in Belleville?" He pointed to the floor as if he meant the shop.

"Genevieve Lacroix," Vianne said bitterly. "And, no. She is not in Belleville, and I hope she never comes back. She was mad, wracked by nightmares and sights of her dead husband, who coincidentally died in the trenches. I told her to leave when she insisted on confronting my mother-in-law to tell her the legend was true."

"Has Genevieve contacted Sandrine since you told her she wasn't welcome any longer and to go back to Verdun?" Colette asked.

"A letter came in the post not long ago," Vianne said.

"A letter? You didn't mention this before. What did she say?"

"I didn't open it. Well, that's not true. I opened the envelope and unfolded the floral stationery, but as soon as I saw her ranting, erratic handwriting, I folded it back up and tucked it away. I should have thrown it out."

"You didn't even read it?"

Vianne had read some, in fact, she'd read the first sentence, but she wasn't about to mention that. "I didn't have to." She let out an irritated sigh; she'd had enough talk about Genevieve Lacroix for one day.

Max looked like he wanted to defuse the situation, especially after Vianne's sigh. "Colette?" He smiled. "Remember that coffee I brought?"

Vianne's eyes lifted.

"Are you able to brew it here in the shop? I'm sure Vianne could use a cup, and maybe we could, too."

Colette paused, looking at Vianne, then back at Max. "I'll be right back." She walked downstairs into the basement where she kept her percolator.

"Coffee?" Vianne asked. "How did you manage to find coffee?"

"I've been saving it. Figure now is a good time to drink it."

"I appreciate your kindness," she said. "It's hard to believe, but the last time I smelled the aroma of coffee was two years ago. In a café that served it to a German officer. Of course, there was nothing left for a regular customer, no matter how much we were willing to pay."

"Of course."

He sorted through some books he'd pulled from Colette's shelves. Vianne studied him the best she could without letting on that she was, and decided they were about the same age. He was distinguished in a way that let her know he had earned his years but wasn't resentful about it.

She turned away when he caught her.

Colette came up the stairs with a tray and three hot cups of coffee. "Oh, perfect," Vianne said, taking a cup. "Shall we make a toast?"

"To the end of the occupation?" he asked.

"That sounds fitting." Vianne clinked their cups before taking a satisfying warm drink, but she noticed he hadn't taken a sip.

"Are you from Belleville?" he asked.

"I was born in Fleury, but my mother died when I was young, and I don't remember my father," she said, then continued on without taking a breath, something she would later blame on the coffee. "After the war, I spent time in Verdun, where I lived with my sister until she grew up. I came here fifteen or so years ago to help my mother-in-law because in many ways she was the mother I never had, and she needed me."

"I see."

"Sorry." Vianne winced. "I didn't mean to tell you my life story in one answer."

"But I asked," he said.

"What about you? Colette said you were from Paris."

"I worked there after the war, but I've been more of a vagabond since the occupation, which is when my research became a full-time job. Now, home is where my briefcase is, and where the information leads me."

"You've devoted your life to it." She took a few more drinks.

"Yes. I suppose I have, now that you mention it."

Vianne hadn't realized it, but she'd guzzled her coffee in just a few gulps despite the warmth.

"Here," Max said. "Have mine. I haven't touched it yet."

"Oh, I couldn't."

"To tell you the truth, I don't like coffee that much. I only offered it because I thought you would enjoy it, and I know how hard it is to find." He poured what was in his cup into hers.

"Thank you." Vianne looked at her watch after drinking a fair amount of what he'd given her. Now, it really was late. "Blaise…" She motioned for him to come along, but he wasn't interested and kept stacking the books. "I hate to take him away from the bookshop, but we do have to go." She hiked the book bag over her shoulder.

Vianne heard Colette whispering what had happened to her sister into Max's ear.

"That's dreadful and heartbreaking," he said to Vianne. He pointed to the slate. "So that is why…"

He stood when she stood, and they shook hands again, but Vianne didn't pull away this time. "It was nice to meet you," she said.

"Pleasure is mine."

Colette walked her and Blaise to the front of the shop. When she sent Blaise behind her counter to pick out a free used book, Vianne knew Colette wanted to tell her something. "Just below the register, Blaise. In the blue basket. Have a look, see if there's anything you want." She pulled Vianne close.

"Don't start with how attractive he is, and how I said it would be lovely if he visited," Vianne said before she could talk. "I was being cordial."

"That's not it." Her eyes shifted to the back where Max was, and then to the counter where they both could only see Blaise hunched over the basket of books. "I'm concerned. I don't know about this couple you have staying with you. What are their names? The Gaultiers?" Colette's voice turned to a

75

raspy whisper. "I've been listening to Max talk about the occult all day, and the Germans, and it's enough to send a chill up my spine. Then suddenly, a rich eccentric couple rents out the entire west wing of your chateau, the only chateau with direct access to the Sorrows—"

Vianne hung her head with a sigh, exhausted from having to explain herself. She went to the counter to collect her macarons and Blaise. "Colette," she said, putting the box under her arm. "I know you are just looking out for me, but like I said earlier, they paid me well, and honestly, it's the best thing that has happened to us in so long."

Before the war, Vianne had started a list of everything she'd sold off to make the estate's obligations. The bigger items went first—the oil paintings in the grand salon and long corridors, the wrought-iron bench in the garden, and some of the more expensive draperies in the suites. Now, with some time and patience, she thought she could start making plans to repurchase them.

"Please don't spoil it."

Colette stared at her for a second longer, as if she wanted to say something else, but Blaise was now by their side and looking up at Colette, batting his big hazel eyes. "All right. I won't say another word. For now, anyway." Colette kissed Vianne's cheek goodbye.

Rain spattered against the pavement, a persistent drizzle that brought Renée indoors, much to Colette's reluctant groans. Vianne watched her follow Blaise, eyes fixed on the teddy bear dangling from his hand. Then, once he was close enough, Renée surprised her, brushing a curl from Blaise's eyes as if she'd done it before.

"If you please," Vianne said, reaching for Blaise, but she grabbed his teddy bear instead and used it to pull him outside.

Renée watched, her brow furrowed and her voice with an air of alarm. "Keep him close, Vianne," she said as the door slowly closed between them. "The quiet ones know…"

Chapter Six

When Vianne turned the car engine off outside the chateau, she encountered a smell she had forgotten existed. Élise's butter-roasted pheasant with cream sauce. She rolled down her window to make sure, taking an even deeper breath than before, and all but tasting the saltiness of the crackling skin floating in the air.

Élise would have had to spend quite a bit of money on the black market to get a pheasant.

"Do you smell that?" Vianne closed her eyes after getting out of the car, thinking that they were in for a treat because of how good it smelled outside; it was only natural for the air inside the chateau to smell even better. "Élise has cooked up something special for us tonight."

Blaise stood beside her, rubbing his stomach, and it filled Vianne with joy. She could give her nephew a proper meal to go with the macarons they'd bought, the kind of meal he probably hadn't had for years—or at least couldn't remember having.

And she had the Gaultiers to thank for that.

The roadster was parked near their private entrance with the passenger-side door opened, as if they were about to get in, or had just gotten out. Either way, they were nearby, and she felt compelled to tell them how grateful she was, once again, for their patronage.

"Blaise, darling. Why don't you take your books to your bedroom and have a read." She handed him the book bag. "Dinner should be soon."

He gave her a squeezing hug. If only he would talk to her. It had been such a good day. Maybe today was the day he spoke to her without his slate? "I love you, Blaise." He looked up from her skirt, his long eyelashes batting slowly, which was enough to make her melt into the gravel. "Is there something you want to say?"

His mouth opened just a hair, words on the tip of his tongue, but then he shook his head, which only slightly disappointed her because it was the closest he'd come to talking since he'd arrived at Chateau Ten, aside from the scream and small noises.

"It's all right." Vianne patted him. "I'll see you inside."

He ran off to his bedroom with dust kicking up behind him before slipping through the chateau's door.

Vianne took the short walk over to the Gaultiers' roadster with the pastry box under her arm. About halfway over, she reminded herself how they paid for privacy, and perhaps she shouldn't bother them, even to express her gratitude, but that only lasted a moment because who wouldn't want to be thanked?

She reached out to close their car door, a natural reaction, then paused. "Hallo?" A magpie squawked from the fence post, followed by silence. She pulled her hand back—she shouldn't have come. They weren't expecting her, and what if she scared them? She could thank them some other time. She slowly stepped backward along the gravel path, one step at a time, before turning to leave.

"Madame?"

Vianne reached for her chest with a yelp, almost dropping the pastry box. It was François, and he had been watching her from a trellis of ivy growing up the chateau's chimney.

"What are you doing?" He casually smoked a thin cigarette, legs crossed at the ankles.

"Monsieur Gaultier." Vianne was still holding her chest. "Your car door was open, and I knew that you were either here or there," she said, meaning inside or outside, "and I wanted to say—"

Vianne cut herself off because it had all happened so fast, and she felt she was rambling.

"You wanted to say…" He took a few hurried steps toward her, his gaze narrowing in on one eye.

"Thank you."

A smile flashed on his tense face. "Oh? For what?"

"For the long-term rental." She nodded once. "I hope you are getting settled and enjoying your day. It is very quiet out here, as I'm sure you've become aware."

"We are. Thank you very much. It is quiet." He took a long drag of his cigarette. "Deathly quiet."

Vianne studied him for a moment as he looked toward the trees. She'd said what she wanted to say and told herself she should leave, but for whatever reason, Vianne hesitated. "By the way, how did you find us here at Chateau Ten?"

Smoked curled from his cigarette. Monique had walked outside, heading to the roadster's open door, oblivious to the two of them standing near the trellis.

"I believe you said—"

"*Ma chérie!*" François snapped his fingers, and Monique turned stiffly around. "Our lovely host wants to know how we found the chateau."

Monique relaxed almost unnaturally upon seeing Vianne. "Is that right?" She slunk over to François after harshly closing the door. "Isn't it obvious?" She rested her arm on his shoulder. "This place is gorgeous."

Vianne realized she sounded more like an investigator, and that was exactly what she didn't want to sound like. She followed up with a more softened approach. "I thought maybe it was Madame Marchand?"

"Oh, her? We found her shop yesterday." Monique pointed to the pastry box. "And I see you were there today. Did you get something wonderfully delicious? Though everything she has is delicious."

Vianne was about to show them the macarons she bought when Monique made a slight gasp. "Oh dear, I see your ears are bare." Monique unclipped her earrings and fastened them to Vianne's earlobes, tickling the nape of her neck with the slightest touch. "They look magnificent on you. Simply magnificent. Don't they, François?" she asked, waiting for him to agree, which he so exuberantly did. "Keep them. They are yours. Blue was never my color."

Vianne felt the weight of the jewels hanging from her ears. They were expensive. "I can't." She started to take them off, though she'd already spent their value in her head. "These must be worth a great deal."

"You will take them, or we will take back our payment and leave." Monique laughed hysterically, which got François to laugh. Vianne couldn't tell if they were serious, but one thing she knew, after years of living with Sandrine, was that when you were given a gift, you should graciously accept, especially when it's from one of your guests.

"Thank you very much," she said. "I mean it. If there is anything else I can do…"

They smiled, holding each other and thoughtfully blinking at Vianne, which she took as their way of letting her know she should leave. They had paid for privacy, after all, and she felt she had taken up too much of their time, and it didn't matter in the end how they found the chateau, did it?

"Have a good evening," she said, turning for the main door. They waved in unison, still smiling. By the time Vianne made it to the front door, they were gone, but that nuisance of a magpie was back, squawking from the gravel near their roadster.

Inside, the aroma of the roast pheasant was almost overwhelming. Upon closing her eyes, Vianne had to reach for the newel post to steady herself. The winds of change had finally come. She'd thought this before, of course, when she set off to Belleville-sur-Meuse with a handbag full of money, but there was something about coming home to a hot, savory meal, and seeing the new tally in her accounting books, now that the day was done.

Vianne opened her eyes when Pierre approached her, mentioning her new earrings and remarking on their incredible sparkle. "A gift for yourself after a good day?"

"These? No. Can you believe our guests gave them to me?"

"I thought they already paid you with francs."

"They did," she said, then clarified. "Monique said blue wasn't her color. It appears they have nothing but money to spend and jewels to give away." She unclipped them from her ears. "Here. See what you can trade them for. I want you to get that new roof."

"New roof?" he asked.

Vianne looked into his kind eyes. He was the most giving person she'd ever met. He would do anything for them, and especially Sandrine. It made her feel good to do something for him.

"You don't wear that ratty threadbare jacket in the mornings because you want to, Pierre. I'm smart enough to know you sleep in it to keep warm. Take the earrings."

His shoulders slumped after trying to push the earrings away.

"I insist. I'm certainly not going to give them to Élise when she asks for more collateral. Drive up the price as high as you can. You'll be able to get more money for them than I could."

"Thank you, Vianne." He nodded. "I will let you know what I get for them."

"Or don't." She wanted him to keep the rest, though she knew he absolutely wouldn't do that. "You know someone in Belleville who has roofing materials, don't you?"

"Yes."

83

"Good," Vianne said. "It will be done quickly, before too many more storms. Hopefully even tomorrow."

"Did the car suit you well?" he asked.

"Yes, it did." She sighed. "But I did hear a bit of depressing news today. Madame Marchand isn't doing well. Rumor is she might be trying to enter the Zone Rouge. I think it was her that Blaise saw out his window the other night and made him scream. Can you keep a lookout for her? I'm worried she might..." Vianne pressed her lips together because it broke her heart to know Madame was having dark thoughts, though she understood how a mother would want to be with her son. "You understand, don't you?"

He nodded.

They made their way into the kitchen, pausing for a close of the pocket doors that separated the foyer from the west wing. "We must keep these closed," she said. "I meant to talk to you before. Between you, me, and Élise, we should be able to handle it."

When they walked into the kitchen, Vianne encountered something else she'd forgotten. The sound of laughter. Élise and Sandrine sat at the table, chit-chatting like they used to before the war, about recipes and old memories of past guests.

Vianne's hand went to her heart, and she was about to say something nice to Élise when the cook looked up, lips thin as a ribbon.

"Dinner is ready." Élise got up to ladle a heaping portion into one of Sandrine's porcelain bowls. "To perfection, I might add, with the finest ingredients I could buy on the black market."

"It smells wonderful," Vianne said. "Thank you."

Élise steeped her tea with valerian root for sleep, adding a splash of liquid from an unmarked amber bottle.

"And I see you found some nerve medicine on the black market as well."

Élise tipped back her teacup, gulping until every last drop was gone. "I did." She untied her apron. "And don't thank me, thank your guests. Angels, they are. Thank God you came to your senses. Otherwise, we wouldn't have any of this." She turned on her heel to leave, but first placed a bowl of pheasant in front of Sandrine. "*Bon appétit.*"

Vianne called Blaise in for dinner, and for the first time in a long time, they ate around the table, all four with no mention of Henri's empty chair, or what was missing from the main dish, because nothing was missing from that pheasant. They talked about how flavorful the sauce was and how hearty the meat, spoonful after delectable spoonful.

"She deserves a raise," Sandrine said, wiping her mouth.

"Élise?" Vianne asked. She wouldn't give Élise a raise even if she could afford it, but indulged Sandrine anyway. "I'll see what I can do."

A gust of wind had kicked up as the sun set, blowing debris over the gardens, but they were safe and sound around the table. Sandrine sat back, her belly full. "I'm stuffed as a pig."

Vianne almost forgot about the macarons. "I have dessert! Fresh macarons." She opened the pastry box, letting Blaise take one first, then offering one to Sandrine while Pierre finished his meal.

"Is today a holiday?" Sandrine asked, suddenly looking confused.

"No, madame," Pierre said tenderly. "Just a good day. Enjoy."

"You asked me to bring home some macarons," Vianne said.

Sandrine bit into her yellow macaron, but Vianne could tell her mother-in-law was questioning more than the day and might be slipping into the past. She felt an urgency to change the subject before Sandrine thought too much more about it.

"Pierre. Oh, my heavens, I can't believe I forgot to mention that I met someone who knows you in town. A professor who is staying with Colette."

He pushed his glasses up his nose. "Whoever could that be?"

"Professor Durand. He said his father was a chemist with you—"

"Max Durand? How wonderful. He's a brilliant scholar. Trustworthy. What on earth brought him to Belleville-sur-Meuse?"

"Research. He wanted me to pass on his regards."

"What kind of research?" he asked.

Vianne wasn't going to bring up occults and secret societies at the dinner table, especially in front of Sandrine. "I don't know all the particulars."

After dinner, Vianne got Sandrine ready for bed, first putting on her own robe and nightgown before wheeling her mother-in-law down to her bedroom. Élise had put fresh yellow roses in a vase at her bedside, something else she must have purchased on the black market.

"Is it still windy?" Sandrine asked.

Vianne saw stormy skies out the window with debris tumbling over the garden. "It'll clear up tomorrow." She turned on the electric lamp, causing Sandrine to squint. "Something wrong?"

"I feel like it's been ages since you turned on that light. Has it been?"

Now that Vianne had paid the electric bill, she had no problem turning on the lamp. "For so long, I liked the candlelight, I suppose." She smiled. "Maybe we can use the lamp more often."

Vianne tucked the sheets around Sandrine's legs after adjusting her pillows. "There," she said.

Sandrine caught Vianne's hand before she could pull away, giving it a weak squeeze against her blanket.

"Yes, madame?" Vianne felt her papery-thin, soft skin.

"I hope Henri brings you flowers often. You deserve it." She winked. "You two have such a future ahead of you."

Vianne was used to Sandrine talking about Henri, but when she spoke about him as if they'd just returned from the Fleury Chapel, as if no time had passed, and they were starting their life together, her words hurt a little more. No wonder she felt stuck. No wonder she hadn't moved on. She kissed Sandrine's cheek. "Goodnight."

She turned off the lamp and closed her door to all but a crack before walking into Blaise's room, finding him lying patiently in bed, waiting for his bedtime story with his teddy bear tucked in next to him. She brushed a lock of hair away from his eyes that always, without fail, flopped back over like a curly cue.

"I love you." She cupped his sweet face with one hand, trying to recall the sound of his voice, but it was getting harder and harder to remember. "Shall I read from one of the books you brought home?"

He smiled feverishly with a little kick of his feet.

She sat in the rocking chair with the book bag from Colette's, when the lamp cut out after several buzzing flickers. Blaise was startled, as was Vianne, but she lit a candle and told him it was because of the storm and not to worry.

Droplets of rain hit the windowpane. "See. Just the storm. By morning, everything will be peaceful and calm. You are safe here, Blaise." Vianne pulled the candle in close next to the rocking chair. "Now, let's see what you picked out..." She examined the cover—a story about a farm boy—and read a whole chapter before she saw Blaise had closed his eyes.

She rocked back and forth in the chair. His room was quiet despite the occasional howl of wind gusts. She reached for the other book to see what it was about, but this one wasn't like the first book at all. There was no title, and it was bound in leather with several protruding bookmarks. "What is—"

It was Max's notebook about the secret society. They must have been switched by mistake. She felt awful that he might be looking for it and vowed to return it the next day. She moved to put it back in the bag, but curiosity had taken over. The occult seemed like a rather frivolous thing to be interested in. Didn't it?

She flipped through the ink-smeared pages, finding his notes were extensive. "Thule Society," she read. "Founders of the Nazi Party..."

The Thule Society believes lost souls can be resurrected, commanded, and used to reshape wars. Steps must be followed, starting with an intent and a desire. The Sorrows and the Zone Rouge are worrisome, considering the legend and the location of the missing relic... Rumors of a sea invasion are imminent, but when? If the Germans can command the Sorrows, France has no hope.

> *Like sirens from the sea, the Sorrows cry,*
> *An eerie melody tangled high.*
> *A ghostly wail of violins unseen,*
> *Drifting through the night in play,*
> *Whispering your name to steal you away.*

Vianne snapped the book closed and was left with her thoughts, and nothing was more debilitating to her than her thoughts, rocking back and forth in her chair a little harder as speckled candlelit shadows danced on the wall. Max knew about the Sorrows when he'd acted as if he didn't. He also knew the rhyme.

Vianne moved to the window and gazed upon the scorched trees of the Zone Rouge, their blunt, branchless trunks looking black on the horizon with an occasional flash of lightning reminding her they were there.

"*An intent and a desire...*" It sounded desperate and fantastical to believe in raising a ghost army, and there wasn't anything more irrational than believing in things you couldn't see. What would that even look like? She almost laughed, imagining something cartoonish—something an old woman would tell children by the fire late at night. Even so, after a few moments of staring out the window with her thoughts, she couldn't resist reaching for the book again.

She flipped to the back.

The Thule Society's belief in a ghost army has roots dating back to Roman times — Virgil's Aeneid, the Battle of Cannae, and the Japanese Myth of the Onryō. Eyewitness accounts, including letters, about the phantom soldiers from the Battle of Mons are current evidence as reported in the Daily Mail.

War stories meant to sell newspapers—that's their evidence?

Vianne sighed. She didn't know much about the Aeneid, the Battle of Cannae, or the Japanese ghost-army myths, but Mons she vaguely recalled. It was a courageous battle between British and German forces during the last war. A short story about the battle was published, talking about angelic warriors and phantom archers, but readers believed it was real. Then, the soldiers started recalling the events as if they truly happened. It was propaganda, as far as Vianne believed, a piece of fiction worth forgetting.

She closed the book for good this time, deciding that not only would she return it first thing in the morning, but she'd remind Max that the Zone Rouge was a burial ground, not a place of restless, lost, and sorrowful souls. Further, what the Thule Society believed was nonsense, and he was full of nonsense to be studying up on them.

She was finished thinking about this and kissed Blaise's

cheek before walking out of the room with her candle in one hand and Max's book under her arm. She padded down the hallway for the stairs, at first not noticing the pocket doors to the west wing were open until she rounded the corner.

She was sure she'd closed them. Didn't she? She must have. She remembered telling Pierre to keep them closed so as not to disturb the Gaultiers, but maybe he forgot? It could have also been Élise.

With her flickering candle, Vianne walked across the foyer to lock them this time, when she experienced another forgotten memory to go with the butter-roasted pheasant, and the laughter in the kitchen: the enchanting sound of music, if ever so soft and fleeting.

But as she listened a little closer, she thought she also heard German being spoken.

She traversed the switchback corridors of the west wing in her robe and bare feet, trying to find where it was coming from. It wasn't coming from one of the suites or Élise's room. She gazed down the longest corridor with her candle to the library door, when all turned quiet.

Vianne briefly considered if she'd imagined it, but she swore she knew what she'd heard, especially after not hearing music for so long. However, it was the German voice she simply couldn't let go of. She reached for the library door because she had to be sure.

The room was unnaturally cold and empty, undisturbed from the last time she was in there with the ladder still where Monique had left it, and the white sheet firmly draped over her broken gramophone.

The candle flickered in the crackling quiet. "Hallo?" She took one step inside on the groaning parquet floor and then froze, entranced by the delicate tap of ivy blowing against the stained-glass window. "Hallo?" she said again, only this time barely above a whisper.

Vianne wondered if she'd gone mad, her grip tightening around Max's book from the idea, before hanging her head. What was she doing? She'd let his ridiculous warnings and lore get to her and imagine things that didn't exist.

Vianne turned, closing the library door when the overwhelming feeling of someone in the dark walking up from behind nearly threw her into the wall.

"Good evening," Monique said, warm and breathy in her ear.

Vianne's candle danced over Monique's glassy cheeks.

"We have paid for privacy, no?"

"I ... I..." Vianne found herself blathering after the initial shock because, yes, of course, they paid for privacy. "I heard music. German voices. I was concerned."

Monique's face changed. "I see." She ushered her away from the library with slender, cold fingers pressed to the small of Vianne's back. "It must be your imagination. There is no music here."

The storm blew violently over the rooftop, only it sounded like a million critters clamoring for a safe home.

They stopped at the pocket doors.

"I'm sorry. But it was so real. Words, German words, and I swore a—"

Monique closed the pocket doors on her while she was talking, leaving Vianne standing in the empty foyer with her candle licking the dark air. The silence was deafening among the nighttime shadows, and the chant in her head was the rhyme.

Their eerie melody tangled high…

She shivered, looking up the walls to the ceiling, then ran up the stairs and into her bedroom, where she closed the door.

Chapter Seven

Vianne woke the next morning from a nightmare, breathing heavily and clutching her chest, the lingering feeling of being chased prickling up her spine. She tried to hold onto the details, but they slipped away with each blink. Normally, she would have blamed it on her financial problems, but things were different now. She blamed this nightmare on Max and his notebook.

She hated that his research and the dark theories had affected her physically and mentally, more so, how she might have upset her guests from imagining things that weren't there.

Vianne entered Blaise's bedroom while tightening her robe tie, finding him on the floor with his slate. He covered what he was drawing with his hand before turning it completely over, but she saw enough to know he'd used the black chalk Colette had given him.

"Good morning…"

He hopped to his feet, latching onto her waist with such

force that she took a step backward. "There, there…" she said, rubbing his back over his pajamas, and eyeing the turned-over slate on the floor.

Blaise looked up from the folds of her robe, his eyes round, innocent, and secretive. After his reaction last time, she resisted the urge to ask him what he'd drawn.

"Why don't you get dressed?"

He took his slate with him to his dresser, running his fingers roughly over the image, smearing the chalk.

"It's cloudy today." She looked gently out the window, pulling back the heavy drape. The warm buttery scent of Élise's home-baked croissants flitted through the doorway. "But it smells like Élise made something special for breakfast, so that is a bright spot." The storm had tossed pine needles over the grass and patio. The fence had been pushed back by the wind, and the trees…

Vianne tied the drape back with a gold cord, gazing into the craggy scorched forest of the Zone Rouge. The trees looked different—the trunks looked browner, not their usual weathered gray, but she had to admit she hadn't examined them that closely before. And are those new branches growing from the dead trunks?

She rubbed her eyes, wiping away the crust of sleep, when she heard Pierre in the hallway. "Pierre?" she questioned.

He poked his head inside. "Yes?"

She pointed at the trees, only now they appeared normal and as they'd always been.

"Something wrong?" he asked.

Her jaw gaped open, trying to understand what she'd seen. "I could have sworn branches had grown overnight."

He looked out the window for himself. "Where?"

Vianne pointed again. "In the Zone Rouge…" She shook her head after staring. "A second ago, it all looked different. Perhaps it's just my eyes."

"A good storm can make you question things. Even the wind can tinker with your mind."

"Like make you hear voices?" she joked.

"Voices?"

"Oh, that reminds me." She snapped her fingers. "Please make sure the pocket doors to the west wing are closed. I'm sure I told you, but they were open last night."

"Yes, I have kept them closed."

Élise had gotten Sandrine and was wheeling her past Blaise's door. "What did you say about the wind?" Sandrine asked.

Élise backed up and wheeled Sandrine into the room.

"We were just talking about how it was quite a storm last night." Vianne kissed Sandrine's cheek. "Did you sleep well despite it?"

"Yes. But I was worried about Henri. He was up all night, checking the doors and windows, and also … I can't find my keepsake key, and it's due for a polish. Have you seen it?"

"I haven't."

"You gave it to Henri, madame," Élise piped.

Vianne gave Élise a look, hoping she wouldn't go a step further and remind her that Henri was dead—and to her relief, she didn't.

Blaise had finished getting dressed, and she thought he was looking for his missing book, checking the empty book bag near the rocking chair, then tugging on her sleeve.

"I need to go to Belleville this morning," Vianne said to Pierre. "One of the books Blaise came home with yesterday wasn't the one we had bought." She turned to talk to Blaise. "I'm going to exchange it first thing. They were accidentally switched. But you'll be all right here while I'm out."

She saw the disappointment in his eyes that he wouldn't be going with her, but she didn't want Blaise hearing about the legend of the Sorrows, the Zone Rouge, ghosts, occults, or anything remotely frightening when she returned Max's notebook. "But, Blaise, you must promise not to go into the west wing while I'm out. Stay close to Sandrine."

He moped, arms long at his sides.

"Blaise, dear." Sandrine motioned him toward her. "Show me the book you do have."

While they were busy, Élise pulled Vianne over to the window by her elbow.

"Don't think about leaving the boy here with me to watch. And just in case you are wondering, I don't mind him. It's you. I'm not your babysitter, and also…" She leaned into Vianne's ear. "I'm not your employee."

"What do you mean, you're not my employee? You work here."

"I'm François and Monique Gaultier's employee. They paid me extra for the term of their stay. Until then, I take orders from them." She peeped over Vianne's shoulder to Sandrine. "I'll continue to take care of Sandrine because she's been my friend for ages. Gave me my first job. But you … you almost lost this place to unpaid taxes because you won't ask anyone for help, and don't think I don't know it."

Vianne was in a difficult spot. She felt she could still leave

Blaise with Sandrine, as long as he understood the rules about not going into the west wing, but what if the pocket doors were left open again? She didn't want Blaise accidentally wandering in there, thinking it was an invitation, after Monique reiterated their need for privacy. Blaise was still delicate, and she wasn't sure if he could endure a scolding, especially from a stranger.

"I will watch him," Pierre said, evidently overhearing.

Élise shrugged. "Suit yourself." She sauntered out of the room to set the table for breakfast.

"Are you sure?" Vianne asked him. "You have so much to do as it is." Pierre was elderly, and she usually wouldn't put such a burden on his shoulders, but all he had to do was make sure Blaise stayed by his side.

"I don't know why she's been so difficult lately," he said. "But no matter. Blaise is a delight. Do you need the car?"

"People might talk if they see me driving two days in a row. I should ride my bicycle."

"I do have one request. I don't think the storm has passed, and I'd hate for you to be caught up in it."

"I'll be careful, and I won't stay long." She kissed both his cheeks. "Promise."

Pierre walked out, wheeling Sandrine to the foyer with Blaise following behind, leaving Vianne alone in his room.

Her eyes wandered to his slate.

With Blaise gone, she decided she'd be a fool not to look. She listened for two heartbeats, making sure they were far away, before grabbing the slate.

He'd drawn the iron fence again, except this time the trees had tendrilled branches that reached out like fingers, but reaching for whom? She pulled the heavy drape back, tilting the slate for more light, becoming fixated on every line, every faded and smudged curve, trying to decipher its deeper meaning, when she heard a noise. A scratch, or maybe it was a gasp.

Vianne covered her mouth, her heart pounding.

Blaise had been standing in the doorway, watching her.

"You came back!" Her voice was unnaturally light and airy, playing it off as if she hadn't been looking, but he had caught her, and there was no mistake about it. But for how long, she had no idea. "Mustn't forget your slate."

She would have to be quicker if she wanted to know what he was drawing without asking.

She hung the slate around his neck as if it were any other morning and walked out of his bedroom door to the kitchen. Once she rounded the staircase, she threw her back against the wall, chastising herself for not being more discreet.

Vianne parked her bicycle in front of Colette's bookshop, finding the storm had blanketed the street in crackling leaves from two seasons ago and thousands of white primrose blossoms instead of the pine needles back at Chateau Ten. Nazi Party banners hanging from collaborators' shop windows looked worn and weathered but nonetheless had managed to stay attached, flipping and flapping in the light breeze.

Vianne looked at her watch. It was still early, and she wondered if Colette's bookshop was open. She cupped her eyes to peep through the window. To her relief, Vianne spied

Colette's dark head of hair between the shelves. After a knock on the glass, Colette waved for her to enter.

"I know you weren't expecting me again after two days in a row. But I swear, it's not to ask for money, and I won't be long."

"No, it's perfect timing! And I love a visit." Colette stood, dusting off her hands. "I have to grab a box out from the back. Tend to the front, will you?" She walked away. "I'll just be a minute. Maybe two."

By the time Vianne answered, Colette was already deep in the back storage area. Vianne had a seat on Colette's stool. Renée wasn't sitting in her usual spot outside, which was a welcome surprise. A few minutes passed. Vianne twiddled her thumbs, hearing Colette rummaging around in the back. She didn't think Colette had many customers on a daily basis, but looked for the money box anyway, just in case one walked in.

"Where's your money box?" she shouted.

Vianne heard a box plummet to the floor in the back, followed by the thump of tumbling books. "Next to my ledger!" Colette replied, from somewhere.

"Ledger," Vianne mumbled to herself, sifting through the books under the counter and finding it stuck at the back, but she was now more interested in the ledger. It was the book Colette used to record every title she'd sold since starting the little bookshop in Belleville-sur-Meuse.

Vianne opened to the current month of May, looking at the names and titles, starting at the top of the month and sliding her finger down each entry. Mme. Marchand bought a book about gardening, and Amélie bought a book about fairytales, presumably for her granddaughter.

It felt a little intrusive, sneaking a peek at what the locals read, but Vianne found it incredibly entertaining. Her finger stopped on François Gaultier's name. *Ceux de 14. The Men of 1914* by Maurice Genevoix, a book about the Battle of Verdun.

Vianne looked up and stared at the blank wall.

She thought it was insensitive for someone to buy a book about the Battle of Verdun in Belleville-sur-Meuse. Vianne was also surprised that Colette even had it available to purchase, as it wouldn't be favorable to the Germans, and she could get in trouble. But Vianne also knew Colette was a sucker for a good sale, and truth be known, it was her private collection that paid her bills.

Vianne was so caught up in her thoughts about François, the book, and rationalizing his purchase that she dismissed the hum of a black Mercedes pulling up outside.

The door swung open with a mad thrash of bells.

Vianne snapped the ledger closed. "Good morning—"

An SS officer wearing silver chevrons and shoulder boards walked through the door. After a brief scan of the shop, he walked up to her at the counter by taking three significant steps in his heavy black boots. He was so close, she could have smelled what he'd eaten for breakfast on his breath if she had inhaled.

Vianne had seen him the other day—she recognized his decorated jacket—but she never thought she'd be in a position where she would have to talk to him.

"Fraulein." He nodded once after taking his hat off and holding it under his arm.

Vianne managed to stand, shakily, but she'd managed it. Colette was still in the back but had gone quiet. She must have seen or heard, and by the lack of noise from the shop owner, Vianne understood she was on her own. All she kept thinking about was keeping her thoughts and words to herself. Talking to an SS—nothing good ever came of it. They were masters at dissecting every word, question upon question.

"I'm looking for a rare book..." He again had a look over the shop, ending with a glance at the children's books Colette had in baskets on the floor. "Is this the bookshop to visit?" A simple smile spread on his lips. It was neither agreeable nor sinister, which made her heart pound.

"A rare book?" Vianne repeated. What he meant was black-market books. She wasn't about to breathe a word about the titles Colette had in her special bookshelves or under the floorboards, and she felt she could play dumb in this case since she wasn't a shop girl, but was filling in.

"Are you the owner?"

"No." She shook her head while answering just to be clear. "There are books on cooking. Gardening, and literature... I don't work here normally. I'm filling in just for the day."

"I see." He fitted his hat back to his head, followed by a check of his watch, and it was a striking white-faced timepiece with silver links—expensive, something Vianne could feed most of Belleville with. "My mistake," he said, turning to leave.

Vianne thought she'd escaped any awkward questions, but then, to her utter dismay, he turned on his boot heel.

"You look familiar." He tapped the counter. "Are you from Belleville-sur-Meuse?"

"I—" Vianne didn't know what to say. Lying to the SS was

dangerous, but so was telling the truth. "I've lived here for a while. The seasons are nice."

He was still staring at her, as if categorizing every nuanced inflection and feature she had, before his eyes trailed down her shoulders and arms, and to her waist.

He shook his head. "It's of no consequence, I suppose. Have a good day." His gaze flitted to the floor baskets again and the children's titles. "Ah!" He reached for the horse book, showing her the cover. "I had a pony when I was a child." He pulled coins from his pocket to buy it.

"So did I." The little voice in her head told her to be quiet— stop talking—but it felt unnatural not to reply. "Such fond memories I have of mine—" She smiled abruptly, cutting herself off.

He handed her a few coins. "No change."

Vianne watched him walk out the door, the coins in her palm. Colette came running in seconds later, yelling for Max to come out of the loft upstairs.

"What was he doing here?" Colette asked, smooshing her nose to the glass and looking in both directions, but he'd already driven away.

Vianne dropped the coins on the counter and backed away. "We had a conversation, and he said I reminded him of someone. His gaze…" She shivered. "It felt like he was undressing me."

Colette grabbed Vianne by the shoulders. "Tell me exactly what he said."

"I can't remember the last time I had to talk to a German. I'm secluded at Chateau Ten. You must be used to it." She felt her racing heart.

"Nobody is ever used to talking to a German, especially the SS," Colette said. "Now, what did he say?"

"He first asked me about your private collection, and I said I was filling in and didn't know. Then he bought a book—a children's book." Vianne closed her eyes briefly. "What if I'd brought Blaise with me today?"

"He knows about my collection?" Colette chewed her thumbnail. "Renée must have told him for a few coins. That's why she hasn't been parked on my bench outside, I bet you."

"What did he look like?" Max asked.

"Like all SS, I imagine. Gray hair that was once blonde, blue eyes." Her eyes lifted to Max's, who had held her gaze. "Attractive, if he wasn't German."

He took off his reading glasses.

She felt like an idiot for mentioning that last part in front of Max, but it was true. Without the uniform—without knowing he was German—he would have been pleasant looking. "I've seen him before, right across the street—he's important, according to his decorated uniform."

"And he bought a children's book?" Colette asked. "That seems strange. I didn't think the SS cared much about children. I hope he never comes back."

"I hope he does come back!" Max said. "I want to know what text he was looking for."

"He was probably looking to extort me. A woman with a private collection is good money in occupied France—money I don't have. I'm going to close the shop. I need to think." Colette checked her watch.

"Maybe I misunderstood," Vianne said. "He asked for rare

books, and I thought that was code for your private collection. My heart was thrashing. It's hard to remember now."

"He's SS, Vianne." She pulled the shade over both the windows before locking the door. "They don't pop into shops and ask for reading material, much less a rare book. He was on a mission." She gathered her candles, then waved them both to follow her into the back. "Let's get out of sight, by the divan."

"I can't stay," Vianne said.

"Well, you can't leave now!" Colette said. "What if he sees you? He'll be knocking on my door next, thinking the owner has come back."

Vianne reached for her handbag and followed Colette since Max had already gone to the back room. Colette's private collection was neatly displayed on two bookshelves. Mainly French criticism of German wars. However, it was what she had hidden under her floorboards that would get her in serious trouble—her Cassini maps. Detailed topography of any given region, most of which were destroyed during the first war after the military used them, but Colette had a way of finding things that were hard to get. Even things that the Germans demanded we hand over years ago for the war effort.

Colette pulled back the rug to lift a section of the floor where she kept her map scrolls. "These need to be moved. I'm not taking any chances." She gathered them in her arms. "They're my most valuable items in this shop. God, I'm so glad you were here when he walked in because I'm not sure how I would have reacted," she said, then stood straight, legs straddling the open floorboards. "Why are you here? You didn't say." She looked over Vianne's shoulder as if she had just realized she'd come alone. "And why didn't you bring Blaise?"

Vianne was still thinking about the SS, his talk about a pony, and how quickly the interaction happened. How easy it would have been for her to elaborate, and maybe he would have figured out where she lived. It was possible.

"Vianne…" Colette snapped her fingers.

"Sorry. I did come here for a reason." She pulled Max's notebook from her handbag. "Your occult book was switched with Blaise's by accident," she said to Max.

"I was looking all over for this!" Max said. "Thank you for bringing it back."

"Why wouldn't I?" Something in his voice made her think. "Did you do it on purpose?"

"Do what?" he asked.

"Switch books with Blaise so I'd read about your fantastical and desperate ideas."

"Why would I do that?" Max flipped through the pages, making note of all his bookmarks and tabs—they were still where Vianne had left them, but she wasn't sure if they were where *he'd* left them. "And to be clear, the legend of the Sorrows isn't mine," he said.

"Speaking of, why did you pretend you had no idea what the Sorrows were?" Colette's eyes popped, apparently, this was new information to her as well. "Clearly, you know all about them, and you believe in them," Vianne added.

He looked up from his notebook. "Do you believe in the Sorrows?" He motioned to his displaced bookmarks, where she'd read about the Thule Society and the ghost army.

"I was curious what you had compiled on that secret

society. I'll admit that, since you can see I thumbed through the pages. But in regard to the Sorrows, no. I believe in things I can see. I made that clear before."

"I'm not here to make you a believer."

"Aren't you?" she asked. Vianne thought that was why he'd lied to her about knowing the legend in the first place—see what she knew and felt first.

"Tell me about the guests at Chateau Ten," he said. "Last time you were here, you said they paid you well." He folded his arms, pressing his notebook to his chest. "Did they pay you in francs?"

"How else would they pay me?" She thought it was a silly question to ask and had a laugh.

"Jewelry," he said.

"Jewelry?" She dropped her arms. She didn't consider the earrings payment, but a gift. "Why would you ask that?"

He paused, making Vianne think he was holding back. "I hope you don't think I've gone mad. I'm sure my question seems strange, and what I'm studying is unusual."

"Pierre called you a brilliant professor, said you were someone to trust, and I trust Pierre. I trust Colette too, and she wouldn't let a mad person rent a room while her husband is away, no matter the price." She paused. "But I can tell you the legend of the Sorrows is nonsense."

The wall clock chimed at the top of the hour. "I better go," she said, after checking her watch. "I told Blaise I wouldn't be long, and Pierre is watching him when I know he has other work to do." She reached for her handbag.

"Vianne," Max said, taking her hand as she tried to leave. "What if it isn't nonsense? What if it's true and the Thule

Society raises an army from the Sorrows before the invasion we know is coming?"

"Have a good day, Max."

She walked to the door, shaking her head. Colette followed, first pulling the shade up to have a look down both ends of the street.

"Come back tomorrow?" Colette asked.

"Afraid not."

"Oh?" Colette looked disappointed after looking back at where Max was pulling books from the shelves for his research. "Well, you can always change your mind, you know. I'm used to your visits now. Maybe Max is, too."

Max was handsome—he was. But Vianne's heart and mind were busy with matters at home, and also, maybe he was just a little mad—the harmless kind of crazy when a professor becomes too close to his research. "To tell you the truth, all this talk about the Sorrows, the Zone Rouge, and Max's research has kept me up at night. I need a break and a peaceful night's sleep."

"All right."

There was still no sign of Renée on the bench. "Where's Renée?"

"Gone, hopefully, forever." She kissed Vianne goodbye.

Chapter Eight

Vianne expected to find Pierre exhausted by the time she rode up to the chateau, but instead found him full of life, hearing him explaining how to use sandpaper as she neared the workshop. She gently pushed the door open. "Hallo?"

Both Pierre and Blaise looked up from the sawdust-covered workbench, smiling.

"I didn't expect you until after dinner," Pierre said.

Vianne smiled. She had nothing to worry about after all. "Looks like you two had a good afternoon." She checked her watch. "I assume Élise made Blaise lunch?"

"She did," Pierre said. "And you saw Max?"

"Yes." She watched Blaise working away with both hands firmly on the wooden sandpaper block, developing a bit of a sweat on his forehead from pouring all his effort into it while Pierre supervised. "Pierre," she said as they sanded. "Can you tell me more about Max? How well do you know him?"

He looked up, pausing, before leaving Blaise to continue

without him. "I know Max well enough that I expect a visit if he's in Belleville. Is that all right, that he visits?"

A smile flashed on her face because he was always courteous to her wishes, even when he didn't have to be. "Pierre, you don't have to ask for permission. You know that."

In many ways, Pierre was the father-in-law she never had, since Sandrine's husband died before she met Henri.

"Thank you, Vianne. Chateau Ten is my home. Has been for many years."

"I know."

He put his hand on top of Blaise's head, giving his blonde hair a toss. "And this boy. I loved having him today." He took off his work glasses for his everyday spectacles. "And as far as telling you more about Max. What exactly did you want to know?"

"What kind of person is he? You said he was smart—brilliant, I think it was. But…" Vianne wasn't quite sure how to ask Pierre what he thought about Max's character, much less his state of mind, without sounding suspicious. "Has he always had a wild imagination and such passion for his research?"

"Depends. Did you find out what he's researching?"

Vianne nonchalantly reached for a piece of sandpaper, feeling the grit between her fingers. "It sounds mythological and unbelievable. I'd feel silly saying it out loud."

"I'll be the judge of that." He folded his arms.

"Can we talk over here?" She waved for Pierre to move toward the door for privacy. "It's a secret society he says is connected to the Nazi Party." Vianne whispered the rest, drawing him in even closer. "He called it an occult, and he has taken an interest in the Sorrows."

Pierre slowly moved away until she saw his eyes again.

"Don't you think that's a strange thing for a professor from Paris to research? And the Sorrows? That's outright fantasy."

"Max is meritorious. If he's researching a secret society, then there's some credibility to it. Does he think this secret society is in Belleville-sur-Meuse?"

Vianne knew the answer to this was yes, since she had read portions of his notebook, but decided to keep it vague. "That was my impression."

"I see." He pulled a crumpled cigarette from his pocket, one he'd probably been saving for a long time, and lit it with a lighter that barely had enough spark. "Does that worry you?"

"No. Because I don't believe in any of it." She looked down at her hands. "He's a nice man. I just wanted to mention it to you and know your thoughts."

"Do you know how his wife died?" he asked.

"No, I can't say I do. Colette didn't tell me, and I wasn't going to ask him."

He walked outside, drawing Vianne to follow him. "On second thought, maybe he should be the one to tell you."

"Is it a tragic story?" Vianne asked.

"Afraid it is." He turned, looking at Blaise through the open doorway, which made her think he didn't want her nephew to hear one whisper about it. "I'm sure being a widower has affected him—his research is probably all he has left."

"I see." Max was complex, had experienced loss, and perhaps they had more in common than she thought.

Monique motioned to Vianne from the chateau's patio door, which concerned her. She looked in on Blaise to see he was still content, sanding the same piece of wood. "Would you mind…" She took a few steps toward Monique.

"Take your time," he said.

She trudged up the grassy hill to the chateau where Monique was now smoothing her shiny hair back. Vianne hoped she wasn't going to say she didn't have hot water, especially now that the bill for coal had been paid. As she got closer, she noted the clean scent of talc from a recent bath, which relieved her, but now she was thinking it had something to do with the pocket doors being opened again. "Is something wrong?"

"I was just waving hello." She pointed away from the patio to the garden. "I'm going on a short walk since there's a break in the clouds today, allowing for a little sunshine between storms. Join me."

She locked arms with Vianne before she could answer. Being so close to Monique, feeling the silkiness of her dress and the smoothness of her lilac-scented skin, made Vianne aware of her age and appearance, which could use a wash and an update.

"Are you having a good stay?"

Élise waved to Monique through the kitchen window, but it was Vianne who waved back, pretending they were the best of friends.

"Yes, very good. Élise is roasting a duck tonight for some dinner guests we will be entertaining in the west dining room. Some new friends, some old. A small gathering."

"That's splendid."

Monique tugged on her arm, drawing her in closer as if they were having a proper girl talk. "That boy of yours, Blaise, is that his name?"

Vianne tensed when she mentioned Blaise's name. "Yes. What about him?"

"Charming young man. I found his slate interesting. He must be a creative."

Vianne stopped walking. "You talked to him?"

"If you can call it talking." Monique smiled. "He wrote a few things down on his slate, which I thought was cute. Efficient, if you ask the right person. But he also carries a teddy bear around like a toddler. Ragged thing. You might have to mend it soon."

Vianne had difficulty understanding. "He was in the west wing?"

Monique hooked Vianne's arm again and led her straight for the Zone Rouge. "Well, technically, yes, he was in the west wing, if you call the pocket doors the west wing. It was right after lunch. But, please, I know how children are. Don't be mad at him."

Inside, Vianne was fuming, but not at Blaise, or even Pierre. She was mad at Élise for leaving the pocket doors open at lunchtime and then blaming it on Blaise, as she clearly had done. "I'll make sure they are locked tonight before I go to bed, and always."

"Excellent." Monique rubbed the opal pendant around her neck. "We'd hate to have to find another place. And you were hidden as it was."

"We are hidden. And did you say Madame Marchand told you about us—"

Monique stopped abruptly with a loud gasp once they reached the iron fence, the scorched trees looming over them. "Sad what happened out there. Simply heartbreaking. And now it's a quiet place with only the rustle of leaves that never fall, reminding us of those who died for France." She moved her lips close to Vianne's ear and whispered. "Have you been in there? It's so quiet at night. Dark." Her breath was sweet.

Vianne blinked. "The Zone Rouge is forbidden."

"Yes, yes, of course. But still, have you?" Monique winked. "You have a gate for goodness' sake."

Vianne's arm slipped out from under hers. "It's forbidden because it's a mass burial ground. It's a place of rest. Honor. Sacrifice—"

"The answer is no, then? I see. Oh, before I forget," Monique said, pointing a finger in the air. "I've instructed Élise to give you our leftover duck roast." She unclasped her necklace. "And this pendant is strangling me. Would you like it?" Monique clasped the necklace around Vianne's neck before she could say a word. "Are there horses on this property?"

"Horses?" Vianne's hands were on the necklace around her neck.

"Yes. What did you think I said?" Monique chuckled. "I see you have a carriage house, but I haven't seen any horses. And what about the orangery?" She turned, looking over the property.

Vianne sold the horses years before the occupation. And the orangery? They still had one. Élise had managed to keep her herbs thriving in there along with some fruits, but you couldn't see it from the chateau because it had been overgrown with brush and tree branches that Vianne couldn't afford to have pruned.

"The horses were a casualty of the war," she said, implying that the Germans confiscated them. "And the orangery is on the western edge of the property and quite functional. Why?"

Monique smiled.

"I assume you have a wine cellar, don't you? And where is the formal dining room?"

"Is the west wing dining room not suiting you?"

"On the contrary. I couldn't help but notice you eat your meals in the kitchen."

Vianne had sold their formal dining table, and they'd been eating in the kitchen for a few years. Her and Pierre told Sandrine it was because of her wheelchair, and the accessibility when she asked. Élise had always remained quiet about what Vianne had sold off, though Vianne saw it in her eyes that she disapproved with each item she secretly had moved out and sold.

"We enjoy the casual nature of the kitchen."

"Hmm."

Vianne was still pressing the necklace to her collarbone.

"This is too valuable. I can't take it." Vianne tried to take it off, but Monique grabbed her arm.

"Yes, you can." Monique gave her a slight look over. "I'm bored with it. Buy some new clothes if you want to sell it." Her eyes slowly shifted to the tree trunks where the wind whistled through their craggy cracks. "I bet these trees have stories. If only they could talk."

She turned on her heel and walked away, leaving Vianne a

bit speechless. She didn't even notice Pierre had walked up to see how she was. "Everything all right?"

It took Vianne a moment to nod, watching Monique as she opened the chateau's patio door and disappeared inside, her hand clenching the opal against her chest.

Blaise had run up to the chateau and stood near Vianne's bicycle with his teddy bear hanging limp and cockeyed from one hand, instead of coming down to them. It was on the tip of Vianne's tongue to ask why, but she quickly focused back on the opal, unfastening it and handing it to Pierre.

"Another piece of jewelry?"

"Get whatever you can for it," she said. "But don't say anything to Élise or Sandrine about it, will you? I have a feeling Élise will get jealous, and Sandrine will have questions that will bring confusing answers."

"It is odd, isn't it?" Pierre asked.

"A little." She wasn't going to mention what Max had said back at the bookshop about paying in jewelry, simply because she was sure it was a coincidence, or at least, that is what she told herself.

"How did they find us, again?" he asked.

"I don't actually know."

"They are being secretive?" Pierre asked.

"I get the feeling she only listens to half of what I say or ask. I'm sure that is all it is. They are rich, that is a certainty, and to our benefit, it sounds like. Roast duck for dinner tonight." Together they walked up the hill toward Blaise. "By the way, why didn't Blaise come down here with you?"

Pierre shrugged. "I thought he was by my side."

Monique was true to her word, and they were given the leftovers from her dinner party. Sandrine didn't ask about Henri's whereabouts, even though they'd set his plate out, which was another nice break for Vianne. Pierre told Sandrine all about Blaise's handyman skills as if they were talking about a grandchild, taking great pride in everything he did.

The duck was rich and tender. The wine was smooth. Vianne tried to take a moment and enjoy it while her good fortune lasted. "It's been a while since we've lived like this," she said.

"I recall a wonderful dinner last night," Sandrine said. "It was last night, wasn't it?"

Vianne kissed her cheek after getting up with her plate to wash in the sink. "Yes, last night was wonderful, too."

Pierre brought Henri's plate when Sandrine wasn't looking. "Quite a few headlamps came up the drive earlier," he said. "Aren't you the slightest bit curious who their guests are?"

"They asked for privacy. I must respect their wishes."

"But shouldn't you check, just to make sure the guests aren't…" he looked once at Sandrine before whispering, "German."

"They signed a contract on that matter," she said, then corrected, "*we* signed a contract." The kitchen smelled of rendered duck fat and wine. Vianne was thankful. "I trust them."

"I would find out who they were," Sandrine said from the table. "If I weren't in this wheelchair, that is." She looked at

Blaise and talked in a sneaky, low voice. "I'd tiptoe around in the shadows and then jump out from the drapes and say—"

"Surprise?" Vianne asked.

"No, boo!" Blaise smiled ear to ear, especially after Sandrine held her hands up like a scary ghost, which was the most delightful sight in the world. "I suppose I mustn't be too loud," Sandrine said, putting a finger on her lips. "What if the guests hear me?"

"They won't hear you. Not over here." Vianne had finished with the dishes and sat back down, sweeping a blonde lock of hair from Blaise's eyes. "I do wonder how it is going over there, however. I hope the duck was as moist and tender as our portions were."

"Did Élise make sure to use the china?" Sandrine asked.

Vianne nodded, though she knew all they had left were the porcelain plates.

"And the silver?"

Vianne had sold the silver off, spoon by spoon, over the years. "Élise would have set them a good table," she said.

"Good. If it was cold or not served on time, a good place setting might be a distraction. But do not worry. Élise is a good cook."

Vianne went to open the kitchen curtains a little wider. "It's so dark tonight," she said, thinking it was the calm before the next storm. She looked for German bombers heading for the channel.

Blaise drew on his slate, and it was quiet for a few minutes while they drank their after-dinner tea. Until Élise burst in with the dirty dishes from Monique's party, plopping them into the sink, which she filled with warm, soapy water.

She whistled to herself. There was no mention of the dinner or the guests, leaving Vianne and Sandrine to stare.

Vianne cleared her throat, but Élise kept on whistling and washing.

Sandrine set her cup down. "Élise. Tell us about the dinner and the guests. Do I know them—are they from Belleville-sur-Meuse or Verdun?"

"I don't know." Élise kept her back to them, but Vianne was glad that at least she'd answered Sandrine. "The Gaultiers asked for plated meals to be arranged before their guests arrived, and when I went in to clean up, the room was empty. Whoever they were had scraped their plates clean. Not a lick of sauce to be had. As I expected, of course. I am the best cook in the Lorraine with the proper ingredients." She glanced over her shoulder in Vianne's direction.

"Did they leave?" Vianne asked.

"Again, I don't know," Élise said, but Vianne had a good idea that she knew. Pierre struck up a conversation with Sandrine, which Vianne seized as an opportunity to remind Élise about the pocket doors.

"Please keep the pocket doors closed. They asked for privacy. All right?"

Élise scoffed, reaching for a rag. "I have remembered."

"But they were open, and I certainly didn't leave them open. Neither did Pierre."

"I don't know what to tell you." Élise had dried all the dishes and was taking off her apron to call it a night. She motioned to Blaise with a point of her head. "Sure it wasn't him?"

Blaise looked up from his slate, then went back to his drawing.

"Leave him out of this," Vianne said.

"Like I said, I don't know what to tell you. Maybe it was Sandrine's visitor."

"What visitor?"

"I don't know."

"You don't know much these days, do you?"

Élise gave her a snide look. "I heard her talking to someone in her room, that's all. I was in the kitchen, and you know that voices can echo down the hallway. Ask her who it was if you're so concerned."

Vianne turned around and watched Sandrine, who seemed happier tonight, joking with Blaise a little more than she usually did, and Vianne didn't want to confuse her.

"Vianne?" Sandrine asked.

"Yes?"

"Where is Henri?"

Vianne closed her eyes. Élise left, tossing her apron in the laundry. They had almost made it through the meal.

"Don't worry about him tonight, madame," Pierre said, getting up from the table to help wheel Sandrine down to her room. Vianne held his hand momentarily when he patted her shoulder.

"And Blaise," Pierre said. "Probably time for you to go to bed, too. Vianne?" he asked, from the doorway. "Coming?"

Vianne followed them out after flicking off the lights. She stopped in the dark foyer to check the pocket doors, to make sure they were locked with a hard pull. Satisfied, she took over for Pierre so he could go to his private quarters, tucking Blaise into bed and then getting Sandrine ready in her room.

Sandrine was standing when Vianne walked in, dressed in her nightgown and reaching for her bedpost. "I'm good for two steps, maybe four," Sandrine said. "That's all."

Vianne helped her get under her covers, tucking them around her stiff legs. "I know."

Clouds had rolled in quickly with a howling gust of wind. In the distance, a crack of lightning. "Another storm. Another night, and another day tomorrow," Vianne said, looking out the window, but she was referring to the Germans and their relentless campaign. How many years would they have to continue to endure the occupation, she wondered, when Sandrine gasped behind her.

"Oh no!" The look of horror had fallen over Sandrine's face with her hands clamped over her mouth, her eyes big and round like an owl's. Vianne had seen this look before, and it sent a ripple of sadness through her body because she knew what was going to come next.

Vianne immediately sat with her.

"Henri left, didn't he?" Sandrine asked. "For the war, and he never came back."

"Yes." She tucked a gray lock of hair behind her mother-in-law's ear, not knowing how much time she had left with the real Sandrine—the one who could remember—before reaching for her hands.

"I'm sure I knew." Sandrine's eyes strained, staring off toward the wall. "It's all so foggy. He died in the trenches, the last weeks of the war." She looked up, pausing. "And he loved you."

A ball formed in Vianne's throat. "Yes, Sandrine. He did."

"But you have wasted a lot of time here with me," Sandrine said. "Why?"

This was the first time Sandrine had asked her that question, and she wasn't sure what to say, other than the truth. "You asked me."

She shook her head. "It wasn't my intention for you to stay this long. I'm sorry. I'm sorry for keeping you here when you could have been living your life."

"You didn't keep me from anything, understand?" Vianne held her hands a little tighter.

"No, Vianne. I did. Don't let me keep you from living your life. Not anymore. Henri wouldn't want that. Take Blaise and go somewhere. Meet someone. Before it's too late."

Vianne turned away when she felt her eyes bulging with tears. She had thought about leaving before, and Colette had never been shy about expressing her opinion on the matter, but now, in her middle years, Vianne didn't know where she'd go, or what she'd do, when for so long her focus was on the chateau. She turned back around.

"Sandrine, I—" she said, but her mother-in-law was fast asleep. Vianne blew out the candle. "Goodnight, madame."

Chapter Nine

The storm inched closer to Chateau Ten as Vianne slept fitfully in a twist of tangled sheets. Sometime around midnight, a thunderous bolt of lightning startled her awake. She sat up, her damp nightgown clinging to her chest, her heart racing, before stumbling in the dark to the window for some air.

The cool night breeze swept over her clammy hands and arms. "Another nightmare," she breathed, only this time, she couldn't blame it on Max and his notebook. It was fragmented and fading, but she remembered trees towering over her and their roots grasping for her ankles.

"*Mon Dieu.*" Vianne needed a glass of water for her pounding head. She found her robe and a candle and padded down the stairs in her bare feet. The pocket doors were wide open.

Élise.

Now, Vianne's head pounded for a different reason. She reached for the latch to close the doors for the second time that night, thinking how she'd have words with Élise over breakfast about this, when she could have sworn she heard her name. She stood still, questioning herself for what she believed was her imagination.

She poked her head between the doors, her candlelight swallowed by the endless darkness. "Hallo?"

The sound of music pulled her to enter—a violin, perhaps, maybe a harp. She knew she should walk away, not set one foot in the west wing, reminding herself that her guests paid for privacy, but for some reason, she could not turn around.

When she heard German being spoken, she gasped.

Vianne slipped through the doors, creeping down the long marble corridors of Chateau Ten in search of the voice—in search of the music—with her silky robe fluttering against her legs.

She stopped once she reached the library.

Candlelight lit up the checkerboard floor under the door. She heard oohs and aahs—more than one person—then with one hundred percent certainty, she heard a woman's voice switching between German and French.

Vianne quietly gripped the doorknob, first thinking about what she was going to say because they could have guests, but they couldn't have German guests. That was it. She'd tell the Gaultiers that their German guest had to leave, and they could never come back.

The strum of strings eerily drifted in the air, soft yet keen, giving her the briefest of pauses before twisting the knob.

"Monique—" she started to say, but she'd frozen in the doorway with her eyes sprung wide open and her candle fighting for its life.

Her departed father-in-law's mahogany writing table had been turned into something diabolical with handfuls of glowing candles in a circle, and François at the helm with the Marchands on one side, and mystic Renée on the other.

"What…" Vianne gulped. "What's going on here?"

François started to get up from his chair, but it was Monique who rushed toward her with a glowing candelabra in her hand. "I'm sorry we woke you." Monique frowned. "François, we need to be quieter. Look what we did."

The Marchands turned to each other as if they weren't sure what to do—stay or leave. Renée looked out of breath and exhausted, refusing eye contact.

"We will be quieter," Monique said. "Is there something else?" She batted her eyelashes.

Mme. Marchand handed François his glassy black necklace, which he immediately placed into a silver box instead of clasping around his neck.

Vianne straightened. "You didn't answer my question." She turned to the Marchands, thinking they would answer, but they remained silent—him rubbing his roughened gray beard, and her with the remnants of red lipstick that couldn't last the night. The gramophone was still covered by a sheet. "I heard music and strange voices—German. I'll ask again, what are you doing?"

Monique set the candelabra down, the flames licking the deep green walls and illuminating the golden filigree swirls. "You have mentioned that before. Interesting. Well, I can't answer for the music, but as far as voices, you are a smart woman, Vianne. Surely you know what we are doing. You know Renée the mystic, don't you?"

Vianne's lips pressed.

Monique motioned to the Marchands with a sway of her arm. "And the lovely couple who run the patisserie are not strangers, are they?"

"No." Vianne lit the oil lamp, adjusting the wick to its brightest setting, which made Renée and François squint.

"Then surely, you know exactly what is going on, no?" Monique pulled out a chair. "Please, sit down."

"I don't want to—"

Monique practically shoved her into the chair. "We insist." Ivy scraped against the stained-glass window high above, casting shadowy vines onto the ceiling as clouds blew swiftly past the midnight moon. "Now, isn't that comfortable?" Monique gave a slight smile to the shadows.

The air felt thick and heavy, with Vianne wrestling between anger and confusion rising warmly through her veins.

"Vianne." Mme. Marchand finally spoke up. "Please, don't get angry. You, of all people, should know what this means to us." She dabbed her eyes with a soaked handkerchief. "We would have done anything to talk to our son Luc again. Thanks to the Gaultiers, and Renée, we have." She smiled tearfully, reaching for her husband's hand on the table to hold as he kissed her cheek.

"You talked to your dead son?" Nothing seemed more absurd and heartbreaking to Vianne, because Renée was a swindler, and she'd do anything for a few coins, even prey on the Marchands' emotions—two of the sweetest people she knew. She wanted to ask them if they really thought this was real, but when she gazed into their sad, yet hopeful eyes, she couldn't bring herself to it, because they obviously did.

"Maybe you'd like to try?" François asked Vianne.

"Yes!" Monique said, snapping at François for the necklace. "That's a splendid idea."

"No!" Vianne put her hand out to stop François, though she wasn't sure what the necklace had to do with anything. "I'm leaving." Vianne knew she didn't have the right to tell them they couldn't have Renée or the Marchands over. "I thought I heard German, and I can see there aren't any Germans here, so…" She got up, nodded once, then left, walking away as quickly as she could.

Monique chased after her, grabbing her by the arm in the corridor before the first turn. "I hope this doesn't sour things between us." Her eyes looked hollow in Vianne's candlelight, intensifying her expression. "We have paid you a great deal."

Vianne knew she was treading a fine line now. "I kindly ask that you don't have séances here at Chateau Ten. Is that agreeable?"

"That wasn't part of the contract."

"I didn't think I'd have to add 'no séances' to our agreement. And who was speaking German?" She looked over Monique's shoulder into the library, seeing the Marchands putting their coats on to leave, and François paying Renée near the oil lamp, or at least, that was what it looked like to Vianne from down the corridor.

"Vianne," Mme. Marchand called from between the library doors. "Please, don't tell Sandrine." She wiped her nose with her handkerchief, then left with her husband through the private, side entrance.

Vianne pivoted sharply toward the east wing with Monique following her. "It was just a little fun," Monique said once they reached the pocket doors. "Sorry we woke you, and we respect your wishes. Won't happen again. We couldn't resist after finding out about the Zone Rouge today."

"You didn't know about it before you arrived?" Vianne asked, but she knew they did because they'd bought a book about the battle.

Monique smiled slyly. "Goodnight, Vianne. Try to get some sleep."

Vianne closed the pocket doors, firmly locking them in place, listening to Monique's heels tapping away against the checkerboard floor. She was disappointed in her guests. The thought that they were trying to talk to the dead, even if she didn't believe in such things, gave her a shiver. Instead of going into her bedroom, she went into Blaise's where he was fast asleep, and quietly curled up beside him, pulling him in close and finding his teddy bear.

What was she going to tell Pierre? What was she going to say to Colette, who'd warned her about the Gaultiers to begin with? She listened to the wind whistle in short bursts through the crack in Blaise's windowpane. She'd say nothing at all.

That was it. She'd stay quiet about it. As if it never happened.

Thunder rolled over the top of Chateau Ten just before the sun rose. Vianne got up to look out of Blaise's bedroom window. Even in the semi-darkness, she saw the devastation the storm had left. Leaves littered the garden, and the shingles she'd heard rattling in the night had finally broken free and lay in the grass, but the scorched trees in the Zone Rouge were as robust as ever. She squinted. In fact, she thought they had grown.

A crack of lightning woke Blaise with a dark cast of the fence's iron bars and pointed barbs displayed on his wall. "Don't be scared," she said, but he pulled the covers to his chin. "Wait for the thunder to chase the storm away." She counted using her fingers. "One, two, three…"

Thunder rolled overhead.

"See." Vianne untied his drapes to let them hang and keep him from looking. "Chasing it away. It's very early morning." She looked at the clock on his wall. "About an hour till sunrise."

She lit the candle on Blaise's nightstand for some soft light and adjusted the covers, tucking his limp teddy bear in close. "Would you like me to read to you?" She felt around for the book hidden in his blanket, but it was his slate. He immediately pulled it away and buried it, but she saw enough to know he'd drawn something secret.

"Blaise, darling…"

She wanted him to talk to her. Tell her what he was thinking and feeling, so she could help him. It broke her heart to know he was suffering. Blaise moved the slate to hold it at his chest, and the teddy bear slipped away and fell to the floor. Vianne picked it up.

"You know your mamma and me were sisters," she said, and he nodded. "I should have been there that night to protect her and you. I should have stayed in Verdun and helped her raise you, or had you both move here."

Vianne hung her head, squeezing the teddy bear because she had never said this out loud before.

It was her decision to move in with Sandrine years ago, out of obligation and loyalty, but if she was honest with herself, she'd also say it was to satisfy a sense of purpose once she realized her youth had passed her by. If she had stayed in Verdun, maybe she could have kept them safe? She could have at least kept her sister from joining the resistance.

"I'm sorry, Blaise. I want you to know that." She tucked the teddy bear back into place under the blanket, its head against the pillow to keep it from flopping over. "I will do everything I can to protect you here and give you the best life I can provide. And after the war, I'll do whatever it takes to find your mother." She saw that his arms were loosening around his slate. "But I can do more if you talk to me."

She smiled hesitantly, not wanting to push more than she already had. She expected him to retreat and roll over with his slate if she said one more word about it, but he surprised her by relaxing his arms enough for her to take it from him, if she wanted.

Vianne pulled her candle inward, gently taking the slate from his arms.

"Oh, my," she said as calmly as she could, but inside she was reeling.

His drawings had escalated into something disturbing; this time, a thin fog had been added to the fence line with thumb-shaped ghoulish faces in black hovering over the tendrilled branches.

She wasn't prepared for something so shocking and wanted to change the subject as fast as she could. "You are quite the artist." She tucked the slate next to him. "Have you used the blue or green chalk yet?" She felt horrible for not being able to honestly talk about what he drew, but she was caught off guard by what looked like the Sorrows.

A few seconds passed before he shook his head.

"Well, maybe today." She found his book on the floor. "Now, shall I pick up where I left off the other night? I should be able to get a chapter or two in before everyone wakes up."

Her hands shook while turning the page, and her head felt light. A deep breath helped, but only a little. She read two or three chapters and had no idea what the story was about because her mind was on Blaise and why he'd draw such a thing.

She pushed the book away once he was asleep, adjusting the teddy bear's head once again because it had somehow flopped over, but it wouldn't stay, no matter what she did, so she buried him under the blanket with a little groan.

It was possible that Monique had asked him about the Sorrows. Vianne also didn't put it past Élise to try and finish the story she started in the kitchen. She planned to talk to Élise about the pocket doors already, and when she did, she'd warn her that if she mentioned the legend of the Sorrows to Blaise again, she'd make sure the Gaultiers wouldn't pay her anymore.

She realized it was an empty threat, but it might work. It was all she had. Vianne simply couldn't have her nephew believing in nonsense, especially in his delicate state. She looked down at his little face, lightly petting his head until the sun had risen.

She blew out the candle. "Morning."

Blaise sat up in bed, and Vianne held her head. Moments later, she heard Pierre walking down the hallway and encouraged Blaise to go to him so he didn't have to watch her. "And take your bear."

Pierre popped his head in. "Good morning." Blaise was quickly tugging on his hand.

Vianne desperately wanted to tell him what happened last night, but that was the last thing she should do, and she had already promised herself she'd stay quiet. "Yes, good morning. I'll get Sandrine," she said. "Go ahead and take Blaise wherever he wants to go."

Vianne had placed Sandrine's dress on the chair the night before, and she was nearly dressed by the time Vianne went to help her, but that was because she only had to take two steps after standing.

Vianne helped her into her chair while Sandrine looked her up and down. "Don't you want to get dressed, dear?"

"I'll get dressed later." Vianne tightened her robe tie and wheeled her toward the hallway.

"The French didn't train for trench warfare," Sandrine said. "Did you know that? They trained with horses and the cavalry instead, and look what happened. That's all the Battle of Verdun was—trench warfare." Vianne stopped. Instead of an elderly woman with memory problems, her mother-in-law sounded like she'd received an education on the matter. "We'd better brace ourselves for the sea invasion meant to save us. It will be a chaotic time, and it's coming. The Germans are making plans."

"How do you know that?" Vianne asked, but Sandrine was now picking her nails. "Sandrine. Who told you this?"

She looked up, confused as ever. "Who told me what, dear?"

Vianne placed her hand on her chest, questioning whether she should ask again when Sandrine clearly had lost her thought. Sandrine's eyes shifted to look at Vianne's ears.

"Where are your earrings?" She reached up, moving a lock of Vianne's hair away. "Forget to put them on, did you? I don't think I've seen a day when you weren't wearing them, even when you were still dressed in your robe."

Vianne continued pushing Sandrine down the hallway where the smell of freshly baked bread was thick. "I let Élise borrow them."

"Why on earth would you do that?" Sandrine was shocked, as she should be.

Vianne searched for an explanation that sounded plausible in the brief amount of time left before Sandrine brought up Henri, because she felt that was coming next. "She asked nicely, and don't we all love Élise? That bread smells good and hearty."

"Yes, it does smell good," Sandrine said.

Vianne wheeled her into the kitchen to find Pierre and Blaise buttering their toast.

Sandrine spied the honey on the table. "Élise, you know how I like my breakfast," she said, but Élise wasn't in the kitchen. "Where is she?"

"She's tending to the guests," Pierre said. "In the other wing."

Vianne walked to the window. So many thoughts ran through her head, especially when she gazed upon the Zone Rouge. Sandrine was not only worse by the week, but worse by the day. The storm had passed, and she thought about the winds blowing through the forbidden forest, what that meant for Chateau Ten, and what it had meant since the end of the war.

Sandrine commented on Pierre's threadbare jacket and how she didn't like something so ratty at her breakfast table. "I'm just being honest."

Pierre laughed. "I know you are. And you'll be delighted to know this is the last morning I'll wear it. I'm getting my roof repaired today."

"I didn't know it was broken." She turned to Vianne. "Did you know?"

Vianne wasn't paying attention and addressed Pierre. "Can you come into my study for a moment?" She didn't wait for an answer and walked out of the kitchen to her study down the hall.

Pierre came in seconds later, closing her door for privacy. "I hope this isn't about the new roof. I sold the jewelry and did as you asked."

"No, it's not that…" Vianne pulled at her hands near the window, not sure how to bring up her concerns about the Zone Rouge, other than to just say it. "Élise said she heard Sandrine talking to someone in her bedroom."

"A visitor?" he asked.

"Did you see anyone on the property yesterday besides the Gaultiers?" Vianne opened the door briefly to see if Élise had made it back into the kitchen. "I thought she recalled a memory of Henri the other day, but I think it was a hallucination. The doctor never said anything about hallucinations." She grabbed his arms. "He didn't mention imagining conversations either. Isn't it possible that we've been exposed to the gases in the Zone Rouge after all?"

"I don't—"

"There's more." She covered her mouth momentarily because she was a little ashamed. "I've been hallucinating. I hate to admit it, but I have." She closed her eyes.

"Hallucinating what?"

"I could have sworn I heard music, and our gramophone is broken, so I know it's not our guests. And don't tell me it was carried in with the wind because I heard it inside the chateau. Also..." She hesitated. "I think the trees in the Zone Rouge are growing. They seem taller and fuller at random times of the day, but after I rub my eyes, I can see they are normal size." She wasn't going to mention Blaise, but now that she thought of his drawings, those were suspect, too. "What if we're all going mad?"

"Have you mentioned this to Max?"

"Max?" she asked. "Why would—" Vianne palmed her eyes. "This doesn't have anything to do with what he's researching, if that is what you are implying." She pulled her hands away after Pierre didn't respond. "Is there a test we can do to make sure the air is safe here?"

"The air is safe."

"I need more than your word." Vianne twisted her hands until she couldn't twist anymore. "Is there a test?"

"You've never been worried about the air before."

"I'm worried now."

"Vianne." He took off his glasses to rub his eyes. "We had a healthy stockpile of gas canisters buried near the front before the German advance—phosgene gas. The Germans had their own mix of gases, and they buried them nearby. We still don't know to what extent, but have you heard of Yellow Cross gas before?"

She shook her head.

"Mixed with chlorine gas, a new gas was created after extensive bombing on both sides, and I can tell you, it causes more than hallucinations. It blisters your skin, and it's not a little rash. Boils erupt right through your clothes, and that's all before your lungs implode. It's one of the main reasons the Zone Rouge is the Zone Rouge. If we were exposed, you wouldn't need a test to prove it."

Vianne squeezed her fists. "Pierre, please. There has to be something. The wind blows every other day, and with the storm, it is something to consider, even in a diluted form from the southern winds."

Blaise burst into her study with his slate, pointing to his sentence and asking Pierre about the wood project they had started. Pierre hesitated, looking at Blaise and then at Vianne.

"Pierre?"

"All right." He nodded. "Come see me at my workshop at the end of the day."

"Thank you," she said, kissing both his cheeks. "Thank you!"

Chapter Ten

Vianne waited in the kitchen for Élise long after breakfast had ended to talk about the pocket doors once and for all, only she never came back after tending to the Gaultiers. Sandrine kept asking Vianne to sit, but her mind was on Renée now and what she did in that library for the Marchands. The more she thought about it, the more she realized she had to go into Belleville and confront the mystic to see if what Max was researching and what happened last night were linked. Colette would have questions as to why she was at the bookshop, again, after saying she wasn't coming back anytime soon, and she'd have to deal with that when she got there.

Vianne twisted her wristwatch over and over, checking the time. When that became too mundane, she switched to tapping her fingernails relentlessly on the tabletop. Sandrine would be all right here, but Blaise…

Blaise played a game with Sandrine where he'd write out words on his slate before Sandrine could erase them.

Vianne wasn't about to question Renée in front of him at

the bookshop, and she didn't trust Élise to watch him. She'd have to ask Pierre again, but this time she would insist that he never leave his side.

Élise passed through the foyer.

"Élise!" Vianne shouted, startling Sandrine, especially when she ran to the doorway as if there was a fire. "Wait, I want to talk to you about the pocket doors—" she said, but Élise had disappeared into the west wing.

Vianne let out a groan, then turned to Blaise. "You asked Pierre about the wood project. How would you like to finish that with him today while I tend to some business?"

His face lit up. Sandrine patted his leg. "What a treat!" Sandrine said.

"You'll be all right if I leave, madame?" Vianne asked, and Sandrine nodded.

"Élise will take care of me, and when she's busy, I think I'll do some reading in my bedroom. Or, maybe outside on the back patio if the wind stays away and it is nice. After last night's storm, I don't think the weather could get any worse."

Vianne looked at her watch again. She thought that the earlier she left, the greater chance she had of finding Renée. "You are sure?"

"I'm all right here," Sandrine said. "Go."

Vianne kissed her cheeks, then set off to the guesthouse with Blaise by the hand. She apologized to Pierre for asking him to babysit on such short notice, especially with the commotion of his roof being fixed that day, but she didn't have a choice. He understood, as usual.

"There's something else." Her chest tightened from holding

her breath. This was the most important request of the day. "Please don't leave his side."

"Well, of course not," he said.

"No, you don't understand. Not even for lunch. I don't want him around Élise or Monique Gaultier alone."

He questioned her first with his eyes. "Is there something I should know?"

She cursed Max silently for planting ideas about the Gaultiers' motives, but once they were under her skin, she couldn't ignore her gut instincts and had to do her own research. She shook her head because she had to be sure and wasn't ready to say.

"Very well. I won't leave his side." He tousled Blaise's hair. "Don't worry."

Vianne rode her bicycle into Belleville, which gave her time to think. If Renée was outside on the bench, someone would hear, just as Colette would hear if she confronted her inside the shop.

Maybe she should just tell Colette? She needed someone to share her concerns with, after all. But Max? Well, she absolutely couldn't let him hear any of it.

She got off her bicycle a few shops down to walk the rest of the way. Girls ran out of the Marchand's patisserie, giggling and sharing bags of treats with the door's bell chiming relentlessly each time the door opened. One girl nearly ran into Vianne because she was too busy shoving cake into her mouth to see her.

"Are the Marchands giving their store away?" Vianne asked, half joking because why would they do that?

One of the girls shrugged. "Maybe. All free."

"Free?" she asked.

"Yes, free!" The girl ran off with her friend, leaving Vianne on the pavement, holding her bicycle by the handlebars. She tried to get a glimpse inside the patisserie, through the throngs of people with outstretched hands, to explain, but she couldn't see much other than the Marchands emptying their glass case.

Amélie from the tax office walked out next with a small bag.

"Amélie," Vianne called.

"Vianne! Good to see you." She hiked her thumb toward the shop. "Better hurry before they are all gone."

Wehrmacht walked in, one after the other. Even from behind the glass, Vianne could tell they were treated with just as much kindness as the rest of the people the Marchands were handing out bags to, which was odd to see considering the way the Marchands felt about the Germans.

"What's going on?" Vianne's jaw dropped. She'd never seen anything like it.

"I don't know, but if it means the Marchands are in a good mood, then what does it matter?"

Vianne propped her bicycle against the building to walk into the shop and ask them herself, gently pushing her way to the front. "Hallo, good morning," she said over the counter as the bells chimed behind her.

Mme. Marchand started passing out pastries faster than her husband.

"Pardon me, madame," a girl said to Vianne to move, hand outstretched as she accepted a gooey pink pastry from over the counter.

"Madame, what is going on?" Vianne tapped the counter with a flat hand. "You are giving all your pastries away. Why?"

Mme. Marchand's husband butted in, telling everyone to come back after lunch, and that they were tired, but Vianne didn't leave, despite the bumping and pushing of others filing out the door.

"Because today is a good day," Mme. Marchand said. "That's all."

"But it's all your stock. All your pastries and sweets, cakes and pies. It's your shop!"

"Vianne. This doesn't concern you."

Vianne was left feeling as if she'd overstepped, especially after Mme. Marchand disappeared behind the curtain, leaving her husband to shoo the last of everyone out, including Vianne. The walls were bare, all the clippings about Luc's achievements and his photograph had been taken down.

"Wait!" Vianne said, but he insisted they had to lock up now. "We need to talk about last night, *monsieur*." She lowered her voice to a whisper. "And why did I hear German being spoken?"

"No, Vianne." He pushed her outside. "We do not need to talk."

He closed the door and locked it behind her, leaving Vianne abruptly on the pavement.

"Vianne?" Colette was digging around for her key ring to open her shop door.

"Colette!" Vianne rushed inside the bookshop and paced.

"What's going on?" Colette rolled up the shades, letting in some light. "You can't stand still."

"I need a second." Vianne looked toward the loft. "Is Max here?"

Colette called for him, but it was dark and quiet in the loft area. "He must be gone." She pulled out a stool. "Have a seat and tell me what's going on right now."

"And Renée?" Vianne asked, twisting to look out the window. "When does she come in?"

"Remember, she wasn't here yesterday. I think she might have left Belleville."

Vianne scoffed. "Oh, she's still here."

Colette sat down behind her counter, reaching for Vianne's hands and giving them a tight squeeze. "What's going on?"

"I don't know where to start, and honestly, I don't know if you'll believe me." Vianne shifted around on the stool before standing again, hand over her eyes.

"Well, start somewhere!"

"Last night. No, it started before then, but last night is when —" Vianne ripped her hand away. "My guests, I think you were right about them. I heard some voices coming from the library."

Colette walked around the counter, her eyes wide. "You're scaring me. What voices?"

Vianne's stomach twisted, but it had to be said. "They were having a séance in the library."

Colette covered her mouth.

"But that's not the troubling part."

"*That's* not the troubling part?"

"Their guests were the Marchands, and Renée was there. I think she was in charge of it."

Colette inhaled a lungful of air. "I knew there was

something off about that couple. We need to tell Max." She slapped the counter. "And you need to evict them."

"No!" Vianne put her hands out. "You must promise me, you won't tell him. Not yet, anyway. I can't act rashly."

"Because of what they paid you?"

"Well, yes. I have to be sure of their intentions. Promise me you won't say anything to Max until I'm ready."

Colette hesitated, folding her arms. "I promise, but what about the Marchands? Did you talk to them?"

"I tried, but I could barely get a word in."

"Why?"

"They are giving away all their pastries." Vianne was pacing again, turning sharply each time she reached a wall. "The whole shop—everything in their case. They are different. Her words were curt, and they were not the same. That's all I can say."

"I really think we need to tell Max about this, Vianne. Whether you believe in the legend or not, if this séance they had has something to do with the Zone Rouge, there could be Germans billeting at Chateau Ten very soon, from what I know about the occult Max is researching."

Vianne's fists clenched. "You don't have to remind me."

Renée swung open the front door, the bell chiming wildly. "Vianne." She slowly took her seat, adjusting her dress and her ratty sweater. "I knew you'd be here."

Although Vianne hoped to confront her, she also couldn't believe she'd show her face in public after last night. She walked deliberately toward her with pounding steps. "Did you? Because you're a sensitive, and know things before they happen?" Vianne crossed her arms, chin up. "Well? What do you have to say for yourself?"

Renée nonchalantly adjusted her dress again over her knees.

"Well?" Vianne raised her voice.

"Quiet down, will you?" Renée pointed to the walls. "Colette has neighbors, and not all of them are friendly." She itched her leg above her stocking, then her head where the mats were thick.

"Take a bath," Vianne said.

Renée rolled her eyes.

"Tell me what the Gaultiers' intentions were with that séance, or I'll tell everyone in Belleville-sur-Meuse you've been visiting the Zone Rouge at night." Vianne paused, but not long enough. "You'll be run out of here if the citizenry believes you disturbed their loved ones' graves. Won't have a coin in your pocket by the time word spreads."

Colette nodded excessively and with crossed arms for what intimidation she could provide.

"I told you not to take on guests. I told you not to do it." Renée shook her head. "You are worried about the quiet one, but you should be worried about yourself. Eventually, they will come for you."

"Who will come for me?"

"They have a way of making people do things."

Max pulled open the front door. "Hallo." He handed Colette that morning's *Le Matin* newspaper. It didn't take long for him to notice Vianne and Colette staring at Renée, eyes shifting. "Did I interrupt something?" he asked.

"Big mistake, Vianne," Renée said. "Sneaking around last night."

Colette pointed angrily toward the door. "Leave. And consider your stay in this bookshop revoked. Bench outside only."

Renée swiped her fringe to the side. "I'm leaving anyway." She pulled the door open extra hard and nearly broke the bell, but Vianne wasn't finished with her and chased her outside.

"Wait!" Vianne said, then hesitated until after the door closed behind her because she didn't want Colette or Max to hear what came next. Her heart sped up—this question was probably more important than the séance. "What did you mean about the trees?"

Renée played with her dress sleeves, looking casual and uninterested. "What trees?"

"A few days ago." Vianne glanced briefly at Max through the window, trying to gauge if he could hear. "You mentioned the trees in the Zone Rouge. Something about when they grow, I'd know. What were you talking about? Know what?"

Two Wehrmacht soldiers walked by, not even batting an eye at Renée, but they did have eyes for Vianne, giving her a once-over, with their gaze lingering on her legs.

"Vianne," Renée whispered once they passed. "Why do you think I haven't taken a bath in weeks, and wear ratty clothes?"

"I…" This question threw Vianne. "I don't know."

"Use your head," she rasped. "I do it because a woman without a husband or someone to watch out for her doesn't have a chance here. It's by choice." She pointed with her eyes to the Germans walking away. "Be smarter than them, Vianne.

You'll have to be, if you want to win this battle." She shook her head, walking away. "I told you not to rent to them."

Vianne listlessly walked back into the bookshop and had a seat on the stool.

"What was that about?" Max asked.

Be smarter than them. Win the battle.

Colette elbowed Vianne, saying something.

"I'm sorry, what?" Vianne asked, looking up.

Max stepped closer. "What was that about with Renée?"

"Oh, you know," Colette said, covering for her and batting her hand. "Renée is always saying crazy things."

Vianne took one last look out the door to see Renée, but she'd disappeared. Colette cleared her throat.

"Ah, Vianne. I think some time away from your guests and Chateau Ten would be good for you. Why don't you bring Blaise tomorrow, spend the day here among the books with me."

"Speaking of Chateau Ten," Max said. "I'm going there now to visit with Pierre."

Vianne came to life, closing the door. "Now?" How was she supposed to talk to Pierre about the test with him there?

"Yes. Is that a problem?"

She sensed he could tell she was hiding something. "No, why would it be?" Vianne realized she couldn't keep him from visiting, and if she resisted, she'd look even more suspicious than she already had. "He'll love a visit."

"Good, how about we go together?" he asked.

"I rode my bicycle."

"I know. I can tie your bicycle to my rear bumper and I can give you a lift." He walked outside with a rucksack of books and got her bicycle before she even said it was all right.

Vianne spun around. "Did he hear me with Renée? Did you hear?"

"I didn't hear," she said. "You know, he's the nicest man you'll meet."

"It's not that. It's his questions about the Zone Rouge and my guests, and I'm not ready." She watched him tie her bicycle up. "What do I do?" She chewed her thumbnail. "How long do you think he'll stay?"

"How am I supposed to know how long he'll stay? Talk about something else." She gently walked Vianne toward the door. "But so help me, if you are still questioning the Gaultiers tomorrow, I'm telling Max, if you don't. I'm worried."

Vianne kissed Colette's cheek.

"And you'll spend the day here tomorrow?" Colette asked.

Vianne thought it was a good idea to get out of the chateau. "Has that SS officer come back into the shop? I'm leery because of Blaise."

"No. Haven't seen him. But, who's laughing now? I have his money after he bought that children's book. I'll have to try and find another one. That horse book was one of Blaise's favorites."

"All right. I'll be by tomorrow with Blaise."

Vianne walked outside to see Mme. Marchand's shop was still closed; only now there was butcher paper in the windows, and the lights were off. Max pulled open the passenger-side door for her. "Ready?"

Max drove away with Vianne sitting quietly with the window rolled down. However, as time went on, she wasn't sure if the silence was because of her or because he knew what she'd asked Renée and he had been thinking about it.

She sat up, the breeze blowing her hair across her cheek.

"Everything all right?" he asked.

"Yes. Fine." She flashed him a smile.

He heard. She was sure of it.

Max didn't drive up to the chateau like she anticipated to drop her off, but pulled right up to Pierre's guesthouse, finding him outside inspecting the repairs done on his roof. Blaise followed Pierre around, nodding and pointing, his slate board under his arm instead of around his neck.

Max took a long look up at the chateau, craning his neck to look at the Gaultiers' roadster parked near the fountain.

"Well, we're here," Vianne said, hopping out before he said anything.

Pierre greeted him warmly. "Max, good to see you." They shook hands.

Vianne didn't want Pierre to mention the jewelry and how he was able to pay for the repairs, and looked for ways to talk about anything other than the roof. She heard a bird squawk from inside the house just as Blaise wrote on his slate that they had caught one.

"A bird?" Vianne exaggerated a bit to keep that topic alive. "How wonderful, I suppose, if it makes you happy." She laughed.

Max was pointing to Pierre's roof, and they started talking about materials and cost.

"And what kind of bird is it?" Vianne asked, interrupting them. "Shall we go inside and see?"

Vianne pulled Pierre back a step as they moved to the door. "Don't mention anything about the jewels in front of Max."

Pierre looked genuinely confused, but she didn't have time to explain because now they were inside. She went straight to asking how Pierre knew Max's father, thinking that would stretch into many stories, and then he'd leave.

"Max's father? We go way back." Pierre opened the chest in his front room, and after rummaging through odds and ends, he pulled out three gas masks. "I still have the masks we invented with our British friends. They don't serve a purpose now, the toxic fumes of the Zone Rouge are no match for these —or any mask in existence for what lurks in the north."

Vianne reached for one at the same time Max did, their hands briefly touching. "Pardon me." She pulled her hand back, a little embarrassed.

"My apologies," Max said.

Pierre pulled a fourth mask from the chest's false bottom. "I mended this one with new technology after the war—a special filter and better sealant. I keep it separate because they are identical." He scratched his head, thinking. "But who would try it? They'd be risking their life."

Max and Vianne both had a look at it. "Then why did you keep it?" she asked.

He shrugged. "Can't seem to part with it, I guess. Though I must confess I've thought about tossing it out many, many times."

Vianne was more surprised that he had a chest with a false bottom than about the masks. After a few lingering words about The Great War and his time with Max's father, time seemed to pass slowly—too slowly for Vianne. She looked at her watch. "Oh, look at the time."

She thought that if she left, Max would, too. It had been more than an hour, after all.

"I should get up to the chateau and see how Sandrine is doing. Come on, Blaise." She took Blaise's hand after he thanked Pierre for watching him, writing on his slate.

"Wait," Pierre said, going into his cupboard where he kept old bottles of wine for special occasions. "I think some wine is in order. Stay." The magpie squawked loudly in its cage, giving Vianne a jolt.

"No, I couldn't possibly..." she said, but mainly she didn't want to add to the amount of time Max would stay.

"I have two bottles," Pierre said, and Vianne's stomach sank. Two bottles mixed with conversation would last three hours, or more.

"Yes, stay." Max opened his rucksack and put his research books on the table along with his notebook.

"I can't. I have Sandrine and Blaise to feed, and..." She snapped her fingers for Blaise to make way for the door, but he was standing right next to it. "We simply must get back."

Max got up from his seat and kissed her cheek as a friendly gesture, which shouldn't have felt awkward, but Vianne made it awkward because she only wanted to talk to Pierre about the test she'd been waiting all day to hear about.

"I'll see you tomorrow at Colette's?" Max asked.

"Yes. See you then." Vianne turned to explain things to Blaise. "Guess what. Tomorrow you're coming with me to the bookshop. We're going to spend all day there."

He grinned.

"Let me walk you out," Pierre said, and once they were in the doorway, with Max out of earshot and Blaise a few feet away standing in the grass, she cornered him.

"What about the test?" she whispered. "Remember? You promised me."

He glanced back at Max, who was flipping through his notebook. "Come down after you've had your dinner. I'll tell you then."

"But what if he's still here?"

"Trust me."

Vianne studied his face. "Very well," she said. But Max didn't just stay through the afternoon—he stayed past dinner, and to her dismay, was still there after she tucked Sandrine and Blaise into bed.

After making sure the pocket doors were closed, she waited in the kitchen, checking her watch every few minutes by the sink while unconsciously tapping her fingernails.

Élise made her bedtime valerian-root tea with Sandrine's favorite kettle. "You are very anxious. If you're not twiddling fingers, you're tapping your foot."

"Me?" Vianne clasped her hands to keep them steady. "I'm not anxious."

Élise scoffed, pouring near-boiling water into her teacup. "You need some nerve medicine to calm yourself and get a good sleep." She pulled an amber bottle from her apron pocket. "But unfortunately for you, I'm not in the mood for sharing. Too expensive."

"It's not nerves." Vianne looked outside at the dark sky as the last sliver of sun sank into the horizon. "It's the gloaming," she lied. "I think another storm is on its way, and only God knows what kind of havoc it will bring."

Élise added a splash of the liquid medicine to her tea, then tested the temperature with a delicate sip. "No storm tonight. The papers said so." She set the teacup aside and took off her apron. "Don't touch this tea. I'm coming back after it's cooled." She looked Vianne up and down after loosely tightening the cap on the medicine bottle.

"I'm not going to drink any of it, if that's what you're worried about." Vianne eyed the tea anyway. "What kind of nerve medicine is it?" she asked, but Élise had started to walk toward the service hallway. "Will it help you remember to keep the pocket doors closed?"

Élise stopped cold. "It's not me leaving them open."

"Yes, it is, and you walked away this morning when I tried to talk to you about it."

Élise folded her arms. "Maybe it's you."

"What's me?" Vianne asked.

"Maybe you *believe* you are closing them, when in fact it's in your mind. You know, someone else imagined things here, once."

"Genevieve?"

"You said her name, not me." Élise turned slowly on her heel and left, leaving Vianne to stew from that comment.

She eyed the steaming cup of tea again, which Vianne knew was still too hot to drink, then the amber bottle next to it. *Too expensive*, she mouthed, mimicking Élise.

In one vengeful motion, Vianne downed several gulps of the medicine straight from the bottle, but it didn't taste anything like what she expected and immediately gagged from the overwhelming flavor of anise. She used a rag to wipe her mouth.

"Damn you, Élise," she breathed.

She had no idea how much she'd drunk, even after holding the bottle to the light. Probably too much, but it would cost Élise and calm Vianne's nerves, in the end, so she did not regret it.

Vianne turned her attention back to Max's car, which was still parked coldly in the dark near Pierre's guesthouse, and waited. Five minutes passed, then ten, then twenty, and his car never moved. It was as if…

Vianne sighed, head hanging.

There was no test. Pierre had already told her he didn't believe they were exposed and must have rung Max after she left the chateau that morning because of it—Pierre wanted him to be there when Vianne returned so they could talk about the Sorrows, armed with Max's research.

Of course.

The medicine had started to kick in, relaxing her shoulders and back when she stretched. It was still early enough to walk down, but even so, Vianne was not going to oblige them. Not now, after feeling tricked. She decided to go to bed herself. She blew out the table candles and walked into the dark foyer to go up to her room. The pocket doors were open.

Her eyes narrowed. *Élise.*

She moved to close them, but the echo of many voices down the corridor stopped her cold. Her muscles tensed. She swallowed hard.

The Gaultiers were having another séance in the library.

Chapter Eleven

The voices were soft at first, gentle as a whisper that grew loud enough for her to imagine they were only a few feet away. Monique laughed while François commanded a seating arrangement around the mahogany table. Renée was there, and another voice—a man with a heavy German accent. There was something vaguely familiar about the way he talked, but she didn't quite know where to place it.

Vianne knew she should walk away, but she was in the foyer about to close the doors, after all, and turned her ear innocently toward the crack.

She fought back a medicine-tasting yawn.

Monique talked about the necklace François wore and other jewelry, namely the pieces she gave to Vianne. "That woman was glad to take the bobbles I offered. I heard they have made their way to the black market already."

"Good," François said. "She is indebted to us now more than before. She isn't very bright, is she?"

"No, and that works in our favor. She actually asked me not

to have any more séances." Monique laughed and laughed. "I wanted to tell her, *ma chérie*, that is why we sought out the chateau. Now, let's talk about why we are here. We had great success with the Marchands, wouldn't you say?"

The German cleared his throat. "Contact was made, but I need to speak with Commandant Lichtenberg's ghost, and time is of the essence. There is an invasion coming."

"I told you," Renée said. "There needs to be a familial connection for me to connect, so unless you are related to this person from The Great War, I can't help you."

"This person?" He scoffed. "Don't you know who he is?"

"How would I know?" Renée asked.

"He's the greatest commandant in German history. If von Falkenhayn, the strategist of the Battle of Verdun, had listened to him, the war would have been over in a few months. Everyone knows this."

"Is that what the book told you?" Renée asked.

Vianne understood that the book he was referring to was the one that Colette sold to the Gaultiers. He must have been studying the battle, the soldiers, and the decisions that were made in the trenches that shaped the war.

Vianne closed her eyes ever so briefly from the medicine, her mind drifting into a dreamy battlefield where she heard bellowing screams and gunfire, her head leaning, leaning, leaning, then resting heavily against the doorframe.

"Commandant Krieger…" Monique said.

Vianne's eyes popped open. *Krieger.*

"We have proved that the Sorrows exist and the stone is worth the price we've asked. Kindly pay the first installment," Monique said firmly.

"One person's ghost isn't enough for payment," he said.

"That wasn't the deal," she said.

"I need to hear from another, in the least instance," he said. "A soldier, from either side of the war, if I can't speak to Commandant Lichtenberg."

"I heard the women who own this chateau have lost someone to the Zone Rouge," Monique said.

"That's not true," Renée piped.

Vianne clamped her hand over her mouth, but it was more of a pulling grab, drawing her lips down. She wasn't sure if she was more shocked over what Monique had asked, or because Renée had lied to protect them. She shook her head to stay alert when she felt her eyes closing again.

"If you don't come up with someone soon, mystic, things won't fare well for you," Krieger said. "I advised you of this months ago, and what would happen if you failed."

"Now that I think of it," Renée said. "There is someone…"

Monique laughed. "*Voila!* Who is it?"

"A woman whose brother died in the Bayonet Trench. She works at the tax office."

Vianne gasped quietly. *Amélie.*

"Perfect. Talk to her tomorrow," Monique said.

"Talk to her yourself," Renée said.

"Watch your tone, mystic," Krieger said. "You are repaying a debt for your treasonous acts, lest I remind you. You will talk to her."

Chairs were scooted back, and some protesting from Renée, who wanted to walk back to Belleville, but the commandant insisted he drive her. Monique and François talked between themselves as soon as their guests were out the door.

Vianne fought back another yawn, and in that brief second she closed her eyes, she heard the gunfire again.

"Krieger's obsession with Lichtenberg is nauseating." Monique sighed heavily. "And if I hear anything about the impending invasion and how we are running out of time, I'm going to scream."

"Like your obsession with this chateau?" François asked.

"What?" she said in a shocked voice. "I am not obsessed."

He laughed. "Then why are you always admiring the bookcases, the checkerboard floors, and those heavy tapestries in the foyer, a place we aren't technically allowed to be. And not to mention the main staircase…"

Vianne knew she had to get upstairs to bed before the medicine took complete control, and delicately closed the doors, but she could still hear.

"*Grand* staircase, François, and who wouldn't admire such artistry? I want a place like this, and at the end of this hustle, with Krieger's money from the Thule Society, we can buy whatever we want. Or, take. They have bottomless pockets, you know, and so does the Third Reich, who will be eating out of our hands next and clamoring to work directly with us."

"It was a marvelous plan of yours, Monique. Finding the stone, even if it cost us everything we squeezed out of Paris, bribing and scheming over the last five years—it's about to pay off. Regardless of whether Krieger changed the deal terms on us."

Vianne took a wobbly step back, rubbing her eyes to stay awake. They were hustlers. Of course, they were hustlers. That's how they made all their money.

"Krieger gives me a headache—he's not like the German

officers in the Latin Quarter or at Hotel Meurice. They were easily charmed by me there. Didn't have to lift a finger."

"I'm charmed by you. Come here," he said, followed by moaning and cries of passion, which was more than Vianne's cue to leave, as if the medicine wasn't.

She tiptoed toward the stairs where she grabbed hold of the balustrade, now wishing she'd left earlier. She could barely stay upright, feeling the full brunt of the medicine coursing through her veins. By the time she made it to her bedroom, she fell onto her bed fully clothed because she didn't have the strength to change. Only instead of falling asleep, she drifted in and out of short, restless dreams before rousing abruptly to the same pop of gunfire she'd heard downstairs. She sat up in a pool of sweat, eyes shifting to the window.

She'd dreamt it, hadn't she? Vianne pressed her hands against her ears when her eyes closed again, but this time, diving headfirst into a nightmare before her head even hit the pillow.

Vianne ran through the forbidden forest with gunfire all around. Pop! Pop! Pop! Soldiers shouted for cover, oblivious to her presence. She turned this way and that, her breath hot and labored, looking for shelter when she heard Henri calling for help from a place deep inside the Zone Rouge.

Her heart thrashed and her ears buzzed, suspended amidst the chaos of the battle.

"Henri?"

Despite noticing that his tone was different, lighter, and not quite right, she ran toward him anyway, tripping her way through kindling and brush, through the tree stumps, and the rusted old danger sign warning to stay out—village abandonné—which she quickly dismissed. Even the tall poplars didn't give her pause, or their robust green leaves glistening with an evaporating dew that crackled into ashen bits the moment she passed underneath.

She came to a fork in the road, dying screams ringing through the cavernous foggy trenches to her right, and the echoes of profound loneliness to her left, where a thick layer of smoke hovered from explosions.

Henri cried out again, his voice thin and farther away, but this time a tone and pitch she remembered.

"I'm coming, darling!" She took an unmarked path to a berm created by the fighting, where ghostly hands grasped at her ankles through field stones left behind by a farm she barely remembered. "Let go of me. Leave me alone!" she screamed before calling out to her dead husband once more. "Henri! Where are you? I can't see you!"

She tripped and snagged her dress on a sharp rock, but for some reason, every step she took was the right one. Once she crested the berm, she found herself in Fleury. She stumbled into the square, coughing uncontrollably from gunpowder and a choking bomb haze. She did her best to wave it away.

Then the air turned strangely still and clear. Every decrepit old building that once held a special memory—the post office, the pharmacy, and the bakery appeared unchanged, yet they were also unrecognizable with dark and soulless black glass windows. When she saw the little stone chapel where she and Henri were married, she felt a crack inside her and was inexplicably drawn to walk up its front step.

She paused for a moment, fingers slowly reaching out for the door, before finally giving it a light push.

Pews were turned upside down, and doors left hanging cockeyed from their hinges. The roof had caved in as if a shell had been dropped on it, exposing the night sky where she saw stars.

"I'm all right," she said to herself, but the moment Vianne decided to walk down the aisle to the altar, the memories of her wedding day flooded over her—her youth, her dreams as a seventeen-year-old bride with her whole life ahead of her, yet what was never meant to be. She saw it in the chapel's walls, like an imprint of the past, forgotten and dead before it was alive.

Now she visited as a ghost of herself, ragged, lonely, and middle-aged, bearing burdens that would eventually bring her to her knees if she didn't find a way to gather strength. She surprised herself with a little cry, hands to her face, her voice amplifying in the eerie silence of the chapel, when a haunting moan that turned into a weep dripped down from the trees and lay heavy as a blanket over her shoulders.

She pulled her hands away, thinking someone was watching her in the dark—eyes on her back.

"Hallo?" A torch appeared on the altar. "Is someone there?" she whispered, then repeated a little louder. "Is someone there?" She waved the flickering torchlight across the tumbled church stones and into the parish's graveyard, barely making out the tombstones.

"Hallo—" A passing shadow that swept through the chapel like a breeze shook her to the core, with her pulse drumming in her ears. She wanted to run, but she was paralyzed in place with her torchlight jittering along the wall from her trembling hand. "Who are you? Come out!"

Another breeze, though this time it was a moaning gust of wind *so fierce, it blew the church doors open with a bang, leaving them flapping forcefully against the wall with squealing hinges.*

"Leave me alone!" Vianne cried, but she'd already run out of there, down the berm, through the fork in the road, and into the poplar trees where she stopped to breathe.

Vianne huffed and puffed, only fleetingly wondering where the soldiers and the war had gone. She sensed she was somewhere in the dark middle of the woods, on a new path that felt hollow and fragile underneath, but that couldn't be right because she recognized the danger sign from before. Shadows swung back and forth on the forest floor from something heavy hanging from the groaning bough above her.

She slowly tilted the torch upward and let out a blood-curdling scream, seeing the Marchands' limp bodies dangling from ropes with all the life draining from their moonlit faces.

"Wake up," she thought she heard, then it was a booming voice in her ear that made her run all the way back to the chateau. "Wake up!"

———

Vianne bolted straight out of bed to her feet, holding her chest with sweat pouring from every crevice of her body. "Another nightmare," she said to herself, panting uncontrollably, then wondered, *wasn't it?* She didn't know.

"The Marchands." She blinked. "The Marchands!"

She tore out of her bedroom to see for herself outside, but once she made it to the gate and felt the prickly brambles through the iron bars, terror flowed through her body. The wind whispered spiraling words of welcome, blowing her hair back and taking her breath away. Vianne realized quickly that she had made a grave mistake attempting to enter the Zone Rouge.

She stepped back and away, feeling exposed in the face of the dark windows of Chateau Ten, and utterly helpless until spotting firelight flickering in Pierre's windowpane. "Pierre!" She opened his door without knocking, finding him standing by the fireplace. Her chest hurt, and now her ears. "Hurry! I think they've hung themselves!"

"Who?"

Vianne grasped his arms, barely able to say their names. "The Marchands."

"Where are they?" Max asked.

Vianne was surprised at first to see Max, who had been sitting at the table with all his research spread out before him. "In the Zone Rouge. Through the brambles—" She gulped. "After the scorched trees on your right, next to the danger sign —*village abandonné*," she said without revealing how she knew where they were.

Max threw on his jacket.

"Wait! You're not scared? The bombs—"

"It's not the bombs I'm scared about, not before the posted danger sign at least." He rushed out the door, leaving Vianne still and numb with the pressure of an elephant on her chest. "My God." She bent over, holding herself, then holding her pounding head.

"You were in the Zone Rouge?" Pierre asked.

She shook her head.

"Then how do you know about the Marchands? How did

you know he'd find them next to the sign? You must have seen them with your own eyes. You must have been there."

"What time is it?" Vianne asked while twisting her watch, and seeing it was close to midnight. She was surprised to know she hadn't been asleep that long. "My head hurts." She held her head again, feeling exhausted and confused. Pierre got her a chair.

"Vianne, how did you know?"

"How did I know?" She thought for a moment, then her eyes flicked up in fright. "Oh no," she said, now worried she'd prompted Max to step into the Zone Rouge for no reason. "I think I dreamt it. Only everything was so vivid—real. The grays and greens. The acrid smell of the air from gunfire. And Henri."

"Henri?"

"I heard him calling for help, only it wasn't him exactly." She stood. "Max shouldn't go. The directions were from my dream—from my nightmare. It's not real. I need to stop him!" She tried to leave, but Pierre held onto her.

"Wait here. Max is expecting you to wait."

"But it was a dream—"

"Vianne, listen to me." Pierre's eyes skirted to her dirty bare feet, and that's when Vianne saw the rip in her dress. She examined it a little closer, remembering she had fallen near Fleury. "You only think you dreamt it."

She shook her head relentlessly. "It was a nightmare. It had to be."

"And what if you were entranced? What if you were lured?"

Vianne's mouth gaped, unsure what to say. "Maybe I'm going mad like Genevive Lacroix?"

"You truly believe that?"

"I don't know what to believe. I drank some of Élise's nerve medicine, and maybe that's to blame. I fought to keep my eyes open and imagined all sorts of things. It could have made me hallucinate and have vivid dreams, too," she said, but that surely didn't explain the rip in her dress. "And if that's what happened, then Max will come back and say they weren't there after all. As long as he doesn't go past the danger sign, he'll be all right, won't he?"

"As long as he doesn't go past the sign, he should be. But, Vianne, if the Marchands were there in the exact place you said he'd find them, will you consider other explanations for what you've been seeing and hearing at the chateau? Max's research is impressive and believable. Will you listen to what he has to say?"

Vianne closed her eyes.

"It's said that they first appear as a shadow. A thumbprint blemish in the dark."

She opened her eyes, chin held high. "A shadow?"

"And in the fog, they take on a human form—what they looked like when they died in battle. It's where they gather, where they get their strength. A soldier might be fighting, reenacting their final battle, or lying in eternal agony."

"I see." Vianne turned so he couldn't see her stricken face. She didn't know what was worse, if the Sorrows were real, or if she'd gone mad after all.

They waited silently at the table, each of them looking at the wall clock as if that would make time move faster. Seconds felt like minutes, and minutes felt like hours, until two hours had passed. "Where is he—"

The door opened, and they both stood. Max looked like he'd seen a ghost.

"Well?" Vianne pulled at her hands. "Were they…" She swallowed dryly. "Did you…"

"They were there," Max said. "Hanging from a poplar tree, right where you said, near the rusted danger sign. I buried them with a shovel from Pierre's workshop."

Vianne blindly felt for the table to hold onto. "I don't need to know the details." Someday she would bring flowers and make it official with a headstone, but that was all too much to think about right now.

Max and Pierre sat at the table next to Vianne. Although her head was down, she felt their eyes on her. She was sure Pierre was waiting for her to ask about Max's research, while Max was probably waiting for her to explain herself.

"I found this near the bodies." Max placed the torch that Vianne had dropped in the forest on the table. In the candlelight, she could see that it belonged to the Fleury Chapel, clearly labeled with an engraving. "It's yours, isn't it? You didn't just walk into the Zone Rouge, you walked all the way to the Fleury and came out unscathed with a torch belonging to the chapel. How?"

"I don't know." The harder Vianne searched for an explanation, the faster the details slipped away from her. "I drank some of Élise's nerve medicine. It must have dulled my senses, made me groggy enough to sleepwalk. And I got lucky. People get lucky all the time," she said, but that didn't explain the things she saw and smelled, or the gunshots she heard.

"Traipsing past the danger sign to Fleury with only a ripped dress hem takes more than luck, Vianne," Max said. "It just does."

Pierre placed his hand on hers. "Now will you consider listening to Max—the Sorrows, his research, and how it correlates to what you've been experiencing?"

She closed her eyes tightly because her mind was spinning, but she did manage to nod. "It's late. Tomorrow? I'll come to the shop in the morning." She got up to leave. "Now, if you'll excuse me…"

Vianne didn't remember walking up the hill to the chateau, or the chill of the checkerboard floor against her bare feet as she padded across the foyer. In fact, she was still so shaken by what had transpired that she completely dismissed the sound of Élise coming up behind her, dressed in a robe and slippers.

"Everything all right?" Élise whispered, scaring Vianne flat up against the wall.

"What are you—"

Élise lifted her candle as her eyes moved downward to Vianne's ripped dress, dirt-smudged legs, then to her toes. "Were you outside barefoot? I thought you went to bed."

Vianne was still clutching her chest, and she realized quickly that she looked suspicious, especially near the pocket doors, let alone still in her day dress. The last thing she wanted was for Élise to think she was eavesdropping on the Gaultiers.

"I couldn't sleep." She dropped her hand. "I thought a few drinks of your nerve medicine would help, only it made me sick and restless. I went to see Pierre…" She hiked her thumb in the opposite direction, not wanting to go into too much detail. "I tripped outside." She tugged her dress into place. "The ground was very moist."

"A few drinks? Vianne, that's three times the dose. Besides, I told you not to touch it." Élise chuckled when Vianne felt her head. "Well, I bet you won't be doing that again."

"I won't. Goodnight."

Vianne walked away as confidently as she could, but her hands were shaking and she was lightheaded. She crawled into her bed after stripping all her clothes off, throwing the blanket over her head.

Chapter Twelve

The next morning, Vianne stood at the kitchen sink as her family ate their breakfast, closing her eyes as the sun rose over the Zone Rouge. No matter how hard she tried, she couldn't get the image of Mme. Marchand out of her mind, particularly the way the moon bathed her calves in soft white.

The path beyond the poplars to Fleury was growing increasingly hazy and unclear, and she completely forgot how she made it out, but the Marchands... That image might just stay with her for an eternity, and it was making her nauseous.

She felt her stomach where it ached.

"What are you thinking about over there?" Sandrine asked from the table.

Vianne opened her eyes. Suddenly, every clinking water glass and every gulp of milk was amplified as if coming out of a tunnel. "Nothing to be concerned about."

She reached for the kettle and started Sandrine's morning tea.

"Let Élise do that," Sandrine said. "And serve the breakfast."

Élise had cooked breakfast before she left—a skillet of eggs with salt and rosemary, and brown bread with butter and honey.

"She must be busy with the guests." Vianne plated their food. "I'm perfectly capable," she said, though she'd rather have a seat.

Pierre came in for the first time that morning. "Good morning." He gave her a pointed look as if he had words to say, then joined her at the sink.

"Not now," she whispered.

"You are going to see Max at the shop this morning? Like you said."

She took a teacup out of the cupboard. "I already had plans to spend the day at the shop with Blaise, so yes."

"You're taking Blaise, still?" He looked at her blankly. "But how can you—"

"I'll seek out private moments and talk to Max." Vianne wasn't about to break Blaise's heart after telling him yesterday of their plans. "It's the best I can do, considering." She turned to Sandrine with her cup of tea.

"Here you are, madame." Vianne added a slice of lemon after setting the cup on the table. "Élise found lemons. Isn't that extraordinary? All the way from Marseille, I imagine."

Élise came rushing in with a tray of dirty breakfast dishes from the Gaultiers' suite. "You can thank our guests for those lemons. Generous people they are."

Sandrine took a sip of her tea, which Vianne made sure was warm and perfectly bitter. "Give them my regards. And yours,

169

too, Vianne? They are proving to be good guests, as good as my friend, Genevieve." Her brow furrowed. "I feel like it's been ages since I've seen her. Has it been?"

"It has been ages," Élise answered. "And she's your close friend. Has she written, Vianne?"

"Who?" Vianne felt even more nauseous than before with this turn in the conversation.

"Genevieve Lacroix," Élise said. "Haven't you been listening?"

"When she comes for her visit, I must insist that we invite Madame Marchand over. It's a good reason to get all three of us together."

"That's a good idea, madame." Élise turned to Vianne. "Isn't that right?"

"Madame Marchand?" Vianne rushed to the sink, about to be sick. Élise watched her with a side eye, then gasped slightly when Vianne vomited all the tea in her stomach.

"What's the matter with you?"

Vianne tried to think up an excuse. The food was excellent, and so was the tea. What possible thing could she say? She wiped her mouth with a rag, glad Sandrine hadn't noticed. "I don't know." It was all she could say, in the end.

Élise reached for Henri's plate on the table.

"He'll be late," Sandrine said, arm outstretched. "Leave it."

"Late, you say?" Élise asked. "You must have talked to him this morning, madame. How is he?"

Vianne glared at Élise for encouraging her.

Sandrine frowned. "He was a little agitated, now that I'm remembering."

"Oh?" Élise said.

"Élise." Pierre stood, but nothing stopped Élise aside from money.

"What on earth could he be agitated about?" Élise continued. "The weather has changed, and with our guests, life is good in these parts. Compared to many in Belleville-sur-Meuse, at least. Are you sure it was Henri and not your visitor yesterday? I heard voices."

"I had a visitor?" Sandrine rubbed her chin. "You know, I can't remember now." She shook her head. "No matter. It will come to me later, I suppose. Or, we can ask Henri ourselves when he arrives."

"Yes. Let's do that," Élise said.

Vianne turned her back on the table to look out the window again. She thought that if she didn't pay attention, then Élise would let the conversation drop. The last thing she wanted was for Sandrine to remember that Henri was dead over her eggs and toast.

Élise placed a dish in the cupboard. "Stare at the Zone Rouge enough, Vianne, and those scorched trees will start to grow."

Vianne whipped around. "Do you think they're growing?"

"No." Élise looked confused, drying her last dish with a rag. "I suppose you'd have to go into the Zone Rouge to find out." She closed the cupboard slowly. "Not that you'd go in there, now, would you?"

It turned quiet between them as Sandrine and Pierre talked about something relating to the garden, which made things even more awkward.

"I wouldn't," Vianne finally said.

Élise wiped her hands on her apron and left without making eye contact.

Vianne held her head.

"Vianne," Sandrine called over the table. "I'd love some of the Marchands' macarons. Would you bring me back some if you go that way?"

"Macarons?"

"Yes. Is that a problem?"

"I'll ah…" Vianne smiled. "I'll see if they are open."

"Why wouldn't they be open?" Sandrine asked. "And make sure to invite her to lunch, tell her when Genevieve visits next."

Pierre left to get the car ready while Vianne wondered how she was going to get through the day, much less the week, until her guests checked out. *Genevieve*. And of all the people to ask about that morning. Vianne sighed.

"I think I'll read my book on the patio," Sandrine said. "Would you be a dear and get it for me in my bedroom on your way out?"

Vianne kissed Sandrine's cheek. "I will."

Blaise went into his room to put on his shoes while she went into Sandrine's bedroom, finding the book on her nightstand, but on her way out, she noticed something new on her bureau. A decorative key made of silver and probably once used as a necklace.

She examined it closely, feeling the bump of an engraving, but couldn't quite make it out. An eerie feeling washed over her with the briefest explanation that it was the keepsake key Sandrine gave to Henri—but that would be impossible.

"Here we are!" Élise startled Vianne who promptly threw her hand behind her back.

"What are you doing?" Élise looked her up and down, and so did Sandrine from her wheelchair.

"Getting Sandrine's book." Vianne showed her the book with her other hand.

"There it is!" Sandrine reached for it. "I think I'll read on the patio today," she told her again.

Sandrine must have forgotten she had asked her for it, and now Vianne was going to ask her a question that would tax her in more ways than one. She rubbed the key endlessly behind her back, knowing she had to be careful, especially with Élise standing right there.

"Sandrine?" Vianne asked.

Sandrine innocently looked up from her chair, with Élise ready to wheel her out of the room.

"Were you at your bureau this morning?"

Sandrine blinked. "This morning?" She looked past Vianne to her framed photographs of Henri and her dead husband. Then to her jewelry box. "Why?"

She smiled. "I found something—" Sandrine's jewelry box had been moved and opened. "A piece of jewelry, lying on your bureau instead of in the box. I wondered if you walked from your bed by yourself."

Sandrine chuckled. "My dear, Vianne. You know I can only manage a few steps." She looked up at Élise. "Patio?"

Vianne motioned for Élise to speak with her near the window. "A word, please."

Élise wheeled Sandrine into the hallway first.

"The keepsake Sandrine gave Henri," Vianne whispered. "What did it look like?"

"The key he went to war with? Have you gone mad?"

"Just tell me what it looked like."

Élise hesitated, looking once at Sandrine sitting quietly in the hallway. "It's ornate. Silver. I remember something about an engraving. Why?"

Vianne felt like her legs were going to give out on her. Instead, she smiled.

"You're acting strange, you know that?" Élise left with Sandrine, talking about breakfast while wheeling her into the foyer.

Vianne stared at the key in her hand, trying to make sense of it—but how could anything like that make sense? It was his key.

Pierre arrived to tell her the car was ready. "Out front with the engine on." His eyes went to her hands. "What do you have there?" He stepped closer.

"Nothing." She pocketed the key. "Thank you for getting the car ready." Blaise ran in behind him, his teddy bear limp and squished under his arm. She gave Blaise a hug, then asked him to wait in the hall.

Between the Marchands and the key, Vianne didn't know what disturbed her the most. Her head pounded behind her eyes.

"Is there something you're not telling me?"

She quickly shook her head.

"You are sure?"

Vianne nodded, putting on a brave face before kissing

Pierre's cheek goodbye. She collected Blaise in the hallway. "Come on, darling. The first one to the car wins." Blaise raced ahead of her, and she thought he went to the car, so she was rather surprised to find he'd stopped in the foyer.

"Blaise, darling—" He was talking to Monique just outside the pocket doors.

Monique straightened, hiding something behind her back. "Good morning."

Vianne subtly pulled Blaise backward by the shoulders, widening the gap between them. If Monique was willing to cross into the east wing, maybe it was her visiting Sandrine in her bedroom. Now was the time to be firm. "Élise said my mother-in-law had a visitor yesterday. Was it you?"

Monique eyed her reflection in a gilded wall mirror, admiring her platinum curls and tucking one behind her ear. Her lilac perfume was stifling.

Vianne cleared her throat.

Monique's eyes shifted. "What were you saying? Oh, yes. Your mother-in-law had a visitor. Now, why would you think it was me?"

"Was it?"

"Is she here now? I don't even know what she looks like." Her tone was joking in manner, which grated on Vianne's nerves, as if Monique had no idea who her mother-in-law was when she was merely feet away in the kitchen and could see her.

"I have gone to great lengths to keep those pocket doors closed. At your request, I suggest you keep to our agreement and stay in the west wing."

Monique scoffed, turning to look at the open pocket doors. "Well, nice job you are doing there. They are open now. They always seem to be open."

"I didn't open them."

Monique laughed. "Well, then who did?" She turned her attention to Blaise, who had been watching and listening the whole time. "At any rate, I'm glad we ran into each other. I have something for you," she said to Blaise.

She revealed a book from behind her back.

Blaise immediately smiled.

"A book about horses. I hope you love it."

"Horses?" It was the book Vianne had sold that SS officer at Colette's bookshop. "Where did you get this?" She snatched it from Blaise's hands, leaving him almost in tears. Though she understood now more than ever, Krieger from the séance and the SS officer from the bookshop were one and the same.

"What a silly thing to ask. At a bookshop, of course. You aren't very bright, do you know that?" Her eyes moved to Blaise, who was trying to grab it back, then to Vianne, who was still shocked. "Well, are you going to keep it for yourself?"

Vianne slowly let go of the book. She had no choice but to let Blaise have it because she certainly wasn't going to take it away from him now. "Blaise. Meet me in the car."

"If you must know, the book came from one of our dear friends we had over."

Vianne waited for Blaise to run off before turning back to Monique.

"You broke our agreement. I heard a German voice last night, and it wasn't the wind, or my imagination."

Monique smiled, slowly showing her teeth. "You must have

been eavesdropping again. Hear anything interesting? And to think you accused me of leaving the pocket doors open." She looked at her painted nails, pretending to be absorbed in the shine. "It's not your curse week, is it?"

"Curse week?"

Monique laughed. "What am I saying? How old are you? Oh, I don't want to fight. We absolutely love it here. You are upset." She rubbed Vianne's arm like a mother to a child. "I can see that. Let me make it up to you."

She unclasped her gold chain-link necklace and put it into Vianne's reluctant hand.

"The only thing that could remedy this situation is for you to leave early on the grounds that you broke our contract. I said no Germans, and you said you hated them. Paragraph five, isn't that right?"

"I think you should read what you signed. Now, I must be off. Ta-ta!" Monique stuck her hand in the air, waving backward with a flutter of her fingers, only to pop back into the foyer after disappearing through the pocket doors. "And, Vianne … we are having guests over tonight. Please, try to resist peeping in on us this time. It seems to have become an infatuation." She snapped the pocket doors closed.

Vianne ran into her study and frantically looked over the contract, flipping through the pages until she found paragraph five. "We shall have guests over that include friends and colleagues…" Vianne closed her eyes after seeing nothing specific about Germans and remembering that they had only agreed while talking.

Vianne realized Monique knew precisely what she was doing when she hurriedly flipped to the last page of the contract upon signing. Now, Vianne needed the help of a professional. Perhaps if she could reclaim her tax money, she could give the Gaultiers back what they paid and void the contract.

She slammed her desk drawer closed, deciding to take the contract with her and see Amélie before Colette's shop opened.

Vianne walked up to Amélie's desk, passing all the other customers who had been waiting since early that morning, and took a seat. Amélie's supervisor gave her a strained look, holding his clipboard and appearing as if he was assessing whether to intervene.

"You have to wait in line like everyone else," Amélie said, then whispered when her supervisor turned his back. "What is going on?"

"I told you about the renters I have. I'm going to try and get them evicted, but that means I'll have to rescind my tax payment."

"Evicted?" Amélie looked surprised. "But why? Aren't they the reason you were able to pay your bills?"

Grumblings from those waiting in line caused Vianne to lose her focus. She whispered the rest. "Can I take back the taxes I paid and get an extension?"

"It doesn't work like that."

Vianne set the contract she signed on her desk. "Well, is there a lodging tax missing from the contract they signed, something this office can add that will, perhaps, be so outlandish they'd leave?"

Amélie took the contract to her supervisor. A hard-nosed little man with a mustache and pointed chin, who promptly shook his head.

Seconds later, Amélie walked back with the contract, whispering. "He said you need a lawyer. A property lawyer. But the only one he knows of is in Verdun."

"I can't go there," Vianne rasped.

She wasn't about to set foot in Verdun after Marion's arrest and disappearance.

"I had a feeling you'd say that. He said other than a lawyer, your only other option is to go to the police."

"Police? No, I can't go to the police, good God, Amélie."

"Only about one in five are collaborators," she said, which made Vianne scoff.

"You mean, one in five has a heart."

"You'll have to take your chances. They are Frenchmen, in the end." She gave Blaise a pathetic smile as he held his teddy bear, slate, and the horse book in a bundle against his chest. "Good luck."

Vianne apologized to those in line as she left, though nobody seemed to accept. The police were just around the block. She thought that if she took Blaise with her, she might garner some sympathy, but only after she reached the front doors, and saw all the uniforms—more than she anticipated—did she understand the mistake she'd made.

She debated turning back, but they had already seen her, and if she turned around now, that would cause more suspicions than what was arguably necessary for a woman with a small child. She should have known better. Marion would have known better than to subject Blaise to so many uniforms, considering what he experienced.

Vianne tucked his slate under her arm, but stuffed the book in her handbag while he held the teddy bear. She knelt on one knee to straighten Blaise's collar and remind him he was safe with her. "French police are our friends," she said, at the same time choking on her own words. "Not like the Germans."

She examined the dark blue uniforms, the double-breasted coats, and the kepi hats. A stark difference from SS uniforms, but still, she looked to Blaise to see if he was all right.

He nodded.

"Stay close." She took his hand and walked inside, talking to the officer behind the counter. "I need to report a crime."

He gave her a scrutinizing look at first. "What kind of crime?"

"I need an eviction."

He itched his chin, pausing, then said he'd be back in a moment. Vianne wasn't sure what to think of it until he came back and said that Officer Lefevre was willing to listen. "Down the hallway. Three offices down."

"Thank you." She and Blaise walked toward Lefevre's office. Officers passed by in the hall, probably wondering what a woman with a child was doing at the police station. Blaise kept turning, watching the police watch them while she hesitated to knock on the door frame.

She hoped Officer Lefevre was one of the good ones, with a heart.

Knock! Knock!

She shifted in her dress, gripping Blaise's hand tightly. A second passed.

"Enter!" a voice barked from inside.

Vianne walked in, finding him behind a desk smoking a fat cigar.

"Thank you for meeting with me, Officer Lefevre."

She placed one of Blaise's hands on the desk so he wouldn't wander off, while the other held his limp teddy bear.

"I have some troublesome renters I need to evict on grounds of a term violation." Vianne slid the contract across the table to him. "We had an agreement, as you can see."

His eyes danced over the contract, page after page. "I can read. What's the problem?"

"They agreed not to have certain people over, and they broke that rule. They violated the contract."

He looked up. "What kind of certain people?"

Vianne gulped. It would be very easy to be truthful if she knew she could trust him, but she had no idea whom to trust. "Just certain people. They won't leave on their own. They should be forcibly removed. Evicted."

He tucked the cigar in the corner of his mouth. "I can't do that."

"Why not?" Vianne stiffened. "I have rights."

"Because of what it doesn't say, right here." He pointed to the white space. "Nowhere does it say that they can't have *certain* people over. It does say they can entertain friends and colleagues, however." He tossed the contract to her on the desk.

Vianne's lips pursed. "The people they had over are not their friends or their colleagues."

"I suppose that depends on who you ask." He stared at her for a second or two before setting his cigar in the ashtray.

"I know who you are," he said, then lowered his voice. "I went to school with Henri."

"You did?"

"I'm surprised they'd rent from you in the first place. Tell them about the toxic gases, and if that doesn't work, tell them about the Sorrows, and that they're next. Wouldn't catch me out there at night." He leaned over his desk. "Not after what I heard from Madame Lacroix. She called your place a ghost house."

Vianne pulled her shoulders back. "Genevieve?"

"Like sirens from the sea, the Sorrows cry—"

"Please!" Hearing the rhyme now had a different feel to it after what she witnessed last night. "I don't need to hear it."

"Can I ask you a question?" He motioned with his hand for her to come closer so he could whisper. "What happens if your guests find out you consulted the police?"

"What happens?"

"I've heard of these people, new to Belleville-sur-Meuse, who seem to have many friends. Powerful friends."

His eyes moved to Blaise, who still had his little hand on the desk, his head turning to look at the police coming in and out of the front door with their guns. Vianne pulled him in close, causing him to step on her shoes.

"Are you implying what I think you're implying?"

"I'm stating the obvious. My advice is to keep quiet and wait out the term of the lease. Once your paying guests leave, the uninvited ones won't be an issue, now, will they? Your guests will be gone in…" He reached for the contract, reading the dates Monique had written in. "A week or so?"

"You knew my husband. Is it safe to say that you will be

discreet about what we talked about just now?" After a moment with him staring at her, she pulled a few francs from her bulging handbag, compliments of the Gaultiers, but did it matter if she spent it now after his warning? "Perhaps this can help?" She slid the money across the desk.

He smiled, setting a stack of papers on top of it for concealment. "It doesn't hurt."

Chapter Thirteen

Vianne walked stoically out of the police station no better off than she had entered, only now she had the Sorrow's rhyme in her head, thanks to him. She hoped Blaise wasn't paying attention and didn't hear, but how could he not? He was right there next to her side. She walked down the street to Colette's, scooping Blaise up in the face of a gusty wind as he clutched his teddy bear, before slipping into the bookshop and finding both Colette and Max waiting for her behind the counter.

Colette kissed her cheek. "I know about the Marchands—"

"Not now," Vianne said, then knelt on one knee and talked to Blaise. "Why don't you go with Colette into the back for a little while. I need to talk to Max privately."

Colette and Max exchanged looks before Colette took Blaise's hand and led him into the back. "I have some new books you could read. Just arrived…"

"Thank you for coming," Max said, once they were out of

sight. "Would you like a seat?" He motioned to the counter stool.

Vianne sat down, head held high. "I know what you are going to say."

"You do?"

Vianne swallowed hard after a long hesitation. Admitting the Sorrows existed after all these years was proving more difficult than she thought. "I told you I only believed in things I could see. Over the last few days, I've seen things—heard, smelled, felt—and no amount of nerve medicine can explain last night away. But if you'll excuse me, believing in the Sorrows is very new to me, and it will take some getting used to."

"I understand. I do. I was in your shoes once, too."

Vianne motioned to his paperwork and notes on the counter. "You have some research to share with me?"

He ripped off his glasses. "Before I start, I must apologize."

Vianne frowned. "Why?"

"You asked me why I pretended not to know about the Sorrows when we first met, and I never did give you a straight answer, and I'm sorry. We had just introduced ourselves, and I needed to keep my research close to my vest. Chasing after something the Germans want—what they've killed for already —could get me hung from the nearest lamppost."

"Are you in the resistance?"

"No, but I am causing trouble for the Reich, and you know what they do to those who cause trouble."

Vianne knew all too well what the Germans were capable of after what happened to Marion. "Start at the beginning."

Max took a seat behind Colette's counter. "I know you

read about the Thule Society in my notebook, their occult beliefs, and their roots in the Nazi Party. Himmler, Hess, and Göring—they are all members. They want to resurrect the Sorrows and create a new army, but not just any army. Soldiers with a thirst for revenge, and ones that can't be wounded or killed."

He paused as if expecting a reaction from Vianne, but she was there to listen.

"And how are they going to do that?" she asked.

"It starts with a stone. Shortly before the Nazi Party gained power, Jewish art dealers were forced to sell a portion of the Guelph Treasure. Specifically, a reliquary box containing countless priceless gems and artifacts to Göring. Only, not all the pieces were accounted for. I believe your guests have acquired those missing treasure pieces."

Vianne folded her arms. "What kind of pieces?"

"Necklaces, loose gems, relics, and bracelets. It's why I asked if they paid you in jewelry. All are inconsequential to me, except one. A demure black stone that's glassy in nature—"

"François's necklace?"

He straightened. "You've seen it?"

Vianne thought her face said enough.

"Be careful. It possesses powerful magic, and legend has it, there are consequences to using the stone. Devastating consequences. I've done extensive research. The Marchands' son died by hanging in that very forest, did you know that? It must have been their worst fear. Otherwise, they wouldn't have—"

"You think a magic stone had a hand in their death?"

Vianne shook her head. "They were suicidal. It's well known they were. They had prepared, giving away all their pastries."

"I can prove it."

"How?"

"Vianne, would you consider—" He paused. "Would you listen in on your guests—their conversations?"

"Eavesdrop? I don't know…" The last thing Vianne wanted to do was create more problems with the Gaultiers after the warning from that policeman about Blaise, and she'd already listened to a fair share, and look what that had cost her.

"If I'm wrong, then you can tell me to go to hell. But if I'm right…" Max had an intensity in his eyes she hadn't seen before when talking about his research. It was both hopeful and desperate. That's when Vianne realized there was more to Max's quest than met the eye. "There's a rumor the stone was broken into two pieces. They'll need both to match the magnitude of their desire—to make it work."

"This is personal for you. Isn't it, Max? You said your research had taken over your life, but it seems to have taken control of it." He looked surprised she would say such a thing, but Vianne thought it was a logical question to ask. "What happened?"

She gave him a moment after he hung his head.

"While in the war, my wife wrote about a mythical stone she had heard about—one that had the power to grant desires. I told her to forget about it, not to believe in folklore, but she became obsessed, fantasizing about raising a ghost army to end the war once and for all."

"Did she find it?"

"Yes. A rare-jewelry collector in the south sold it to her."

"A good hustler can make a person believe anything they want."

"Normally, I'd agree. But in the last letter I received from her, she said to watch for angel warriors to rise and fight from the skies. I was in battle, near Mons at the time."

"Mons?" Vianne blinked a few times. "Are you saying—"

He nodded.

"That you believe she—"

He nodded again. "She used the stone for selfish gains and paid the consequence for the ghost army at Mons. The doctor said she died of a broken heart, but I know it had to do with the stone."

Vianne turned her back to think. She understood the layers of his quest more deeply now, but her first priority was Blaise and his safety. She wasn't prepared to give Max an answer right then. The Gaultiers only had a week left to their rental, and then they'd be gone—like Officer Lefevre said. No more séances and life would return to normal, Sorrows or no Sorrows, because life had been peaceful before the Gaultiers arrived. She wasn't about to risk all she held dear trying to find out about a magic stone when all she had to do was wait for her guests to check out.

"Will you help? Eavesdrop if you get a chance—"

"I can't," she said. "Not right now, anyway."

"Why not? After all you've learned and experienced. The Sorrows—"

"I understand that the Thule Society is dangerous, and I'll go far enough to say I think the Gaultiers are dangerous, but not for the reasons you believe. I tried to get them evicted, but that made things worse. If they find out, they could retaliate against me using their connections with the Reich, and my heart can't take losing Blaise on top of everything else I've lost."

She called Blaise in from the back.

"Wait—" Max reached for her shoulders when she turned. "Vianne, the Sorrows are haunting the land at night, getting closer and closer to your property with each passing midnight hour. What will you do once they are in your home?"

"Why would they come into my home?"

"Once that happens, they are mere days away from fulfilling their quest, finding the other stone—"

"This is about Blaise, his safety. I can't risk—"

"Vianne—" he held her firmly "—listen to me. What the Gaultiers have planned with the Germans—the Thule Society—is far more dangerous than any kind of retaliation you'd receive for trying to evict them."

Colette came walking in with Blaise. "All finished?" She had a smile on her face that quickly changed when she saw Max and Vianne's demeanors. "I'm sorry, should I—" She pointed to the back to give them more time.

"No. I'm leaving." Vianne took Blaise's hand. "Both of us are leaving."

"But you promised to stay all day. Remember? Yesterday, we discussed that you need time away from the chateau."

Vianne had pulled the door open, dinging the bell.

"Will I at least see you tomorrow?" Colette asked.

Vianne knew better than to tell her no after all her visits the last few days. "Maybe." She kissed her cheeks and said goodbye to Max. "I'm sorry. I..." She turned away when he looked at her. "I have to go."

Vianne walked Blaise to the car, avoiding the Marchands' shop at all costs, but saw Renée sitting on a different bench a few shops along. She thought she could put an end to what Max had talked about with one conversation.

After putting Blaise in the car and giving him his slate, the book, and the bear to keep him busy, she walked as discreetly as she could the few strides over to Renée and had a seat beside her. The stench was almost unbearable.

"What is wrong with you?" Renée rasped.

Vianne reached for her chest. "Me?"

"I'm sitting by myself. Please leave."

"Stay away from my library and stay away from Chateau Ten. You hear me?"

Renée bolted to her feet and disappeared between two buildings. Vianne chased after her for a short distance because she could still see Blaise's head in the front seat from where she was standing. "Did you hear me? I'm not leaving until you answer."

"Evidently, you aren't." Renée reached into her pocket, pulling out a crumpled cigarette. "And you're willing to risk both our lives to do it."

"What do you mean, risk our lives?"

"I told you to be smart." She lit her cigarette with a sparking lighter, puffing it to life. "You're not doing too well."

"Whatever the Gaultiers are offering you for your services, I'll double it." Vianne dug into her handbag for a few francs to pay her off, because if they were up to something devilish like Max said, they couldn't succeed without Renée. "Just stay away—"

Renée shook her head, looking off into the clouds that had rolled in. "Money has nothing to do with it."

"Then what does?" Vianne asked.

There was a commotion nearby. Girls skipping down the pavement for Mme. Marchand's to see if she had more free pastries to pass out.

"I'm not telling you here."

"Then where?" Vianne asked.

Renée stomped on her cigarette after only smoking a small part of it. "I'll find you." She snatched the francs from Vianne's hand before she had a chance to pull it back. "I told you to be smart. Do better, Vianne."

Renée stuffed the money down the top of her dress, then left, crossing the street to catch up to Amélie, who'd just come out of the tax office. Vianne watched from the pavement, feeling uneasy when Renée put her arm around Amélie, who would never normally allow Renée to even get close enough for a touch.

Girls pulled on Mme. Marchand's locked door. "Why aren't they open?" one said, then turned to Vianne.

"Do you know?" The girl stomped her foot. "Madame? Do you know?"

Vianne stumbled back to her car, shaking her head.

That night's dinner was chicken cutlet with roasted potatoes slicked with a drizzle of warm olive oil. Élise prepared it but refused to serve them, and instead sat at the table talking with

Sandrine. Vianne supposed Élise thought she could get away without serving while the Gaultiers were paying her.

Vianne felt compelled to gaze out into the Zone Rouge, even though the sun had set and it was already dark. Her thoughts lingered on the memory of the Marchands' bodies— laid to rest in the mourning ground among earthworms and the bones of countless others, decaying, and oozing fluids. Then out of nowhere, like an unwelcome guest, she repeated the rhyme to herself.

> Like sirens from the sea, the Sorrows cry,
> An eerie melody tangled high.
> A ghostly wail of violins unseen,
> Drifting through the night in play,
> Whispering your name to steal you away.

She closed the kitchen curtains with one swift yank. Vianne wasn't going to do that now—she couldn't. Not if she planned on keeping her sanity while the Gaultiers were still there. The Marchands were with their son, like they wanted, she reminded herself. And her guests would be gone in a little more than a week, taking their German friends with them, and life would return to normal—whatever normal was.

She turned around, a platter of chicken in her hands. "Dinner is served." Vianne set it down in front of Élise.

"Yes, it is served, isn't it?" Élise used a big spoon to scoop out healthy portions for herself and Sandrine before setting the platter off to the side. "Where is Pierre?"

"I guess he decided to eat in the guesthouse." Vianne

turned to Blaise, picking up the platter since Élise didn't bother passing it. "Chicken?"

Blaise nodded, fork in his hand. She skipped over Henri's plate, leaving it clean. Sandrine didn't appear to notice, though her gaze scanned the table.

"How was your day?" Vianne asked as a way to distract her. "Did the weather cooperate well enough to read on the patio like you hoped?"

"I had a lovely afternoon," Sandrine said, and Vianne nodded, but she was thinking about the Gaultiers now and what they had planned that night. "Élise made a strong tea, just how I like it, didn't you, Élise?"

Élise nodded. "The Gaultiers are generous with their pantry budget. Black tea. Very expensive."

Vianne thanked Élise for taking care of Sandrine while she and Blaise were out.

"Why wouldn't I?" Élise said sharply.

Vianne held her tongue. It wasn't worth getting into an argument in front of Sandrine. Élise had cooked a nice meal, and the ingredients were fresh, most likely purchased from the black market that morning. Vianne understood that she needed to pick her battles.

She marked off the days that had passed on the wall calendar, circling the day the Gaultiers would leave. "Cooking for our guests tonight?" Vianne asked Élise.

"Not tonight." Élise ate with zest, forking a chunk of meat and swirling the brown sauce around the rim of her plate before gobbling it up.

"Oh?" Vianne tried not to look overly interested, but she wanted to know if they were having guests over for a séance again. Élise got up to pull some rolls from the oven while Blaise held up his slate, trying to get Vianne to look. He even tapped her arm.

"In a second, darling." Vianne glanced at his drawing, but not really, pushing the slate to the side and talking to Élise.

"Do you know…" Vianne thought up her words carefully. "Are they planning on using the library tonight?"

"I don't know."

"Have you joined them in the library before?"

Élise looked up after shoving a roll into her mouth. "Why would I do that?"

Vianne sighed internally for two reasons. They hadn't included Élise in their séances, and also, maybe they wouldn't be having one that night. "I see. Hopefully a quiet evening, then."

"I suppose." Élise lit two candles near the sink when the lights flickered from the storm. The curtains were open again.

"Close the curtains, please," Vianne said from the table.

"Why does it matter? The Zone Rouge is blacker than tar tonight." Élise sat down with one of the candles, forcing Vianne to get up from the table to close the curtains herself. The lights flickered a little longer this time, causing them all to look up in silence before they went out for good, leaving only the two melty candles near the platter to finish their dinner.

Vianne took an opportunity in the dim candlelight to place a napkin over Henri's plate.

"Finished, madame?" Vianne took Sandrine's plate to the sink while also placing Henri's clean plate in the cupboard without Sandrine noticing. She made a lather with the dish soap, glad to have escaped the question about Henri's whereabouts.

"Vianne?" Sandrine said.

Vianne thought she'd spoken to herself too soon—it was coming—she was going to ask about Henri. "Yes?" she asked guardedly.

"What about the macarons?" Sandrine asked.

"What?"

"The macarons from the Marchands. You said you'd bring some back. I was hoping for a blue and pink one. Where are they?"

"Oh! Yes, I did. Didn't I?" Vianne didn't think Sandrine would remember, and now she had the unpleasant opportunity to talk about the Marchands at dinner, knowing their bodies lay not that far away. "They were gone. The shop was closed."

Vianne turned on the tap to drown out Sandrine's voice, but Sandrine asked Élise to intervene, forcing Vianne to turn off the water.

"Gone where?" Sandrine asked.

"I don't know. Maybe—" Her gaze drifted through a split that had opened in the curtain, making out the black silhouettes of the scorched trees from a crack of lightning. She couldn't say anything about picking the macarons up next time because there wouldn't be a next time. "Élise can make some macarons here at home tomorrow."

Vianne reached up, not just tightening the curtains this time, but making sure not a sliver, not even a tiny pinprick of the Zone Rouge could be seen through the curtain split.

"Can't you? Make some tomorrow?" Vianne sat back down at the table where Élise tore another bite from her dinner roll.

"For Sandrine? I will see what ingredients I can find."

Blaise tapped Vianne's arm again. "Yes?" She smiled, realizing she'd been ignoring him most of the meal because she'd been so wrapped up with Élise and finding out about the Gaultiers.

She tousled his blonde hair while he pushed his slate at her.

Élise and Sandrine's conversation turned to talk about the weather, and in particular, the storms that had been roaring over the Meuse. "It is odd…" Sandrine said, going on to talk about the wind and the lightning, "Such violent weather for this area…"

Vianne took the slate in her hands, and her stomach dropped. This time, he'd added the chateau to his drawing, but with one of the black ghoulish faces from the trees hovering inside.

"Isn't that right, Vianne?" Élise asked, but Vianne was too busy looking at the slate, her eyes fixed on the drawing.

Blaise squeezed her wrist with his cold little hand, his hazel eyes wide and round, looking up under his long eyelashes, waiting for her to acknowledge what he'd drawn.

"Blaise…" She pointed. "Darling, is this the chateau?" she asked, because she had to be sure, even though he'd clearly drawn the iron fence and the scorched trees.

He nodded, and she moved her finger to the face hovering inside the chateau. "And this—"

"Vianne!" Élise clinked her fork against her water glass. "Isn't it true we had weather like this last year?"

Blood pumped in Vianne's ears. She managed to shake her

head at Élise's question, but she hadn't a clue what she'd asked.

Sandrine and Élise began chatting again, but she couldn't think with all that noise and got up to stand by the sink. She adjusted the curtains again out of nervousness. Her head pounded. Her eyes ached.

Élise kept talking, but somewhere in between, she heard Sandrine yawn. Vianne turned around, her voice unnaturally elevated to cut them off. "Is it time for bed?"

Both Sandrine and Élise looked up. The kitchen turned quiet. Blaise squirmed in his chair. After a moment, Sandrine nodded, and Élise offered to wheel her down to her bedroom.

"You didn't have to shout," Élise said before wheeling her away.

Vianne roughly rubbed her forehead, waiting until she heard them enter the hallway before turning to Blaise once more. The candles flickered on the table.

"Blaise, I—" she'd started to say when a whisp of air blew across the back of her neck, followed by a sound—a brush of the curtain fabric, and it wasn't faint, giving Vianne an icy shiver and thunderous heartbeat that pulsed fear through her limbs.

Blaise slowly looked over her shoulder to the window, eyes wide as moons.

Chapter Fourteen

Vianne turned around, clamping her hands over her mouth. The curtains had been thrown wide open by something unseen. She shrieked, running from the kitchen with Blaise in her arms to stand in the dark foyer, her heart banging like a fist through her chest.

Boom! Boom! Boom!

She needed to think, but she also wasn't going to let Blaise stay in the chateau one more second.

"Pierre," she said, all breathy.

She raced down to Blaise's bedroom to throw some things in a bag with only the candlelight from Sandrine's room across the hall for light.

"Vianne, is that you?" Sandrine called, but Vianne didn't have a voice to answer back and left out of the side door for the guesthouse. She scooped Blaise up in her arms the last few yards, calling for Pierre to open the door as she ran down the hill.

"I'm sorry!" she said, rushing in. "I know it's late." She set

Blaise down by the fire and tossed his things on the divan as the magpie squawked madly in his cage. "I need him to stay here tonight."

Pierre threw a blanket over the birdcage to keep it quiet. "What's wrong?"

"Is Max here?" she asked, taking a frantic look around the front room, but she could see he wasn't. She wanted to tell Pierre what had happened and what she thought, but Blaise was looking up at her, and she didn't know what to do.

Headlamps flashed up at the chateau, driving around the fountain to the west wing. At least two cars, but what kind she couldn't tell. "*Mon Dieu…*" She held the window curtain to the side, watching until they disappeared.

"I must go. I'll come down and get Blaise in the morning. Don't come up." She gave Blaise a kiss and a hug, leaving as quickly as she had entered, going back up the hill for the patio door.

She took a moment to get her bearings in the dark corridor, where it was deathly quiet, her back against the wall. Every hair on the back of her neck stood on end.

She inched toward the foyer, trying to focus on the beginning of the stairs instead of the kitchen where she felt pulled. "You're not allowed in here," Vianne said, trying to sound forceful. "You're not invited!"

Élise snuck up on her in the darkness. "What are you doing?"

Vianne clutched the newel post with both hands. "No— nothing." She forced a smile when Élise raised her candle to see her face.

"I heard what you said all the way from Sandrine's room.

Who's not invited?" Élise gave her a scrutinizing look after Vianne shrugged. "You are acting very strange." Vianne watched her check the pocket doors. "You can't blame me now," Élise said, before walking off with her flickering candle.

Vianne raced down to Sandrine's room as soon as Élise had disappeared, finding her mother-in-law sitting up in her bed and reading by candlelight.

"Oh, Vianne." She closed her book. "How are you? I called for you."

Vianne stood in the doorway longer than she should have before smiling. "I came to say goodnight." She felt her chest, thinking she might be having a heart attack.

"Sit here." Sandrine patted the empty space on her bed.

"What is it, madame?" she asked, looking over her covers where Élise had clearly tucked her in. "Are you comfortable?" Her wheelchair was beside her bed, and her clothes were laid out on the chair for tomorrow. Everything was as it should be, except her velvet drapes, which had been tied off to the side, allowing a glaring reflection of her bedroom in the glass.

"Keep these closed," Vianne said, closing the heavy drapes as tightly as she could, placing books on the gold fringe to hold the velvet in place. "Promise me you'll keep the drapes closed."

"I'll tell Élise."

"No. You must do it!" Vianne wasn't sure if she could trust Élise, considering all the times she'd left the pocket doors open. "Promise me," she said, for what it was worth, considering Sandrine's memory.

Sandrine placed her hand on Vianne's when she sat next to her on her bed. "Something is bothering you. What is it?"

Vianne stared into her eyes, afraid of saying the wrong thing, or maybe afraid of saying the right thing. She definitely didn't want to upset her.

"Vianne, tell me. What is on your mind?"

Vianne got up, tightening the drapes once more and smoothing the gold fringe until it lay flat, making sure not even a crack of moonlight could be seen. "There is something I want to ask you about. Has our guest, Madame Gaultier, visited you?" A few moments passed without a reply. "Madame?"

Vianne turned around to find Sandrine fast asleep. She sighed, sitting back down on her bed, though this time she placed her head in her hands to think.

She knew she couldn't sit and hide in Sandrine's room all night, not after what had happened, and seeing all those cars drive up. They were having another séance, and Max had asked her to eavesdrop, but that meant she'd have to move, walk past the kitchen, and into the west wing, and how was she going to do that?

Vianne held her hands out, watching them tremble and unable to control herself. "But Blaise…" She would do anything to keep him safe, except now the situation had changed. She had to decide if it was riskier to eavesdrop, or to stay in the dark and not know what their plans were after what happened in the kitchen—Sorrows in her home.

Marion would eavesdrop, she thought, and put her own fears aside.

Vianne made herself stand.

She had to be careful—she had to be quick. But above all, she had to be quiet.

Vianne blew out Sandrine's candle and crept down the hallway to the foyer, stopping only to gently slip off her shoes for noise and tuck them behind the staircase.

She gulped, wiping her brow of perspiration after gently opening the pocket doors, but there was no going back now, and bravely stepped into the dark west wing, feeling her way to the library with her hand tracing the wall.

Shadows passed through the dim light that shone under the library's door. Whispers could be heard, followed by weeping.

Vianne peeped through the keyhole.

She caught glimpses of the Gaultiers and Renée sitting at the mahogany table, laden with drippy candles and candelabras on both ends, before spying the German from the bookshop, which didn't surprise her, but then her heart sank. Amélie was their guest of honor.

Renée groaned with her eyes closed and hands lying flat on the tabletop, moving continuously in a sweeping figure-eight.

"I said that's enough," Amélie said, but Renée's hands were still moving, faster and faster. "Enough!" She jumped from her seat to cry in the corner near the book ladder.

Renée sank into her chair, huffing and puffing as if she were exhausted. Monique rushed to comfort Amélie near the books, trying to get her to lie down on the chaise, but Amélie was adamant about standing.

Monique reached for the candelabra.

"We have confirmation." Monique passed François his necklace after taking it from Amélie. "The reliquary stone works and the Sorrows exist in strong numbers. We have demonstrated that twice now."

"I don't know why I allowed you to talk me into coming here," Amélie said to Renée, but she didn't appear to be listening. "I wish I never knew how he died—a pool of blood gushing from his head from a bayonet. What a horrible thing. I wish I hadn't come!"

"Shh! Shh!" Monique said. "You must be discreet."

François adjusted the oil lamp's wick to burn brighter.

Renée finally roused, hand to her head, talking about a headache. "Let her leave," she said. "You don't need her now."

Vianne looked for a place to hide in the dark and managed to feel her way into an empty suite before Amélie rushed out the library door for the private side entrance. Vianne watched her start up her car through the window and tear out of there with a burst of rock and dust that ticked against the glass. Everyone had remained calm—nobody ran after her. In fact, François had quietly closed the library door as if it were a customary reaction.

Vianne tiptoed back into the corridor.

"As Monique was saying," François said. "We have proved the Sorrows exist. Kindly pay the promised fee for services rendered, Commandant Krieger."

"I'm not paying you anything until we find the other stone —I need both pieces in my hand," Krieger said. "Not half."

"No!" Monique interjected. "That was not our bargain. You agreed to pay half once we proved the existence of the Sorrows, and the rest of it once the stones are joined."

Krieger scoffed. "No, I would not agree to that, and I can speak for the others, we don't think the Sorrows can be raised without both pieces, not for a desire this complex. Payment will occur when I have the missing piece in my hand, joined with the one around François' neck. We have writings about it, prophecies. It is the only way you'll get the fee you requested." He pointed to Renée. "And you! You still have work to do."

Renée dug her palms into her eyes. "I've fulfilled my bargain. I have given you everything you asked for, and now I have all but given you my life, as I'm surely dead once the citizenry of Belleville-sur-Meuse find out what I've participated in, what I've told you, and what I've done."

"No," Krieger said. "You have not given us everything. Tell us where the missing piece is."

"I don't know," Renée said through her teeth.

He pounded his fist on the table, which gave Vianne a shake. "You do know!"

Renée stood her ground even after Krieger got in her face and shouted with spittle. François asked him to step back, and he did, which Vianne couldn't believe because he looked and sounded red hot, even after he sat down and tugged his uniform back into place.

Monique swung the stone back and forth as if a reminder of what they possessed.

Vianne tried focusing on the stone, but her eyes were drawn to the stained-glass window where she swore dark shadows had turned the glass silky black.

"Would you like us to try and summon the lost souls ourselves with only half?" Monique asked. "We could do it. I know about your past in Mons."

Krieger crossed his arms. "What do you know about the Battle of Mons?"

Monique slunk around the table before facing him, taking her old seat like a queen in her castle. "I heard only half the stone was used in resurrecting the ghost army there. Angels, as they were called by the *Daily Mail* because they were British soldiers helping their own. Only, if we raised the Sorrows—François and I—we could raise the French army, turn them against you, and annihilate the German forces occupying the country in the present." She looked up at François. "Isn't that right?"

"You are misinformed," Krieger said, then he stood. "But one thing is for certain. Using half the stone for something so delicate could only end in disaster. This is why I'm insisting on finding the other piece, and also why I'm not willing to pay for only half. The Third Reich and Commandant Lichtenberg deserve the precautions I am taking. Take note."

Monique stood, challenging him with a snarky smile from across the table. "Your obsession with Lichtenberg is clouding your judgment." She pressed the stone between both hands. "I command—"

The oil lamp flickered relentlessly. "Don't!" The candelabra blew out. "Stop it!" Krieger lunged for her and missed.

"It's in the Zone Rouge," Renée blurted, and both Monique and Krieger looked at her. "Hidden. Safe. But another is looking and … and…" She held her head again. "I can't see beyond that."

"We know it's in the Zone Rouge!" Krieger barked. "But where, exactly—for the sake of all who are damned. Walking into the forbidden forest without a map is a death trap. The risk of stepping on a mine, or worse, coming in contact with one of the leaky gas stockpiles…"

"What about a Cassini Map?" François asked. "Those have detailed topography notes, down to scale."

Krieger scoffed. "I haven't seen one in twenty-five years. Besides, even if we found one, the information on that kind of map predates the war and would be useless. We need to know a clear and safe path." He rubbed his face, only to drop his hand and look at Renée. "Did you say someone else is looking? You never mentioned this before."

"I don't know who," Renée said, shaking her head. "I can't see a face. There might be two. A woman, I feel."

Krieger looked incensed. "Where is the stone?" he demanded.

"I have fulfilled our deal," Renée said. "If you want more information, then you'll have to pay me like everyone else." She motioned to his shiny white-faced watch. "I'll take your timepiece."

Krieger grabbed Renée by the throat, pulling her right out of her chair and tossing her to the floor. She lay coughing and gasping for breath, and somewhere between it all, she let the words escape her.

"The Fleury Chapel."

"There, there," Krieger said. "That wasn't so hard, was it?" He adjusted his uniform cuffs while Renée crawled away, holding her throat. "The map for safe passage." He looked pointedly at Monique. "Find it, if you have any hopes of collecting that outrageous fee you asked for."

Vianne blindly stepped back into the dark suite before Krieger stormed out.

Renée was still coughing and hacking, trying to catch her breath. "Bury the stone and run if you know what is good for you. The land belongs to the Sorrows. It's theirs. They will not take kindly to those who try to command them. Be warned."

"Don't warn us," Monique said.

"Nothing good will come of it," Renée said. "Nothing of you will remain."

"Is that a threat?" Monique chuckled. "François, darling. The putrid mystic from the streets is warning us."

François joined Monique in an uncontrollable laugh. Renée stumbled out, leaving them both in the library alone with the door ajar, forcing Vianne to stay in the dark suite next door. She pressed her ear to the floral wallpaper.

"François. What are we going to do with her?" Monique asked. "Two people are looking—one of them a woman. I thought the mystic was about to tell Krieger our plans to take his money and steal the stone for ourselves once he raises his army."

"What if she wasn't talking about us?" he asked.

"I didn't think about that. Regardless, Renée better keep her mouth shut from now on."

"What can we do about it?" he asked. "She doesn't have much family left, not after that incident in Verdun, so there is little leverage in that regard…"

Vianne wished they'd keep talking about what Renée did in Verdun, but they moved on to more about themselves.

"We will be the ones the Führer will consult for delicate operations when this is over," Monique said, followed by an angry pound of her fist on the table. "We will have the power and the riches. Damn Krieger for changing the deal on us. We deserve payment for what we've done thus far, and when we are done, I want this chateau. Tell me I can have it when this is over."

"Relax, *ma petite*," François said. "All will work out. I promise."

"Let's use the stone now. We have proved it has the power to grant certain things. Let's try our hand at asking for something we want."

"Without the missing piece? Krieger said this stone has a fraction of the power."

"We've proved it can work, for smaller uses. I'm not talking about raising an army of our own. I'm only wishing for something small, like beauty, to keep me satisfied before we steal both stones for ourselves."

"You are already magnificent, as you must know from looking in the mirror all day. I don't think it is a good idea to use half."

"Watch it, François. You sound like that ridiculous mystic and her warnings. Also, I don't look in the mirror all day. Give me the stone. Shall we?" There was a pause, as if she had indeed asked the stone for something, but Vianne couldn't be sure. "Now, what will you ask for, my darling husband?"

"The opportunity to follow you anywhere," he said.

A brief quietness ensued before she heard Monique's seducing moans. Vianne took that as an opportunity to sneak out of the suite, padding slowly back toward the pocket doors, when she heard muffled footsteps in the dark behind her.

Vianne gasped, briefly turning back, thinking she saw shadows following her, and entered the foyer out of breath. She delicately closed the pocket doors while her heart was thrashing. She had made it. But every shadow on the floor and ceiling played with her imagination as she stood still in the empty foyer with her heart in her ears, especially the moonlight streaming through the front window where ivy tittered against the glass.

She thought of what had been in the kitchen, what could be in the foyer by way of numerous windows, or in any one of the long corridors…

A prickling shiver shot up her arms. "Hallo?"

The pocket door rattled from something pressing on it from the other side, sending her bolting up to her room where she jumped into her bed, throwing her blanket over her head with her eyes blasted open and her heart hammering.

She breathed heavily, the air suffocatingly warm, with her mind racing.

What if it was Monique? She wouldn't follow her into her side of the chateau, would she? She'd been so careful, and so quiet. Vianne was beginning to think it was safe. She'd only imagined she'd been followed, she thought, but then she definitely heard something—something that made her tremble and sick.

Another person's breathing.

She slowly pulled the blanket below her eyes. *It's nobody*, she thought. It was nothing. Then her heart nearly stopped.

A woman stood in her doorway.

Vianne jumped out of bed on guard. "Who are you—" The rancid smell of Renée's matted hair and soiled dress hit her. "Renée?" She immediately collapsed onto her bed, her head light and her vision tunneling from standing up so fast. "*Mon Dieu*, what are you doing here?"

"Shh!" Renée rasped, barging into her room and going straight to the window, closing her heavy drapes with one pull of the tieback cord. "You want them to hear?"

"They can't hear from the west wing."

"Not the Gaultiers, Vianne." She lit the candle by Vianne's bedside after closing the door. "I'm talking about the Sorrows."

"Sorrows?"

"Tell me you believe, and that they don't scare you."

Vianne hung her head. It was the first time she would admit out loud that she believed. "I didn't believe it before, but now I do."

"What changed?"

"I believe, and that should be enough."

"I know you were listening to us, but not because I saw or heard you. You were smart this time, and the Gaultiers are none the wiser. Good for you. But you'll need to be smarter." She tossed the shoes Vianne had hidden behind the stairs onto the floor.

"Why are you here?" Vianne asked. "We are not friends, but this is the second time you've warned me. Third, if you count the warning not to rent to the Gaultiers in the first place."

Renée pulled a cigarette from her pocket and had a smoke near the window. "This isn't easy, and what I'm about to tell you will come as a shock." She looked up after taking a long drag of her cigarette, the candlelight flickering over her cheeks. "I've met Blaise before."

"What? When? How could you have—"

"I knew Marion. Not well, but well enough. I was there when she was arrested."

Renée was right about Vianne being shocked. "You were there?"

"Blaise recognized our connection when you came out of

the bookshop the other day. Sensitives do that. If you had been paying attention, you would have noticed."

Vianne gathered some strength, sitting up tall. "Tell me everything you know about my sister. Now."

Renée flicked ash into Vianne's empty rosebud vase. "We were in the resistance together, and we were trying to protect the stone. I failed, and I must go before it's too late. They don't know Marion had a son. I wanted you to know that." She paused, taking another drag from her cigarette. "I know you've been worried."

Vianne covered her eyes. This was hard to hear, and a little unbelievable, but she needed to listen to it.

"The boy has seen the Sorrows," Renée said. "You know this?"

Vianne dropped her hands. "I think there's one in the chateau. What do I do?"

"Pray."

"That's what got me into this!" Vianne said.

"Listen, Vianne." She dropped her lit cigarette into the vase. "You're about to be tested. You must be strong. Not only does Blaise depend on you, but so does the world."

"The world?" she asked. "How am I supposed to save the world?"

"The stone is dangerous. The commandant has the potential to turn the Sorrows into a powerful army—trained German soldiers rising from the scarred remains of the battlefield, taking the shape they had the moment they died. Blood-soaked, driven by sorrow, revenge, and orders."

"I don't know if I believe that. A magic stone—"

"It doesn't matter what you believe." Headlamps shone

through a split between the drape and the window. Renée watched carefully, pulling the fabric subtly to the side for a peek. "The Germans are drawn to the stone, and so are the Sorrows. They'll do whatever it takes to find it, and use whoever they want." She closed the drapes when the lights grew too bright, followed by a long, studying look of Vianne's face. "You're not sleeping well at night, are you?"

"How do you know?"

"It's just a feeling I have." She ripped one of the drapery cords free. "Tie your wrist to the bedpost. It might help." After tossing it to her, Renée moved to open Vianne's wardrobe.

"What are you doing?"

Renée hurriedly picked through all her dresses, pulling a yellow one out with a matching spring sweater that was neither old nor new, but clean and presentable. "In the wild west, Americans traveling through hostile territory used to circle their wagons. Have you heard of that?"

"Wagons? What are you talking about, Renée? You're sounding mad."

"Wagons. You know, horse-drawn, settlers, loaded with all they held dear. To protect themselves from thieves and hostiles, they'd band together by circling their wagons at night, putting their most valuable possessions in the middle, which the enemy understood. But some of the settlers would remain on the periphery for an ambush. Sometimes it meant the difference between living and dying."

Renée stepped out of her tattered rag of a dress, leaving it in a crumple under her shoes, and slipped on Vianne's. She reached for a scarf next, covering her hair.

"Where are you going?" Vianne stood.

"Now that I've told them what they wanted to hear, I'm a liability. They only need a map for a safe passage into the Zone Rouge, and I fear they will have a solution to their problem in short order. I feel it." She grabbed Vianne by the shoulders. "Be smarter than them. Listen to your gut. You'll know what to do. Listen to the trees for God's sake to know when they're close."

"The trees?"

Renée went to Vianne's bureau and searched her perfumes. "Haven't you figured out what you are, Vianne?" She sprayed the air above her with Vianne's last mist of Chanel No. 5. "The forbidden forest is alive with roaming souls. I know you've felt them in the trees, a sigh that creeps yet conceals itself in a fog. A sensitive can see through the veil." She pocketed a costume brooch and what few francs Vianne had lying in a change dish.

"I'm not a sensitive. In fact, I've lived here for years and haven't sensed anything until—"

"Until Blaise showed up? He was the spark that lit the fire inside of you. Then the stone was used on your property, and that made the Sorrows stronger. Prepare yourself, Vianne. You're going to see and hear more things you can't explain. Worse, if the Germans find out, they will use you like they used me."

"Use me," Vianne repeated.

Renée poked Vianne hard in the chest. "Now is the time to circle the wagons, Vianne. Ask for help and gather your people. Pay attention to the signs." She turned, and like a shadow, Renée slipped out the door and disappeared down the darkened hallway.

Chapter Fifteen

Vianne woke the next morning with a gasping, clawing breath. In her dream, the Sorrows had called her name—their voices sweeping over the treetops of the forbidden forest like a powerful gust of wind. Her heart pounded, but she lay still, waiting for her eyes to adjust to the dim light of her bedroom. "Oh, thank God," she whispered, discovering the cord Renée told her to use was still around her wrist and tied to the bedpost.

She sat up, rubbing the raw welt left behind, thinking of Renée's cryptic messages and words of warning. "Sigh in the trees, creeping..." Vianne's stomach sank. She didn't remember the terms last night, but she had heard this kind of language before—in the opening sentence of Genevieve's letter.

Vianne pulled back her covers, and after trying to talk herself out of going downstairs to find it, she slipped on a dress and padded downstairs, unable to resist. She pulled open all her desk drawers, one after the other, trying to remember where she'd last seen it, rummaging through her loose papers, then her old bills, when a yellow envelope fell effortlessly to the floor near her feet.

She unfolded the letter carefully.

Dear Sandrine,

Do you see them, too? Tell me you do. A passing shadow in the night. Soft music drifting, a sigh in the trees, creeping through the leaves.

But now—oh, now they know my name and they drag it through the wind after calling to me in a dream. Genevieve … Genevieve … Genevieve…

Vianne gasped, hand to her mouth.

Day and night, night and day, no rest, no peace, just their voices threading through the mourning grounds all the way to my ears. I cannot sleep. I cannot breathe. I cannot look outside. I know what is coming next.

I shut the curtains, but they are there. I lock my suite's door, but they are in the ghost house you call Chateau Ten. They wait. They watch. They whisper.

Don't listen. Don't look. Don't talk to them.

—Genevieve

Vianne shakily tucked the letter back into the envelope.

"Vianne?" Sandrine called to her from her bedroom down the hall. "Is that you, I hear?"

She placed the letter in her top drawer, unsure what to do with that information. She certainly couldn't pretend she hadn't read it. "I'll be right there, madame."

Vianne took a moment with her eyes closed, doing her best to collect herself with a smooth of her hair before walking down to see Sandrine.

"Good morning." She stepped into the room, finding Sandrine dressed and getting into her wheelchair. "Let me help you!" Vianne ran over to her, but Sandrine had managed and sat heavily in the chair.

"I'm all right," Sandrine said, then chuckled. "Sorry if I gave you a fright."

Vianne kissed her forehead. "Everything gives me a fright these days."

"Open the drapes," she said. "I'd like to see the sun."

"It's a dreary day, no sun. Why let all that grayness inside?" Vianne grabbed hold of Sandrine's wheelchair to roll her out of the room, when she protested, insisting that not only she open the drapes, but that she wheel her closer to the window before heading down to breakfast.

Vianne thought of ways to get around it, but nothing sounded plausible. Sandrine turned, looking up at her over her shoulder. "The window, Vianne."

Vianne gingerly tied the heavy velvet drapes back, then turned to keep from looking into the Zone Rouge. Her heart pounded.

"Everything all right?" Sandrine had been eyeing Vianne as she rubbed the burn on her wrist.

Vianne smiled. "Mmm."

She wrapped a shawl around Sandrine's shoulders,

thinking how alert she was after waking up, and maybe this was another chance to ask about the visitor Élise had heard. She had to find out if it was Monique, more than ever now, after Amélie attended the séance.

"I need to ask you something." Vianne's back was still to the window. "It's all right if you don't remember. Has Madame Gaultier, our guest from the west wing, visited you in your room?"

Sandrine appeared to think for a moment before looking up at Vianne.

"When?"

"Anytime. Has she ever talked to you?"

"Someone was visiting me in my bedroom?" she said, tapping her chin. "Now that you mention it, yes, I remember that much, but also Élise. She told me to be quiet about something, but I..." Her face strained. "I'm sorry, I don't remember what she told me to keep to myself."

"She told you to keep a secret?" Vianne was thrown by this and wasn't sure what to make of it. "From me?"

Sandrine placed a gentle hand on Vianne's.

"Madame. Promise me. If Élise asks you to go into the library at night. Don't."

"The library?" Sandrine was clearly confused. "Why would she do that?"

Vianne decided it was best to have her question hang. The likelihood that she would remember not to go with Élise into the library was stronger that way. She wheeled Sandrine into the foyer, parking her chair at the front windows.

"I'm going to check on breakfast," she said, leaving her, but only as a way to talk to Élise privately.

Vianne walked into the kitchen where the curtains were still thrown open from last night. She felt utterly pulled to look toward the trees, as hard as she tried to resist and focus on the crackle and pop of eggs in the frying pan.

"We're out of grease again." Élise scraped the eggs from the bottom of the pan with a metal spatula, then switched to the wooden one when Vianne closed in on her, as if she'd been using it the whole time.

Vianne crossed her arms. "I know what you did."

"What have I done?" Élise took her pan over to the table and started scooping eggs onto plates. "I'm using the wooden spatula."

"You gave Monique access to Sandrine, let her talk to her in her bedroom, then told my own mother-in-law to keep quiet about it—not to tell me."

"You're mad!" Her face was one of surprise, but Vianne didn't know if that was because she'd caught her or for some other reason. "I haven't done anything close to that."

Vianne uncrossed her arms. "Élise, the Gaultiers are not your friends. They most certainly are not Sandrine's."

"They're friendlier than you've been, especially these last few months. I've let some things slide because of your sister and Blaise, but Sandrine—"

Sandrine wheeled herself into the kitchen a little out of breath. Vianne rushed to help her. "I heard my name," Sandrine said.

Vianne changed course with Sandrine in the room and smiled. "Did you? I was just saying that I'll be taking breakfast down to Pierre and Blaise. They are in his workshop already," she said. "Nothing to be concerned about."

"I see. Well, Élise and I will have a nice breakfast up here, then."

Élise looked at Vianne with the pan still in her hands. "Of course, we will have a nice breakfast. We always have nice meals together, and this has been the case for decades. Isn't that right, madame? Even before Vianne moved in. It was just you and me—me and you."

"And Pierre," Sandrine said.

The kitchen turned quiet aside from Vianne gathering Pierre and Blaise's breakfast on a tray. She had already decided she needed to talk to Amélie about last night, and Max, but she was going to have to be quick about it because she didn't want to leave Sandrine at the chateau very long without her, even after Élise said the Gaultiers would be out most of the day.

"I'm going to Belleville. You'll be all right on the patio again while I'm gone?" Vianne asked Sandrine, but then turned to talk to Élise. "But just so you know, I won't be long."

Élise rolled her eyes. "I don't care how long you're gone."

"I'm always fine here," Sandrine said, giving Élise's hand a pat on the table. "If you see Amélie, will you give her my regards? I'd love for her to visit."

Vianne stopped cold in the doorway, tray in her hands. "Amélie?"

"Yes. If you see her."

Vianne nodded, then left for Pierre's, carrying the eggs and toast down to the workshop where she heard some activity. She had a moment to talk to Pierre privately as she set out breakfast on a worktable before Blaise was finished with his sanding project.

"I saw what he drew on the slate last night," was the first thing Pierre said. "The chateau, and the face inside."

Vianne was quiet for a moment, making sure Blaise's plate had the most eggs and the biggest piece of toast. "And what do you think about it?"

"I think you saw a Sorrow, or felt one. That's why you were frantic."

She looked up. "It was in the kitchen," she said, matter-of-factly, because she knew Pierre wasn't going to say he told her so. "Max told you about the stone. Do you believe in that as well?"

"It's possible, isn't it? If the Sorrows are real, then why not the reliquary stone too?"

"Reliquary stone. Monique called it that last night." Vianne put one hand to her forehead, briefly thinking about telling Pierre about the key while reaching for it in her dress pocket with the other.

"What is it?" he asked.

"I don't know what to believe about the stone. Now, I'm afraid of doing the wrong thing. I only want to protect my family."

"As do I," he said. "But ignoring the challenges that we face isn't going to keep anyone safe."

"I'm going to see Max again today and tell him what happened." Vianne set out the water glasses. "Would you mind watching Blaise again? I don't want him visible in the streets, and I also don't want him anywhere near the Gaultiers in case they come back early. I know you will keep him safe and away from them. And away from Élise, whom I'm not sure about right now since she technically works for them."

He nodded. "You have my word. Have you tried evicting them? This is your family's chateau to run. You make the rules."

Vianne looked into Pierre's eyes, ashamed to admit the restrictive nature of the contract she'd signed. "I have tried. I met with someone of authority. They advised me not to make a fuss and mentioned Blaise as a reason why—retaliation."

His face changed. Then he sat down heavily and rubbed his eyes. "And I sold the jewels and spent the money, didn't I?" he said. "I'm sorry. You have no leverage now."

"I told you to do it."

She called Blaise over to have a seat and eat breakfast together, and they ate quietly, only the noises of their fork tines against their plates and the crunch of the toast and sips of water could be heard.

"What about praying?" she asked.

"Praying?"

Vianne hesitated to mention that Renée had also told her to pray after Blaise looked up from his plate. "Can I ask you a personal question?"

"Personal? Yes."

"When has it worked for you?" she asked. "Praying, I mean."

He took off his glasses again, though this time he set them on the worktable and sighed. "After the war, home didn't feel like home anymore. The air smelled like the trenches, soggy peat and iron, even on a sunny day. I had changed and didn't know where to go or where I fit in. I was on my knees and prayed for a second chance at life, one where, instead of killing, I took care of someone. Sandrine was an old friend, as you know. I never told her my situation, but that next day I received a letter in the post asking me to come help with the estate, and I've been here ever since."

Vianne placed her hand on his.

"So, yes. I think praying for help works."

"Oh, Pierre. I'm sorry for never asking, and I'm sorry for not knowing this part of your life. You have been a godsend to us here, and in particular to Sandrine."

He gave her hands a squeeze. "You'd better get going. Leave the breakfast dishes."

Vianne wiped her mouth with her napkin. "Thank you."

When Vianne left, she told Blaise to stay away from Élise and also the guests in the west wing. "Do you understand?" She nodded to get him to nod. "Stay with Pierre at all times."

He threw his arms around her.

"I love you, Blaise," she said softly in his ear, and for a moment she thought she heard a noise as if he was going to say it back, but instead he scribbled out a heart on his slate.

"Don't worry about him here with me," Pierre said. "Do you need the car?"

Vianne doubted she could ever rent to another guest again after this and wanted to save the petrol now. "I'll ride my bicycle."

Vianne didn't remember the ride into town because her mind was spinning as fast as her wheels, thinking about the Gaultiers, the séance, and also poor Amélie and what she went through last night.

She stepped into the tax office expecting to find Amélie at her desk, but her chair was empty. The door closed abruptly against her heels with a clang of bells. Heads turned, and she gripped her handbag a little tighter. Instead of asking for Amélie or waiting for her to come out of the back, she cut to the front of the short line and sat down at her desk.

She barely had time to gather her thoughts before the clerk next to her whispered, "Amélie didn't come in today."

"Where is she?" Vianne asked.

The woman shrugged. "How am I supposed to know?"

Amélie's supervisor walked by with his clipboard, eyeing Vianne. She pulled her shoulders back when he paused, quickly thinking up a lie because she couldn't tell him the truth.

"I had an appointment with Amélie today." Vianne tapped her watch. "I don't have time to wait." She got up and left, only to hold her chest outside. Amélie never missed a day of work.

How can this be?

Vianne noticed more Germans on the pavement than she was used to, but if she had been fully paying attention, she would have noticed that a small procession of Wehrmacht was about to march through the square. Instead, she leaned against the nearest building and found herself looking at Henri's key, which she pulled from her pocket. A stiff wind blew over her, swaying the tree branches and rustling the leaves.

"Vianne!" Colette came walking up quickly from the opposite direction. "What are you doing out here?" She reached for her hand, getting a look at the key. "What is that?"

Vianne shoved the key back into her pocket, but she was

still in a daze, with her eyes like a deer's in headlamps, now looking at the tittering leaves where she heard a soft chant that seized her limbs.

> *Like sirens from the sea, the Sorrows cry,*
> *An eerie melody tangled high.*
> *A ghostly wail of violins unseen…*

"The Wehrmacht is about to pass through." Colette gave her a shake. "Vianne—"

Vianne covered her ears with a yelp.

"Shh!" Colette pulled her in close from watchful eyes just as an open-top Mercedes full of SS drove by, their heads pivoting side to side and little Nazi Party flags near the headlamps. The tack-tack-tack of a Tiger Tank followed. "What's the matter with you?"

Vianne took a few heavy breaths.

"Where's Blaise?" Colette asked. "Has something happened—"

"Safe," Vianne said. "With Pierre."

The crowd grew thicker, and the police were out with their truncheons, urging people to move along. One stopped next to Vianne's bicycle to have a short chat with an SS officer, which made her tense back up.

"Come with me," Colette said. "We'll talk in the shop."

"But my bicycle." Vianne tried to reach for it.

"Leave it." Colette looked down both ends of the street. "If we don't hurry, we'll be stuck."

They cut across the street, through the weak and the old with mothers shielding their children, trying their best not to look into the eyes of the Germans, but it was shocking to see so many SS in Belleville-sur-Meuse.

Somehow, they made it across the street without a whistle being blown at them, and before the procession passed through and the police stopped all traffic.

Vianne burst through the bookshop door behind Colette, her face stricken, finding Max going over his notes on the counter.

"What happened?" Max tore his glasses from his face. "You overheard something? Saw something—" He grabbed Vianne by the shoulders. "A séance?"

Vianne nodded, then went on to tell him all that she'd learned, starting with Renée facilitating the seances, how she helped them connect with the Sorrows, and Amélie's dead brother. "Amélie ran out of the library, crying. I went to see how she was doing at the tax office just now. She wasn't there. It's not like her to miss a day of work."

"The Gaultiers let her use the stone. That's the second time they let someone—"

"What?" Vianne asked. "What does that mean?"

"It means they are proving the stone works for the right price."

"The German was there again, the one I helped in this bookshop. Commandant Krieger."

Max's lips parted slightly, but no sound came, only stunned silence.

"You know him?" Vianne asked.

He covered his mouth momentarily, then nodded. "Rudolf Krieger. He fought at Mons and believes firmly that he witnessed the resurrection of the ghost army as it happened on the battlefield. It's what drove him to find the stone in the first place."

Vianne paced the shop, feeling a little sick. "I don't know what to do. I don't know how to keep my family safe. How to keep Blaise—"

He helped her sit down and got her a glass of water because she was shaking all over.

"Something else happened last night." Vianne took a drink of water that ended with her guzzling the entire glass. "There was a ghost in the chateau." She gulped. "A Sorrow—a dead soldier from the forbidden forest."

"You saw one?" Colette breathed.

She nodded incessantly. "I finally read Genevieve Lacroix's letter. She wasn't mad. She saw them, too. Her warnings were dire, and I didn't listen. I didn't even give her a chance."

"And what about the stone? Remember what I said, Vianne? If there is truth to the Sorrows, then isn't it logical to at least believe the stone has some importance?"

"Importance? Yes, it is important, insofar as the Germans want it. But magic? Conjure a ghost army?" Vianne held her stomach where it ached.

"The article." Max retrieved his briefcase from his upstairs loft. "Maybe have a look at this." He pulled out a crackling old newspaper article from the last war and handed it to her. "This is the *Daily Mail* article that came out after the Battle of Mons. Eyewitness accounts of how the army was raised, letters, interviews, recounting what it looked like."

Vianne talked as she read, her eyes growing. "Ghostly archers … shimmering beings…"

"The event is well documented by many. They disappear as

soon as the threat is over, inflicting catastrophic losses to the other side."

"Customers!" Colette announced.

Vianne handed the newspaper to Max, who stuffed it away just as the door swung open with a clattering of bells.

"Hallo. Good morning," Colette said, smiling.

A woman, her daughter, and an older man with a cane. The man hobbled over to the counter, handing her a coin. "For your trouble. I just wanted to get off the street."

"It's all right." Colette smiled. "Do you know … why are the Wehrmacht here?"

"This panzer division is moving north, and that can only mean one thing." He leaned over the counter, whispering. "They are planning for the invasion we've all been praying for. Moving whole detachments to the northern coast. I heard to Pas-de-Calais." He paused while the bulk of the tanks passed the shop, rattling the bookshelves and the glass windows.

"So that's where they think it will happen?" Colette asked.

"That's what I overheard on the street between two Germans. I'll tell you one thing, I'm from the sixth village that died for France, but I'm not ready to die again. God help us," he said on his way out.

The woman looked up over the bookshelf, then took off with her daughter once it was clear, following the man out. Colette put her face to her hands when the shop turned quiet again, elbows on the counter.

"Vianne, I'm worried about Amélie," Max said. "Do you know where she lives?"

Vianne nodded.

"You can't go to her house," Colette said. "What if the SS

are there? It's not out of the question if she was involved last night, and you know how they are, they'll bombard you with questions."

"Well, Max can't go. She doesn't know him, and it would look suspicious. I have to go," Vianne said.

"Then I'll go with you." Colette tucked some books in a basket. "If we are stopped or asked what we are doing, we can say we are delivering her books—just came in today."

Max put his hand on the basket, keeping Colette from lifting it away. "Promise me you'll both come back here right after."

Colette promised, then he turned to Vianne, and without a second thought, she reached for Max's hands and held them. "We promise."

Chapter Sixteen

Two young girls pulled at the Marchands' locked door. "Strange. They are never closed," their mother said, looking around and spying Vianne. "Madame, have you seen the Marchands?"

Vianne didn't have to close her eyes this time to imagine the silhouette of Mme. Marchand's milky white calves dangling in the fog.

"Let's go." She hooked Colette's arm and walked the other way, through the square and toward the row houses.

Vianne hoped they wouldn't see the officer she had talked to yesterday, but he had already noticed her after approaching the police station. His back was up against the brick building, smoking with other officers.

"Why is he staring?" Colette said through her teeth.

"Because I spoke to him yesterday," Vianne mumbled, head down.

"What?" Colette whispered.

Vianne gently looked up after they walked past. Then, in a

bold move, she glanced over her shoulder and saw Officer Lefevre was not only still staring but tipping his hat.

"I needed someone to look over my contract with the Gaultiers. Amélie suggested I go to the police. I was desperate." Vianne tightened her arm, pulling Colette even closer. "I'm sure Max has talked to you—told you some of the more disturbing things that happened to me that night the Marchands died, and what he believes. I know you'll tell me the truth. What do you think about the stone?"

Colette's eyes shifted to Vianne's as they walked. "It scares me, and I'm worried. Not just for Amélie, but for you and Blaise, and hell, Pierre and Sandrine, too."

"There's something else…"

When Vianne told her about Renée's late-night visit to her bedroom, Colette practically had to pick her jaw up from the pavement.

"But I don't think we'll see her again. She said she knew Marion from the resistance and had met Blaise. Apparently, Marion knew about the stone and was trying to keep it safe."

"And you trust what she said?" Colette asked.

"I know it sounds like a coincidence, but I believe she was telling me the truth." Vianne tapped her heart. "I felt it."

"Then that means Marion was taken because of the stone," Colette said.

Vianne hadn't thought about it that way until Colette said it out loud.

"Like I said, Vianne." Colette looked up at her. "I'm worried."

"But do you believe the stone works?"

She nodded without hesitation.

They made it to Amélie's cobblestone street to find it was unusually quiet, aside from the clack and tack of two children playing jump rope. "Which house is it?" Vianne asked. All of the row houses looked a little desolate and abandoned in some way from years of wartime neglect. A neighbor motioned to them from her window, talking through her open curtains.

"Are you here to see, Amélie?"

Vianne and Colette briefly looked at each other. "Yes, why?" Colette held up her basket of books. "I have a delivery."

"Shh!" The woman shook her head at them for being too loud. "I heard some noises early this morning."

"What kind of noises?" Vianne asked.

A car drove by slowly, and she backed away from the window, allowing the curtains to flap closed.

"Madame?" Vianne called, and a hand reached up from the inside and closed the window sash.

Vianne tugged on Colette's arm to walk next door. "I'll knock." They walked up the two stone steps where Vianne rapped twice. The children stopped jumping rope.

"Now the children are staring," Colette whispered.

The trees rustled from a breeze, one that caused gooseflesh to bump up Vianne's arms.

"Knock again," Colette said, but Vianne was studying the trees, looking for a sign. "What's wrong?"

Vianne didn't know how to explain. "It doesn't feel right."

"What doesn't feel right?" Colette asked.

"I don't know. The air. Do you feel the static?" Vianne shivered.

Colette gave the door a gentle nudge. "It's unlocked."

Vianne poked her head in. "Hallo?" she called, followed by

a pause. "Amélie? It's Vianne…" They walked inside to stand in her front room where the silence was magnified by the cut of Vianne's concerned voice. "You weren't at work today."

Colette closed the door. A moment passed with them waiting for Amélie to answer back.

"Where is she?" Vianne asked.

Colette shrugged, setting the basket down on a side table where Amélie kept old photos of her family. She picked up the one with a dried flower next to it, Amélie's brother, taken after he enlisted in the French army in 1916.

Vianne took three steps into the kitchen, arms folded, taking in every nuanced clue. "Look at this." She pointed to the two uncooked eggs on a plate and a pot of water yet to be boiled on the cooktop. "She was making breakfast."

"You mean, she was either interrupted or stopped."

Vianne turned around, looking at the table, which was set for one, and at the icebox, which had been left open and had turned warm. That's when she noticed the cellar door was ajar. A strip of black and stark cold air.

Colette pointed with her head for her to go first.

Vianne didn't want to, but felt she had no choice. She lit a candle and slipped through the door with Colette following closely behind. Upon first step, she could tell the wooden stairs were as old as they were loud, each board splintering from their weight. They both paused.

The flame illuminated the darkness like a dull glimmer, only lighting up the next step down. "Hold onto the rail," Vianne said.

"I am," Colette said, but she also had a hand on Vianne's shoulder in front of her. "How much farther?"

"I don't know." A wispy cobweb brushed Vianne's forehead, but she couldn't swat it away because she'd have to let go of the rail, leaving an annoying tickle trailing down her face.

Colette's fingers dug into Vianne's shoulder. "You were right. It doesn't feel right. Let's turn back."

Another step. "We can't turn back now," Vianne rasped.

"Fine," Colette whispered. "Go."

Vianne's eyesight narrowed from the candlelight, hand sliding down the rail until she got to the bottom step and stopped cold from seeing Amélie's twisted body lying like a wrung towel at the bottom of the stairs.

Colette screamed, hands to her mouth, but Vianne was still frozen with her heart plummeting to her stomach.

"Is she…" Vianne examined her feet first, with one heel caught on the stairs, then her floral dress as it lay above her crooked legs, and her head lying in a slow-growing pool of blood.

"She's dead," Colette said.

Vianne turned away, fiercely holding onto the handrail for support and taking a few panicked breaths. However, the image of Amélie's lifeless body remained, right down to the jar of peaches still in her hands, coupled with the warm smell of iron in a damp and drafty cellar.

"What are we going to do?" Colette cried.

Vianne shook her head because she didn't know.

"But we have to do something—"

The clunk of jackboots pounded on the floor above them. "Shh!" They both searched the ceiling as whoever it was traveled from one side of the house to the other, shaking the support beams, until stopping at the top of the stairs.

They held each other, Vianne's pulse a frantic thrum, and her hands squeezing Colette for dear life.

Creak! A hand pushed the door all the way open, and the flit of fresh air snuffed their candle out. A dark silhouette of a man in uniform appeared.

"Who's down there?" He flicked on a torch. "I heard a scream." His light scanned the cellar, landing on Vianne and Colette, who were squinting, trying to see.

He thumped downstairs with another man behind him, finding Amélie on the floor. His light cast on her limbs, but now Vianne's eyes had adjusted to the brightness of the light and saw it wasn't just a man in uniform. It was Krieger.

"Oh, hallo," he said. "What are you doing here?"

Vianne was a jumble of words, the least of which made sense, until finally she found her footing. "My ... my friend. I came to check up on her. She fell." Vianne wiped her eyes. "She's dead, and we don't know what to do."

He addressed the other officer with him, who said he would find someone to help. Krieger turned to Vianne, giving her a look up and down. "I know you." He snapped his fingers. "You sold me a book!"

Vianne mustered up a nod.

"Come. I will drive you both back." He ushered them both up the stairs.

"I'm glad I happened to be passing by. Otherwise, I wouldn't have heard that scream. What a fright for both of you." He took his coat off after seeing Vianne shiver violently.

"Please. You'll catch your death after being in that damp cellar."

Vianne stood paralyzed as he slipped his wool SS jacket over her shoulders, doused in a citrusy cologne she detested. He clomped outside where he chatted with another officer, pointing down the street, and then toward the cellar. His tone, his kindness—just as she remembered from when he bought the book from her—crawled up her skin.

"We can't go with him," Colette said.

"We have no choice." Vianne grabbed the book basket from the side table and handed it to her. "If we don't, he'll wonder why."

They followed him outside to his car where he held the door open. "Officer Muller will notify the undertaker."

"Officer Muller..." Vianne saw he was an Abwehr officer, yet while their uniforms were starkly different, they wore the same shiny white-faced timepieces on their wrists.

He nodded, and she nodded back, then he pointed at the front seat. Vianne got in while Colette stiffly got in the back with her basket of books. Neighbors either turned away or closed their curtains.

Vianne thought she might get sick, right there in the front seat, wearing his SS jacket with silver shoulder boards. She rolled down the window for some relief after they drove off, thinking of poor Amélie and how she could have fallen in her own home, and on the stairs she must have walked thousands of times. And that pool of blood. Just like her brother.

Vianne closed her eyes. *Mon Dieu, just like her brother.*

"This isn't the way," Colette piped, and Vianne's eyes opened.

They were headed in the opposite direction, out of Belleville.

She gripped the armrest. "Where are you taking us?"

"I have one other stop," he said.

Colette was nearly silent in the backseat, and so was Vianne. When he turned away from the square and drove across the bridge to the other side of the Meuse, Vianne's heart took a beating, thinking he was going to take them all the way to Verdun.

"Where's your stop?" Vianne clawed the armrest.

He smiled after pulling off the side of the road where other cars were parked. A black Mercedes, and also, the Gaultiers' roadster. People mingled in the grass as if they were having a garden party. "Wait here." Vianne sank into the seat after he got out.

"What is going on?" Colette sounded as breathless as her, also lying low.

Vianne's eyes barely peeked over the dashboard. The other cars were SS, but the men were dressed in suits as if it were their day off. Krieger talked to Monique, who was one of many joking and smoking during a break in the weather. He turned and pointed to his car as if making a mention of them. Monique smiled.

"I don't know," Vianne whispered.

After the quick exchange, Krieger started walking back to the car.

"He's coming." Vianne sat up as if she'd been sitting that way the entire time.

"That wasn't so bad, was it?" he asked, getting in.

She expected him to mention the chateau after talking to

Monique, and when he didn't, she felt that was a strategic choice, and braced for when he would.

He drove back onto the road, the tires rolling over loose gravel, Vianne hearing every pop and scrape between the thumps of her heart. Just before they made it back over the bridge, he turned to her.

"Where are you from? Verdun? One of the nine villages? Where? I heard you haven't lived here your whole life."

"I'm…" Vianne fumbled her way through telling him she was from Verdun because she wasn't going to tell him she was born in Fleury. "Why?"

"And you own Chateau Ten. For how long, and where is your husband?"

So many answers ran through Vianne's mind, and not one of them made it to her mouth. She pulled his woolly jacket away from her throat.

"Why aren't you answering me?" he barked, which made Vianne shudder. "I know you from somewhere else, don't I?"

"What? No, we haven't met, aside from at the bookshop." She held her head. "Pardon me, I just lost my friend. I can't think."

"Did you hear about the Gaultiers?" Colette asked, and both Vianne and Krieger whipped around to look at her. Vianne could tell she was nervous from the sound of her voice. "I heard whispers about them."

"What kind of whispers?" he asked.

"Whispers that they aren't who they say they are."

Vianne turned back around, gripping her handbag now instead of the armrest. Colette might buy them enough time to get to the bookshop.

"I'm half German, and I feel it's my duty to share. Though not too many people know my lineage. My family is from Bavaria. You?"

Vianne thought that one look at Colette's documents, and he'd know the truth. But Krieger seemed taken with the idea that she was half German.

"Cologne." He pulled up to the curb outside the bookshop.

"I've visited," Colette said. "Lovely city."

Vianne wasted no time tearing off his coat and leaving it on the seat. "Thank you for the ride," she said, hopping out of the car.

She managed to hold herself together until she walked into the shop, then she and Colette nearly hyperventilated against the bookshelves.

"Was that—" Max ran to the window and watched the car drive away, taking his glasses off to get as close to the glass as possible. "Krieger?"

"Yes." Vianne stumbled to the back with Colette where the candelabra was ablaze with candles, providing a warming light against the dark blue walls. "The questions—he wouldn't stop." Vianne sat heavily on the divan, punching the velvet pillows. "Damn him!"

Colette clutched her chest. "My heart." She looked at her shaking hands next. "I can't believe I spoke out. I'm glad it's over."

"I don't think it's over. He knows where I live and who I am." Vianne let out a little weep. "And Amélie…"

Colette moved to the divan where they embraced and cried together for what they had seen.

"What happened?" Max asked.

Vianne pulled away from Colette, sniffling and wiping her eyes. "She's dead. We found her lying in a pool of blood at the bottom of her cellar stairs. Looked like she fell. Krieger said he heard us scream from the street and insisted that he take us home."

"She's dead?"

"She must have fallen," Vianne said, clinging to the little bit of doubt still floating in her mind like a life raft. "Or maybe she was pushed? She knew too much, and the SS wanted her dead."

"You honestly believe she had an accident?" Max looked at her as if she were delusional. "She used the stone, Vianne, and the ones to use it before her, you found hanging from a tree. There are no accidents when the stone is involved. Krieger showed up too late to kill her himself. He either doesn't know about the consequences or is too blinded by his greed to care about such details."

"But, but…" Vianne said. "She still had a jar of peaches in her hand."

"Are you saying you didn't think about it? Stairs Amélie must have climbed up and down a thousand times. Stairs, she knows. Every creak and wobble, every loose board. What are the chances?"

Vianne palmed her eyes. She could explain away the Marchands' deaths, but together with Amélie, it was too much of a coincidence to ignore, even for a skeptic like her. The stone had powers she couldn't explain, and if that was explained away as magic, then so be it.

"What are the chances—"

"There aren't any," she blurted, pulling her palms away. "I believe you. But what can we do about it?"

"We have to find the missing stone before they do. The Sorrows are drawn to the stone's powers, and the stone is drawn to the Sorrows, feeding on the people who use it. We must find and destroy the pieces, at all costs." He opened his notebook after putting his glasses back on. "My research is pointing to Fleury."

Vianne gasped, remembering what Renée had blurted in the library. "Fleury?" Then she stood, chewing viciously on her fingernail.

He took off his glasses. "Did you overhear the same?"

She was still chewing her nail. Colette stepped in. "Vianne—"

"I'm sorry," Vianne said. "Yes, and I should have told you right away, but that was before Amélie…" She swallowed hard. "Renée told them it's in the chapel during a séance. She left town because of it, saying they got out of her what they wanted. I don't think she would have fled like that if it wasn't true."

Max's mouth hung open in shock, then he looked relieved. "I thought it was there. I just never could prove it." He faced Vianne after taking a few moments to think. "Are they going into the Zone Rouge tonight to get it?"

Vianne shook her head. "Krieger won't go in without a map. He's especially afraid of the explosives still buried in the ground."

"Unless he finds someone who knows a way," Max said. "Someone who's been inside the Zone Rouge already."

"No…" Vianne felt nauseous. "You think they'll force me to take them—show them the way? But how would they know?"

"Are you sure nobody saw you the other night?" Max asked.

The windows at the chateau were dark when she ran outside. Élise had some odd comments the following morning, but she didn't say anything when she caught her in the foyer upon her return that night, and if the Gaultiers had seen her, they would have already mentioned it. "Did anyone see you?" she asked back.

"I was dressed in black and walked flush against the fence line before slipping through the gate," he said. "Besides, I didn't make it all the way to Fleury like you." His tone had changed, and so had his face after a long pause. "Vianne, would you—"

"I can't." She turned with a close of her eyes. The thought of walking the mourning ground with the Sorrows hovering unseen in the trenches and among the trees terrified her more than anything, knowing what she knew now. "So please stop looking at me like that."

"Even for the sake of the war?" he asked.

"I was lured there while I was under the influence of a heavy nerve medicine. I can't remember anything beyond a few hazy steps."

"But at one time, you knew every safe step to take, a pathway. Maybe you can try—"

"I don't want to try," she cried. "The Sorrows know my name. They called for me in a dream, just like they called for Genevieve. It's only a matter of time before it happens when

I'm awake. You know how the rhyme goes, you know what will come next."

Colette gasped. "Whisper your name to steal you away," she said, then turned to Max. "She's right. It's a miracle she walked into the Zone Rouge and escaped. There won't be a next time, not when they are calling for her by name."

Vianne slung her handbag over her shoulder. "I have to go—I—I have Sandrine and Blaise to take care of." She walked to the front of the shop and found that Colette had a customer, a man, standing with his hat in his hands.

"Hallo." He nodded once. "I'm sorry to bother you. My aunt and uncle run the patisserie next door."

Vianne's face turned slack. "The Marchands?" She adjusted her handbag. "Yes. How can I help you?"

"Have you seen them?" He looked genuinely confused and concerned. "They asked me to visit them weeks ago, but their shop seems to be shuttered, and their apartment on the second floor is cold and empty as if they left in a hurry."

"I'm sorry, I have not seen them."

"Hmm." He looked down. "It just doesn't make sense that they'd leave, especially when we had plans."

Colette had walked up just in time to hear the tail end of the conversation. "The Marchands? I heard they gave away all their pastries." She looked once at Vianne. "Is it possible they went on a journey somewhere? Paris or…"

"I suppose it is possible," he said.

"Do you have a number where you can be reached?" Colette asked. "I can phone you if I hear from them."

He wrote down his travel arrangements and where he was

staying in Verdun. "I am only paid up until the end of the week. Please, let them know I came by." He handed Colette the paper.

Vianne nodded once, and Colette showed him the door, the bell chiming softly. Once he was gone, Vianne placed her hand over her eyes.

"His face was so sad, you could feel the despair," Colette said. "Maybe I shouldn't have lied. Maybe I should have told him the truth."

"You can't tell him the truth," Vianne said. "It'll ruin their reputation. They wouldn't want that."

Her head pounded. She said goodbye to Colette again, giving her a kiss on the cheek.

"Vianne?" Max gingerly approached her, his glasses in his hands. "I owe you an apology. I didn't mean to pressure you or make you feel guilty in any way. I understand why you don't want to go back to the Zone Rouge. But what about me? Tell me which way to go."

"I told you I can't remember."

Max looked defeated and a little embarrassed for pushing her still. "Can I give you a ride home? What if I stayed overnight at Pierre's?"

Vianne thought about the ride, but she needed time to think and decided to take her bicycle. "No. I want to ride, and we can talk more tomorrow. It's been a very long and sad day."

"I understand."

He kissed her cheek, and then so very slightly reached for her hand. "I'm here if you need anything."

Vianne knew he was being sincere, and she appreciated it,

but it did nothing to quell the uneasiness in her gut when she thought about going back to the chateau—and going back to the Sorrows.

Chapter Seventeen

Vianne pedaled home as fast as she could, the image of Amélie lying in a growing pool of blood dominating her thoughts, making the relatively easy ride feel like it was stretching into eternity, becoming more arduous and strenuous with each spin of her wheel.

She leaned her bicycle against the chateau, exhausted in both mind and body, just as Pierre called up to her from his workshop that Blaise had run ahead.

She scooped him into her arms. "Did you have a good day?" She hugged him tightly with her eyes closed, resisting a peek over his shoulder into the Zone Rouge where the wind was raging.

Pierre joined them seconds later. "Were you successful?"

Vianne held Blaise a moment or two longer before finally pulling away. She sensed Pierre knew something important had happened—perhaps even traumatic—when her eyes welled with tears.

"I'll tell you at dinner." She smiled, putting on a brave face when Blaise looked up at her.

"I see," he said.

"You can go back down," she said. "We'll be fine here."

"You are sure?"

She nodded. "For now."

Vianne paused in the foyer after Blaise ran off to his bedroom, eyes shifting to the closed pocket doors, then to the kitchen where she expected to hear Élise grumbling away about the state of the chateau, but it was quiet, with a dim grayness cloaking every open window. She'd never felt so exposed, eyes on her front and back, eyes she couldn't see, eyes that were watching.

Her heart sped up, hurriedly closing every drape she could get her hands on, pulling the gold cords loose to let the window coverings hang heavy and long—two in the hallway and three by the door—when she heard Sandrine talking to someone in her bedroom.

Vianne turned still, listening to her mother-in-law's soft voice echoing off the walls against the beat of her heart.

It didn't sound like Sandrine was talking to Blaise, because why would she speak to him about repairs to the chateau, and how lovely the dinners had been lately?

She took a guarded step down the hallway, followed by another and another, her heels methodically tick-tacking against the marble checkerboard floor.

She paused, her back against the cool wall, and her fingers searching ahead to Sandrine's door.

"Hallo?" Vianne said, just loud enough for her to hear.

Sandrine laughed, the kind of laugh when she heard a joke,

while footsteps cracked against the parquet floor from someone pacing. Vianne's heart pumped a little faster. She had caught Monique visiting her mother-in-law—she had done it.

She prepared herself for the confrontation with a close of her eyes before stepping inside, expecting to see Monique and possibly even François. Instead, she saw Sandrine sitting in her wheelchair by the open window, her hand in a wave to someone outside.

"Oh, Vianne." She folded her hands in her lap. "Lovely to see you are back."

Vianne clutched the doorframe for dear life, her eyes locked on the velvet drapes where they had been tied off to the side. "Keep these closed!" She haphazardly fixed them, tucking the edges under knick-knacks and figurines she snatched from the bedside table.

"Whatever for?" Sandrine asked.

There was no use in reminding Sandrine that she'd already talked to her about the drapes that morning. "Just keep them closed." Vianne pressed her head to the window frame, clutching the long velvet drapes together, making sure no split or fold had escaped her.

"I'll do my best." Sandrine stood shakily from her chair. "Help me to my jewelry box, will you?" Vianne assisted her across the room where she picked through her rings and necklaces. "I just saw it not that long ago."

Vianne was still trying to understand what she'd heard. The footsteps, the laughing. "Saw what?"

"The keepsake I gave Henri. You know what it looks like, don't you? It's decorative silver with a flat face and has an engraving on the back."

Vianne reached into her pocket for the key. "This key, madame?" She opened her palm, and Sandrine's face lit up.

"You have seen it!" She put her hands together in a quiet clap. "Better yet, you have it. Good. I thought it was lost. Henri said you needed it, and not to delay."

"You talked to Henri?"

"You are acting quite peculiar, Vianne. Yes, you must have heard him talking to me right here in this room seconds ago. But sadly, he had to go," she said, looking briefly at the floor.

"What?" Vianne breathed.

"He said he woke you up but realizes you only believe in things you can see, and he doesn't blame you for not knowing."

"What are you talking about?"

"When you were lured into the Zone Rouge, don't you remember? He did his best to ensure that each step you took was a safe one. It wasn't easy for him to visit." She picked through the rest of her jewelry until she found a pair of earrings. "Here. I asked Élise for your pearls back."

Vianne sat heavily on Sandrine's bed, the earrings Henri had given her curled up in her hand against her chest, and the key he carried into the trenches in the other. "I can't breathe."

"I promised her that I wouldn't give them to you until after the guests checked out—our little secret—but since you are here, might as well give them to you now. But there was something else I was supposed to tell you…" Sandrine shrugged after a few thoughtful moments. "I guess I forgot. I forget so much these days. When's dinner?"

Vianne still couldn't breathe.

"Dinner, Vianne?" Sandrine asked again.

Vianne slipped the key and her earrings into her dress pocket and bolted for the door. "I'll check," she said, but once in the hallway, she put her back up against the wall and inhaled a gulp of air. She held her forehead where her head was splitting, then her chest where it felt like her ribs were cracking. In fact, everything hurt or ached—every part of her body, including her wobbly legs.

She staggered off to her bedroom, somehow making it up the stairs, and feeling for her bedpost to keep from falling before sitting guardedly on her bed.

Blaise walked in with his teddy bear after watching her from the doorway.

"Hallo, darling..." She smiled, doing her best to act like nothing was wrong, like Marion would have done, but it was nearly impossible. She gave her cheeks a rough swipe where a few tears had snuck down. "You shouldn't have to see me like this."

He sat next to her on the soft bed, placing his little hand on hers. She thought about his drawings and wondered if he had also seen Henri—maybe she'd missed it, and perhaps he had been trying to tell her the whole time. She squeezed her eyes painfully shut to gather courage because she had to know.

"Have you..." The lump in her throat made it hard to talk. "Seen Henri?" She wiped her cheeks again.

He nodded sweetly, his innocent eyes looking up at her from under all those lashes.

A whimper escaped between her lips from this acknowledgment. "Is he one of them?" She heard the desperation in her voice and briefly clamped her hands over her mouth. "Is he a Sorrow?"

Blaise frowned with a shake of his head, and Vianne burst into tears.

"What did he want? Why was he here?"

She frantically wiped the puddles from her eyes and noticed Blaise didn't have his slate, but before she could scan the room for it, he reached up, cupping his mouth to whisper in her ear.

"To help you."

Vianne's gaze was fixed on something insignificant across the room, unable to move and unable to blink with her heart thrumming not only from the sound of Blaise's voice but his message.

"Dinner!" Élise was suddenly at the top of the stairs. "It's ready and warm." She stood in the doorway, presumably waiting for Vianne to answer her, but she was in no condition to talk. "Did you hear me?"

A moment passed, maybe two, with Vianne's back to her, but Blaise was staring.

"Thank—" Vianne adjusted her strange posturing and tried to hide her heavy breathing. "Thank you," she finally managed to say, and as normally as she could.

"All right," Élise said, her tone strange and suspecting. "See you downstairs. Beef and vegetables."

Vianne nodded feverishly, then waited a few seconds until she was sure Élise had made it downstairs before turning to Blaise. "My darling, you talked." They embraced, Vianne squeezing her eyes closed just as hard as she was squeezing him.

"He says you're the one who can destroy the stone," Blaise said.

Vianne pulled sharply away, looking at Blaise. "Me?" she asked, but he just stared at her with his big hazel eyes. "But how?"

He shook his head, shrugging, and the last thing she wanted to do was upset him or push him too hard. "It's all right, darling. It's all right." Vianne wasn't sure what she was going to do beyond getting Blaise to safety and out of the chateau. "Listen to me. After dinner, you're going to Pierre's for a few days."

He nodded.

"Go pack a bag with your favorite things, then meet me in the kitchen for dinner."

He started to run to his bedroom, but before he was gone, she pulled him back for another embrace.

She remained on her bed thinking about the stone. "*Mon Dieu,*" she said when voices coming from the register drew her attention to the floor.

"Monique," she wondered aloud, creeping over. "François…" She carefully slipped off her shoes for noise and bent to her knees, placing her ear to the metal register where it was cold and smelled of dust.

They were in the library, and their voices were uncannily loud for being so far away.

"Time is running out," Monique said. "What if Krieger abandons his efforts? After all we've sacrificed, draining our savings to find the stone around your neck, and then waiting around while he changes our agreement daily. We'll be penniless if we don't get the map he ordered us to find."

"Now, now, darling. Don't get upset."

Monique growled. "What if we find someone who's been in

the Zone Rouge—someone who's forged a secret path? Surely someone in Belleville has breached the fence line and opened that gate—for curiosity, for lore. I don't care what the people say."

"The women of the chateau," François said, and Vianne covered her mouth. "We need to pressure Élise into telling us more about them." He paused. "If what we overheard in Belleville is true, they may have had a loved one who died in the battle. I don't care what Renée said."

Monique's heels tapped across the floor. "Hmm."

"What is it?"

"Things were easier when it was just the stone around your neck. I'll tell you one thing, if Krieger thinks he's going into the Zone Rouge without us by his side, he's mistaken. I don't trust him to pay us if we don't. Then we will kill him, take both stones for ourselves."

"Have patience, darling. All will be ours shortly, once we get to the chapel. Be glad there isn't a third piece out there—"

Vianne adjusted her head, accidentally brushing the register and making a scraping metal noise. She shut her eyes, waiting for them to talk again, but they must have heard her because the conversation had ended.

She stood as carefully as she could without making another noise, nervously rubbing the engraving on the key with her thumb.

"Vianne!" Élise rang the dinner bell. "Dinner!"

Clang! Clang! Clang!

Sandrine didn't say much at dinner and pushed food around on her plate. Vianne thought she was exhausted from all the earlier activity. Blaise ate quietly, and so did Pierre. It was clear Vianne wasn't going to discuss anything with Pierre about what happened in Belleville at dinner.

Élise watched them all, eyes shifting with each chew. "Why are the curtains closed?"

Sandrine's eyes lifted. "I don't know—"

"In case of a raid." Vianne ate a small potato covered in beef juices from her fork.

It turned quiet again, aside from chewing and swallowing.

"So," Élise said. "You went into Belleville today?"

"Mmm," Vianne said.

"And how was Amélie?" Sandrine asked.

Vianne coughed on her food. "Amélie?" She reached for her water glass. "Why do you ask?"

"Didn't you say you were going to see her and pass on my regards? Or am I imagining that?"

"You did say that, Vianne," Élise said.

"I didn't see her." Vianne had set her glass down but took another drink that ended with her finishing the entire glass and giving Pierre a pointed look.

Vianne saw Élise notice her earrings and used them as a way to change the subject. "Thank you for giving my earrings back."

Élise took her plate to the sink. "It was Sandrine's idea. However, she was supposed to wait. I guess she couldn't remember."

"What was my idea?" Sandrine asked.

Élise kissed Sandrine on her cheek. "Nothing, madame. Good to see you up and well. A little tired, though?"

"Yes." Sandrine smiled.

Élise wadded up her apron to toss in the laundry and made her way out, stopping by the window with a reach for the curtain.

"The raids!" Vianne said, and Élise's hand retreated.

"I forgot," Élise said.

Vianne poured herself another glass of water from the table pitcher, and they sat, quietly eating their stewed beef and root vegetables, though Sandrine was back to pushing food around.

"Pierre, Blaise will be spending a few nights with you until I get things sorted out here."

"Oh?" he said. "Max will be by later."

"I will be down after dinner, and we can all talk."

Vianne felt bad for telling him he was babysitting Blaise instead of asking, but she saw it as an emergency. She was also not going to accept no for an answer.

They cleaned up the dinner dishes without another word between them. Sandrine sat watching Blaise, and Blaise watched Vianne rinse off the plates.

"And the curtains?" Pierre asked.

"Keep them closed. Forever."

He turned, holding his hand out for Blaise, who scooted from his chair. "I'll see you shortly."

Vianne nodded once, then turned to wheel Sandrine down to her room. "I hope you don't mind going to bed early. Another storm is expected."

The storm Vianne was referring to was the one created by François and Monique Gaultier. Sandrine wouldn't know, in the end, as long as she locked the door. Vianne adjusted the velvet drapes, making sure they were still tightly pinned down, before going to the bed to tuck in the blankets, when Sandrine grabbed hold of Vianne's hand.

"I owe you so much."

"You don't owe me anything, madame. You're my family. Always have been."

Vianne tried to pull away, but Sandrine resisted, giving her hand a squeeze.

"Did you read the back?"

"Back of what?" Vianne asked.

"The key. I remember now what I was supposed to tell you. You must read the engraving. Henri said it will help."

Vianne dug the key out of her pocket. It had never occurred to her that the engraving was for her.

"Use the light," Sandrine said, just before her gaze drifted to the wall about to fall asleep.

Vianne held the key to the flickering candlelight on the nightstand, but couldn't make out any words from the engraving, both from the quality of light and the tarnishing. The electric light only made it worse with a horrible, brassy glare.

"Madame?" Vianne snapped her fingers, and Sandrine roused slightly.

"What is it, dear?" She sounded confused now.

"I can't read it." Vianne frantically polished the key using her dress hem. "What does it say?" She rubbed again. "Madame? What does it—"

Sandrine had fallen asleep with both hands peacefully on top of her chest.

Vianne let out a frustrating groan, then thought Pierre would have a torch for extra light.

She locked Sandrine's bedroom door before she left. Nobody was going to get to her mother-in-law while she was away, and certainly not Monique or François.

Outside, the wind howled, and the sun had set into a deepening gloaming. She kept her eyes on the guesthouse and ran down the hill, covering her ears, but she couldn't cover them and knock at the same time.

Bang! Bang! Bang!

"It's me!" Vianne's heart pounded more than her fist on Pierre's door, waiting for him to answer. "Open up!" She twisted the knob in both directions when she heard the dreaded beginnings of music, a haunting, sorrowful cry coming from the forest. "Pierre!"

The door flew open. "What's the matter?"

She blew past Pierre in the doorway for his lamp, pulling the key from her pocket and doing her best to read through the dark tarnishing. She didn't even notice the magpie squawking in its cage.

"What do you have there?" he asked. "Your hands are shaking."

"I need a torch," she said, but was able to catch just enough light to read. "Wait—" She blinked a few times in the face of the lamp glow. "I am a Catholic, call a Priest?"

Pierre put his glasses on. "A last rites token. The last time I saw one of those..." He slowly looked up at her. "Soldiers carried these keys in their pockets during the war, or around their necks." He yanked his glasses away. "Where did you get this?"

Blaise had gotten up from the carpet where he was reading to see what the alarm was about. She kissed his forehead and told him she just needed a moment before sending him back to his horse book by the fire. Pierre draped a blanket over the birdcage to muffle the noise.

"Vianne? Where did this key come from?"

"Sandrine's bureau," she said. "It's the key Henri took with him to war."

His mouth slowly gaped open. "But it's supposed to be in the Zone Rouge."

"I know."

"Then how can you explain—"

"I can't," she said. "Ah, Pierre. There's so much to tell you." Vianne sat heavily in his chair. "You better sit for this, but I'm not sure where to start."

"How about the beginning?"

She waited until he had a seat at the table, and started at the beginning like he asked, from the Gaultiers' first séance to when she locked Sandrine's door just minutes ago, no detail too small. "Renée warned me, saying unexplained things would happen—"

Vianne covered her mouth, thinking how could she have been so obtuse? "The pocket doors."

"What about them?"

"It's been the Sorrows this whole time. They wanted me to attend the séances. They were luring me."

"*Mon Dieu*." Pierre took off his glasses to rub his eyes. "You've been dealing with so much in such a short amount of time and seemingly by yourself. I'm sorry you had to bear witness to Amélie's death. She was a good friend to Sandrine.

This is troubling... And the key? I don't understand what it all means."

"Me either, and it is troubling. The only good thing that came from this is that Blaise used his voice."

Vianne held her head.

"I don't want you to stay at the chateau any longer." He put his glasses back on and looked at Blaise, who was still absorbed in his book. "Sandrine, either. You can all stay here until this is over, starting tonight."

"I can't." She gave Blaise a parting embrace, telling him she'd see him in the morning.

"Why?" Pierre asked.

"Because you know what it will do to Sandrine if I wake her up and move her at this hour. She'll be more confused than ever, and it will last for days."

"All right. But will you move down tomorrow?"

Vianne nodded reluctantly because she wasn't sure what excuse she'd tell Sandrine, but she'd have to come up with something. "I'll bring breakfast down in the morning. Don't come up." She turned toward the door.

"Vianne?" Pierre stopped her with his voice. "Be safe tonight."

Vianne nodded, her back to him in the doorway.

She didn't think about the walk back to the chateau until she was outside alone in the dark. The grounds were encased in a heavy stillness, with the roar of a turbulent wind she could hear in the distance but couldn't feel. She gulped sourly, her heart speeding up, thinking of the trees. She vowed not to look at them, no matter the pull.

And she walked.

Slow at first, trying not to be seen. Then the music came, soft and gentle like a breeze tittering through the strands of her hair that turned into tendrilled reaching fingers.

Like sirens from the sea, the Sorrows cry…

She covered her ears like she did last time, but it was too late.

"Vianne … Vianne … Vianne…" she heard from the trees, and she took off in a panting sprint.

Chapter Eighteen

Vianne threw her back against the wall after running inside, squeezing her eyes shut and clutching her chest where her heart pounded. She allowed herself to question whether she was trapped in a nightmare and sleepwalking, pinching her arm to make sure. "Why me?" she said between silent gasps.

Monique's laugh spiraled down the corridor, and her eyes sprang open.

Sandrine!

She felt her way toward Sandrine's bedroom with a searching hand, disoriented from having all the drapes pulled, but finally finding the doorknob in the dark and giving it a twist. Still locked.

Vianne sighed heavily, but the moment of relief was eclipsed by the retreating tap of Monique's heels.

She turned toward the noise, hand still tracing the wall, finding the foyer dead quiet and empty, from the front door to the drawn window drapes, then to the solid black space between the open pocket doors.

Vianne pulled her shoulders back.

Yes, she could hear them now in the library. A cacophony of noises echoed off the marble checkerboard floor—men and women. She didn't think they'd have a séance unless…

Vianne covered her mouth. Unless they found a way into the Zone Rouge. But who—

Vianne's heart sank when she heard weeping.

"Élise."

She tiptoed over to the pocket doors, poking her head into the darkness. Monique and François barraged Élise with garbled questions, but she was only able to make out a few words.

"Give us a name … we demand it…"

The foyer turned chillingly cold a second before Vianne stepped through the doors into the west wing. Step after careful step, she slowly made her way toward the library. Around the first corner, her heart was thumping, but by the second corner, it was nearly out of her chest. Now, she heard Krieger.

"Tell us about the woman who lives here," Krieger said.

"Sandrine?" Élise sounded exhausted. "She's helpless. Doesn't know what day it is most mornings—"

"Not her," he growled. "The other one. Vianne. She was in my car today and smartly managed to resist my questions. Has she been in the Zone Rouge?"

There was another German besides Krieger, and another voice Vianne didn't recognize, a man with a flat voice. He mentioned his medical bag.

Vianne slipped her shoes off for noise and walked the rest of the way, scooting along the dark wall until rounding the last corner. The library door was cracked open at the end of the hallway, splitting the darkness in two with a burst of bright electric light, allowing her a peek inside without moving another inch.

Monique sauntered around the table in a fancy maroon dress, her perfectly set platinum hair barely moving, telling Élise that she paid her a great deal, but would give her even more if she'd just tell the truth.

"I have told you the truth."

"Have you been in the Zone Rouge?"

"No, I told you already. Let me go." Élise twisted and grunted in her chair, trying to get up, but Krieger was there to hold her in place. Tears followed. Vianne had never seen Élise in such a helpless state, which scared her.

Monique turned, nodding once to the doctor. "Administer the sodium pentothal."

"Are you sure—" François started to say when Monique shushed him. "But Monique, darling. We only have one dose."

"Élise knows more than she should. I can feel it. Out of all the people in Belleville, she's the one who knows more than that mystic we let slip away."

She nodded to the doctor to continue. He opened his black bag with an insatiable grin, pulling out a syringe followed by an ampule of medicine. "I could manage a second dose for the right price."

"You took almost all that we have," she said, then turned to Élise. "I hoped it wouldn't come to this, but you've left us no choice. You are a very expensive woman."

"What is that?" Élise yelped.

"This will help you tell the truth. A drug perfected by the Third Reich." The doctor loaded the syringe without saying a word. He gave the glass a flick.

"Get that away from me!" Élise scraped her feet against the floor, scooting her chair back along with the rug, trying to get away. "I'll scream!"

Monique pressed her hand to Élise's mouth as the doctor came toward them with the needle. "Relax," he said. "It won't hurt as much if you just relax."

Élise yelped when the doctor plunged the syringe into her arm before turning as limp as a sopping wet rag. Vianne clamped both hands over her mouth. The way Élise lay in the chair, her lifeless, pale limbs heavy on the table, reminded her of Mme. Marchand's body in the tree.

"How long does this take?" Monique asked the doctor, then stepped back, and to Vianne's relief, she saw that Élise was still alive, but she looked lost with a continuous roll of her eyes.

"A few minutes to half an hour. Truthful answers come when you wait for the medicine to take effect." The doctor put his syringe away, and a German escorted him out. "But I was told I'd get the necklace, too."

Monique ripped a pearl necklace from her neck and threw it at the doctor. "Leave and don't tell anyone about what you saw here tonight. Do you understand?"

Vianne pressed her back to the wall, hiding in the thin strip of shadowy darkness as they made their way out. She thought he looked like an Abwehr officer in uniform next to the doctor, though she couldn't be sure in the dim light. The library door started to close from a hand inside, and she padded closer, ducking into a recessed doorway before the air turned as dark as black chalk.

"Time is running out," Krieger said on the other side of the door, followed by what Vianne thought was a fierce bang of his fist on the table.

"Do you have news to share?" François asked.

"The invasion is imminent," he said. "Weeks, possibly days, and if it is days, then our time is even more precious and limited. Is she ready?"

Monique's heels tapped around the table and then turned soft on the rug. "Élise. Are you in there?"

Élise's voice wavered between groggy and coherent. "What did you give me?"

"Something to help you tell the truth," François piped, but Monique wasn't pleased with his intrusion, and there was a small argument about who would do the questioning when Krieger slammed his fist on the table again, but this time to get them to be quiet.

"Have you been in the Zone Rouge?" Krieger growled.

"No," Élise said.

"Start with easy questions," Monique said. "Ones we know the answers to."

"How long have you worked here?" Krieger asked. "Months? Years?"

Élise took a few seconds to answer. "Years."

"And you see the old woman and Vianne regularly?"

Her delay was even longer than last time. "Yes."

"And the old man I heard of just today. Lives in the guesthouse. What is his name?"

Monique answered for Élise when it was clear she wasn't in

a state to do so, saying his name was Pierre. He was a handyman, but possibly more. "Isn't that right?"

"Why isn't that other woman here—Vianne?" Krieger asked. "She was quite skilled in evading my questions earlier today. I will bet you she knows more than this one."

"No. Élise knows more than all of us, including Vianne," Monique said. "She's the eyes and the ears of Chateau Ten."

"Pierre," Élise finally said, followed by unintelligible sounds. "He's…"

"He's been in the Zone Rouge," Krieger said. "And so has Vianne. Tell me!"

Everything turned quiet, aside from Élise's breathing, which was loud and panicky. But Vianne was panicking most of all, feeling that her heart, which once pounded so fiercely, had fallen out of her chest to the floor. A burst of rain tapped heavily on the roof from the incoming storm. The wind would sweep over next, and what would it say?

She made the decision to leave—if only she could get her legs to work—taking a few stiff steps backward with her hand over her mouth, regretting not taking Pierre's advice in the first place and staying far away from the chateau.

The German she thought had left with the doctor was back, grabbing Vianne's arm in the darkness. "Who are you?" he growled.

Vianne was too shocked to scream, which allowed him to easily push her into the library.

"Well, well…" Monique folded her arms.

Krieger smiled. "Speak of the devil."

In the light, Vianne saw he was an Abwehr officer like she

initially thought. Muller, the one who was at Amélie's. "I caught her outside the door." He forced her to sit.

Vianne did her best to look to Élise for help, but what could she do? Élise looked unwell, with her droopy eyes, and her back slouched from being drugged. Froth formed at the corners of her mouth.

The chandelier buzzed as if it was about to cut out, causing everyone to look up except Monique. "Listening in the hallway, were you?" She lit the candelabra.

"I heard crying. I can see now that the crying came from our cook." Vianne tried to look tough by jutting her chin's razor edge. "You said you were done with the séances."

"This isn't a séance." Monique turned to François as he adjusted his black smoking jacket. "Is it?"

François laughed, taking the stone from the middle of the table and slipping it back around his neck. "We are past that."

"Useless middle-aged woman," she mumbled, lighting a cigarette. "One of many in this chateau I could do without."

"Not long now, and your lease will be up," Vianne reminded them.

Monique exhaled a plume of thick smoke from her mouth. "Come now, Vianne. You are smarter than that, aren't you? We aren't leaving until we get what we came for." She pointed her cigarette at Élise. "And it starts with her."

François kicked Élise's chair. "This is fruitless. I don't see why you need a map to get to the village. The stone's not hidden in the trenches."

Krieger jeered at them both. "You have no idea what dangers exist out there, do you?"

Vianne looked to the ceiling as they argued, thinking about

the last people to sit in her chair—Mme. Marchand, then Amélie. Both of whom were now dead. Vianne's eyes fluttered closed.

Krieger tapped the table in front of Vianne, jolting her back into the conversation.

"Have you been in the Zone Rouge?"

Vianne scoffed, thinking that was enough, but he pressed on.

"Why not?"

"Because it is forbidden for a reason," Vianne said.

Krieger rubbed his chin. "There is something familiar about you. I saw it earlier today. A mannerism I couldn't quite put my finger on. And before in the bookshop."

"You've said that before."

"Yes, and now I'm repeating it." He studied her, looking around the table to see how she sat in the chair, then got up and pulled a lock of hair out from her collar where it had gotten tucked under, allowing her a smell of his citrusy cologne. "And you have a child?"

Vianne's hands tightened under the table. She'd rather die than talk about Blaise with those people.

"I haven't met him," he said. "Your boy is the one Monique gave the book to, is he not?"

Vianne shifted in her seat.

"My, oh my," Monique said. "That question made an impression on you, didn't it? Where was the boy earlier? I didn't see him after dinner, in the foyer with one of his books, being quiet and silent. How come he doesn't talk?"

"Why were you in the foyer?" Vianne asked.

Monique smiled. "Why, indeed." She paused, playing with

her cigarette before finally flicking the ash into a crystal ashtray. "Oh, no matter. I want to find the old man, too. Is he with him?"

"I'm leaving." Vianne stood, only for Muller to push her back down.

"No. You are not leaving," Monique said. "Why were you eavesdropping? Something you were hoping to hear?"

"Like I said before, I came to see what the crying was about. I made my home your home, or I did until you broke our rules. It's only natural I would walk into the west wing and try to find out why someone was weeping, especially after the last few days."

"Such attitude." Krieger clip-clopped slowly around the library in his tall black boots, hands behind his back, inspecting the titles on the shelves before moving on to the globe near the gramophone and giving it a spin. "For the amount of money the Gaultiers have paid you, you'd think you'd be a little more thankful. In fact, you could replace this broken gramophone with an electric model, if you wanted."

"You have been ungrateful," Monique chimed in, agreeing.

Krieger perused the liquor trolley, inspecting a bottle of Scotch before settling on a bottle of brandy. Rain tapped against the stained-glass window, which only got him to briefly pause for a look.

"Did you want to thank me for the book I bought for the boy?" He took his time pouring the brandy. "On second thought, I should make sure he still has it and you didn't take it away." He crossed his legs leisurely before taking a slow sip.

Vianne pressed her lips together, thinking that if she just

stayed quiet, they'd lose interest and move on—he was just trying to intimidate her, though sadly, it was working.

"You have lived here a long time, haven't you, Fräulein?" Tell us what you know about the Zone Rouge." Krieger placed a book on the table, which Vianne quickly recognized as the book the Gaultiers had bought from Colette. He tapped the hard cover with his finger. "First-hand accounts of the battle talk about gas canisters hidden in secret stockpiles. What do you know of them?"

"Nothing, obviously." Vianne was just glad to change the subject and not talk about Blaise. "Have you asked anyone in Belleville? They would tell you the same. Nobody knows."

"It is not obvious," Monique said, slinking around the table to have a seat next to Krieger. "And we have asked."

Vianne slipped her hand into her dress pocket for a feel of Henri's key out of nervousness, feeling the engraving as the rain tapped viciously against the window.

Monique reached over the table to pull Vianne's hand out. "What do you have?" She made Vianne drop the key on the table with a few hard shakes.

"It's a keepsake. That's all." When she thought her explanation wasn't good enough, she added, "I wear it around my neck, but the chain broke."

Krieger picked it up for a quick inspection, then moved on to talk about the gases and finding a safe passage.

Vianne shoved it back into her pocket, waiting to see what Élise was going to say—waiting for them to let her go— rubbing the key with the fat of her thumb until it felt raw.

"Wake up!" Monique shook Élise to sit up straight. When Élise didn't, Monique became visibly agitated. "Forget this path nonsense. Time is wasting! François and I will go in without one if need be and report back." She turned, as if she was about to leave right then, when Krieger cleared his throat.

"Officer Muller." Krieger looked to the Abwehr officer. "Tell her what the gases will do."

"Gladly." Muller sat up even straighter than he had been. "You will feel a burning in your chest, quickly followed by your skin, if not at the same time, as if being thrown into a raging fire. Once the boils appear…" He inched forward, elbows on the table. "You have only a few seconds before you collapse and die in agony."

Krieger nodded. "Unless you step on a mine. In that case, you would have no limbs to crawl out of the trench you'd found yourself in, an arm over there—" he pointed indiscriminately "—a leg over there. Blood splattered on tree trunks, soaking into the soil…"

François looked horrified, holding onto his arms.

"All right!" Monique looked like she'd had enough and got in Élise's face, yelling at her to wake up, and that was what finally roused her.

Élise blinked a few times. She was no longer sluggish and groggy.

Krieger waved the others to lean in a little closer over the mahogany table. "Do you like Vianne? She is a good employer?" he asked.

Élise nodded, then she shook her head. "No. I do not like her. I'm angry at her for spending all of Sandrine's resources." Élise burst into tears. "If only she'd ask for help. We could all pitch in, but instead, she treats me like I'm not part of the family, and I've been here longer than her. It hurts."

Vianne was surprised to hear this come from Élise, having no idea she made her feel that way. She wanted to tell her she was sorry, but wouldn't dare, not right then.

Monique raised one eyebrow, looking at Vianne.

"What about Monique and François?" Krieger asked. "Do you like them?"

"I hate them both."

Monique smirked, cigarette high in the air.

"But you liked them before?" he asked.

"I liked them when they gave me money for a stocked pantry. François is weak and will do whatever Monique says. He is not a man."

Monique giggled. "This is fun. Keep going."

François dropped his arms to hang.

"And Monique is not a real woman," Élise said. "A real woman doesn't keep another hostage, or have to look in a mirror all day to affirm her beauty."

Monique straightened with that comment. "It's not all day, surely." She cleared her throat. "All right. Enough with the basic questions. Ask her what we need to know."

"Have you seen anyone go into the Zone Rouge?" Krieger asked.

Élise shook her head.

Vianne closed her eyes, relieved. Élise was either resisting the sodium pentothal and lying, or telling the truth. She hadn't seen her enter, just like she thought, but what if she saw her coming out? She had caught her in the foyer afterward.

Krieger paced, hand to his chin. Vianne knew he was a cunning man, and it would only be a matter of time before he changed the order of his questioning.

"Leave us alone," Vianne said. "Like Élise said, you've held us hostage. You've done everything possible to make us miserable. We only live here. We only—"

Krieger turned on his heel, cutting Vianne off with a direct and piercing gaze. He bent down to whisper into Élise's ear.

"Yes," Élise said. Then she nodded.

The only person in the library who didn't straighten with intrigue was Vianne, who shook her head at Élise to be quiet.

"Who?" Krieger asked, now loud enough for the whole library to hear. "Who is it you've seen coming out of the Zone Rouge?"

Élise raised her arm slowly, pointing to Vianne.

Monique stood, her chair screeching back. "I told you the cook knew more than she let on!" She tapped all the way around the table to Vianne and bent over, both hands on her hips. "Tell us everything you know, or—"

Vianne refused to look into her eyes.

"I'll find the boy. That's what I'll do. I'll find the boy and make him show us a way into the Zone Rouge."

"I haven't been in the Zone Rouge." Vianne stood again, only this time she managed to fight Muller's hands as he tried to restrain her. "Nobody has, Monique. Not a soul in Belleville!"

Krieger had been watching Monique and Vianne spar and seemed more interested in the way they reacted to each other than what was necessary, until he snapped his fingers. "I don't believe you. You have been. I can tell. The only question is, how? Do you know a safe passage, or have you built up a tolerance to the gases by living so close? I'm betting you know a safe passage."

"I haven't been."

"You will lead me into the Zone Rouge tomorrow night," Krieger said. "Be here at ten o'clock. Do not be late."

"But I don't know a safe way." Vianne's eyes welled with tears. She wasn't sure how she could walk into the forbidden forest, knowing the Sorrows were waiting for her in the mourning ground with welcome arms. Her face ticked with emotion, but it was a gush of tears she worried about as her eyes pooled heavily.

"Aw. What is this we see?" Krieger moved in close as the rain beat relentlessly against the window. "A little actress. Watery eyes like the rain outside."

Vianne tried to flick her tears away, but it was nearly useless. "I'm not an actress…" She sniffed and wiped her nose, then broke down in a silent cry. "I'm telling you the truth."

"I know who you remind me of!" Krieger turned to Officer Muller. "That traitor from Verdun. Awful woman, cried over everything and everyone, begging for her life." He tried recalling her name with a tap of his head. "What was her name?"

"They all cry," Muller said.

A gust of wind roared over the chateau's roof, the sound of shingles tearing off one by one as the windows shuttered. The chandelier flickered—zap, zap, zap—before finally cutting out, leaving only the candelabra with Monique and François embracing each other.

"Yes, they cry, but not like that one. The mystic's friend—" Krieger snapped repeatedly.

"I don't know," Muller said.

"Marion Moreau!" he said, and Vianne lost her breath.

"That was her name. You have the same eyes. What a little liar she was." Krieger laughed from the back of his throat. "She got her comeuppance, didn't she?"

He flailed his arm while making a devastating face, giving Vianne a glimpse of what Marion must have suffered in her final moments.

"Marion…" Vianne struggled to stay standing, the room fading to gray while grasping for the back of her chair in the dim candlelight. "Marion Moreau? Is she…" Vianne's throat turned dry. Her head, light. "Is she?"

"Dead. You know her?" Vianne remembered him asking, just before she fell backward in a faint and knocked herself unconscious.

Chapter Nineteen

Vianne woke slowly the next morning with an ache in her bones and a sense of not knowing where she was. She vaguely recalled her dream once realizing she was in her bedroom and had been sleeping, then sat up in bed, reliving the terrifying details.

Skeletal trees watched over her as she stood deep in the misty Zone Rouge. A dense fog rose in the distance along with a sound—a penetrating beat of phantom drums signaling the rise of the Sorrows. She tried to run, but something tethered her ankle, and she fell fast and hard into a trench, landing on a bed of bones.

She panicked, thinking she'd been lured away again, but saw her wrist had been tethered to the bedpost. "Oh, thank God. I'm safe," she reminded herself, but not a moment later, her heart thrashed for a different reason.

Her shoes had been tossed on the floor against the wall with the heels pointed upward—a place and position she wouldn't consciously leave them. She didn't even remember getting into bed and struggled to remember anything that happened after dinner. A piercing pain on the back of her head perplexed her even more, and she was surprised to find a goose egg of a bump under a sticky mat of hair. On her fingertips, she saw blood.

She sluggishly made her way to the dresser, using a hand mirror to get a better look, but went back to her shoes. She didn't put them there, did she? She thought she remembered slipping them off in the west-wing corridor. Or was that a dream? She had trouble distinguishing what was real and what was not.

Élise.

She turned around, looking at her door where the smell of morning eggs had slipped under the crack. Things were a little clearer now, remembering she'd talked to Élise. She reached to take off her nightgown, only to realize it was the dress she wore last night.

"*Mon Dieu*," she said to herself, taking a few shuffling steps to her door, then back to her closed window, hand on her head, remembering bits and pieces—the library, the SS, and a doctor —but mainly the torturous tone of Élise's voice when she wept.

Vianne tried desperately to recall what happened in the library while holding her head. Krieger. *He asked me something. What was it?*

Élise could tell her what happened. She ran a moistened rag over her face and smoothed back her hair the best she could over the painful lump.

She checked on Sandrine first, unlocking her door to find

she was up and dressed, and thankfully unaware that Vianne had locked her door last night.

"I'm taking my time this morning," Sandrine said.

Vianne helped her into her wheelchair after giving her a kiss on her cheek. She could feel Sandrine's heavy eyes on her, examining her unkempt hair and her limp dress that smelled like her sheets.

"Open my drapes, please," Sandrine said.

"I'm taking you to breakfast." Vianne wheeled her down the hallway, but once in the foyer, Sandrine insisted she stop for her morning gaze.

"The window, Vianne. I must have a look outside, like I always do."

Vianne couldn't get out of it this time. She pushed her to the window where Sandrine swept the heavy drape to the side, spying the Gaultiers' roadster parked near the fountain. "What a splendid car. Whose is it?"

"We have guests staying with us, madame."

"We do?"

"Yes, the Gaultiers."

"Oh, right. I think I remember now." Sandrine looked again, and Vianne saw her chance to talk to Élise privately about last night and left her by the window unattended.

She paused in the kitchen doorway, watching Élise scramble eggs at the cooktop, before cautiously stepping up to the counter, thinking maybe Élise would ask her instead. "Good morning."

Élise set the wooden spatula down, letting the eggs brown in place, before turning down the heat. "Hallo."

"Eggs smell good," Vianne said.

Élise gave the eggs another stir. "Yes."

The few moments of silence that passed between them only made things worse.

"I set Henri's place," Élise said.

Vianne glanced briefly over her shoulder, seeing that all the place settings had been neatly arranged. "Élise…" She twisted her hands. "I—"

Élise walked away with the pan. "Yes?" she said, her back to Vianne as she plated the eggs.

"Ahh…" Vianne rubbed her forehead next because her palms had turned sweaty. Élise piled way too many eggs on Blaise's plate. "I'm bringing breakfast down to Pierre and Blaise."

Élise froze with a spoonful of eggs over Blaise's plate. "I see." She walked back to the cooktop with the frying pan and let out a heavy sigh, eyes closed. "Vianne?"

"Yes?" she asked, hopeful that now was the time, just as Sandrine wheeled herself into the kitchen.

"Good morning to you both!" she said.

They turned, surprised by Sandrine wheeling herself in. Élise promptly wiped her hands on her apron. "Let me help you."

Vianne closed her eyes at the moment she'd lost. Now, she'd have to wait.

"I don't need help," Sandrine said, shooing her away, then managing quite well and finding her seat. "Smells good." Sandrine glanced over the table, remarking about the salt on the table and the plum jam, which was one of her favorites. Élise also had sliced buttered toast and steaming hot black tea. "I love this menu."

Vianne and Élise barely touched their food while Sandrine dug in.

"We must extend an invitation to the Gaultiers to join us for dinner," Sandrine said.

"Why?" Élise asked.

"Vianne said they are our guests."

Vianne reached for her tea, but she was overthinking and couldn't bring herself to drink it.

"Is it a nice day outside? Looked nice from the front window." Sandrine motioned. "But why are the drapes always closed in the bedrooms and the curtains in the kitchen? And where's Pierre, and Blaise?" Sandrine paused, then asked again, because Vianne was staring straight ahead with her cup pressed to her lips. "Vianne?"

Élise elbowed her.

Vianne set her cup down. "What was that?"

"Where are Pierre and Blaise?"

"They are in the guesthouse. I'm bringing their breakfast down to them this morning."

"Ah! I see." What followed were a few moments of quietness, with Sandrine watching Élise push her eggs around with her fork and Vianne looking into her lap. "Is something wrong?"

"No." Vianne slipped her hand into her pocket, feeling the key and giving it a squeeze. "Nothing is wrong."

"What about you, Élise? Anything wrong?"

"No." Élise turned to Vianne. "I'll get the tray ready once we are finished here."

Vianne nodded. Then it was quiet again with Sandrine still watching them both and Vianne pretending everything was normal—just another morning—but all she was thinking about was how to bring up last night with Élise.

"And Henri," Sandrine said. "Where is he?"

Vianne pressed her thumb to the engraving. "He left, madame. Remember?"

"I suppose I do," she said, but it was Vianne who remembered something after feeling the engraving.

Krieger had touched the key last night in the library. She pulled the key out and stared at it in her palm. She was sure of it, wasn't she? She could see his face and smell the tartness of his cologne. But why was she also thinking of Marion?

Élise pushed her plate to the side and lit a cigarette, her hands trembling uncontrollably as she struck the flame. A lungful of smoke billowed in the air—the smell, acrid and familiar. Another memory from last night. Vianne looked up.

"Monique," Vianne said.

Élise turned, cigarette perched in her fingers. "What?"

"Monique smokes," she said.

Élise stood, screeching her chair back, and went to the sink. "Maybe. I don't know."

Vianne was starting to put the pieces of the night together all on her own, but she was missing the main piece; she could feel it. She groaned, touching the painful lump on the back of her skull. "Don't you know?"

Élise smoked her cigarette over the sink, staring at the closed curtains.

Sandrine had fallen asleep in her chair, and Vianne saw her chance again, but this time she'd have to be direct. She couldn't afford for Élise to run off, and Vianne sensed she was looking for an excuse to leave.

"Élise." Vianne got up from the table. "Be truthful with me."

Élise took another drag from her cigarette. "About what?"

"That was you I heard, weeping in the library last night. Wasn't it?"

Élise took two gulping puffs from her cigarette with her eyes closed, causing Vianne to lose her patience. She grabbed Élise's shoulders, turning her around. "Look at me!"

Élise opened her eyes.

"You were there?"

"Yes," she said, finally, and somewhat exhaustedly. She lifted her sleeve, showing Vianne the bruise where the doctor had stuck her with the syringe.

Vianne nearly collapsed on the counter with her hands over her eyes, confirming what she had been piecing together. "I remember now. You told them I had been in the Zone Rouge." She ripped her hands away, standing straighter. "*Mon Dieu*, Élise. He wants me to take him to Fleury—through the mourning ground."

Élise cried, head hanging. "I'm sorry. I know we've had our differences, but I'd never—" She wiped her eyes with the back of her hand. "I'd never wish this on you."

"It wasn't you. It's what the doctor gave you. You couldn't resist."

"What was it?"

"Something that made you tell the truth." Vianne hugged Élise, and they cried on each other's shoulders.

"What are we going to do?" Élise asked. "Monique thinks you went into the Zone Rouge to find the stone."

"Why does she think that?"

"Renée told them a woman was looking for it. They think it is you," she said. "If they touch one hair on Sandrine's head, or Blaise's, I don't know if I can live with myself."

"Did they say they would touch them?" Vianne's heart raced. "Did they? Tell me?"

"I think they did. I remember something about Sandrine, and saying that she has a dead son, and … and…" She wiped her eyes again. "But it's what you said after reviving from your faint that I remember the most."

Vianne dropped her arms. It never occurred to her that *she* had said something after falling backward and knocking herself out.

"They were pressing and pressing you about taking them into the forest. You pointed to Krieger, saying you'd take him into the Zone Rouge, but he'd better call a priest because he'd need one."

Vianne couldn't move, her eyes fixed on Élise. "I said that?" she asked, then turned toward the closed window curtains, trying to breathe because she remembered why she had been thinking of Marion. "He killed my sister." Her hands slowly closed into fists. "He was the one who arrested her and made Blaise an orphan." She bent over the sink, about to retch. "I feel sick."

She drank a glass of water to try to wash the urge from her mouth.

Élise rambled on about fleeing in their car, but how they probably wouldn't get too far with the SS setting up checkpoints. "Monique told François that they had to press the doctor for another dose of the medicine they gave me. What if they use it on Sandrine? What if they use it on Blaise?"

Vianne gasped at that prospect. "Blaise?"

"You'll die in the Zone Rouge—you'll die!" Élise's voice turned shrill. "If not from the Sorrows, and whatever else lies buried in the ground, then after Krieger gets what he wants from you, he'll shoot you dead. Maybe even in a trench—"

"Listen to me." Vianne gave her a shake. "Listen! Sandrine and Blaise aren't safe here. Neither are you."

Élise nodded incessantly.

"Get the car and take everyone to Colette's. Tell her what happened. Whatever you do, don't let Sandrine or Blaise hear. Sandrine will ask questions. You'll have to tell her a lie. Do you understand?"

Monique and François stepped out onto the patio, their voices dangerously close to the window. Vianne's eyes shifted just in time to see their shadows passing underneath the closed window curtain. She thought Élise had stopped breathing.

"Do you understand?" Vianne whispered.

Élise's nodding returned. Sandrine started to rouse at the breakfast table.

"I'll help you into the foyer, then you must go, and straight down to Pierre's to get Blaise and the car."

"But what are you going to do?"

Sandrine sat up, rubbing her eyes. "Did I fall asleep? What time is it?"

Vianne hugged Élise fiercely, whispering in her ear that she was going to take care of their guests once and for all, and Krieger, though she actually had no idea how she was going to do it.

Élise pulled at her hands near the counter.

"There, there, madame," Vianne said. "Élise has a surprise for you."

"Oh?" Sandrine looked at Élise, still pulling her hands.

"Yes, indeed." Vianne helped Sandrine from the table and into her chair, then walked with them into the foyer while Élise told Sandrine a lie—she had a day planned for her in Belleville. Sandrine reached for Vianne's hand.

"Aren't you coming with us?" Sandrine asked.

"I can't, madame." Vianne did her best to smile. "Not today." She handed over the wheelchair to Élise, then blew them both a kiss as they left.

"Can we stop at Madame Marchand's?" Sandrine asked as Élise wheeled her away. "I miss her."

"We'll see, madame…" Élise said, then they were gone, and Vianne was alone in the foyer at the bottom of the stairs in the big empty chateau.

Vianne walked back into the kitchen as quietly as she could, positioning her ear near the window, listening for a footstep or for one of their voices. She slowly lifted the curtain by its corner, until she saw the blue sky and let all the morning light spill into the kitchen, and found herself gazing upon the scorched trees of the Zone Rouge.

Bang! The kitchen door closed behind her, but before Vianne could turn around, Monique had her hands clamped over her mouth, and François had a knife to her side.

"We have business to discuss." Monique pointed to the narrow servant's hallway that Élise used to travel between the east and west wings, and forced her to walk down to the library.

"What are you going to do?" Vianne asked, but Monique

refused to answer, and François only followed Monique's orders. "Didn't you get what you wanted last night?"

"No, we did not. You fell." Monique opened the library doors, and at first, it looked empty, but when Vianne stepped inside, she saw the doctor was back and had his black bag open.

"Sit here." He pointed to an empty chair.

Vianne shook her head, but there was little she could do with the knife held to her ribs. "What do you want to know? Just ask me."

Monique scoffed. "I don't trust you."

"Just ask me." Vianne folded her arms tightly so they couldn't inject her. "I'll answer your questions. I promise."

"And you'll lie. It's what I would do, so I know you would, too. Besides—" she glared at the doctor "—I sold every piece of jewelry I had left for this ampule, and by God, we're not going to let it go to waste."

The doctor held out his hand while Monique unclipped her earrings and took off her glittery necklace set with pearls. François handed him a few coins from his pocket and the gold chain he was wearing, until all that was left between them was the black stone around his neck.

The doctor grinned, nodding once to Monique—the debt had been paid, and he was going to do what he'd promised. "Pleasure doing business with you."

"Shut up," Monique growled. "Stick her with the needle, then leave."

It was then that Vianne realized he was a German doctor. His accent was almost undetectable. She should have known. His sharp nose and cheekbones, and that dark blonde hair that was probably golden in his youth. He loaded his syringe as Monique lifted Vianne's dress sleeve.

"Get your jewelry back, Monique," Vianne said. "You don't have to do this."

"Be quiet and relax," the doctor said to Vianne. "Otherwise, it will sting more than it should."

Vianne remembered Élise falling asleep and looking drugged, in addition to telling the truth. "Am I going to die?" she asked.

The doctor loaded his syringe, and she braced for the moment of impact. There was little she could do but think of ways to avert their questioning. She knew from watching Élise that they'd have to be specific. *Think about the question. Do not infer. Do not tell them more than they asked for.*

The doctor moved to a chair next to Vianne as her eyes welled with tears. He leaned in close, close enough for her to know he liked his cigarettes. Vianne's heart beat a little faster, then pounded in her ears when he held the needle to the light and gave it a flick with his finger. "Please don't," she said, as if it would make a difference. She thought her heart was going to explode from panic.

"Breathe," he said. "It will hurt more if you don't."

Vianne panted, then tensed uncontrollably a second before the doctor stuck the needle into her arm like a dart. A little yelp followed.

"Now you wait," he said, slowly pulling the needle from her arm. "This ampule was half the dose I gave the woman last night. I don't think you'll have much time."

Vianne remembered the doctor leaving because she suddenly had an awareness of just the three of them in the library, and looking up at the ceiling when she sank into her chair. "You didn't have to do this…"

"We did. I told you that already."

"Shh, shh…" François said, and Monique crossed her arms.

"François," Monique said through her teeth. "If you tell me to shush one more time—"

Vianne closed her eyes, but she wasn't sure for how long. When she woke up, she sat bolt upright. The room spun. "What did he give me?"

"The same as Élise had. Sodium pentothal. It's supposed to help you tell the truth."

"But why me?" Vianne asked.

"Because I don't want my skin to fall off my bones from the gases, and you said something last night that I couldn't quite shake."

"What did I say? I don't remember much after I fell."

"You told Krieger he would die, essentially. But if you know a safe route and have lived to tell about it, why would you say such a thing? It occurred to me that you must have used a gas mask, a special mask for multiple visits. Even the Wehrmacht wouldn't have ones to protect against the mix of toxic gases buried out there from The Great War."

"Not me." Vianne hesitated because she felt compelled to tell her the truth; it felt unnatural not to. "Pierre was a chemist. A brilliant chemist. Probably the best in the world because everything he does is the best—"

"Yes, yes…"

"Be specific, darling," François said.

Monique sighed. "Are there gas masks on this property that would protect against the specific gases in the Zone Rouge?

You are the proprietor. You must know every nook and cranny by heart in this chateau. If anyone knows for certain, it would be you."

"I do know every nook and every cranny."

"Then tell us about the masks, Vianne," she said through her teeth.

"They are gray." Vianne held her hands up and modeled how they looked. "Big, bulky, smell like rubber."

Monique huffed. "You are exhausting." She glanced up at François, who shrugged, and Vianne understood that they didn't believe her, or at best, they thought she was being a pain on purpose. "And we are running out of time, François."

"Maybe she needs more?" he asked.

Monique slapped the table. "We don't have more!"

"Then what do you want to do?"

Monique paced the room, tapping back and forth in her heels before sitting back down and looking casual. "Do you want a cigarette?" She lit herself a cigarette that she pulled from a shiny silver case. A swirl of smoke hovered over them.

"Yes, but not from you." Vianne smelled Monique's sour perfume. "Lilac smells awful on you."

Monique laughed, looking up at François, who nodded once.

"It is working, *ma chérie*. Just be specific."

Monique got situated. "You mentioned Pierre. The chemists in the last war were privy to quite a bit of information. Some even invented masks. Now, one more time. Do you have gas masks on this property?"

"Yes."

"How many and where are they?"

"Four." Vianne's eyes grew heavy. She had no idea how much longer she could keep them open and grasped for the edge of the table. "In the guesthouse."

Monique was still smiling. "François, we need to talk to the handyman," she said, then turned back to Vianne. "Stay here. Do not leave the chateau, do you understand?"

Vianne collapsed with her cheek on the table.

Chapter Twenty

Vianne woke minutes later in the cold library with Monique's spent cigarette in the ashtray. She stood and fell a few times from the weight of her wobbly legs before she was able to stumble her way out, catching herself on the table, the bookshelves, and then the wall before finally stepping into the corridor.

Vianne knew she had to find Pierre before the Gaultiers. It was the only thing that mattered.

She didn't remember passing through the pocket doors or the foyer, but she did remember the feel of the morning air against her skin when she made it outside where the sun was bright and warming. She squinted, trying to focus on the workshop, then ducked behind the hedges when she saw the Gaultiers' roadster parked outside Pierre's.

François knocked and knocked on the front door, yelling for him to answer, followed by equally forceful raps on the window that echoed up the hill. Pierre had either sent Blaise to

Colette's with Élise and was hiding, or had left with them. God, she hoped he'd gone with Élise.

François busted the front door open and disappeared inside for a minute, if not less, then charged out the door for his roadster and drove back up to their private entrance, with Vianne still hunkering below the hedges.

With him out of the way, Vianne saw her chance and hurried down the hill as fast as she could—only to hesitate in Pierre's doorway. A shiver shot up her spine from the quietness. "Pierre?" She peered inside where the door was lightly squealing on its hinges. "It's Vianne."

She cautiously stepped into the guesthouse and closed the door.

"Pierre," she said again, but this time a little louder. Blaise's book and teddy bear were by the fireplace, presumably left in place after leaving in a hurry with Élise. The bird cage was open, and the magpie was nowhere to be seen.

A car drove up outside, and before Vianne had a chance to react, its doors opened and closed. François was back, but this time he brought Monique. If she moved, they might hear her, but she couldn't stay still either.

"I looked everywhere, darling," he said to Monique. "I was here for five minutes, at least."

Vianne's eyes shifted back and forth between the divan and the closet, where the doors had already been thrown wide open, and then back to the divan. Underneath was a space just big enough for a woman her size to squeeze under.

"Well, you didn't look hard enough!" Monique snapped back.

Vianne dove under the divan where it was dusty, tucking in

all her fingers and toes, squeezing her eyes shut. They stopped at the door. A moment of silence followed, but Vianne's heart pounded all the way up into her ears.

"You said you left the door open," Monique said.

They know. They know, they know, they know.

When the door opened, Vianne forced herself to watch. They walked around the front room, Monique's heels tip-tapping against the wood floor, and his shoes turning soft from stepping on the rug.

She picked up Blaise's teddy bear near the fireplace, giving it a squeeze and adjusting the button eyes. "Check the closet," Monique said.

"I did."

She threw the bear angrily on the divan. "Recheck it!"

François checked the closet, but Vianne's eyes were on Monique's shoes, and which way her toes were pointed, because that was where her gaze was. Vianne heard François rummaging through Pierre's jackets in the closet, the hangers sliding to one side on the dowel. She prayed for them to leave, afraid of what they might inject her with next if they found her.

Monique was the one to open Pierre's chest and find the masks. "Look what we have here, François." She counted out three. "Vianne said he was a chemist, and a chemist living so close to the Zone Rouge would have masks fit for any combination of gases."

"Have you told Krieger we are going too?"

"I will tonight. When I show him the masks."

François ticked his tongue as if he disapproved.

"Don't worry. Krieger won't put up a fuss, not when I use the mask as leverage."

François dug into the chest. "Where's the fourth mask?"

"I'm convinced now more than ever that Vianne is the woman Renée said was looking for the stone," Monique said. "It makes sense that if she's venturing into the Zone Rouge regularly, she'd have the mask with her."

They turned to leave, but Monique was now interested in Blaise's book, which was left on the floor. "Look at this. The book Krieger bought."

François walked to the fireplace to have a look. They discussed Blaise and what he might know before tossing the book back on the floor like trash.

"François, what happens if she refuses to lead us? Aside from the gases, there are bombs to consider, so we still need her. We won't get our payment if she backs out or goes missing."

"Krieger said he will punish her by killing the boy and the rest of her family until she reveals herself."

"And once it is all said and done?"

"If she's not on a train headed to the east, then she's dead just the same."

"Yes…" she said with an air of deep satisfaction. "Either way, we will take the chateau for ourselves. It is the least we are owed for our troubles on behalf of the Thule Society."

"That sounds fair."

Vianne bit her tongue, watching them walk out the open door. She waited until she heard them drive away, but that was mainly because she was still too shocked and couldn't move. Eventually, she did manage to crawl out, but she could barely stand and sat clutching her stomach where it ached. Blaise's limp teddy bear sat on the divan where Monique had thrown it, button eyes twisted as if it were watching her, studying her, and judging her.

Vianne angrily turned it face down on the divan cushion, closing her eyes and squeezing the bear tightly. She felt beaten and at her lowest point, moving to her knees on the floor. There was only one thing she hadn't done—not ever.

Vianne folded her hands and talked up to the ceiling, a little cry escaping from her lips. "I need help!" she exclaimed. "God, do you hear me? I can't do this alone..."

Her eyes trailed to Blaise's horse book. There was a wagon on the front—something she hadn't noticed before. She reached for it, taking a few heaving breaths. It wasn't just a book about horses. Vianne swiped the tears from her eyes.

The book was about the American West, with pioneers and wagon trains and how they'd band together to help one another, circling their—

"Circle the wagons," she said to herself.

Mon Dieu. It was what Renée had told her to do—gather her people for help.

She didn't have to do this alone, in fact, she wasn't supposed to, and she realized what Sandrine truly meant when she said Henri was with her when she was in the Zone Rouge, making sure every step was a safe one—Vianne had been drawn to the chapel for a reason. She was meant to destroy the stone, as Blaise had relayed to her, but now she knew a way to do it.

Vianne felt a shift inside her, scrambling to throw open the window curtains. She gazed out into the Zone Rouge—

the scorched trees and the gate. She had buried the memory, but now, like a match flaring in the dark, clarity sparked.

"The brambles," she breathed, remembering the sodden ground beneath her feet, the air thickening with rot, sorrow, and agony, and the towering poplars looming in the dim light. Then she saw it—clear as a photograph in her mind: the fork in the road.

She had chosen to go left. Not by chance. Not in confusion.

But because Henri had called to her.

Step after careful step, through the old farmland with raised field stones where she fell, then up the berm to Fleury.

Vianne whipped around, nearly out of breath. She needed to find the other mask. A quick search in the false bottom lent no clues. Pierre. She had to find him before the Gaultiers did. And she didn't have a lot of time.

Vianne snuck up to the chateau and retrieved her bicycle, pedaling as quickly as her heavy legs could go into Belleville. She had full intention of riding right up to Colette's storefront, but the police had the road blocked off to allow for a fleet of German military lorries to pass.

She got off her bicycle to watch, one after the other, with clanking chains and roaring engines that shook the ground under her feet.

Krieger crossed the street to talk to Officer Muller. She stumbled backward, pulling her bicycle with her and moving closer to the nearest building for concealment, and right next to Officer Lefevre from the Vichy police, who was also watching.

Vianne stood stiff as a board.

Krieger got into the backseat of a chauffeured Mercedes

and slammed his door closed, clearly angry about something Muller had said or hadn't said.

"Tensions are rising among the ranks." Lefevre blew his whistle at a passerby. "But no matter." Krieger sped off with Muller watching him from the pavement with crossed arms. "There's always another waiting to take his place."

Lefevre marched off to see about the passerby, leaving Vianne to consider what he'd said and watch Muller slowly walk away.

A child tugging on her skirt broke her gaze. "Yes?" It was one of the girls from the other day trying to get a free pastry.

"Madame?" The girl waved her down to her level. Vianne leaned down.

"Do you know where the Marchands are?" She batted her eyes.

"The Marchands?" Vianne repeated, turning toward the cold and lonely patisserie, completely shuttered with a few leaves tumbling past. She straightened. "They left."

The car Krieger drove off in had turned around and was now headed in her direction, filling Vianne with dread.

She dumped her bicycle on the pavement, slipped into the bookshop under the clang of bells, and ducked. If Krieger had looked, he would have seen her bicycle wheels spinning on the ground outside.

Colette ran up from the back. "Oh, thank God, it's you."

Vianne leaned against the window, hand on her chest where her heart was beating wildly, taking a moment to realize she was safe, then hurriedly retrieved her bicycle and brought it inside. "Where's Blaise?"

"In the back. With Sandrine and Élise."

Vianne rushed to the back and thankfully not only found that her mother-in-law and Blaise were safe and sound, but also Pierre.

Blaise got up off the floor where he was reading to throw his arms around her waist. Vianne squeezed him back, never wanting to let go. "I love you, Blaise," she said, barely above a whisper.

"I love you," he said back.

Sandrine's face lifted. "He talks?"

Vianne's eyes filled with tears as she nodded. "How about you spend the night here?" she said to him. "Right here with the books. Would you like that?"

His eyes widened. It was probably his dream to fall asleep in a bookshop.

She hugged Pierre. "We need to speak privately." Max walked down from his loft apartment. "Max and Colette, too."

Colette found a spot for them between the bookshelves. Another wave of German lorries rumbled slowly past, rattling the windows and scooting the books from their place on the shelves. Colette tried her best to hold them in place.

"I need help," Vianne said. "From all of you."

"Help?" Colette looked even more alarmed, and Vianne didn't blame her. "Élise said you are taking Krieger into the Zone Rouge. She's the last person I'd believe, but then you told Blaise he could sleep here, so now I'm not sure what to think."

"I am not only taking him, I'm also taking the Gaultiers."

"You can't do that!"

"They know I've entered before, and if I don't do it, they will kill Blaise."

Colette gasped, hand over her mouth, while Pierre grabbed for his heart.

"Pierre." She gulped. "The gas masks in the chest by your fireplace, those are the ones you showed me the other night—the ones that don't work?" she asked.

"Yes, those are them."

"Where is the other mask, the one you refitted?" Vianne hoped he'd kept it, hidden it somewhere safe, instead of tossing it out like he mentioned. She held her breath. "Please tell me—"

"It's in my workshop."

Vianne sighed in relief. "Perfect. That's perfect." She turned to Colette. "Take me to your private collection."

"What are you looking for?"

"A Cassini Map."

"Follow me." Colette locked her front door, then escorted them to the very back of her bookshop, where a narrow spiral staircase took them into her rudimentary, dark, and damp basement with a dirt floor. They lit several candles, and together helped Colette pull several map rolls out from behind a secret compartment in the wall.

Vianne picked through them on the table, looking for the right one.

"A Cassini of that area predates the war," Max said.

"It doesn't matter. I remember the way—I remember the path." Vianne found the map she was looking for and unrolled the brittle scroll, holding the edges down with more candles. Vianne found Fleury easily, then pointed to the blank space where the chateau was built. "This is where the chateau is now."

Max gave her a pencil, and she drew a path to the village starting with the poplars, marking the posted danger sign, where the poplars thinned, and drawing a dark line for the fork before Fleury. When she closed her eyes, she remembered distances, and how long it would take to walk one stretch of the path compared to another, and noted them.

"Taking a left at the fork is a safe route to the chapel, passing through old farmland. You can feel the stones from its property line still in the ground just before a berm rises unexpectedly, protecting the village. A right at the fork leads into the heart of the Zone Rouge, toward the battlefields and the deepest trenches." Vianne looked at Pierre through the flickering candlelight. "I'll be taking a right at the fork. To the trenches and up north to the leaking chemical stockpile."

"That's suicide," Pierre said. "You'll kill them and yourself by traveling north."

"Not if I wear the mask you adapted for the mix of gases—the new filtering system and the sealant."

"It's not tested." Pierre shook his head. "Don't you understand?"

She put her hand on his. "I have to go."

"And what if the mask fails?" he asked.

"That's a chance I'll have to take."

Vianne turned to Max, tapping the map with her pencil where all her illustrations had been meticulously drawn out. "Here is the map they were looking for. The stone is in the chapel at the end of the square. The air is safe there. Otherwise, I wouldn't have survived. Will you help me? Will you meet me in Fleury?"

He nodded, giving her hand a squeeze. "Yes. Absolutely, yes."

"Wait a minute." Colette crossed her arms. "You said you don't have a choice, but you do. You can leave on the night train to Paris, Lyon, or even Marseille. They won't find you—"

"But they will find me, eventually. Just like they found Marion." Vianne paused, taking a heavy breath. "Krieger killed my sister, Colette. After he arrested her, he killed her."

Colette gasped. "He told you that?"

Vianne nodded. "Now, do you understand? I not only have to go. I want to. I've never thought of myself as a killer, but in this case, some people are best in a grave."

Vianne's own words struck a chord inside her. She never thought she would talk this way or believe the things she did, but she felt stronger because of it.

The basement turned quiet for a moment, with all four of them looking at each other in the dim flickering candlelight. Vianne didn't think there was anything else to say, except something to help Pierre.

She reached for both his hands. "Pierre. I know you are worried about me, and I confess, I feel like a mouse thrown in with the snakes, but I need your help most of all. Otherwise, we have no future. Will you show me on the map where the canisters are?"

Vianne could tell he was conflicted, but that was because he was protective. He had to know this was their only chance.

"Give me the pencil," he said.

Pierre drew an X north of Fleury where the stockpile was. "There's a trench you'll need to follow. A trench unlike any other, right here," he said, drawing another line that branched off the fork in the road Vianne had drawn. "It's wide as a creek, but deep as a river. It must have roots and trees growing from it now, but also…" He looked up. "You need to look out for bayonets sticking up from the ground. Follow the edge only. Promise me you'll watch for them."

"I promise." Vianne leaned over the map, studying every twist and turn of the trench.

"There's one more thing." Pierre took off his glasses. "There's a mine near the stockpile. Look for barbed wire and a flattened area that looks out of place among the mounds of earth."

She nodded. There was so much to remember.

———

They waited until the evening to leave the bookshop, after Colette provided a simple dinner of a baguette and cheese. Colette assured Vianne that if she didn't hear from her in the morning, she'd take them all to her apartment across Belleville for safekeeping.

"Sandrine noticed the Marchands' shop was closed. She wanted to go over there and talk to them. What do you want me to do?" Colette asked.

"Tell her they left to be with their nephew, cleared out their inventory. She'll understand if you tell her they felt there were too many Germans in Belleville."

Vianne said goodbye to Blaise first, explaining in the simplest terms that it wasn't safe at the chateau, but she'd be back in the morning. When it was time to say goodbye to

Sandrine, Vianne was lucky that she had fallen asleep on the divan and didn't have to explain. She hugged Élise.

"I'll never forget what you did for me, bringing my family here when I asked. I remember what you said in the library. I am grateful to you, Élise. I'm sorry for the tension that has developed over these past years. We only wanted the best for Sandrine and Chateau Ten. We've been on the same side this whole time."

Élise gave her a slight nod. "Be careful."

At the front door, Colette held her hands. "Vianne, I—"

"Don't say it." Vianne hugged her. "I'll see you in the morning."

"You promise?"

Vianne nodded, tears welling in her eyes and refusing to let go, because the goodbyes were starting to sound like goodbyes forever. "But if I don't…" She couldn't manage to say the rest.

"I'll take care of Blaise," Colette said.

Vianne swiped the tears from her eyes before hugging Pierre.

"Remember, follow the edge of the trench up north—only the edge."

"How will I know when I've made it?" she asked.

He pulled away. "You'll know."

Colette reached for Vianne's wrist. "And whatever you do, do not look down."

"Why?" she asked.

"Because of the legend, because of the—"

"Wait," Vianne said, eyes closing briefly. "Don't tell me. It's probably best I don't know why."

Colette stiffened. "Just don't look down."

Vianne turned to Max, and together they walked out to his car. The streets were quiet, and the air was oddly stagnant after the lorries had rumbled through. Max opened the door for her, and she caught sight of the Marchands' shop.

"What is it?" he asked.

Vianne didn't want to talk about the stone, other than how to find it. "Nothing." The sun had started to set, cloaking the street in a diminished, dull light. "The gloaming," Vianne said.

"What about it?"

They got in the car and drove off to the chateau.

"It feels so final—the setting sun with the mixes of orange and gray. So many favorable possibilities, yet also the chance to fail. Truth is, the last time the sky looked like this, I found the Marchands hanging in a tree." She unclipped her earrings. "Max, if something happens to me, can you give these to Colette?" She handed them to him. "They're the only thing I have worth a damn, and she could use the money."

"Of course." He put them in his pocket.

They drove up to the guesthouse close to eight o'clock, taking the back road to avoid being detected by the Gaultiers. When Vianne got out of the car, they heard an engine or two at the chateau and saw a flash of headlamps near the fountain, followed by voices. "Krieger must be here already."

"Do you think they'll come down to the guesthouse?" he asked.

"I suppose if I'm not in the library by ten o'clock, they will."

Pierre's home was dark, as expected, and it looked unchanged from when Vianne was last in it. She took in the emptiness, rubbing her arms for warmth, but she was still trembling for other reasons. Max lit a candle, providing a soft glow. The kitchen clock ticked.

"Does Pierre have any of that wine left?" Vianne went to Pierre's pantry, finding he had one bottle of wine left in his cupboard. "I don't think he'll mind," she said, pulling the cork and sloppily pouring a glass.

The first gulp was refreshing, but the fourth and fifth started to feel heavy in her stomach, and she regretted opening it in the first place. "I thought I needed that, but now I'm not sure." She wiped her mouth with the back of her hand. "I'm sorry."

"Sorry for what?"

"I'm not acting very ladylike."

He poured himself a glass. "It's all right. I think we both deserve a pass," he said, just before he matched Vianne's healthy gulp of wine.

"Did you ever think your life would end up like this?" she asked him. "Rather hard to believe, isn't it?"

"It is. Never did I think I'd be a widower at such a young age. I had plans to teach science at the Sorbonne, raise a family, and live a life of peace. I certainly didn't expect to spend my best years chasing Germans around Europe looking for a deadly, magic stone."

"I wanted—" Vianne stopped herself. Her dream wasn't that far off from Max's in regard to raising a family and living in peace; and if they were successful, perhaps she would get a second chance through Blaise—see him grow up at least, for Marion's sake. "I wanted something similar."

They sipped the rest of the bottle, listening to the kitchen clock tick closer and closer to ten o'clock and sitting with their thoughts. Soon enough, it was time to prepare. Max retrieved the mask from Pierre's workshop and brought it inside. With Max's help, Vianne fit it to her head to make sure it was snug.

"I think I have it." She brushed her hair back to life after taking off the mask.

"Do you want to go through the plan one more time?" he asked.

Vianne didn't want to think any more about what could go right or wrong—the gases, the Sorrows, and whether she'd come out of the Zone Rouge alive because she had no choice but to go. She would protect her family at all costs, and Marion deserved justice for what happened to her.

She shook her head. "No."

He held her hands. "After we destroy the stones, and the others are dead, I'll spread a rumor that will end this once and for all—nobody will look for the reliquary stones near Chateau Ten again."

"What will you say?"

"That the Gaultiers hustled Krieger with a fictitious story about the stone as bait, killed him, and fled south with his money."

"And then this will be behind us," she said.

"Forever."

She nodded.

Once it was five minutes until the top of the hour, they moved to the door.

Vianne wasn't sure if this would be the last time she saw Max or not, and for what it was worth, she wanted to thank him. He had challenged her when she clung to her beliefs, but when she took a hard look inward, she realized that he was

ANDIE NEWTON

making her aware of her own fears. If only she had come to her senses earlier.

"Max?" She turned near the door, her heart in her throat.

"Yes?"

Before she could talk herself out of it, Vianne reached up and gave him a quick hug. "Thank you." She let go just as quickly and left, swiftly closing the door behind her.

She took a moment with her back against the door, feeling for the key in her dress pocket and looking toward the Zone Rouge, which was eerily void of all voices and sounds. The Sorrows knew she was coming, and they'd been waiting.

"God, help me."

Chapter Twenty-One

Vianne entered the library with her lips pressed and her gaze direct, finding François leaning against the dark green wall with his arms folded, and Monique sitting on the edge of the mahogany table wearing trousers and holding her gas mask. The glow of electric light from the crystal chandelier competed with the candelabra, casting a brassy glare.

"Vianne." Monique smoothed her platinum hair behind one ear.

Vianne remained silent and still and couldn't help but notice the library had a different feel to it, just like the outside. The shadows were gone, and there was no hint of music —quiet.

"I told you, François." Monique lit a cigarette after tapping her silver case. "She'd come, and she's a whole minute early." A second later, the clock chimed at the top of the hour, sending a bolting shock through Vianne's veins. Monique motioned to the lights. "Flip the switch, it's horrible for my complexion."

"Forget the lights." François stroked the stone, sliding his hand up and down the chain. "Where's Krieger?" He moved away from the wall to walk to the ladder and wait.

Monique studied Vianne, taking a leisurely pull from her cigarette. "I see you brought a mask for yourself, Vianne. I knew you had the other one. Probably under your bed. Maybe in your wardrobe."

Monique slipped off the tabletop, her boots tip-tapping along the parquet floor, slinking toward Vianne. "You little liar. How long have you been looking for the missing stone?"

"I haven't."

Monique exhaled a lungful of smoke from the corner of her mouth. "The mystic said there was a woman." She pushed Vianne to sit.

François pulled Monique back. "Easy now, darling. Like you said, we need her."

Monique shrugged his hands off her and reluctantly went back to her cigarette, sitting on the tabletop, but this time, she became enamored with her reflection in a hand mirror. "For now, we do." She fixed a stray curl.

Vianne gulped—Monique's exact words had not escaped her.

For now.

"Look at all these books." Monique set her mirror down for a walk around, her finger delicately grazing the spines as she passed. "How much do you think these are worth?" she asked François instead of Vianne. "After the war, a great deal is my guess."

"Yes. A great deal," François said.

Monique climbed the ladder. "I do love this ladder," she said, cigarette bobbing on her lips. "Give me a push, François."

He returned to the wall, arms crossed and holding the stone hanging around his neck.

She climbed back down. "Very well, then." Another sigh.

Vianne shifted in her chair, watching Monique move on from the books to inspecting everything from the oil lamp to the gramophone records as if they were her own, or would be soon. All she kept thinking about was her dear sister, Marion, and how Krieger's face was the last face she saw.

Her hands curled into fists around the mask strap, feeling from one end to the other. Vianne was looking forward to seeing him gasp for air. She only hoped she'd make it into the heart of the forbidden forest and out of the mourning ground before something happened to her. She closed her eyes, saying a prayer as Pierre would advise her to do.

"What are you doing?" Monique snubbed out her cigarette in a crystal ashtray.

Vianne relaxed her fists. "Waiting, like you said."

Monique studied her. "Hmm."

Moments later, Vianne heard the clip-clop of Krieger's boots coming from the private entrance as if he were billeting in the west wing himself. "Is she here—" He looked at Vianne, a little surprised as if he didn't quite believe she'd show up.

Monique showed him the masks. "We are accompanying you to make sure we get paid after all the changes you've made to our deal. And before you ask, this isn't a request. This is non-negotiable."

He examined the mask she gave him.

"It's a special mask," Monique said.

"How so?"

Monique smiled sheepishly. "Turns out the handyman had

one-of-a-kind masks from The Great War—the only ones suitable for the Zone Rouge." She motioned to Vianne. "One dose of sodium pentothal and she became a chattering little bird, that one. We are fully protected now—she's been using one herself for protection for God knows how long."

Vianne stood. Waiting felt like uncertainty, and she just wanted to get on with it. "Shall we leave?" She moved toward the door with her mask.

"Not yet." Krieger pulled the Verdun book he'd been carrying around from his jacket pocket. "I want to show you something."

Vianne watched quietly as he flipped through the pages, many with bookmarks and margin notes and loose papers tucked inside. Vianne saw where he wrote in "Commandant Lichtenberg."

"Here." He pointed.

Vianne leaned over, trying to hold her expression. They had found a map after all. Though not quite what they were looking for, without a direct path to the village, but it was a map, nonetheless. There was also a diagram of the reliquary stones, and how they fit together—looked like Krieger had fastened a pattern together with a single brad to show how the two stones fit together.

He swiftly covered it with his palm when she tried to get a better look.

"It clearly shows the ninth village right here," he said, tapping the page. "Now, show me the route to Fleury."

François and Monique suddenly became interested, leaning over the table.

"This map isn't to scale," Vianne said, pretending to give

the map a thorough examination. "Not from what I remember. And the forest isn't marked." She tapped her temple. "It's up here."

"What do you remember?" Krieger asked. "In case we get..." When he braced the table with both hands, Vianne caught sight of a Luger under his jacket in a chest holster. "Separated."

Vianne did her best not to let on what he meant—they did plan to kill her either way.

She flashed them a smile. "Let's hope we do not get separated. It is dangerous out there." Vianne realized quickly it was to her benefit for them to believe she'd been in the Zone Rouge multiple times. They would trust her directions and keep her alive as long as they could. "I have a tested, trusted path starting with a fork in the road after the poplars." She scratched out a line for the fork but made sure not to mention the berm to the left, or the particulars about walking the edge of the trench up north. "We take a right and go this way," she said, finger trailing in a general direction. "That's where each step will be technical and precise. Follow me exactly. One wrong move and..." Her eyes lifted slowly.

"We better not get separated because of something you've done," Monique said to her.

"It won't be because of me. Sometimes there's a fog that could be thin or thick as paint," she said, knowing that the fog came with the Sorrows. "If you fall behind, you risk walking into an old minefield—or worse. Your torch won't help you in the fog."

Her eyes went to the stone's diagram after Krieger momentarily lifted his hand, but he quickly tucked it in the back pages, keeping her from fully seeing how the stones fit together.

Krieger examined the map one more time.

"Ready?" Monique asked.

Krieger snapped the book closed. "Ready." Vianne watched him tuck it into his inside pocket.

They were finally leaving, and Vianne tried to find relief in that, but she didn't know if Krieger had read about the berm or not in that book. He didn't seem to know or question her about it.

Monique passed the torches out. Vianne and François both reached for the last one.

"I'm leading the way," Vianne said. "I have to have a torch."

Krieger nodded once to give it to Vianne.

"Follow me," she said, turning for the door, but Krieger grabbed the mask that was dangling from Vianne's fingers before she could make it into the corridor, snapping it back. "What are you doing?" Vianne's eyes sprang backward, refusing to let go.

Krieger took a good look at the mask stretched between both their hands. Some might say he studied it. "I am making sure they are the same, of course."

"Why wouldn't they be?" Her gaze shifted between him and the mask, unsure what to do. If she fussed, she'd look suspicious. If she gave in too easily, then she might be stuck with a mask that absolutely didn't work.

"I want to check." He grabbed her wrist.

"I've already fitted it to my head." She yanked her hand

away, causing them both to lose their grips, and now both masks were on the floor.

Vianne's mouth hung open. She didn't know which one was hers.

Krieger picked them up for further inspection before pushing one at her. "That wasn't so hard, was it?" He walked past her into the corridor, leaving Vianne utterly breathless.

Monique slunk by.

"After you." François directed Vianne to follow Monique out, but she still hadn't taken a breath and was staring at the mask in her hands, trying to discern if it was hers by feeling for warmth on the strap where she had held it last, and examining the fit, but she had no idea. "Go!" he yelled, and they both walked out.

Vianne stood at the iron gate where the air was unnaturally still and humid, the scorched trees casting heavy shadows that darkened the brambles. Not a breeze, a flick of air, or the sound of a crackling leaf in the night. Her eyes gently glanced toward the guesthouse, wondering if Max was already nearby like he had promised.

"What are you waiting for?" Monique flicked on her torch. "Go." She gave her a push from behind, but Vianne dug in.

"You know what's in there, don't you?" Vianne asked. "We must be careful. Every step counts."

"Of course. That is why you are leading us through the gases and the bombs."

313

"I'm talking about the Sorrows," Vianne said through her teeth.

All three of them looked at her, and she thought what imbeciles they were. They'd focused on the stone, their greed and desires, and never considered the bodies in the ground, and what the sorrowful souls of the Zone Rouge could do.

"Commandant Lichtenberg will not harm me," Krieger said.

"Can you hear them?" Vianne asked, but it was more of a test.

Monique whipped her head around to look at François, who appeared unsure. Krieger searched the night sky, the twinkling stars, and the distant moon that cast dim light on them in the garden.

"Stop trying to scare us because it won't work," Monique said, attempting to sound strong, Vianne could tell, but she must have been a little scared. "What do we do if we hear them?"

"There's nothing you can do." Vianne unlatched the gate and led them through the brambles to the other side.

Monique stepped forward. "Why, what happens?"

Vianne flicked on her torch. "You become one of them." She took a withering, shaky breath because she was petrified. "Now, stay close." She pointed her light toward the poplar trees up ahead, walking slowly so that Max could keep up, listening to twigs snap under their feet with each careful and measured step.

"Go faster." Monique brushed cobwebs from her hair before moving to a snag on her trousers. "This is taking too much time."

Vianne stopped. "I'm going as fast as I should, not as I can. And it is a walk. Didn't you know?"

Krieger pushed Vianne to move. "Just go!"

The poplars slowly swallowed all glimpses of the moon, the thick darkness creating glowing halos around their torches. Vianne saw the tree the Marchands had been hanging from and prepared to pass underneath, but she wasn't prepared to see the rope that hung them still attached and wound around the branch. She said a little prayer, remembering that Max buried them nearby.

"What are you whispering?" Monique's voice was shrill. "Are you conversing with the Sorrows? Is this a trap?"

François had had enough. "Stop it, Monique." He grabbed her hand to point her torchlight behind them as heavy boughs shifted above, creaking and moaning in a language all their own. "I..." He looked conflicted. "I thought I heard footsteps."

"Those are ours," Vianne said, hoping he'd abandoned his efforts, especially after she got a few steps ahead, and he did, but Monique was struggling to keep up, worried about her hair and the dirt on her boots.

Vianne heard François apologize to her, and they had a private conversation of raspy whispers, which infuriated Krieger, and there was an argument. Payment details and the deal they had agreed to were discussed again.

"Shh!" Vianne scanned the trees up ahead, checking for the fog. The tremble in her hands was evident from her shaking light.

"Save your arguments for after we find the stone," Krieger said to them.

At the fork, Vianne veered to the right, but Krieger

stopped, shining his torch the opposite way and barely grazing the field stones several yards away. "This doesn't feel right."

Vianne didn't know if she should insist, risk causing attention to herself in the forest, or keep walking like she'd done with Monique. She eyed the shiny black stone hanging from François's neck.

"Put your mask on." She fit her mask over her head and walked as calmly as she could north.

"Follow her," Krieger finally said.

She closed her eyes briefly.

The forest had changed into a mix of trees, short, tall, and thin, with a quiet hush about them. Keep north, was all Vianne kept thinking. Keep north and find the trench.

A brush of peaty coolness flitted through her hair like ghostly fingers, making her dizzy. She held onto a silvery birch tree. Monique piped up with a complaint.

"Shh!" Vianne rasped. They were close. So close, but her torch had dimmed. She searched the ground with her foot, unsure where the forest floor ended and where the cavernous hole of the trench began because it was so dark, feeling the firmness of the soil, and where it turned soft. Pierre said to get as close to the edge as she could.

Vianne inched closer and closer until she was leaning over the thick and impenetrable darkness of the trench. Krieger yanked her back with a firm grab of her dress.

"You'll fall in," he said, voice muffled from the mask.

Vianne nodded, her inhaling breath as shocking as the sound of her heartbeat.

Monique stomped past François to walk next to Vianne.

"Someone needs to keep an eye on you." She adjusted her mask as if she were fixing her hair.

Krieger pointed. "Get going."

Vianne imagined the dead soldiers' rotting bones in the trench beside her. In the faint distance, she heard weeping. She looked to Monique to see if she heard it, too, but she was either looking up at the trees or taking an extra step to keep pace.

Vianne's palms turned sweaty, and her heart skipped more than it pounded, turning into a rhythmic cadence that hummed throughout her body. She knew she looked suspicious with every turn of her head, especially as the trench went on for an eternity, but she was waiting for so many things to happen, the stockpile, the fog, the Sorrows—

"How much longer?" Monique whined. "We must have walked for an hour."

"Be quiet!" Krieger shouted.

Barbed wire emerged from the shadows, blocking their path and directing them to walk toward a mound, when a mournful wail of violins drifted through the hollow woods, shaking her bones and a million leaves in the trees.

Like sirens from the sea, the Sorrows cry,
An eerie melody tangled high…

Vianne turned right and then left, huffing and puffing and fogging up her mask.

"Where's the village?" Krieger grabbed her arm. "Answer me!"

Monique stomped forward, grabbing the other arm. "Where's the village, Vianne?"

The weeping Vianne heard earlier built and built, no longer in the distance, and about to roll heavily over the top of them if she didn't move. "Don't you hear that?" Her voice was shrill.

Monique let go of her to clutch François with both hands. "What is that?" She searched the air. "I hear moaning. Weeping…"

"No," François said, breaking away. "It's a song."

Vianne whipped around, checking the trench and then the trees, discerning how close the Sorrows were by looking for the fog. Hissing came from behind the barbed wire, followed by a greenish-yellowy gas gurgling into the air and flowing over the ground like a babbling brook.

"What's happening to me?" Monique held out her shaking hands, but the shaking had traveled up her arms, and now her entire body was convulsing. She gasped and clawed at her throat. "Help!"

She reached out to Vianne, but she took a step back.

"It's burning!" Monique said, pulling off her mask and letting out a bone-chilling scream. Her eyes bugged from their sockets as she scratched and bloodied her face and pulled her hair. "Help me! Help me—"

François pleaded for Monique to secure her mask. He even tried to force her, but she stumbled away, throwing herself on the wire before falling limp, hair flopped over her head. François was next, having a coughing fit of his own that had him walking into the unknown, yet still calling out for his wife. "Monique!"

Boom!

The blast of a stray mine blew both Krieger and Vianne to the ground on their backs, and amidst his chaotic screams and the deafening pierce of the blast still in her ears, Vianne heard her name being dragged through the wind and sung in the trees.

She scrambled to her feet at the same time Krieger did. Her heart pounded. They had found her—the Sorrows were here and watching. Her eyes shifted to François, struggling on the ground to stand without his legs, and then to Krieger, who was frozen in place.

Vianne had to move, she had to run, but her torch was unreachable in the dirt. She could tell Krieger was on to her for what she'd done. He reached for his gun, and in a moment of clarity, Vianne snatched the necklace from François's disembodied torso and ran for her life through the forbidden woods without a path to save herself.

Chapter Twenty-Two

Vianne darted through the trees. Panicked breaths came hot and shallow, fogging the inside of her mask and smothering her with stifling pressure. Branches snagged her clothing and scraped her legs, each touch making her want to shriek.

"Vianne!" Krieger was close enough for her to hear him yell through his mask, threatening to kill her when he found her. She turned, seeing him as a gray figure running toward her, gun drawn, but not sure where to shoot.

Pop! Pop!

She ran a few hobbled steps to get out of the way and found herself at the edge of the trench, arms flailing to stay upright. "Ahh ... ahh..." Her feet slipped right out from under her, revealing herself with a scream, sliding down the dirt wall into the deepest, darkest part of the trench, landing on a bed of clattering bones. With searching hands, she felt metal buttons on dewy, torn fabric and old leather, which drew a whimper.

"Vianne!" Krieger shouted right above her at the edge of the trench, which made her jerk in place.

She held her breath, watching him through her cloudy mask, aiming his gun at every creak and bristle from the trees. He coughed violently from the gas exposure, ending with him pulling out tufts of hair before disappearing.

A second passed in the quietness. Vianne still had her wits and her health, which meant she must have the working mask after all, and Krieger had the faulty one. The revelation gave her immense relief.

"Thank God," she whispered to herself. "Thank—"

The trench cooled with a ripple of putrid, sour air, followed by a waterfall of moonlit fog that settled at the bottom of the trench, revealing the tips of bayonets poking out of the ground from soldiers buried beneath. She struggled to stand, grasping at roots and clumps of dirt. Seconds felt like minutes, knowing she should run, but she could barely feel her legs.

"Vianne…" Her name threaded through the rusty bayonet blades. "Vianne … Vianne…"

Her heart nearly stopped. She'd been here before—in her nightmares. Only this time…

Vianne gulped. Silvery silhouettes took shape in the thickening fog—soldiers on the march, trembling the forest floor and growing in strength with each breath she wasted standing in place, squeezing the stone.

"No." A phantom drum vibrated every nerve. "No—" She grasped at bones and roots alike to move, leaving her dizzy with legs as sturdy as cotton.

She felt Krieger behind her, an imposing, heavy force of his own, followed by the sound of footsteps as he fought the full effects of the gases. Renée had told her to pay attention to the signs, but where were the signs now?

Faster and faster she moved until her chest felt like it was about to burst, when she heard her name again, though it was different this time. She stopped between two dirt walls of tangled roots. The tone didn't sound ghostly or threatening, but worried.

"Vianne, where are you—Vianne!"

"Max?" she called up.

"Thank God. Oh, thank God!" He reached down and helped her out. "You're safe."

She had made it to the fork where the air was clear and breathable. "What are you doing here? You're supposed to be waiting in Fleury."

"I heard gunshots and was worried, so I ran back in search of you—"

Vianne ripped off her mask, and they embraced, but they didn't have a second to spare. "The Gaultiers are dead." She turned, looking into the murky trench behind her, slowly filling up with fog. "And Krieger is after me. We must hurry!"

They found their way to the berm and made it swiftly to the village, running straight up to the chapel and searching for the stone amid the overturned pews and bookcases, to the fallen altar. Another gunshot, only this one followed a howling wind. "He's coming. Max, he found us!"

"The rectory," Max said, turning, but there was nothing left of it.

"What about the parish graveyard?" Vianne asked.

"You think the priest was buried with it?"

"The priest?" Vianne covered her mouth with one hand and

reached into her dress pocket for the key with the other. "*Mon Dieu*. That's it." A gust of wind whistled through the church stones, blowing her hair back. "That's it!"

"What's it?" he asked.

Vianne rushed to show him the key. "Henri left this for me. It's a sign. A sign of where to look!"

He pointed his torchlight at the engraving.

I am a Catholic… Call a Priest.

"It's buried with the priest."

Another gunshot ricocheted through the night, and he tugged on her hand, racing out to the graveyard, pointing his torch at the tombstones, trying to find the priest's.

Vianne gasped. The fog had found her, curling down the cobblestone street through the square, approaching the chapel. Krieger called to her from its thick middle.

"I'm going to find you…" he said, but his voice had changed, and he sounded sad and as mournful as the Sorrows calling her name. "Vianne…"

Her heart pounded in her chest. "It's happening. He's turning into one of them!" She tapped Max's shoulder as he searched the ground with his torch. "Hurry!"

His torchlight grazed an ornately decorated tombstone. "There!" She pointed. A black stone glistened in the light just below the epitaph. Obscured but in plain sight.

Max kicked over the tombstone, cracking it into pieces, and pulling the stone from the crumbled bits. Vianne snatched it away to get a closer look and compare them herself, and they appeared to be two pieces of one whole, but in the dark with a fading torch, she didn't have the light or the time to do anything other than destroy what was in her hands.

"We need a hammer, something," she said, looking over the ground for something to use, then remembering the chapel. "The bricks!"

They burst through the front doors and down the aisle to the altar. Vianne placed the stones on the steps and got ready to smash them, grabbing for a brick.

"Wait!" Max stopped her with a reach, his eyes glazy and wide. "We should keep them—keep them for ourselves."

"What? You told me we had to destroy them. It's dangerous if we don't!" Vianne couldn't believe her ears, but the fog had rolled in quickly and thick, curling around Max's legs and wrapping around his waist as he grunted and strained.

She turned back to the stones, hurling her arms into the air.

Krieger stomped down the aisle. "Give me the stones!" he bellowed, his gun drawn, eyes blazing red, and most of his hair pulled out. "Now, or I'll shoot!"

With a single, decisive blow, Vianne shattered the stones, sending them splintering into a thousand shards of black crystal that disappeared into the night.

"No!" Krieger cried.

The fog recoiled, retreating into the depths of the forest as though a door had opened, releasing Max from its influence.

The Sorrows were gone, but the gases in the north had left Krieger crazed and delusional, looking for retribution, and there was nothing Vianne could do to stop him. He pointed his Luger at her as she knelt on the altar steps.

She winced, bracing for the shot, when Max lunged for the gun, stepping into the line of fire and falling to his knees holding his arm.

Krieger fell to the floor holding his head and dropped his

gun. Vianne saw her chance, snatching the Luger for herself and aiming at his heart.

"Commandant Lichtenberg?" Krieger asked her, hallucinating. "No... No!"

She smiled. "Yes."

Pop!

The blast kicked her feet out from under her. The next thing she saw was the stars, lying on the chapel floor with Max next to her. A moment passed in the piercing quietness with only the sound of her heart beating in her ears.

"Are you all right?" Max asked, his voice normal, and himself.

She blinked. "Yes. Are *you* all right?" She could tell his wound was superficial from the little bit of light they had, thank God, with the bullet grazing his arm, but that didn't mean it wasn't painful and bloody. She helped him to a stand.

"Vianne, I didn't mean any of that. It wasn't me—"

"I know." She held him close until he found his footing.

He grimaced, holding his wounded arm. "I'm just glad you didn't listen to me." He looked into the sky, the stars, and then the graveyard. "Do you hear anything?"

Vianne listened; she even felt her heart. The Sorrows' cry had extinguished when she crushed the stones, and now, hopefully, they were at rest. "No."

"Good. Let's get out of here." They stepped over Krieger's body.

"Wait!" She turned back, pulling Krieger's book and all his notes from his inside pocket. She tucked it down the front of her dress.

"What's that?"

"I'll tell you later." They put their arms around each other for support and walked down the aisle and out of the chapel.

Vianne's face stung with nicks and scrapes, but the pain in her legs was worse—raw and chafed after falling in the trench. But it could have been worse. She gently looked up at Max, thinking of his poor wife and the consequences she paid.

"Ready?"

She took his hand, and in the early dark hours of the morning, they maneuvered their way through the twisty, knotted brambles and through the gate to the chateau's garden.

They looked up at the chateau, made darker by having all the drapes and curtains pulled. "How much time do you think we have before someone comes looking for the Gaultiers or even Krieger?" she asked. "There were other Germans at the séances."

"Hours, maybe days, maybe never," he said. "There is no way to know. We'll have to erase all traces of the Gaultiers from the chateau just to be safe, starting with their suite."

They made their way through the pocket doors and down the long corridors to the King's Suite. The air smelled overwhelmingly of Monique's lilac perfume even before they made it to the door.

Vianne flicked on the lights, the brightness making her squint. The bed was unmade with the duvet Vianne had spent a lifetime taking care of wadded up in a ball at the foot of the bed, sheets in disarray, and the pillows on the floor.

"Grab everything." Max reached for their travel trunk. Vianne yanked Monique's satiny dresses from their hangers and tossed them inside.

"Dresses from Paris, and shoes from Milan." She picked up a pair of Italian slingbacks from the floor and threw them on top. "Something to sell after the war."

Max was busy looking for something in every crevice of the desk, in the wardrobe, and even in the bathroom, before looking under the bed.

"What are you looking for?"

He pulled a silver box out from under the covers. "I found it." Max was nearly breathless, placing the box carefully on top of the fluffy duvet. "What remains of the Guelph Treasure."

Vianne's fingers went to her lips. She'd seen this box before, in the library with François. Though up close, she could see it was more ornate than at first glance, and it was heavy, probably made of pure silver rather than plated.

Max delicately lifted the lid. Inside, a few gold chains and loose jewels were along the silk-lined bottom. But the most interesting find was a booklet of notes written by Monique herself. He thumbed through the pages. "Look at this."

Vianne turned on the lamp for extra light.

Max had opened to a page with a drawing of the stone's two pieces, how they fit together, and a list. "Names and dates of every Thule Society member she had contact with."

"Muller," Vianne read. "He was here—in the library."

"Remember that rumor I said I'd spread? This list will make sure it reaches the right ears."

Vianne examined Monique's drawing. "I've seen this diagram before." She reached for the book she had taken from Krieger, flipping to the back—the diagram she had only gotten a glimpse of in the library before they left. A piece of paper, divided in half, and held together by a brass brad, allowing the two pieces to move apart like wings.

Max let out a slight gasp, thumb on the brad as if considering the possibility of a third piece, something that would fit nicely in the middle.

"Max, you don't think…"

"No." He smiled after the slightest hesitation.

"Thank goodness," she said. "You looked like you were thinking about it. I suppose it will take some time to make sense of all that has happened and realize the search is over. Especially for you, after all your research." She handed him Krieger's book.

"I'll keep this safe and hidden." He tucked the book in his waistband.

They'd cleaned out the suite, making it look just as it did the day Vianne had rented it to the Gaultiers, and hid their belongings in the attic where nobody would find their trunk, but where they could have access to the valuables after the war.

"And their roadster?" Max asked.

"Nearly everyone in Belleville will recognize it as theirs." Vianne paced for a few moments, then thought of the perfect place. They could lift away a section of the iron fence, drive the roadster into the Zone Rouge just enough to conceal it in the brambles, then replace the fence as normal. "After the war, we can sell it. By then, it won't matter whose it is."

"That's a good plan." Max winced, looking at his arm where the blood had crusted.

Vianne felt bad, as she should have tended to his wound first thing when they came inside. "Come with me into the kitchen to clean that up." She led him into the kitchen and asked him to have a seat at the table while she looked for the hydrogen peroxide and bandages.

The morning sun rose gently on the horizon. She reached for the kitchen curtains to let in some of the light, but stopped cold with her fingers on the fabric.

"Like you said, Vianne. It will take time. It's safe to open them."

She nodded, then spread the curtains open just enough to see each other clearly. Her hair was matted and filthy, as was her dress, its pattern now barely visible beneath the grime.

"I can take care of my arm," he said.

"And so can I." She flashed her eyes after sitting next to him. "Besides, I want to do it. It's the least I can do." She rolled up his sleeve, exposing the wound now caked in blood from having happened hours ago. She dabbed some cotton in hydrogen peroxide. "This will sting a bit."

Max hissed, but only slightly as she cleaned the wound.

Vianne thought he was brave for stepping in front of Krieger's bullet for her, a hero even. "Max, I..." She didn't know how to thank him for what he did. If it wasn't for her continual denial, they could have moved quicker—she sure would have saved herself some agony. "I'm going to insist that Pierre move into the main house. He shouldn't be our handyman anymore, with him as elderly as he is, and he does so much already with Sandrine."

He had been watching her fasten the bandage.

"Would you..." she hesitated, because she didn't want to sound forward or out of line, but she felt safer with Max around, and also, there was something about him she liked.

"Consider moving into the guesthouse?" As soon as she said the words, she worried about how she sounded, and spoke fast. "Pierre will feel better knowing someone will take his place—someone he trusts—and you don't have to stay very long, maybe until the war is over, and then who knows—"

"Yes." He smiled. "I'd love to."

They hugged, right there in the kitchen. Vianne couldn't remember who reached out to who first, and she didn't care. It was the first step in taking control of the chateau and taking control of her life, and she was content with her decision. She gently opened her eyes, looking over his shoulder and spying the window curtains.

"These aren't open enough." She threw the curtains wide open so she could see the scorched trees of the Zone Rouge. "And the others..." She walked out of the kitchen to the front windows in the foyer. "All these heavy drapes." She was tying them back with their gold cords, illuminating the marble checkerboard floors, when a car drove up to the chateau and around the fountain.

"Pierre!" Vianne ran outside as his car pulled to a stop near the fountain. Élise popped out first to open the door for Sandrine. Colette scooted out from the back.

"I thought you were taking them to your apartment," Vianne said.

"We were worried and thought we were safer together. Our hunch paid off." Colette hugged Vianne. "Were you ... did you..."

"We succeeded." Vianne nodded incessantly. "We're safe."

Colette clutched her chest, eyes closed. "Thank God."

Blaise burst from the backseat and ran straight to Vianne.

"You are all right, my darling?" Vianne asked, lifting him tightly in her arms and kissing his cheek over and over.

He nodded, and she squeezed him again before setting him down. She kissed Élise's cheek next, then Pierre's before moving on to Sandrine. "And my dear Sandrine."

"Yes, yes. What is it?" Sandrine asked.

"Oh, nothing," Vianne said, wiping her eyes of tears. "I'm just happy you are back."

Sandrine looked up at Pierre, who explained they had been gone overnight.

"I remember," Sandrine said. "My back remembers." She stood to get into her wheelchair after Pierre pulled it from the car boot.

They all headed inside the chateau. Max had been watching from the doorway. Just as Vianne passed, she reached for Max's hand, and their eyes connected. "Thank you," she mouthed.

Chapter Twenty-Three

Three days had passed, and Vianne yawned after waking up slowly to the sun warming her bedsheets, content that her nightmares were gone and she didn't need to tie her wrist to the bedpost any longer. After giving her hair a quick brush and her face a wash, she wrapped her robe tie around her waist and walked downstairs to check on Sandrine, finding her already up and in her chair with Élise about to wheel her to breakfast.

Sandrine wore her favorite floral dress with her silver hair combed into a loose bun. "Vianne, is the water pipe all fixed?" she asked.

Élise and Vianne exchanged glances.

Colette had told Sandrine that there was a water break at the chateau, and that Max was going to fix it as an excuse for the overnight stay. Since coming home, she still asked about it, surprisingly, when normally she would have forgotten.

"Yes, madame." Vianne smiled. "Max fixed it."

"Max, that friend of Pierre's?"

"Yes," Vianne said. "That friend of Pierre's, and mine, too."

"Oh, that's nice."

Vianne placed her hand on Élise's before she started to push Sandrine's chair into the hallway. "You should have woken me. I would have helped."

"I wanted you to sleep in," Élise said, then whispered. "Sandrine asked about Genevieve and when she was going to visit. What do you want me to tell her?"

Vianne turned to Sandrine. "I wrote Genevieve a letter, madame. I'm sure it's the war that is keeping her tied up. Hard to travel these days."

"Yes, I suppose you are right."

Vianne had indeed written Genevieve a lengthy letter, first apologizing for not listening to her concerns when she was a guest, and then not replying to her letter. She also told her that she had experienced something similar and hoped they could talk.

Sandrine patted Vianne's hand. "Thank you, my dear."

Vianne kissed Sandrine's cheek before Élise wheeled her away, watching them disappear into the foyer, listening to Sandrine talking about the weather, and how she had the strangest dream.

Vianne walked into Blaise's bedroom. "Good morning—"

"Auntie!" Blaise ran to her from the window to wrap his arms around her waist. "Good morning." He squeezed extra hard.

She patted his back warmly. Since she destroyed both stones, the chateau had been quiet, and Blaise talked more and more each day. He seemed finally at peace with his new surroundings at the chateau, comfortable, given the circumstances and what had happened. "Did you sleep well?"

He looked up from the folds of her robe, nodding, and she sent him on his way to breakfast. "I'll be right behind you. Take a book."

Blaise picked a book from his shelf before padding down the hallway with his teddy bear, leaving Vianne near the window.

Max and Pierre stood in the courtyard, pointing at the damage the magpie had done to the garden while the bird perched itself on the iron fence.

They had paid a doctor to stitch Max's gunshot wound in secret and apply sulfa from the black market to keep infection away, though it took Vianne's pearl earrings to afford it. She was glad to do that for him, and she knew Henri would have approved.

After adjusting the drapes on the rod, Vianne walked to the kitchen where she smelled brown toast, lightly pan-fried eggs, and piping hot black tea.

"Smells wonderful in here." Vianne closed her eyes briefly, taking a deep, satisfying breath.

Élise used a dollop of butter for the grease. "I'm going to miss this black-market butter. And this is the last of our tea."

"Why would you miss butter?" Sandrine asked from the table. "Surely, we have funds for necessities. Tea included."

Sandrine didn't remember the guests who'd checked out or the money and valuables they'd brought with them.

"There's a shortage," Vianne interrupted. "Isn't that right, Élise?"

"Yes, madame."

Vianne helped Élise set the table, a place for all of them, including Max, but no plate for Henri. Vianne thought it was time to let Henri go, just as much for Sandrine as for herself.

"We'll be all right," Vianne said privately to Élise near the stove. "The loose jewels the Gaultiers left behind provided some funds, and after the war, we have the roadster. We won't lose the chateau. That's the important thing. And Pierre says the garden will be plentiful even with that magpie back. We're from the abandoned villages, and this is Chateau Ten—we've been through tougher situations."

"Yes, you are right, and I'm relieved to hear this," Élise said. "Thank you for telling me, but if things change, you'll ask me for—"

"Help," Vianne said with a pat of her hand. "I will ask you for help. I promise."

Pierre and Max came in from outside and joined them, having a seat around the breakfast table and enjoying the tea.

Élise plated the eggs, moving around the table from place setting to place setting.

"Vianne…" Sandrine noticed Henri's missing plate. "Where's—" She sighed heavily, rubbing her forehead. "Henri passed away, didn't he?"

Everyone looked up from their plates.

Vianne nodded. "He did, madame." She pulled the keepsake key from her pocket. "But he left us this to remember him. I had a chain put on it and gave it a proper polish."

"The key," she breathed. "And you want me to have it?" She held her chest as Vianne slipped it over her neck.

Vianne thought it was poetic that Monique and Krieger

briefly held the key in the library, considering it was quite literally the key that had held the answer.

"Henri would want it this way," Vianne said. "Keep it close." Vianne squeezed Sandrine's hand when tears spilled over her cheeks.

Pierre reminded Sandrine that they were there for her if she had any more questions, but told her that Henri was at peace and not to worry. Vianne believed Henri had answered her prayers and visited because Blaise and Sandrine both said they saw him, but she wasn't sure if Sandrine had the key the entire time or not, and had just forgotten. In the end, it didn't matter. She was thankful and would always be grateful to Henri for his help and for the sign.

A rapping knock at the front door startled them all. Vianne went to answer, seeing Colette peeping through the front window. "I have good news! Let me in!" She had something heavy in her arms. When Vianne let her in, she was surprised to see it was a radio.

"What on earth? Colette, radios are illegal—"

"The allies have landed." Colette stood in the foyer, struggling to keep the radio from slipping out of her hands. "The invasion! It finally happened."

"You're going to drop it." Vianne took the radio from her, then passed it to Max, who came up seconds later.

Colette and Vianne hugged. "It was a surprise to the Germans, landing farther down the coastline than they anticipated, in Normandy."

Vianne pulled away. "That is good news, indeed." She took her hand. "Join us in the kitchen."

They followed Max into the kitchen, where he announced that Colette had brought them a gift.

Sandrine set down her water glass. "I like gifts."

Pierre moved glasses and plates to the side so Max could set the radio down. Élise stood, gulping the mouthful of eggs she had in her cheeks. "What is going on?"

"There's been an invasion," Vianne announced. "Plug in the electrical cord." Vianne pointed to the outlet. "Right there."

Pierre plugged the radio into the socket and they were greeted with a blast of music—Chopin, Sandrine's favorite.

Sandrine's mouth hung open. "Oh, that's lovely. Simply, lovely. I haven't heard music in so long." She looked up at Vianne. "Isn't that right?"

"That is right, madame. Our gramophone is still broken."

Pierre spun the dial to find the broadcast from Radio Londres through the static and strange voices cutting in and out. "I found it." They huddled around the radio and listened to the report. The details of the invasion were hard to imagine.

"They did catch them by surprise," Vianne said just above a whisper. "Which means the Germans must have been outnumbered."

They were stunned initially, then overwhelmed with relief. The broadcast ended abruptly, but it was long enough for them to understand the particulars. There was still a lot that needed to happen before they were liberated, but this was the beginning—the rescue they had been waiting for.

Pierre turned the volume down when the station returned to playing Chopin.

"Well, here's to keeping us in suspense and in the dark for years." Colette raised her glass of water, but it was Pierre who insisted on getting the last bottle of wine he had in his guesthouse to celebrate.

"I drank it," Vianne said, then looked at Max. "We drank it. Before we…"

Vianne wasn't going to say she was afraid she'd die in the Zone Rouge in front of Sandrine and Blaise, and that's why she guzzled his wine.

She smiled. "I was nervous."

"Rightfully so," Pierre said. "Élise, are there any bottles left in the cellar?"

"Most are spoiled, but I'll check." Élise disappeared for a spell, down the stairs to the wine cellar, before gleefully running back up moments later with two salvageable bottles of red wine.

"I'll pour." Vianne retrieved the wine glasses from the cupboard. Colette went to help.

"News of the invasion has traveled fast," Colette said. "Couldn't find a policeman or an Abwehr officer in the square today. And I had some customers early this morning. Good news makes people want to spend money. But the biggest difference is the atmosphere. It's changed. I can't put my finger on it. Neighbors are out talking to one another in open circles."

"Talking? Right on the open street?"

Colette nodded.

Vianne uncorked the wine and began to pour.

"Madame Marchand would have loved today," Colette said quietly, watching her glass fill to the rim.

"I know."

They'd decided to tell the Marchands' nephew the truth about what happened to his aunt and uncle, leaving out the Sorrows and the stone's roll in their deaths. He said he understood why Vianne and Colette had kept it from him initially—that they didn't want to stain the Marchands' reputation.

Behind them, at the table, Sandrine told Blaise about her son. Afterward, Pierre shared stories of his early days with Max's father.

"When are you going to tell Blaise about his mother?" Colette whispered.

"I'm going to wait. He's improved so much these last few days, and I fear I'd set him back with bad news. Besides, there is a part of me that…" She briefly dipped her eyes. "I know it sounds like wishful thinking, but—"

"I understand. What if Krieger was lying? He was a Nazi, in the end. Hope is a wonderful thing to have, especially now." Colette subtly motioned to Max, which got Vianne to playfully roll her eyes.

"Stop it, Colette. Saving each other's lives brought us closer, that is true, but we are friends." She picked up Blaise's teddy bear from the counter.

"Sure, if you say so. But I can still be hopeful."

Vianne turned to look longingly out into the Zone Rouge with her family's laughter and chatter behind her. A silent breeze swept through the bushes and tittered the blades of grass. The Sorrows were attracted to the stones, she reminded herself, crushed to dust in the depths of the Zone Rouge. They wouldn't be bothering her anymore.

She propped the teddy bear against the curtains with its head flopped over.

Colette downed two or three drinks of her wine, making her voice wet. "Have you seen Renée?"

Vianne shook her head.

"I bet she's sitting back, counting her money, and celebrating the news just as we are."

"Only she's not matted and dirty because she's wearing my yellow sweater and matching dress."

Colette laughed. "I'm sure she is." She held her glass up, and they toasted. "I'm surprised that's all she took from you, honestly." Colette went back to the table, sitting next to Blaise, who wanted his teddy bear facing toward them on the windowsill.

Vianne adjusted the bear ever so slightly against the curtains until Blaise approved, then gave his button eyes a twist. A few seconds passed, studying him. She moved the bear's leg, and then his arm.

"Vianne?" Max asked.

She looked away after a long pause. "Coming." She brought the glasses to the table. "Ready for a toast?"

They raised their glasses over the breakfast table.

"To the end," she said, but in addition to the end of the war, Vianne was toasting an end to the Gaultiers, the Thule Society, and an end to those damn stones.

"To the end," they said back, glasses clinking.

Chapter Twenty-Four

Saint-Lô, France
D-Day + 4

Renée sat on the edge of the wooden chair, her hands tied behind her back with two Abwehr officers staring down at her, their arms crossed and wearing unkempt uniforms from being up for days on end. Outside, and about a mile away, Allied tanks slowly advanced while Messerschmitts tried their hardest to stop them with daring air raids, morning, noon, and night. Saint-Lô was crumbling, and while the Germans fled the city in droves, a small detachment from the Thule Society remained, refusing to leave until they'd pulled Renée from her hiding spot embedded with the locals.

The whistling of an incoming bomb made Renée duck in her chair, eyes to the rafters, praying and praying for a missed target. The officers never moved.

Boom! The building shook, and women screamed in the street. Somewhere, a baby cried.

"Leave me alone." The air was thick and stifling in the small room, a mix of damp stone from a day of rain and dust from fallen brick and plaster, making it hard to talk, much less breathe. "I've told you everything." She coughed into her sleeve.

"We will not leave you alone," one officer said.

Renée tried to still her breath as the door swung open. An Abwehr officer from her past, and one that had just as much presence as he did the day he arrested her in Verdun, strode deliberately into the room in his jackboots, his heels grinding against the debris-ridden floor.

"Hallo, mystic." He shone a torch in her face. "We meet again. You remember my name, no?"

"I'm not a mystic. And we haven't met," Renée said, but she knew damn well his name was Officer Muller.

He bent down from the hips, hands behind his back, looking at her dead in the eye. "Is that so?"

Renée immediately turned her face. It wasn't often Renée felt intimidated, but in this particular instance, she was shaken and wondered if he could hear the secrets pounding in her chest as if a second heartbeat.

"You look different." He examined her blonde hair, slick and shiny, not the matted nest it usually was. And a yellow dress and sweater instead of the faded frock she was known for, straight from Vianne's wardrobe. "I will give you that, but your little disguise failed to work this time."

He pulled a small notebook from his inside jacket pocket. "I made copies of Krieger's notes," he said, and Renée's gaze shifted. "Ah! You know him?" He smiled, but not really. "It's all right. I knew this already—how could I forget the deal we made in Verdun? I heard the Gaultiers killed him before they fled, but your deal was with me as well, and it is, shall I say, not complete."

"I upheld my side of the bargain, and it's very complete."

"Is it, now?" He tucked the notebook back into his inside jacket. "The Thule Society wishes for you to be truthful, for once, and tell us where the other piece is."

Renée scoffed. "What other piece?"

A slow smile spread on his face before he spun on his heel and paced, his boots skimming over the crumbled bits of brick and stone all about the floor.

"You lied to us. The stone was broken into three pieces."

"I didn't lie."

"We know, Renée."

Renée opened her mouth to respond, but her voice faltered. She had lied to them about the stone, but not entirely. She could still remember Marion's voice the last time she saw her, making her promise to never reveal the whereabouts of the most valuable piece, and most importantly, never to tell her sister, Vianne, that the truth lay with Blaise.

Marion's directions had been clear: if she was arrested or disappeared, do whatever possible to keep the Germans from the stones. Then vanish. But now, as she sat under Officer Muller's gaze with her hands tied behind her back, vanishing seemed impossible. The last thing she expected was for Marion's sister to be living at Chateau Ten, and she most certainly didn't expect Blaise to be living with his aunt. She had done her best regarding the stones, or at least that was what she kept telling herself.

"Well?" He gave her a violent shake. "Where is it?"

By the tone of his shouting voice, Renée wasn't sure if he already knew the answer and was seeking validation, or if he absolutely didn't know that a third stone had been sewn into Blaise's teddy bear.

Renée saw that teddy bear numerous times when Blaise was at the bookshop, and even tried looking for it in his bedroom the night she fled, but he kept it close at all times. He wouldn't let it out of his sight! She had to leave it if she wanted to live, but if she had managed to grab it, she would have tossed that teddy bear in the Meuse.

A fresh round of explosions rattled the walls. Muller barely blinked, but Renée seized the momentary distraction to throw him a red herring. Whatever he thought she knew, he couldn't prove it one way or the other—yet. All she had to do was survive the interrogation.

"Untie my hands and I'll talk. For a price." She eyed his wristwatch—a white-faced beauty of a timepiece with shiny, silver links. She'd seen one before on Krieger; it was worth more than she could dream of. "That luxury watch of yours. It must be worth the information you seek."

He laughed from his throat. "I'm not giving you this watch."

"You don't have time to *force* me to talk, if you know what I mean, because those tanks are coming, and you're running out of time. Give me the watch."

Another blast, this one shaking the floor and the ceiling. The officer hurriedly untied her hands, and she took a moment to admire the watch on her wrist, but she was actually planning her escape, looking for the door and also spying a broken window without a curtain. The other two officers were distracted by a rumbling lorry they didn't think was their own, by the way it was driving.

"Get down!" one of them yelled, followed by the zap of rapid gunfire, popping against the interior walls from an outside sniper. Renée saw her chance and ran for the door, making it clear across the rainswept street before she heard Muller yelling for her somewhere in the dark behind her.

"We'll never give up, Renée!" Another explosion, this one close enough to throw her against a building but not enough to stop her. "This isn't over!"

Author's Note

The story of the nine villages that "died for France" is both inspiring and heartbreaking, and, like so many places in France, the Zone Rouge carries echoes of war that still linger today. For those interested in learning more about the Battle of Verdun and the Zone Rouge, there are numerous online resources available if traveling to the site isn't possible. If you're curious about the Third Reich's fascination with the supernatural—or wish to explore the Thule Society further— one book I kept reaching for was *Hitler's Monsters* by Eric Kurlander. It breaks down the regime's obsession with the occult and the strange (very strange) ways it shaped their worldview.

As with all my novels, my goal was to tell a story that entertains while honoring the history it's rooted in. Since the only thing I love more than a good WWII story is a ghost story, this was my chance to bring the two together.

Thank you for reading! I hope this book moved you, surprised you, and kept you turning the pages.

Acknowledgments

Thank you to Charlotte Ledger, my editor at One More Chapter, for suggesting I write a ghost story, and to my agent, Kate Nash, for encouraging me. I also want to thank the incredible team at HarperCollins UK for my gorgeous covers, superb audiobook narrators, and expert packaging. A special shout-out to Aimee Brown for reading my rough (very rough) draft and giving me early feedback. Thank you to my readers! I hope you loved this story and were thoroughly entertained.

SISTERS. TRAITORS. SPIES.

When a British RAF Whitley plane comes under fire over the French coast and is forced to drop their cargo, a spy messenger pigeon finds its way into unlikely hands…

The occupation has taken much from the Cotillard sisters, and as the Germans increase their forces in the seaside town of Boulogne-sur-Mer, Gabriella, Martine and Simone can't escape the feeling that the walls are closing in.

Yet, just as they should be trying to stay under the radar, the discovery of a British messenger pigeon leads them down a new and dangerous path. Now, as the sisters' secrets wing their way to an unknown contact in London, they have to wonder – have they opened a lifeline, or sealed their fate?

AVAILABLE IN PAPERBACK, EBOOK AND AUDIO!

**A GRIPPING EMOTIONAL WW2 HISTORICAL NOVEL
INSPIRED BY A TRUE STORY!**

Since her husband, Josef, joined the Czech resistance three
years ago, Anna Dankova has done everything possible to
keep her daughter, Ema, safe. But when blonde haired, blue-
eyed Ema is ripped from her mother's arms in the local
marketplace by the dreaded Brown Sisters, nurses who were
dedicated to Hitler's cause, Anna is forced to go to new
extremes to take back what the Nazis have stolen from her.

Going undercover as a devoted German subject eager to prove
her worth to the Reich, the former actress takes on a role of a
lifetime to find and save her daughter. But getting close to Ema
is one thing. Convincing her that the Germans are lying when
they claim Anna stole her from her true parents is another…

AVAILABLE IN PAPERBACK, EBOOK AND AUDIO!

The author and One More Chapter would like to thank everyone who contributed to the publication of this story...

Analytics
Imogen Wolstencroft

Audio
Fionnuala Barrett
Ciara Briggs

Contracts
Laura Amos
Inigo Vyvyan

Design
Lucy Bennett
Fiona Greenway
Liane Payne
Dean Russell

Digital Sales
Laura Daley
Lydia Grainge
Hannah Lismore

eCommerce
Laura Carpenter
Madeline ODonovan
Charlotte Stevens
Christina Storey
Jo Surman
Rachel Ward

Editorial
Janet Marie Adkins
Rosie Best
Kara Daniel
Charlotte Ledger
Lydia Mason
Jennie Rothwell
Sofia Salazar Studer
Emily Thomas
Helen Williams

Harper360
Emily Gerbner
Ariana Juarez
Jean Marie Kelly
emma sullivan
Sophia Wilhelm

International Sales
Peter Borcsok
Ruth Burrow
Bethan Moore
Colleen Simpson

Inventory
Sarah Callaghan
Kirsty Norman

Marketing & Publicity
Chloe Cummings
Grace Edwards
Katie Sadler

Operations
Melissa Okusanya
Hannah Stamp

Production
Denis Manson
Simon Moore
Francesca Tuzzeo

Rights
Ashton Mucha
Alisah Saghir
Zoe Shine
Aisling Smyth
Lucy Vanderbilt

Trade Marketing
Ben Hurd
Eleanor Slater

The HarperCollins Distribution Team

The HarperCollins Finance & Royalties Team

The HarperCollins Legal Team

The HarperCollins Technology Team

UK Sales
Isabel Coburn
Jay Cochrane
Sabina Lewis
Holly Martin
Harriet Williams
Leah Woods

And every other essential link in the chain from delivery drivers to booksellers to librarians and beyond!

YOUR NUMBER ONE STOP

ONE MORE CHAPTER

FOR PAGETURNING BOOKS

One More Chapter is an
award-winning global
division of HarperCollins.

Subscribe to our newsletter to get our
latest eBook deals and stay up to date
with all our new releases!

<u>signup.harpercollins.co.uk/
join/signup-omc</u>

Meet the team at
<u>www.onemorechapter.com</u>

Follow us!

@onemorechapterhc

Do you write unputdownable fiction?
We love to hear from new voices.
Find out how to submit your novel at
<u>www.onemorechapter.com/submissions</u>